Devil's Move

LESLIE WOLFE

ITALICS PUBLISHING

This is entirely a work of fiction. Characters, organizations, agencies, corporations, places, aircraft, and incidents depicted in this book are the product of the author's imagination or are used fictitiously. Any resemblance to actual persons, living or dead, business establishments, or events, is entirely coincidental.

The publisher does not have any control over and does not assume any responsibility for third-party websites or their content.

Italics Publishing Inc.
Cover and interior design by Sam Roman
Editor: Joni Wilson
ISBN: 1-945302-01-1
ISBN-13: 978-1-945302-01-5

DEDICATION

For my husband, who never stops believing in me.

...Chapter 1: Ready to Play
...Thursday, May 21, 7:58PM Local Time (UTC+1:00 hours)
...Restaurant La Cordonnerie
...Paris, France

The loud ringtone shattered the cozy atmosphere of the exclusive restaurant and caused a few diners to frown and throw disapproving glances.

Oblivious and rude, the phone's owner took the call in a loud, raspy Russian. "Da?"

"Vitya? It's Misha. We're in play," the caller said and then hung up.

The Russian continued his dinner. A spark of excitement in his eyes and a faint flicker of a smile at the corner of his mouth were the only visible effects of the call. He loved playing God.

...Chapter 2: An Offer
...Thursday, December 3, 11:22AM EST (UTC-5:00 hours)
...MedStar Georgetown University Hospital—MedStar Heart Institute
...Washington, DC

Waiting. Waiting is the absolute worst part of having to deal with hospitals. Robert Wilton nodded to himself absently, letting his weary mind wander. He had waited for almost two hours, counting every minute right outside the conference room whose opaque doors read "Transplant Committee" in black, bold lettering. The impersonal label on the door and the way it stood out against the white, impenetrable glass held a menacing look. It felt surreal to know that some complete strangers had such decisive power over the destiny of a family.

Robert tried to picture the faces of the committee members. Would they be favorable? Would they say yes? What does a transplant committee do, anyway? His mind wandered again, recalling the articles he had read in preparation for this day. They meet, they review the details of each patient, and they decide if that patient makes it to the waiting list and with what priority. They decide who gets a heart and who doesn't. They decide who lives and who dies. A shudder disrupted Robert's thoughts, and he stifled a sob. *She can't die...she's all I have. Please, God...*

"Mr. Wilton?" A man's hand gently touched his shoulder. The man had a sympathetic smile and sadness in his green eyes, brought forward by the pale teal of his scrubs.

Oh, no... "Yes," Robert managed to articulate.

"The transplant committee has finished its session, and I'm afraid the news is not so good. Your wife does not qualify for a transplant."

"No! This can't be. I'm sure this is a mistake..." Robert's voice was gaining momentum. "This must be a mistake, because you don't know her. She's wonderful...she's all I've got! Please...?" Robert grabbed the man's sleeve, pleading with him, his breathing shattered by uncontrollable sobs.

"Sir, I understand this must be very hard for you to hear, and I can assure you this decision was not taken lightly by our committee. Your wife is almost at the age limit, which is sixty-five, and, unfortunately, our rules are very clear about transplant candidates with a history of substance or alcohol abuse. I am very sorry."

Hope flickered in Robert's mind. "What are you talking about? She's not an addict! You got it all wrong...there must be some mistake. Please tell the committee they can give her a heart, because she's not an addict. You have all your facts wrong. Please."

"Sir, I am afraid our information is accurate," the man continued in the same professional, sympathetic, almost whispered tone of voice. "She might not be an addict, but she has a DUI on her record in the past ten years, and that's an instant disqualifier." The man stopped for a minute, letting Robert process the information. Pallor took over Robert's tired, tear-stained face as he grasped the finality of the transplant committee's decision. "I wish there were more we could do. I am very sorry." The man paused again for a few seconds. "Is there anyone we can call for you?"

Robert stood with difficulty, barely aware his muscles were crying with pain from the tension he had been accumulating on that waiting room chair. *I need air*, he thought, heading with unsteady steps toward a door at the end of a very long corridor. His mind had registered the sunshine coming through that door whenever someone had walked through it. *How do people walk these corridors? How do people leave here and tell their families it's over?* Robert's mind was wandering again. *If these walls could talk, they would scream.*

He sat down on a bench right outside the building in the warm sunshine offered by a mild December. He didn't feel able to walk any farther. *This isn't happening...This can't happen...Please, God!* Holding his head in his hands and rocking back and forth, he finally let the uncontrollable sobs out, gasping for air.

"Mr. Wilton?" a man interrupted.

"Go away...there's nothing you can do for me," Robert said, not even looking up to see who was standing there.

"That's not true, Mr. Wilton. There might be something I can do for you," the man said, taking a seat on the bench.

Robert looked at the stranger. He wasn't dressed like a hospital employee, and he was definitely not the man from the committee. He absently registered minor details about this man: pricey suit jacket worn on top of a black turtleneck, expensive watch, a faint scent of high-end cologne. Light, short-trimmed, thinning brown hair; high forehead; intelligent eyes; but cold as ice. Wrinkled face. Very wrinkled.

"My name is Warren Helms," the stranger continued, "and I have only one question for you." He paused, waiting for Robert to shake his hand. Hesitantly, Robert shook the man's hand. "What would you do to save your wife's life?" Helms asked.

"Anything," Robert answered without thinking, "anything at all. Just ask. I have some money. I could raise more." Hope flooded his heart.

"Oh, it's not that complicated; it's not about money, Mr. Wilton. It's much easier than that." Helms paused, looking at Robert with inquisitive eyes. Robert was hanging on every word. He was ready. "We'll just need a small favor from you, at the right time."

"What kind of favor?" Robert asked, concern seeping into his voice.

"Nothing you wouldn't normally do, nothing out of the ordinary." Helms stopped for a second and then continued, while starting to get up. "But if you're uncomfortable, just say so and I will be on my way—"

"No," Robert almost yelled, grabbing the man's arm. "No, I'll do it, whatever it is. I'll do it."

"All right, then we have a deal. Now go home to Melanie and tell her you both are going to Vermont, where she'll be getting a new heart. I will call you with the details. Start packing today. The surgery will happen sooner than you think."

...Chapter 3: Overhaul
...Monday, December 14, 9:02PM EST (UTC-5:00 hours)
...News of the Hour Special Edition Report
...Nationally Syndicated

"Good evening, ladies and gentlemen." The anchor paused slightly, the way she normally did for dramatic effect. Her wavy blond hair and perfect makeup showcased a face filled with excitement. "In an announcement that took everyone by surprise earlier today, the White House confirmed that President Mason has signed off on the initiative to have the next presidential elections 'brought to the twenty-first century,' as the president himself phrased it.

"The American presidential election, a democratic institution in itself and the single most important process in our democracy, has been maintained almost unchanged for more than a century. Traditionally handled via paper ballots marked with pens or by punched holes, the election process has had little innovation brought to it, with the exception of sporadic, county-level initiatives. For next year's presidential elections, we are now looking at a completely overhauled process involving technology, such as touch-screen monitors and centralized electronic data storage and analysis."

The camera zoomed out, allowing the studio guest to become visible on the screen.

"Our guest tonight is the initiator of the elections process overhaul, California Senator Sidney Mulligan. Senator, thank you for joining us tonight."

"Thank you for the invitation, Stephanie, always a pleasure." The senator smiled at the camera.

"Senator, please tell us what made you decide to spearhead this initiative?"

"Very simple, Stephanie: it was way overdue. Election data is crucial information, highly sensitive, and time critical. Until now, on numerous occasions, due to the imperfect process we currently have involving paper ballots and all the processes related to paper voting, we have seen allegations of tampering, miscounting, and influencing, just to mention a few. Like the situation we had in Florida in 2000, if you recall." The Senator stopped talking, allowing Stephanie to engage.

"Yes, I do recall. Wasn't that when the machines punched holes in the ballots that were not clearly associated with the ballot options?"

"Precisely. Based on that experience, and on other situations where I felt—we felt—that the democratic process of elections is jeopardized by its own archaism, I have decided to not sit idle and instead to drive this change. That's what motivated me to rally some resources and begin exploring the possibility of an overhaul."

"How difficult was it for you to see this initiative approved?"

"Relatively difficult, I might say." He paused for a little while, thinking. "Although, in retrospect, the electoral process has been maintained almost unchanged for more than a hundred years because my fellow legislators are mostly risk averse. With the exception of a few isolated precincts innovative enough to deploy some form of technology to this process, the majority of the country still votes on paper today."

"Then how exactly were you able to see this through? Walk us through what it took to get this overhaul approved."

"It wasn't extremely hard, once we formulated it and submitted it for debate—just more difficult than I had anticipated." Senator Mulligan paused, arranged his already perfect tie, and then resumed. "Before submitting it, I met with several technology leaders in Silicon Valley and worked through some scenarios, identified some of the pitfalls, and worked through a proof of concept. I wanted to make sure we're not wasting time and effort or running the risk of overlooking any potential issues."

"I guess it helps having Silicon Valley right there by your side, doesn't it?" Stephanie interjected.

"Sure, it does." The senator smiled right back, open and friendly.

"Was this a democratic initiative?"

"Well, not at the start. At first, when I suggested it, the voices of opposition were on all sides of the political spectrum. Now it has the full support of the Democratic Party. We worked through that, and we were able to rally enough initial support to make it go to vote. I think the strategic and historical dimensions of this initiative transcend party lines and reach deep into our very cores as political leaders."

"What were the main reasons legislators voted against it?"

"Fear of change, risk aversion, fear of technology, just to name a few. The opponents are intimidated at the thought of changing anything in one of the cornerstone processes of our democracy." The senator thought for a few seconds, and then a mischievous smile appeared in his eyes. "But let's keep in mind that America builds the same home designs it did fifty years ago, just because it's safer, easier, and cheaper to do so. No one wants to take on the risk of building new, modern houses that people could potentially be reluctant to embrace. The typical neighborhood in suburban America looks exactly the same way it did halfway through the last century, because at the end of the day, Americans are, simply put, risk averse. Change averse. And that is the biggest roadblock in the path of innovation and progress."

"Maybe we should have started with this question: how will it all work? What will change in the voting process? How will the voters experience change?"

"Very little will actually change in the voter experience, but this change will be critical. The voters will still be registered, as they are now. Nothing new there. Their voter registration cards will be reissued every two years; again, nothing new. The registration cards will have bar codes on them, still nothing new. On Election Day, inside the voting booths there will be touchscreen devices, very similar to tablets, only mounted on small stands inside the booths. These devices will have bar code readers, so the voter will be able to scan their registration card to start the voting process. Once they scan their card, they will be presented with information on the screens, walking them through the entire voting process.

"So, for example, the first screen will show 'President and Vice President' options, and voters will simply touch the names they want to cast their votes for. When touched, that specific candidate's section on the screen will be highlighted in green, and the device will prompt the voter to touch 'continue' if they accept the selection. Then they advance to the next screens, one vote at a time. Very simple and straightforward."

"Yes, absolutely," Stephanie approved. "What happens in the background? How does it all work?"

"That's where all the beauty is. The voting system will be housed by a data-processing government contractor, vetted by the NSA—that's the National Security Agency—with the highest levels of security in place. The versatility of this new system enables the device to offer all the state-specific and local ballots after scanning the registered voter cards. This system will aggregate and process all information as votes are collected, so we will have our ballot results within minutes after booths close. Additionally, having a precise record of each and every vote, time stamped and location stamped, will completely eliminate all the suspicions about vote tampering or manipulation, thus cleaning up our voting process."

"Very interesting. Who's building all this technology? Will it be ready in time for November elections?"

"We have selected a government contractor, DCBI, with decades of experience delivering impeccable service to assist with the technology deployment. For those of your viewers who might not be entirely familiar with the name, Donaldson & Campbell Business Intelligence is one of the top three technology-consulting firms in our country. It has a history of delivering strategic government contracts on time, within budget, and with the highest security. DCBI will deploy the entire solution, based on very specific requirements that include every single aspect of the new system, from how the devices will look, feel, and work to how the data will be captured, interpreted, and stored."

"One last question, senator," Stephanie said, suddenly turning serious. "Are you worried? Do you have any concern this overhaul might not go as planned?"

"No, I am not worried, not at all." The senator's calm smile lingered.

"Thank you very much for your time with us here tonight, senator. This was very interesting and informative. We are looking forward to having you join us in the studio again with progress updates."

"Thank you, I would be happy to."

The camera zoomed back in, centering on Stephanie's elegant features.

"That was Senator Sidney Mulligan, the pioneer of electronic voting. On January 7, we will welcome to our studio the voice of opposition against this highly disputed overhaul, New Jersey Congressman Jim Archesi, one of the most conservative voices in the Republican Party." Stephanie paused briefly before delivering the final phrase of her show. "Live from our studio, this is Stephanie Wainwright, with *News of the Hour.*"

...Chapter 4: A Contract
...Friday, December 18, 1:33PM PST (UTC-8:00 hours)
...Meadowood Mall Starbucks
...Reno, Nevada

"Hello?" Coffee spilled on the table, as the cup tipped over in the man's rush to pick up the call.

"This is Helms. Travel arrangements are made. She's arriving on the twenty-third at 8:25PM, American Airlines flight 1075 from DC via Dallas/Fort Worth. Get the job done."

"Yes, sir," the man answered as the caller hung up.

...Chapter 5: Training
...Tuesday, December 22, 8:07AM PST (UTC-8:00 hours)
...Carmel Valley Beach
...San Diego, California

Alex Hoffmann landed hard on her back, the air knocked out of her lungs despite landing on sand. She grunted and spat out some of the sand that had stuck to her tongue. She tried to get to her feet, but then gave up and settled on the wet beach, still dizzy, eyes open under the fine December mist.

"I hate you," she said, giving Lou a look of deep resentment. "I hate you very much right now. Words cannot describe."

"Yeah, whatever," Lou said unmoved, "now get back on your feet. You're very vulnerable when you're down."

"Don't care anymore," she whimpered. "Just go away."

"No can do, boss, we only have a few days to get you in shape. Up!"

"I *am* in shape," she grunted angrily. "I look great." She got up, shaking the sand off her sweats and trying to arrange her wet hair. "I am in great shape, and I can take care of myself, thank you very much."

"Wrong and wrong," Lou said. With a swift movement of his arm, he grabbed her and twisted her in the air. This time she landed face down in the sand.

"Ugh," she spat. "Enough already, I think I get your point." She curled on her side, not caring about the wet sand anymore. "But I am in great shape, even if I don't know martial arts, or whatever this is. I'm not GI Jane, nor do I intend to be. Not ever."

"Sure, you're in great shape to go clubbing, nothing more, and you look great in one of those short skirts. But when things got rough I had to bail your ass, if you so kindly remember."

Alex felt the sting. "So what? That's what we do for each other in this job. That's what we're supposed to do: have each other's backs. Plus, I already thanked you."

"Yeah, but what if I'm not there? What if none of us are there when you need help? Do you want to die before your time? Are you in a hurry or something? Or do you want the last thought that goes through your head before you die to be 'I now die of laziness because I could have learned how to defend myself, but I was too complacent to get my ass off that sand and work with one of the best close-combat trainers I could have hoped for'?" Lou approached her and offered his hand to help her get up. "Up you go."

"You don't ever lose an opportunity to list your talents. Modesty sure ain't one of them. You also should have started with hacking, which I'm sure is the strongest skill you have. You should have stuck to hacking. It would have hurt less." She grunted with a smile and patted him gently on his very well-developed forearm. "OK, but whatever you do, don't throw me on the ground again, or I will start crying."

"Deal, but only for today. And you get to do whatever I ask you to do, without argument. We've already wasted forty-eight minutes squabbling. We only have a few days, so let's make the most of them."

"Yeah, OK, but you know it's Christmas week, right?" She flashed him a full-blown manipulative smile.

"Don't care. So please give me twenty ab crunches on my count. Go!"

She sat on the wet sand, scowling. Lou started counting and coaching her.

"One, two, breathe, four, five, keep it coming, faster, seven, eight, keep going!"

The deserted beach, just north of Torrey Pines State Reserve, was one of her favorite places to come and relax, enjoy the constant crashing of the Pacific waves, and bask in the gentle sunlight. Today, and most probably for quite a few days to come, it had become their own private dojo. Louie Bailey, Lou for short, the newest addition to The Agency team, had just finished his first case. It made Alex feel competent, tenured, and a bit protective: although Alex was only one case ahead of Lou in terms of experience, he obviously didn't need any of her protection. Six-foot-three and built like a rock, the ex-SEAL seemed very able to take care of himself.

"Up," he interrupted her ab crunch session, "let's run." He sprinted ahead of her, and she struggled to catch up. He was leading her where the waves touched the shore, making running a splashy, annoying, and difficult exercise.

"It sucks here, in the water," she complained, "why not run six feet to the right? What's wrong with that? My feet are wet now."

"You can't postpone or reschedule a fight because your feet are wet. This is not about comfort; it's about focus and pushing your limits outside your comfort zone. So push yourself, focus, and endure." He smiled discreetly, his head turned away from her.

"Bastard," she mumbled.

He was right, and she knew it. The Agency work was very dangerous. Infiltrating organizations and conducting undercover investigations without being part of any law enforcement entity was a risky existence that could turn deadly at any time without warning. It had happened in the past and would definitely happen again in the future. She hated him for being right and hated this cold, wet, and miserable alternative to what could have been a day of luxurious indulgence in front of the fireplace, complete with Belgian chocolates, martinis, and a good book.

"OK, we're stopping," Lou said, "now drop down and give me twenty."

"You're joking, right?"

"Wrong. Drop and give me twenty pushups, now. On my count. One, two, three. Good."

Yep, great sacrifices I'm making for my job today, Alex thought, *but well worth it, I might say*. Her job had been a continuous adventure since the day, not so long ago, when she had walked through The Agency's door to interview with its founder, Tom Isaac. Tom and his small team had since become like a family to her, a closely knit group of top-notch, highly intelligent professionals, with Lou Bailey as the latest addition.

Each assignment required a different approach, and her low tolerance for repetitive, boring work was fully satisfied. The job was challenging and dangerous, but very rewarding. *And quite well paid too*, she thought, letting a smile of satisfaction make it through her effort-strained features. This was going to be her first financially comfortable Christmas ever.

"Enjoying yourself, huh?" Lou's voice brought her back to reality.

"No, not at all, let me be very clear about that." She laughed. She stood up, panting, knees and arms trembling from the prolonged effort.

"All right, let's start some real training now," Lou said and winked.

"Kidding me? What was this I've been doing here since 8AM?"

"Well, mostly bitching, and *some* warm-up." He laughed. "Now we're getting into the interesting part. The purpose of our training is to give you the basic self-defense knowledge required, at minimum, to deter relatively simple attacks. Tom briefed me about your past. So please pay attention: this is important." He sat on the wet sand, crossing his legs in a relaxed half-Lotus pose. She followed suit. They were both wet from the rain and their sweat and covered in sand, but the warm-up had left Alex indifferent to any environmental factors.

"I will teach you how to deter attacks by hand, knife, and gun. Typically, when going after a woman, aggressors will not come heavily armed or in large groups. Due to their reduced body mass and overall lower strength, women don't seem as threatening. The bad guys are most likely to think you pose zero threat and will tend to underestimate any risk associated with you putting up a fight. We'll learn how to make them regret it."

"Will you teach me how to throw my legs in the air and kick them in the head?" She grinned mischievously.

"No, and please forget every single fight you've seen in movies. This is real life, not some carefully choreographed John Woo combat scene, where actors just fly through the air without any respect for the laws of physics." He was not smiling anymore. "This is real, as real as it gets."

"OK," she said, her attention in full gear.

"The techniques we are going to practice are part of a family of combat techniques called CQC, or close quarters combat. Specifically, I will show you two different CQC techniques. One is borrowed from Krav Maga, the self-defense system invented by the Israelis, and the other from Systema, developed by the Russians. Between these two fighting systems you will have a good base of defensive and offensive strategies to counter an attack."

"I see," she said. This was getting serious. "Did you learn these when you

cutthroat Russian intelligence officers, friendships he cultivated carefully throughout the years.

One day it was over, one cold November day in 1991. Communism was done and finished; the KGB was falling apart, and Vitaliy was free again. He left the dissolving KGB without giving any notice, just scribbling a one-line resignation letter to get his papers released from the personnel department. He exited the Lubyanka KGB headquarters edifice without looking back and started building his fortune.

With the USSR falling apart and all the former Soviet Republics seeking their independence from Russia, there was chaos in the streets. Many of his Russian friends and contacts were in Russia, including the majority of his former KGB contacts, who had decided to return home instead of immigrating to or seeking asylum in the West. Russia was also not a communist economy anymore. It was the dawn of Russian capitalism through a painful passage from communist, state-owned structures to the capitalist, free-market economy, a period one could call transitionism.

However, no one knew how to be a capitalist, how to think like one. Being citizens of a communist country for generations, never traveling outside the USSR, having mandatory but guaranteed jobs, and having lived in a system that made owning any kind of property or wealth a capital offense, no one knew how to become a capitalist overnight. No one except Vitaliy and other foreign intelligence officers who had stashed their cash outside the country, had contacts in the real capitalist world, and the knowledge of what capitalism was, how it worked, and how it can make the right people rich.

Vitaliy Myatlev wasted no time. Within months of his departure from the KGB, he had opened several companies in Russia with foreign capital he'd been able to raise rapidly. He brought into the country luxury household items, such as ice-free refrigerators, washing machines, dryers, convection ovens, and microwave ovens. He knew not many Russians had money to buy these at first, but he would hold the stake in the appliance market, and once all the known brands had been deployed through his companies, no one else would be able to grab that distribution market from him.

Moreover, all the KGB officers and party officials who were loaded, but had decided to keep their accumulated savings in Russia, had heaps of rapidly devaluing Russian rubles to spend. Myatlev's prices were ridiculously high, but his merchandise moved fast nevertheless. From Whirlpool to Kenmore to KitchenAid, he brought them all to Mother Russia, for a substantial profit.

He moved on to bring wireless cellular services into a country that had almost no telecommunication infrastructure outside the major cities and citizens were forced to wait months for a new landline, despite the copious bribes they were willing to pay. The mobile phones addressed that need, and, within a few years, almost eliminated residential landlines.

He still didn't stop. Next, he built a few banks. He finally held the capital reserves needed to attract partner names like Credit Suisse and AIG, and to issue a credit card product of his own. After all, the Russians needed a financial institution to lend them money at predatory interest rates to pay for the highly expensive appliances and overpriced cell phones. Once the foundations of his financial empire had been laid, he proceeded to acquire vast amounts of real estate at ridiculous prices, knowing those prices would soon rise. He was able to foresee the inflation that soon took over Russia and moved his liquidities to hard currencies and gold.

He had already made the list of the top 100 richest people in the world, and that was before he started his oil and gas endeavors. He wasn't going to stop; it was never going to be enough. His lust for power was tireless, and the thrill of the hunt was too exciting for him to give up.

Vitaliy Myatlev had moved to Kiev a few years before, when his wealth had grown to be large enough to cause him sleepless nights. Some of his old KGB friends had climbed the ranks of political power, achieving interestingly strategic and useful roles in the Russian government. One had just become president; the other had been the minister of defense for a while, holding that seat for a few years now. Their influence, kept motivated by large cash payouts, luxury cars, and custom-built villas, had proven very advantageous throughout the years.

But Myatlev was not stupid. He knew their favor could turn into scorn overnight, and he couldn't trust any of them. Therefore, Myatlev acquired Ukrainian citizenship in addition to the Russian and Iranian citizenships he had gained at birth, bestowed on him in a hurry and without due process by the deputy minister of the Ukrainian Ministry of Internal Affairs. Of course, now the minister had a new Mercedes S65 AMG, lunar blue metallic, and there was a rumor spreading that a dying aunt from Germany had willed him the exquisite vehicle.

Myatlev opened the door to his suite as soon as Ivan swiped the access card and entered the imposing living room to find his guest reading a magazine, installed comfortably on the plush sofa. *Shit*...he thought, remembering he was wearing only a white spa bathrobe.

His guest rose and extended his hand with a slight nod. Myatlev shook the man's hand vigorously.

"Welcome, Mr. Zaidi," he said in his most dignified tone of voice, trying to compensate for his inappropriate attire.

His guest, dressed to the nines, smiled and responded, "Or maybe *I* should say welcome, yes?"

"Yes, indeed, indeed. My deepest apologies for keeping you waiting and for having you endure seeing me dressed like this," Myatlev responded, making a hand gesture to apologize for his improper appearance.

His guest, Samir Jamal Zaidi, an Iraqi national of considerable wealth, was rumored to be well connected to both sides of the political battlefield in his country. Welcomed in the high circles of American political power and equally honored in Iraq by various political factions otherwise at war with each other, Zaidi was highly influential and a great partner to have for any endeavor. In his late forties, Zaidi had an appearance of determination and calculated calm, never showing any of his thoughts or feelings. His face, covered with the typical beard that Iraqi nationals liked to wear, was impenetrable and seemed entirely immobile and expressionless. He wore sunglasses at all times, even indoors, hiding his eyes behind dark lenses. He was a hard man to read.

Minutes later, after Myatlev had dressed appropriately for the occasion, he and Zaidi took their seats at a dining table brought up by the hotel staff, set to perfection with white brocade linens, silver accessories, and Bohemia crystal glasses. Myatlev's bodyguards had taken positions from a polite distance, guarding the men as they ate.

"I have a proposition for you, Mr. Zaidi," Myatlev said, immediately after his guest had finished the soup.

Zaidi made an inviting gesture with his hand.

"I am assembling a small group of very influential, very wealthy individuals," Myatlev continued, "whose global interests are aligned. Several countries are represented in our council, and yours is one of the countries that should hold a seat in this association of common goals." Myatlev paused, gauging his guest's interest level. Zaidi's eyes flickered for a split second, barely visible behind his tinted lenses, but he remained silent.

"There are many things we can do for each other," Myatlev continued, "and even more things we can do together. United." He stopped and focused on the schnitzel in front of him, savoring a piece of it with his eyes half closed in delight.

Finally, Zaidi spoke. "Which countries are represented on your council?"

"So far, Iran, Afghanistan, India, Pakistan, and, of course, Russia."

"How many representatives are you inviting from each of these countries?"

"Only one," Myatlev said gravely.

They ate silently for a few seconds.

"And what is the mandate?"

"During the past few decades we have observed how America has turned into the world's most arrogant bully, fortifying its super-power position in the world and stopping at nothing to maintain that power and increase its wealth. The American domineering way to meddle in other countries' internal affairs has reached an unprecedented level of insolence, causing significant concern for several countries."

"Oh...so your mandate is anti-American?" Zaidi asked abruptly.

"Our mandate is to establish a new world order, where we don't have the high-and-mighty Americans dictating how we conduct our internal political and economic affairs. Our mandate is to fix the balance of power in the world and restore other nations' rights to decide for themselves."

Myatlev took another bite of schnitzel, allowing Zaidi time to consider his proposal.

"How are you planning to pursue this goal? Politically? Engaging in violence?"

"That would be for the council to decide, depending on what actions we decide to take."

"I see," Zaidi said and then promptly touched his mouth with the white napkin, marking the end of his meal. "I am very honored by your consideration, but this is not something that I am inclined to be a part of. I would also like to wish you all success with this initiative."

"Would you like some dessert?" Myatlev asked, unperturbed. His eyes encouraged Zaidi to accept his offer, then shifted slightly to catch Ivan's gaze. Myatlev nodded almost imperceptibly, and his bodyguard nodded in response.

"No, I have to decline, I'm afraid. It has been a very satisfying meal; thank you for your hospitality," Zaidi said.

Ivan approached Zaidi from behind and grabbed his head with his right arm, immobilizing it as he placed a napkin soaked in chloroform over his nose. Zaidi struggled for a few seconds and then fell inert. The two bodyguards grabbed Zaidi quietly and took him to the other room. At some point in the very near future, they would get him out of the hotel in a suitcase, shoot him in the head somewhere, and throw his body in the Danube.

You can't win every time, Myatlev thought bitterly and took a sip of wine. He had to be more careful next time.

...Chapter 7: The Drive to Tahoe
...Wednesday, December 23, 8:52PM PST (UTC-8:00 hours)
...Reno–Tahoe International Airport, Rental Car Terminal
...Reno, Nevada

"Here you go, Miss Roberts, if you'll sign here, and here." The courteous car rental employee pointed out several places on the form. "We'll get you ready to go in just a second."

"What kind of car are you giving me? May I have a GPS, please?" Laura asked impatiently, running her fingers through her long, black hair and placing a few rebel strands behind her left ear. The man she was traveling with put his arm around her, but she didn't welcome his gesture of affection. She continued to lean against the car rental counter, ignoring him, focused on getting the paperwork done.

Laura Roberts was tired and a little irritated with her new boyfriend. He seemed to have absolutely no interest for what was on her mind. She wanted more than just easy-breezy companionship and great sex; she wanted a human being she could exchanges ideas with, a partner. Maybe he was not Mr. Right material, after all. Too bad. He did look gorgeous, this one.

"Umm...you've reserved an SUV. We have a Chevy Tahoe," the clerk giggled. "You might want that since you're driving to Tahoe, right? We have a Honda CR-V, and...umm...and a Jeep Wrangler, but that's a gas guzzler."

"This time I'm not gonna care," Laura said decisively. "What color is it?"

"Red. And it's convertible," the attendant added humorously, "Very useful feature in the dead of winter."

"Great. I'll take it." She was starting to feel better again. She had endured eight hours of flying from DC through a boring stopover in Dallas. Her morning had been challenging, and her boyfriend moody.

She hopped behind the wheel and programmed the GPS, while Bo struggled with the luggage. The Jeep was fairly new; it still carried the unmistakable new car smell.

"This car has no space for luggage. This trunk is a joke," he mumbled.

"Use the back seat, baby; there's enough room there. Let's go already. It's late."

He climbed in, slamming the door shut. He was going to give her some attitude, by the looks of it.

The GPS acquired satellites and gave her a route. Their destination was almost an hour away, an hour of driving in the dark on icy mountain roads. She groaned.

"It's far, but it's going to be great, you'll see. Totally worth it."

"Especially if you decide to leave the office behind and enjoy whatever we came all the way out here to enjoy. You know, it was cold enough in DC. We didn't have to fly all the way out here and lose twenty degrees in the process. It didn't have to get any colder than DC." Bo had a way of complaining, half-jokingly, that drove Laura crazy.

"Baby, we're gonna warm up by the fire and have a couple drinks, and the cold will be gone." She made every effort to cheer both of them up. They needed it. She needed it.

"OK, but promise me not a word about your work. I really don't understand why you give a crap anyway." He was still mad.

Laura felt a pang of anger taking over her self-imposed calm.

"I give a crap because my work is important. Because I have to care. Someone has to care. This is a strategic decision for everyone involved, and they're gonna do it wrong. They're not thinking straight. There's no other choice; *I* have to think for them, and I *do* care." She stopped and took a deep breath.

"There's no escaping this matter, is there? You're so riled up; there's no way you'll leave it alone. OK, then, let's hear it. What's making you so mad?"

She turned and looked at him for a split second. Was this the same guy she had boarded the flight with? What, now he decided to give a damn? Maybe there was some hope for him after all. She took a deep breath, letting it out slowly, a long and elaborate sigh.

"OK. Here it is, in a nutshell. DCBI, the company I work for, just won an incredible contract. We've known about it for a while, and we were already preparing for it, but it just got confirmed this month. Can't tell you what it's about: it's highly confidential. But it's very large and strategic, one of those contracts that can make or break companies and people. I'm their senior director of vendor assessment, which makes me directly responsible for selecting the vendors to execute this contract. There are several people on our sourcing team who decide which vendors come to the table and become part of our vendor list or supply chain. Do you follow me, baby?" She wanted him to understand and maybe even offer some advice. A second brain examining things could only help.

"Yeah, I get it. I might not be in business for a living, but so far, I'm with you. I still don't see the problem though."

"The problem is that most of the people on my team want to outsource the work on this strategic contract to offshore vendors. And that is just wrong."

"This is what got you mad? Everybody is offshoring everything these days; no one cares anymore. So why do you care?"

She gripped the wheel tighter with both hands. The road was dark and curvy, quite treacherous to drive at the end of a very long day. A wall of stone on her left, a pitch-black abyss on her right.

"Jeez! I care because it's wrong. There's no room for error in this contract. I've worked with offshore vendors enough to know how deadlines are missed, quality is not respected, promises are not kept, and products are substandard. In the end, it costs you double anyway. We just can't screw up this particular contract, and if we send it offshore like we're doing everything else these days, we're screwed." She stopped talking for a while, concentrating on driving the curvy, slippery mountain road. "Plus, there will be a lot of media involved."

"Media? So it's *that* kind of strategic, large project, huh? I think I might have an idea what project you're talking about."

"No, you don't; you're not supposed to, shush," she silenced him. "But yes, it is *that* kind of strategic project. We're all going to look like absolute idiots—no, even worse, like traitors—giving such a contract to an offshore company when this country's labor force has still not recovered after the last depression. Reckless, deluded idiots, that's what they are."

"Baby, I know how you feel about this entire offshoring business, and trust me, I feel the same way too. Everyone knows this is one of the things that has robbed us of our standard of living and our jobs and everything. Politicians and business leaders are the only ones who don't wanna see it, because they make more money putting everyone else into the ground. But this is old news. Why get so angry now? What changed?"

"It's just this particular contract, that's all. I cannot agree to send it offshore. I can't tell you what this contract is about, can't even confirm your guess, but trust me: for this specific contract, offshoring is terribly wrong. I have a very bad feeling about it."

"Are they forcing you to accept it?"

"My boss has a very balanced way to select vendors. The entire team weighs in; it's not top-down driven." She corrected her approach on a tight, descending curve at the last moment, making the Jeep's wheels squeal.

"Then?"

"My team is filled with idiots too, just like the rest of this shortsighted world of greedy fools. They only see the apparently low prices of offshore outsourcing. They don't, or won't, see beyond that. They don't think, and they never learn, even from their own bad experiences."

"OK, I get it, or I think I do. Listen, baby, here's what I think. Unless you are very calm and relaxed about this situation, you cannot persuade anyone of anything, You'll just throw spaz attacks like you did with me on the plane. No one will take you seriously. You have to let go and stop caring before you can begin to care effectively."

"Huh...What line of business did you say you were in? 'Cause you definitely do not talk like a biologist."

Bo laughed, relieving the tension in the car. "I'm full of surprises, baby; we'll explore a few in just a little while." He put his hand on her leg, right above the knee, and squeezed playfully.

She squealed, then touched him on his arm to get his attention. "Hey, what's that?" She pointed at a red flicker, coming from the woods ahead of them.

"Where?"

"It's gone. No, here it is again. It comes and it goes."

"Looks like a signal, or maybe a laser. Maybe someone is playing."

"It's brighter; now I see it all the time." She squinted, as the red laser beam started to blind her. She slowed down, but it wasn't helping. "I'm pulling over," she said, worried.

"No, keep going," Bo said. "Step on it. I really don't think stopping now is such a good idea."

She hit the gas, partially covering her eyes with her hand to escape the blinding glare of the red laser. Then she felt the Jeep hit the railing and plunge into the darkness, ripping through tree branches and brush. She heard herself shriek. Then nothing, just silence and darkness.

...Chapter 8: Thank You Dinner
...Saturday, December 26, 5:16PM PST (UTC-8:00 hours)
...Tom Isaac's Residence
...Laguna Beach, California

Alex loved going to Tom and Claire's place. Following the gentle curves of Cliff Drive and passing by houses decorated for the holidays, she let the Christmas spirit invade her. It had been more than ten years since she had left her parents' home, and she had never looked back. She couldn't look back, even if she wanted to. Many Christmases had been lonely and sad since that day in her past, but not anymore. She had a new family now.

Pulling up in front of Tom's perfectly landscaped front yard, she noticed a black Bentley stopped along the curb. *Oh shit, the client is here already*, she thought. *Sucks to be late.* She entered through the side gate, going straight for the backyard.

"There she is." Steve cheered, raising his beer bottle to greet her.

"Women love to make an entrance," Richard announced humorously. He gave her a hug, clumsily, so he wouldn't disturb Little Tom, hanging around his neck. Alex wondered how this relationship had started. Little Tom, the resident Siamese cat, had eyes for no one else but his owner, Tom Isaac. Yet, whenever Richard was around, the cat jumped and wrapped himself around Richard's neck like a scarf, letting his paws hang loose on both sides. Looking at the two of them, Alex couldn't decide which one of them enjoyed the relationship more.

Richard Fergusson, financial and business genius, was a key asset to The Agency. He stepped in whenever clients needed a strong hand taking over on an interim basis. He was comfortable leading in any C-suite role, and still looked classy and distinguished while wearing a Siamese cat around his neck, on top of his Versace suit. As for Little Tom's choice of venue, that remained a mystery. *Maybe Richard is wearing catnip cologne*, Alex thought with a silent giggle.

"Hello, dear." Claire Isaac gave her a warm hug. "Merry Christmas!"

"Merry Christmas to you too, Claire. Are you having a good time with this invasion?" Alex pointed toward the rest of the guests, scattered in the Christmas-lit backyard. Most of them had gathered around the barbecue, where Tom was making large gestures with his tongs, generating waves of laughter. It was a rare occasion to see everyone assembled. It had to be Christmas, or the end of a client engagement. Today it was both.

"Loving every minute," Claire said, and then took a sip from her drink, a tall glass filled with a clear liquid, small ice cubes, and herbs.

"What is that you're drinking? Always wanted to ask."

"It's an angry mojito, dear," Claire said with amusement.

"Why would a mojito be angry?"

"'Cause it doesn't have anything sweet in it. It's just Bacardi, mint leaves, lime juice, Pellegrino water, and ice."

"Interesting," Alex said.

"Would you like to try one?" Claire offered.

"I'll stick to martinis for now, but later," she said, dropping her voice to a whisper, "after the client leaves, I'll take you up on that offer."

"Deal," Claire said, wrapping her arm around Alex's shoulders and giving her a quick side hug.

Alex relished Claire's affection. As the only female on the team, she had sought Claire's advice many times. Her balanced manner, resourcefulness, and wisdom had helped guide Alex's development from the young, ambitious, and vulnerable kid who had taken a dangerous job just a year before into the driven investigator she had become.

Alex went over to greet Steve. He was leaning against a retaining wall and holding a beer bottle with one hand and a cigar with the other; his demeanor reflected calm and satisfied accomplishment. It was a feeling the whole team was sharing, except maybe for the calm part. Alex felt more enthusiastic, more energetically satisfied with their latest accomplishment, rather than calm.

Steve Mercer, however, a veteran with The Agency and a psychologist, would definitely be the one to remain calm about things, no matter how things evolved. He helped everyone on the team understand motivations and analyze social and organizational processes that broke down within organizations. Steve was the profiler, predicting behaviors and narrowing lists of potential suspects. Steve was also the one who assisted clients through the stressful, many times afflictive, unfolding of events that usually followed most of The Agency deployments. Alex had Steve's number on speed-dial; he was her closest friend, the first to become her friend when she had joined the team.

"Hey," Steve said, giving her a quick hug.

Alex blushed slightly. Their relationship could have been more. She had wanted it to become more, but she had withdrawn, afraid to ruin their friendship and impact their work together. It was complicated.

"Hey to you, too." She smiled warmly.

Just a few feet away, there was Brian, engaged in a four-way conversation with Tom, Lou, and Blake Bernard, their client. Brian stepped sideways, allowing her to approach the small circle. Lou, still the shy new guy when everyone else was around, waved briefly to say hi.

"Good evening, young lady," Tom greeted her ceremoniously, waving his tongs in a mimic of a hello.

"Miss Hoffmann," the client greeted her with a head nod.

"It's Alex," she said, extending her hand.

"Blake," the client responded. "I guess we can drop the formalities; we're from a very large cup filled to the brim. Ellen took her seat next to him and immediately started shuffling through some reports, getting ready to present her update.

Jimmy walked in next, greeting everyone. He took himself very seriously and did not know when to relax. He thought his job was stressful, and he let that stress show on his face and in his behavior. Robert had worked with him on this, trying to resolve the issue, but somewhere inside Jimmy there was a lot of stress going on. Maybe it was his personality or the nature of his role. Most quality professionals are used to focusing on what's broken or not working, their entire world populated with defect and failure. Over time, that can influence one's perspective on life. Jimmy took a seat across from Eddie. He looked pale and preoccupied, even more than he usually did.

Brad was the last to walk through the door. He was forty-seven now, but he must have been quite the playboy in his earlier life. A powerful presence, he held a combination of charisma with high intelligence and an awareness of both, fueling his self-confidence almost to the point of arrogance, but not beyond. Pleasant to work with and very resourceful, Brad's cooperation was sought by the most senior of project managers in the company, who recognized his value and wanted him on their side. Brad sat across from Ellen and left the door open. They were still waiting for Laura to take her seat at the end of the table, across from Robert.

Robert stood up and slowly moved to close the conference room door.

"Good morning, everyone," he said in a sad tone of voice.

They looked at him with various levels of surprise and concern.

"There's no easy way to say this," he continued, "so I'll make it quick. Laura died last week on her way from the airport to a Tahoe cabin she had rented. Her boyfriend, Bo, was killed too. Some of you knew him."

"Oh, my God..." Ellen said, covering her mouth, her eyes welling up instantly.

"How? How did it happen?" Brad asked.

"Road conditions were bad. Light snow turning into ice, very dark and slippery roads. Their car hit the railing and plunged into a 300-foot ravine. I was told they died on impact."

"Anything we can do," Jimmy asked, "for the family?"

"There will be a memorial service," Robert continued. "We will set up an account to collect donations in support of the family. I can't think of anything else right now, but I will let you know. Let's observe a moment of silence for Laura and Bo."

They bowed their heads and silence took over.

Robert interrupted it a minute later, clearing his throat quietly.

"Let's move to the first item on the agenda. The electronic vote contract. Laura's expertise will be greatly missed. We are in the final stages of vendor selection for this project. I don't need to tell any of you how important and highly visible this project will be. It's also on a very tight schedule. We cannot fall behind. Please think thoroughly before making any recommendations."

He cleared his throat again and breathed deeply before continuing.

"We are moving to finalize the selection for two separate vendors for this project. One is for the hardware manufacturing; we have four vendors shortlisted there, all offshore. The other one is for the voting software; there are five shortlisted vendors for that part of the project, with four offshore vendors."

Robert paused a little, allowing his team to catch up with taking notes. "We will divide and conquer Laura's workload. Even if we start recruiting now, we can't bring in a new director of Vendor Assessment in time to help us select these vendors, so this team will have to compensate. Get organized, book your travels, ask questions, do what you have to do to help this company select the right vendors for this project. We can't make a mistake on this one."

They all agreed, silently. No pressure.

"Keep on going!" he shouted to make himself heard over the earmuffs.

She shot the entire clip, getting more used to it with every shot.

"Let's see how you did," he said, bringing the target closer. "You nicked his ear, took a couple of fingers off his right hand, and gave him a flesh wound in his left thigh. This bad guy's still coming at you, and you shot an entire clip. Now you have to reload, and he's still coming! We have work to do."

She watched Lou change her clip with lightning-fast precision. This was her new reality, and she was going to be ready for it. *Time to grow up, girl, and fast,* she thought, putting a bullet through the target's head for the first time after several wasted clips.

...Chapter 14: First Council Meeting
...Sunday, January 3, 1:07PM Local Time (UTC+2:00 hours)
...CANWE Headquarters
...Undisclosed Location, Greece

The property spanned several acres of forested land, showing some glimmer of blue toward the west, where the Mediterranean was visible between two mountain peaks. The owner of the property didn't care much for that view though. A high security fence surrounded the main property, eight-foot tall and two-foot thick, made of concrete, its top covered in glass shards cemented into the structure. The fence was equipped with motion sensors that triggered silent alarms anytime something passed through their invisible rays. An electrified spiraling barbed wire roll, too wide to hop over, would also greet any daring intruders.

The barbed wire was installed on the inside of the fence, making it almost invisible from the outside. Inside the fence, there was a neatly mowed lawn, about ten acres or so, surrounding the main house. Security guards with Dobermans patrolled the yard, walking along the fence and around the house. A gardener was the only other human being who would normally make an appearance in this yard, tasked to keep the grass neatly trimmed. He also had the unpleasant duty of picking up the numerous dead birds and squirrels killed from climbing over the wall or getting zapped by the electrified roll of barbed wire.

Behind the house, there was a small heliport, equipped to handle night flights. At night, the pilots had little trouble finding it. Tucked in a clearing within acres of thick forest, it was equipped with an airport grade lighting system, inset LED lights in green, yellow, and orange, marking the approach and safety zone for inbound choppers.

The landlord's helicopter, a black Eurocopter EC145, was able to accommodate up to six passengers. The EC145 could come and go as needed, unnoticed by any neighbors, who were too far to have any suspicions about anything out of the ordinary. The villagers thought the place belonged to a famous Hollywood movie star who wanted to lead a secluded life in retirement, hiding away from countless paparazzi.

The house appeared quite normal on the inside. The graded roof covered the best part of the house, extending over a large living room with very high, vaulted ceilings. Nothing was unusual about it, other than how it was equipped and what it was used for.

Entering the house, one had to go through three layers of security screenings. The first step was to pass through an imaging device that detected, using resonating ultrasound, any unexpected items hidden in the visitor's clothing. A thorough pat down was next, followed by passing through another portal, this one meant to identify any recording or transmitting devices the visitor might carry. All this happened while the visitor's personal items were screened via a high-resolution, X-ray machine, a few generations more sophisticated than the ones the TSA currently used in high-traffic airports.

Then the visitor could enter the living room, leaving his cell phone and any other electronic devices with security personnel. That's where most new visitors stopped and stared before proceeding. In the middle of the huge living room sat a structure housing an eight-seat conference table and chairs. It was elevated two feet off the floor on posts, and built entirely out of thick transparent glass. A room within a room, completely transparent and lifted from the floor of the house; the structure made it absolutely impossible for any surveillance device to be placed inside those walls.

This type of structure contained all vibration within its walls, making even passive surveillance impossible. Most visitors hesitated before stepping onto the transparent floors, but they were thick and sturdy enough to hold eight elephants instead of people. House staff referred to the glass room as "the Aquarium," but no house staff was allowed to enter it without supervision, not even to clean the shiny surface of the glass conference table.

There was chopper traffic expected at the property, and the helipad lights were on. The EC145 landed and dropped off one passenger. The moment Myatlev set foot on the heliport surface, lowering his head slightly under the moving rotor blades, his chief of security greeted him promptly.

"Welcome back, Mr. Myatlev."

"Thanks," Myatlev answered and then hurried into the house.

The black chopper took off and almost an hour later brought four more men. As they disembarked, they went through security, then hesitantly entered the Aquarium and took their seats at the glass table. Myatlev greeted every one of them personally as they arrived. After the last visitor had taken his seat, Myatlev pushed a button to close the door to the Aquarium, then another to turn the glass walls opaque.

"Welcome, gentlemen," Myatlev said, "to the first gathering of our newly formed council. As you have already noticed, we are in a highly secure location, where we can discuss the matters at hand freely and without concern. I will start with some introductions, and then open the floor for discussions and ideas." Myatlev turned to his left and gestured toward the man sitting next to him. "The first man to join our new council was Mr. Karmal Shah from Afghanistan. Then we were joined by Mr. Mastaan Singh from India, followed by Mr. Ahmad Javadi from Iran, and, finally, Mr. Muhammad Sadiq from Pakistan."

The men greeted one another; some reached across the table and shook hands.

"Our small yet powerful organization, aptly named the Council for a New World Equity, or CANWE, is welcoming today a few very powerful men from various countries, united by common goals. We all want to establish a new world equity, one where we will rid ourselves of the self-righteous, uninvited, and unwanted interference of America in everything we do in our own countries." As he spoke, he looked the other men in the eyes, one by one, and what he saw made Myatlev very happy. He had chosen well.

"America is powerful, the strongest economy of this planet, and that makes Americans think they have the right to police the world. All of us here want to end that. All of us here are disgusted by having to deal with their obnoxious interference in everything we do, in our countries and in our homes. All of us here want them gone from our lives and their supreme arrogance kept in check. America is powerful, the strongest economy of this planet," he repeated his earlier statement.

"For now. We, too, are powerful, and we can end their arrogant supremacy once and for all and throw them spinning into a bottomless hole of economic decay and despair. All of us are powerful as individuals. Some of us have our powerful countries supporting our interests as they are stated here today, in this first formal meeting of our council. We can be the architects and strategists of the future, the five of us." He stopped talking for a little while, evaluating his audience.

"The future belongs to the bold, gentlemen, and we are going to take back what was always rightfully ours, the freedom to do as we please in the spaces of our own countries." He let a few seconds of silence go by, and then invited the group to the conversation with a wide hand gesture. "Let's discuss."

"It's an honor to meet everyone here," Javadi opened, "and I want to thank you for inviting me to be a part of CANWE."

Myatlev nodded in response.

"I wanted to ask," Javadi continued, "are we considering adding more members? Syria, China, and North Korea come to mind."

"Syria might be a good idea," Sadiq seconded.

"I beg to differ," Shah intervened. "If my understanding of what we are here to do and how we are looking to achieve our goals is correct, we have no business bringing the Syrians to this organization. They are reckless fanatics. They have no respect for strategy. They are primal and bloodthirsty, and, in my opinion, they're unable to execute complex plans that require forethought and self-control."

"They are devout Muslims, though, hence anti-American," Sadiq insisted.

"CANWE is not about Muslims against America," Myatlev intervened. "CANWE is not about religion. It's about politics and economics. Not all of us are Muslim, and that's not even by design; it's by accident."

"I assume we are going to coordinate attacks against America, retaliatory missions. In that case, Syrian fanaticism might come in handy," Sadiq added.

"We might," Myatlev responded, "we might if we have to. Such missions are just one device in our toolbox holding many different weapons. My vision is a little different, and I am hoping you will embrace it. Americans are equipped to identify terrorist attacks early on, and that makes it relatively hard for us to orchestrate a major attack, major enough to destabilize them for centuries to come."

"What if we nuke them?" Sadiq offered. "We could find ways to smuggle numerous nuclear bombs into the States and detonate them from anywhere. They wouldn't see that coming; they wouldn't have a defense against that kind of massive, coordinated attack."

"Then what? Nuclear winter for the entire planet?" Myatlev asked.

"It would be well worth it to see them suffer and pay, finally, for every bit of blasphemy they engage in every single day. Millions of them are guilty of blasphemy against Islam, and they never see punishment. It has to end."

"Yes, but we shouldn't rush into doing things that are short-lived and plain stupid," Myatlev said bluntly.

Sadiq's face flushed, which made his olive-toned skin turn a dark shade of purple. "This is insulting. I will not stand for it!" He stood abruptly, throwing his chair back. "I thought we had the commitment to do something, not just talk like impotents!"

"And we do have commitment, but we also want to have a good strategy," Myatlev said firmly. "Just think about it. If you nuke a couple hundred million Americans, would they even know what that was about? No, they'd end up having lived a life of luxury and ignorance. They would die quickly, painlessly, without having seen or understood what they've done wrong. You would punish them for their countless blasphemies by killing them, but they wouldn't know the reason. They wouldn't understand. You wouldn't punish them for their arrogance because they would die. still thinking they're better than everyone else on this planet."

Sadiq held Myatlev's gaze sternly for a couple seconds, still angry, and then lowered his eyes. The Russian had a point, albeit hard to admit.

"What if the Americans saw it coming, and there was no place to hide from it?" Myatlev continued. "What of their arrogance then, when chaos, fear, and poverty will take over their lives, day by day, minute by minute, while they sit powerless, unable to do anything about it? What of their arrogance when they'll have to watch the peoples of the nations they have despised rise to unprecedented power, while they lose everything they have? That's what I would call vindication. That's what I would call punishment for their many blasphemies against Islam. That's when I would be satisfied that they can no longer feel entitled, and that's when I would agree the new world equity has been established."

"Do you have a plan, or is this just wishful thinking?" Singh asked.

"It is a goal for now. But if we keep this goal central in our minds, a strategy will soon be set," Myatlev answered. "Once you've all had time to think about some potential strategies, we will meet again and finalize a plan of action."

"What about money?" Javadi asked. "Whatever we decide to do, it will require tens, maybe hundreds of millions to make it happen."

"Although we are all among the richest people in the world, we cannot directly fund this initiative from our personal accounts," Myatlev answered. "We will find and organize sources of funding, and it's entirely up to each of us what or who those will be. After all, we're business people, aren't we? We should be able to put something together to fund this organization. Please remember, there is significant opportunity at the time an empire falls. Our businesses will thrive beyond our wildest dreams. Consider your fundraising efforts nothing more than what they really are: seed capital investments for our futures."

He stood, signaling the meeting was over. "Only one question remains. Can we?" Myatlev asked, the pun with the council's acronym noticeable to everyone. An unexpected question, they all answered in different tones of voice, but quite forcefully.

"Yes, we can."

Myatlev escorted his guests to the helipad, while his staff radioed the chopper to come back and pick up the passengers. He watched them interact casually with one another while waiting. They were a good group: strong, motivated, and bold. They were ready to hear his strategy and adopt it; although it was already in play.

with difficulty.

"Get a cab, don't drive," Robert said as he was departing. No one else said anything.

Robert braced himself and went to see Campbell.

...Chapter 16: Democratic Candidacy
...Monday, January 4, 3:01PM EST (UTC-5:00 hours)
...Flash Elections: Breaking News
...Nationally Syndicated

"Another member of Congress announced his intentions to run for president this coming November," Phil Fournier said. "This time, Democratic Representative Robert Johnson from Illinois is seeking support for his candidacy."

The screen displayed the portrait of a well-known politician who enjoyed being the center of attention and was frequently calling press conferences to make announcements of little importance.

"Famous for his vision on immigration reform as well as healthcare, Bobby Johnson, now sixty-seven years of age, has declared that his presidency would restore the glamour that America used to have when the entire world was dreaming of our promised land. His statement made reference to recent statistics showing that, due to increased poverty and unemployment levels, fewer people every year decide to file for permanent immigration status in the United States, confirming that our country has ceased to present an attractive destination for people looking for a better future. Representative Johnson's commitment is toward 'righting the wrongs of our society,'" Phil stated, making quote signs with both his hands. "As of right now, support for Representative Johnson's candidacy is registering modest levels, at only 17.6 percent. He needs to gain support not only from the Democratic Party but also from the electorate in general. Vice President Mark Sheridan is a very strong opponent in Johnson's race to secure the Democratic Party nomination."

The anchor set his hands gently on the news desk in front of him, preparing his exit.

"We will keep you informed with reactions to the announcement of Bobby Johnson's candidacy. From *Flash Elections,* this is Phil Fournier, wishing you a good evening."

...Chapter 17: A Full Tank
...Monday, January 4, 4:47PM EST (UTC-5:00 hours)
...Benning Avenue near Anacostia
...Washington, DC

Light snow flurries melted on impact with his windshield. Jimmy Doherty groaned and turned on his wipers. He was struggling to see straight as it was, but the wet windshield was making it worse. He slowed down a little bit more, crawling at twenty-five miles per hour or so and receiving angry scowls from drivers forced to pass him. He was not feeling that great, he had to admit.

A light chime caught his attention. His gas level indicator came on. He looked around, and with difficulty, he forced his blurry vision to identify the familiar markings of a gas station. Maybe it was time to stop. He wished he had taken a cab. With a sigh, he pulled into the Shell gas station on Benning.

He climbed out of his car, and the effort left him breathless. He leaned his forehead against the car's cold and wet roof and closed his eyes for a minute, trying to regain his strength. Very slowly, he pulled a credit card out of his wallet and authorized the transaction at the pump. Getting the pump nozzle into the gas tank and starting the flow of gasoline took every ounce of energy he had left. He turned around and leaned against the car, looking at the snow flurries coming down in a blur.

A shot of pain froze his left arm. He gasped for air, but he wasn't getting any. The pain expanded up to his neck and jaw, compressing his rib cage and leaving him almost paralyzed. He reached for the call button on the side of the pump but stumbled and fell on his knees, then buckled on his side. The pain was more bearable like this, lying down. Maybe all he needed was to lie down for a while. Eyes half open, he watched blurred flurries hurry down, melting one after another, until he slipped away.

The pump nozzle clicked shut with a loud noise. The tank was full.

...Chapter 18: A Difficult Conversation
...Tuesday, January 5, 9:24AM Local Time (UTC+3:00 hours)
...The Kremlin
...Moscow, Russia

Mikhail Nikolaev Dimitrov unbuttoned his coat and relaxed a little on the back seat of his black, bulletproof Mercedes G-Wagen. The car heated well and fast, and his driver, Sasha, knew how to keep the car on the road despite the slippery layer of ice on top of last night's snow. *Ah, the Russians still don't know how to clean the streets.* Dimitrov sighed. *Winter always takes Moskva by surprise.*

Dimitrov looked out the window. They were approaching the Kremlin from the south, from across the river Moskva, now frozen solid. Sasha was preparing to turn off Bolshaya Polyanka and onto Mokhovaya Street, approaching their destination.

Dimitrov fidgeted uncomfortably. He dreaded the meetings with his boss, President Abramovich, despite their life-long relationship dating back to their early KGB years. He was one arrogant, unstable, dangerous bastard, hungry for power like no one else. And a drunk, of course, a loud, uncontrollable, violent drunk. Most Russians liked their sauce, and that's no wonder, considering the cold weather and crappy economy; people needed an outlet. In Russia, drinking is a culture, and vodka is present in all houses, no matter how poor. *But there has to be a limit, there has to be control,* Dimitrov thought, *especially when you hold a public office of such importance.* Dimitrov liked moderation, which was an essential balancing feature for the minister of defense of the Russian Federation.

Dimitrov wondered for the tenth time that morning what the meeting was going to be about. Was it Crimea again? Abramovich simply could not get it in that thick and conceited skull of his that one cannot invade a foreign independent country like Ukraine and have no consequences to deal with. Now the crazy bastard wanted to invade half the world to make someone pay for the reactions to the Crimea situation. He scratched his forehead, thinking hard of new ways to calm the psychotic rages of his boss, if today was going to be one of those days.

"Dobroye utro, gospodin ministr." The door to the Kremlin was being held open for him by a young and enthusiastic Kremlin guard.

"Good morning," he responded as he walked through the door.

He walked the familiar corridors and cringed a little when he was told the president would see him right away. It was serious this time.

"Come right in, Dimitrov," President Abramovich invited him in with urgency. "You have to tell me how we get rid of these bastards and their stupid sanctions. They're insulting us every day. They're spitting in our faces, and we do nothing about it. Why?"

The bastards were the leaders of the Western world, who had united in support for Ukraine and had imposed numerous sanctions on Russia following the annexation of Crimea. Those sanctions had not ceased and were causing Abramovich immense irritation.

Dimitrov chose his words carefully before speaking. Abramovich was famous for throwing his opponents, or anyone else for that matter, in jail with or without cause. That's why Dimitrov wasn't about to tell him that there was little he believed could be done combatively.

"Gospodin president, there are several things we could do. We could respond with sanctions in return and prepare a strong statement advising them not to meddle in Russia's internal policy. We could—"

"Are you the minister of fucking industries?" Abramovich interrupted brutally. "From you I expect military action, not economic sanctions. What's our military response to this insult?"

"Gospodin president, we cannot attack the whole world at the same time," he spoke hesitantly.

"Don't come in here and tell me what we cannot do. We can do many things. We have tanks and planes and guns. We have satellites, and we have soldiers. We have Mother Russia to defend!" Abramovich ended his statement by slamming his fist down.

Mother Russia was not under attack. Mother Russia had attacked another country, but Dimitrov was not going to insist on that point of contention. On occasions, his passion for logical reasoning and for stating the truthful facts had caused him serious trouble. But he was learning.

"Who would you like us to start with?"

"The Americans! Who do they think they are, telling me what I can and cannot do in my own house, with my own people? They think me impotent, and they laugh at me. Yet they're sanctimonious, arrogant, and entirely screwed up. That son-of-a-bitch Mason tells me that I have no right to Crimea, any more than Cuba has a right to Florida. Ha!" He stood and started pacing the floor, his anger building and his self-control vanished. "Crimea is about the Russian people coming home to Mother Russia. It's our land, it always has been, and always will be."

"Did you receive another call from President Mason?" Dimitrov asked, as calmly as he could.

"Yes, yes, what have I been telling you? Are you even listening to me? What are you going to do about it?"

"The sanctions are hurting the West more than us—"

"The hell with the sanctions! They threaten me, and I threaten them back ten times worse! We've done that! Give me military action!" He stopped to catch his breath and let out a long sigh. "I miss the days of the great KGB.

Those men knew how to get the job done, any job! I never had to tell them twice. If people needed to be killed, they would be killed. Or removed. Or whatever was needed. With honor and love for the motherland."

Abramovich's career had started in the KGB, where he had risen through the ranks with a speed fueled by his unlimited ambition, monumental hubris, and willingness to sacrifice anything and anyone to reach his goal. Or for no reason at all. Before he had turned forty, he was feared more than he was respected, but in the ranks of the KGB that had worked quite well in his favor. During Gorbatchev's time in the Kremlin, Abramovich had risen to be the youngest KGB general in the history of the feared State Security Committee. He had also grown to be deeply disgusted by Gorbatchev's obvious pro-West policy, and by his famous transparency and openness. Gorbatchev's damned glasnost and perestroika had led, ultimately, to the fall of the USSR, to the destruction, the devastation of Mother Russia. History was never going to forgive him, and neither was Abramovich.

Abramovich had sworn to himself he would right this wrong one day and restore the greatness of Russia. Now the Kremlin was finally his, and no effort was spared to restore that greatness, the magnificent power of the nation that, not so long ago, had ruled over, or influenced half the civilized world. His battle had started there, in Crimea, where the strategic port of Sevastopol held the key to naval access to the Black Sea, and through the Mediterranean, to the Atlantic Ocean. This was too great a strategic advantage to back down from because of some measly economic sanctions or some borders that shouldn't have existed in the first place.

Russia's big business was on his side, supporting him with unlimited funds in return for privileges and the unofficial right to pilfer the land, speculate, and exploit the Russian work force. Moscow was now one of the world's leading cities in terms of luxury cars seen on the streets, while the majority of the people starved, froze in shanties, and wore rags, regretting the good old days of communism. That's what capitalism and the damn glasnost had done to Russia. Robbed her of her pride, values, and power.

"The Muslims put America on its knees from a goddamn cave, and we have armies!"

"The answer is not our armies," Mikhail Dimitrov said. "Armies anyone can see from their satellites. We wouldn't be stealth in our approaches, and we'd have terrible losses for minimal gains. We'd be humiliated again." He stopped talking, watching carefully for Abramovich's reaction. He seemed deep in thought, looking out the window at the gray winter sky.

"You miss the old KGB? Well, so do I," Dimitrov continued. "I miss the rigor, the procedures, the cleanliness, the discipline, and the resourcefulness. What if we brought it back?"

Abramovich turned and faced him, intrigued.

"What do you mean, bring back the KGB? We have the FSB; we have the SVR," Abramovich asked, referring to the two agencies created from the remains of the old KGB when it had ceased its existence, also in the ill-fated year 1991. FSB was the Secret Police Agency, or Federal Security Service, with main duties covering counterintelligence, counterterrorism, and overall security within the country's borders. SVR was the post-1991 spy agency, named now the Foreign Intelligence Service.

"And everyone knows we have them, so we're cats wearing bells. We'll never catch any mice. Impotent and naked." Dimitrov resented his powerlessness just as much as Abramovich did. Although a moderate politician and not prone to unnecessary, excessive violence, he had wondered many times whether he was doing his country any favors by being a moderate and allowing Russia to be toyed with by the Western powers. He took a deep breath and continued. "Let's bring the KGB back, but do it right. No one will know. Reactivate networks, place people, re-establish protocols. Then strike."

Abramovich turned to look at him, not moving from the window, as if to see if Dimitrov was serious. Dimitrov decided to let Abramovich in on his secret agenda; although he hated bringing him in the loop too early when things were still uncertain.

"I have already started rebuilding the old KGB, unseen and unknown. One of its best former assets is now executing his first post-glasnost mission, reporting strictly to me. Our common friend, Vitya, is working to get things started out there in the field, with America as his first target."

Abramovich walked toward him so determinedly, so forcefully, he almost flinched. He grabbed Dimitrov in a bear hug, patting him on the back.

"Mishka, Mishka, that's why I love you," Abramovich said, while Dimitrov struggled to breathe in his endless bear hug. "You will make us great again, yes? Let's drink to that!"

Abramovich filled two cut crystal glasses with vodka, readily available on the coffee table. A fresh bottle of Stolichnaya was always kept on ice and waiting to be served. He handed a glass to Dimitrov and cheered. "Ura! Na zdorovie!"

"Ura! Na zdorovie! To our future!"

They drank enthusiastically, downing the generous shots in one gulp each. They had a plan.

...Chapter 19: Memento Two
...Tuesday, January 5, 10:03AM EST (UTC-5:00 hours)
...DCBI Headquarters, Sixth Floor Conference Room
...Washington, DC

Robert sat at the conference room table, head in his hands, sadly contemplating the announcement he was going to make. Jimmy had been a close friend for so many years. Beyond the sense of loss he felt, he was also blaming himself for not calling 911 when Jimmy had been so visibly unwell at the meeting. He hadn't even offered to drive him home. Why? He had become so engulfed in his own guilt and fears that he had ceased being human. There was no excuse. He had stopped being the leader of his team, and had become the corrupt, threatened, and manipulated puppet of very dangerous men. Just a pawn in a treacherous game he did not understand. He only knew they meant business, whoever they were. His wife's life was in their hands. He had to deliver his end of the deal today.

"I'm guessing Jimmy called in sick, huh?" Brad interrupted Robert's pensiveness.

Robert did not answer. Ellen and Eddie were already in their seats. They were ready to start. An eerie feeling of déjà vu froze the blood in his veins.

"I have sad news for you," he commenced his announcement in a trembling, hesitant voice. Three pairs of concerned eyes from around the table looked straight at him, and they all widened with concern. "Jimmy died yesterday on his way home."

"Oh, my God." Ellen sobbed.

"What?" Eddie asked. "How did it happen? Car crash?"

Brad stood silently, not uttering a single word, sad eyes and a deep frown indicating his reaction to the news.

"No," Robert said. "He stopped to gas his car on Benning and had a heart attack right there at the pump."

"And no one was there?" Ellen asked in a tearful, outraged voice. "No one could help?"

"It was very fast, they said. There wasn't any time. The heart attack was massive, causing extensive damage to the wall of his heart. He was gone in seconds."

Silence fell around the table, thick and filled with sadness.

"We should have called 911," Eddie said after a minute or so, voicing everyone's thoughts. "We should have done something."

Everyone nodded. They all felt it. Silence fell again.

"Yes, you're right, Eddie," Robert answered. "I thought of that too. I can't find an explanation, other than we didn't expect it to be so serious. Jimmy was visibly upset yesterday, but he had been upset before. He was always very passionate in his beliefs."

"Not like yesterday, though. Yesterday was different," Eddie insisted.

"You might be right, Eddie, but there isn't anything much we can do about that now, other than learn a sad lesson about caring more about one another, about paying closer attention," Robert said.

"How do you suggest we proceed?" Brad asked, bringing them abruptly back to the work agenda. "I don't want to be insensitive, but we do have a deadline at noon today."

"Yes," Robert confirmed, "we do. Resuming where we left off yesterday, then." He looked through some notes in his portfolio, getting his thoughts in order. "We decided yesterday manufacturing was going to Taiwan, right?"

They nodded all around, Ellen sniffling and wiping the tears from her eyes.

"Yesterday we got stuck on software. We were dealing with the dilemma between deciding based on data and on our tested-and-true points system, and the ethicality of offshoring a project of such strategic importance to our democratic values, and the subsequent PR risk." Robert summarized where they had left off the day before. "Any new thoughts about that?"

"Did you get a chance to see Campbell?" Brad asked.

"Yes, I did, and he supports our tested decision-making system without any hesitation. He agrees we shouldn't change methodologies under such pressure, and he says he'd be fine handling any PR flack coming our way."

"In that case, the decision is simple," Brad said. "None of us here today opposed the traditional vendor selection process with respect to this contract, so I guess we're ready to award it?"

Robert's thoughts raced. *None of us here today opposed...None of us here today opposed...*He kept repeating Brad's words in his mind, over and over, wondering why he felt sick hearing those words. Then he realized why, and his heart skipped a few beats, blood draining from his veins. His face turned pale, and he grabbed the edge of the table to steady himself in the wave of the dizziness that had gotten a hold of him. Goosebumps prickled his skin; his heart pounded against his chest with a deafening sound.

All those opposing the selection of ERamSys as a vendor for the e-vote contract were now dead.

"Boss?" Eddie startled him. "Are you OK?"

Robert struggled to regain control over his racing thoughts and his pounding heart.

"Umm...yes. You were saying?"

"We're awarding the software deal to ERamSys from New Delhi, for $179 million. Any objections?"

"No, let's proceed." He did not feel the relief he had expected to feel reaching approval for this decision. He was petrified. If Laura and Jimmy's deaths were more than just coincidental accidents, what were the implications of that fact?

"Vendor engagement?"

"We will have our own team on-site for the entire contract duration. With Jimmy gone, we need a strong quality leader to take this over, and no names come to mind. I think this is our main priority from an engagement perspective," Eddie responded.

"I can deploy analysts on-site until we have a quality resource we like, just to keep things moving in the right direction," Ellen offered.

"All right." Robert approved. "Let's do that. I will have the contracts taken for signature to Campbell this afternoon, so please go ahead and start the engagement process."

His team started toward the door, whispering softly. He felt a hand touch his shoulder. He looked up into Ellen's tearful eyes.

"I'm sorry for your loss; I know he was also your friend." She stopped, stifling a sob. "Hell, what am I saying? I'm sorry for *our* loss."

He thanked her with a slight nod, deep in his thoughts.

"The hardest thing to accept is that these things just happen," Ellen continued, "and they have happened twice, in such a small team, and that makes it very hard. But there's nothing anyone can do...these things just happen."

Robert looked at her, tormented and speechless. *May God forgive me for what I have done.*

...Chapter 20: The Challenge of Change
...Thursday, January 7, 9:01PM EST (UTC-5:00 hours)
...News of the Hour Special Edition Report
...Nationally Syndicated

The studio setting had two large, comfortable armchairs, one taken by the show's host, Stephanie Wainwright, and the other by a dark-haired man displaying a determined, passionate demeanor.

"We have invited into our studio tonight Congressman Jim Archesi from New Jersey to discuss the potential pitfalls of the proposed e-vote system. Welcome, congressman." She concluded her introduction with a flash of her megawatt smile.

"Thank you for your invitation, Stephanie, always a pleasure," the congressman responded. He seemed tense and almost sullen.

"Congressman, please tell us what the main points of contention are from your angle. Why do you think e-vote reform poses a danger, and what kind of danger does it pose?"

"There are three main areas of concern, all are very serious. First," he said, counting with the fingers on his left hand, "we have a vast lineup of privacy concerns. Second, we have the heightened risk of vote manipulation and errors. In short, by deploying e-vote we are making election fraud very easy. Third, if such serious concerns regarding the new voting process are contaminating the electorate, we will have the worst participation in our history. If people are afraid for their privacy or don't trust the effectiveness of the system, they will not show. We will cripple our entire electoral process."

"Let's examine the privacy concerns. What do you think is front and center on people's minds?"

"If the voter registration scan will be happening on the same terminal and at the same time as the actual vote, this will open the door for the voter's identity to be associated with the actual vote input somewhere in the application's background. The architects of the e-vote system have reassured everyone on repeated occasions that this will never happen because the system isn't built that way. They are affirming their intention to make voting mobile, allowing a voter residing in New York City to vote in San Francisco for the full ballot registered under his county of residence. Nevertheless, the vast majority of the voters we have interviewed are very wary. Let's admit it; the government has made little progress in the past decade in winning the confidence of the electorate, especially in matters of privacy and individual rights. The scanning process will ensure voter mobility, which brings some value to the 1–3 percent of the voters who will choose to travel that very day. That only goes for some states, not for all."

"Help me understand," Stephanie said, "why the big concern now, when some voting precincts already have electronic voting machines in use and have had them for a while?"

"So far, only some of the states have deployed voting machines, and even those states have not deployed them in all precincts. States and counties are free to choose what voting mechanism will be deployed. New York still votes on paper. Washington, DC, is set up on DRE, or direct-recording electronic, on digital terminals. However, the majority of the existing electronic voting equipment is aged and has become a security risk. Yes, the opponents of e-vote reform all understand this issue, and we all agree something has to be done. However, this reform calls for the deployment of a unified ballot method, standardizing the devices used across the nation, as well as the software. This layout will effectively centralize the data processing of all ballots. That's why any privacy issue becomes so scary, whether real or not."

"Interesting," Stephanie said. "Do you think most concerns are real? Or not?"

"If the software does exactly what we are promised and it will not associate the voter's identity with the actual ballot, then the majority of the privacy concerns are not real. That is a big if. We also have to think of the perceptions about this issue. How would we gain the voter's confidence, even if we inspect that software inside and out? What would suddenly make the average American trust the government on matters of privacy? The latest polls indicate that less than 38 percent of Americans trust the government on how security, privacy, and civil rights are respected. The same study reflects that most Americans value their privacy over security. So it would take nothing short of a miracle to shift that distrust to a vote of confidence for the e-vote reform, where privacy and vote secrecy are concerned."

"How about the second major concern you have? Vote security?"

"That is a *major* one," Archesi said, underlining the word with hand gestures. "Here's why. If hacking a voting system in a county only jeopardizes the local votes, hacking into a centralized system will give access to the entire election. Until now, any national-scale wrongdoing would have had to coordinate attacks on various vote systems, terminal types, paper versus digital, etc. The lack of centralization and organization in this process helped our security. In short, chaos was helping us stay secure. As we're structuring and centralizing our data processes behind voting, we're eliminating that chaos, but we're also making it very easy for election fraud to happen on a major scale."

"That is a very scary thought," Stephanie admitted. "What's being done about it?"

"The NSA participated in designing the security module that will be installed on top of the voting software, ensuring the impenetrability of the software on all networks and all devices. A team of the best NSA people are guaranteeing that no one will be able to hack into the system come November. The security protocols also call for renewed security modules each ballot year."

"It seems really tight, doesn't it?"

"It does, and I tend to trust the NSA when it says the challenge is taken care of. But this reform is also the biggest challenge one can throw in the face of countless hacker communities, so anything can happen. Your strongest defense is only good until someone invents a bigger weapon and come after you."

"Let's hope the NSA is as good as we all hope it is. How about your third concern, voter participation?"

"With everything I mentioned until now, voter privacy poses the biggest threat to voter participation. I don't think there's much we can do to persuade the American people that we have somehow changed our DNA and we will suddenly start respecting their rights and their privacy."

"My understanding is that the e-vote reform has been signed into law, so it *will* happen this November. What do you suggest we do to mitigate some or all of these concerns?"

"There is a single, minimal change," the congressman said, "that will mitigate the first point and help immensely with the third. That is removing the voter registration card scanning from the digital process. Have humans look at it and validate it, just like it's done today, and forfeit mobility for privacy."

"That doesn't sound so bad," Stephanie said. "Seems like a small compromise to achieve a great deal."

"Precisely. We are introducing a motion to have the scanning component removed. I am hoping my colleagues will see things the way you do, Stephanie, and forfeit a minor piece of progress in favor of major voter confidence and participation."

"It seems to be the logical thing to do, so good luck! And thank you for your time tonight."

"Thank you for your invitation, Stephanie. Have a good night."

The camera zoomed in, leaving Congressman Archesi out of view and focusing on Stephanie.

"Live from our studio, this is Stephanie Wainwright, with *News of the Hour.*"

...Chapter 21: Public Opinion Woes
...Friday, January 8, 6:47PM CST (UTC-6:00 hours)
...Johnson Campaign Headquarters
...Chicago, Illinois

Anthony Fischer glanced at the in-dash time display while pulling into his reserved parking spot in front of Bobby Johnson's campaign headquarters. It was late...He was going to have another late night, and he felt it in his bones. The money was nice though. Very nice. Just as nice as the best presidential campaign manager of the moment could hope for, and then some. He had helped two other presidents get the job, and he was going to help this one too. Johnson had been his second choice; Krassner was way better candidate material, but the prize associated with Johnson's name was almost double. Fischer always followed the money and made the rest follow him: voters, media, and results.

With the right kind of support and two half-decent brain cells, anyone could make it to the White House. Fischer was the best America had to offer in creating and securing that kind of support, the kind that made presidents out of simple candidates. He had the devious, contriving capacity to wile, ploy, manipulate, or seduce anyone into believing anything, into believing the good stuff about his candidate and the bad stuff about the opponents. And not just believing. He had the gift to turn followers into leaders of opinion and beguiled voters into fanatic disciples. He was Johnson's only shot.

He opened the main entrance door to Johnson's campaign headquarters. The lively chatter ceased for a few seconds; that's all it took the staff and volunteers to recognize him and resume their activities. He walked straight to Johnson's office door and entered without knocking.

There he was...plastered again. Slouched on a two-seater couch, his tie knot loosened and top shirt button undone, a half-emptied bottle of single malt Scotch on the table in front of him. He was shitfaced this time, tears running freely on his fallen-apart face. Fischer swallowed his anger and prepared himself for yet another session of babysitting, of handholding one of the lamest politicians in the history of the US presidential runs.

"What's the matter, Bobby?" Fischer almost sounded like he cared. He did care, deeply, for his payday. He was in this loser's boat, and the loser had to win for him to get his millions.

"What if they don't like me?" Johnson whimpered and slurred, reaching out with trembling hands for the single malt. "Did ya hear what they said about me, the assholes? The fuckin' assholes?"

"What did they say, Bobby?"

"That I would be a...a dangerous president for the American foreign policy, 'cause I don't know the difference 'tween South Korea and North Korea." He sniffled. "Who does, huh? Who fuckin' does? Aren't they all the same?"

Fischer swallowed a bitter response to Johnson's geopolitical dilemma.

"Bobby, Bobby, look at me. Who are you, Bobby?"

"Huh?" Johnson poured another two inches of Scotch into his glass, spilling some on the table.

"Yeah, you heard me, who are you?"

Johnson squirmed a little, and then attempted an answer.

"I am Bobby Johnson, and I am running for president."

"Damn right you are!" Fischer stood up, grabbed the glass of liquor from Johnson's hand, and emptied it in the fireplace. The fire responded with an angry burst of flames. "So why the heck would you care what they like and dislike? Huh?"

Johnson was not answering. Still confused and very much drunk, he needed another shock.

"Answer me, God damn you!" Fischer yelled, grabbing Johnson by his loosened tie and lifting him onto his unstable feet. "Are you a pushover? Are you a pussy?" With each question, Fischer shook Johnson a bit, enough to rattle him and dissipate some of the liquor fumes in his head. "Pussies don't belong in the White House, you hear me?"

"Yes," Johnson muttered.

"What did you say?" Fischer pressed on.

"Yes, pussies do not belong in the White House. You're right."

"So what are you gonna do, then? Huh?"

"Umm...Not be a pussy anymore...?" Johnson's hesitant reply came half-affirmation, half-question.

"Exactly right," Fischer said, dropping the force in his voice to an almost normal conversation level. "So here's what you're gonna do." He let go of Johnson's collar, went straight to the whiteboard, and started scribbling.

"One," he said, then wrote the number on the whiteboard. "Stop drinking like this. One a day and a couple before bed, but that's all. You exceed that, I catch you drunk again, and I am out of here, got it?"

"Yes, understood," Johnson said, swallowing hard.

"Two," he said, writing the number under the first one, "stop acting stupid. Think before you speak. Deter questions you don't know the answer to, and prepare for God's sake, prepare before those interviews. You have PR support, use it! They'll write your stuff; you make sure you understand it and memorize it. Is that clear?"

"Crystal," Bobby Johnson confirmed.

"Three, start acting like the future president. Watch how you dress, how you speak, how you act. Make the people like you, trust you, and believe you.

I'll do the rest."

"Got it," Johnson confirmed again, subdued.

"One more question for you, but think hard before you answer." Fischer held silent for a while, for emphasis. "What are you willing to do to become president?"

"Anything, absolutely anything." Johnson's alcohol-powered confidence took over, eliminating all hesitation.

"OK. Remember what you just said, because the time will come when I will ask you to do some out-of-the-ordinary things to get you there. Is that clear?"

"Absolutely clear, I will do anything you ask me to."

Fischer scrutinized him, top to bottom, but found little reassurance. Disheveled and wobbly, a man of weak resolve and wavering commitment, demonstrating very limited practical sense, Johnson could prove real tricky to put in the White House. Maybe that's why the prize was so substantial.

"All right. Sit down and let's discuss funding."

Johnson sat back down on the two-seater, sitting straight this time.

"We need to make friends with the right people and fast. We need serious funding for your campaign, and we need to get organized. This is a quid-pro-quo game: remember that. I will make introductions for you with some very rich and influential people, people who have interests. Some want a policy abolished or a piece of legislation overturned. Others would like tax breaks or new legislation pushed through. You promise them help, and they promise you support. The good part is they have to deliver first. Got it? Zero risk for you."

"But what if I'm unable—"

"Bobby, what are you willing to do to become president?"

"Anything," Johnson stated cockily, "anything whatsoever."

"Then remember that and don't make me ask you again. Show some spine, be decisive, and get the job done!"

"Got it. Who are these rich people?"

"The best corporate America has to offer: fat checkbooks and full agendas. You have nothing to fear."

"Will we keep it legal? There are limits to contributions, you know," Johnson asked.

The man was stupid, and that was that. Fischer exhaled in frustration.

"Of course we keep it legal, Bobby. Our rich friends will only help us fundraise and get to what we want sooner and easier. Not every form of support has to be in cash, you know. One more time: what are you willing to do to become the next president of these United States?"

"Absolutely anything, I swear," Bobby Johnson concluded, hand held firmly over his chest, like taking a solemn oath.

...Chapter 22: Ideas
...Monday, January 11, 10:12AM Local Time (UTC+3:00 hours)
...Russian Ministry of Defense, Arbatskaya Square
...Moscow, Russia

The more Dimitrov thought about it, the more he liked it. He was building the masterpiece of his career. Bringing back the KGB, the way it used to be, but undetected by the West, and fast enough for the irrationally limited patience of President Abramovich. What a stroke of brilliance! Of course, he wouldn't be bringing back the entire KGB, just the part they needed the most and had somehow lost over the years. Being one of the best intelligence units in the world. The teams who got anything done, anywhere. The black-ops capabilities that the entire world had learned to fear and respect. The honor, the glory, the loyalty, and the self-sacrifice of countless agents.

The momentous success he had known in his career had always depended on knowing what move to make and when. He was a great chess player. He knew exactly what he had to do.

Taking his personal encrypted cell phone out, he dialed a number from memory.

"Vitya? It's Misha. I have another business proposition for you."

...Chapter 23: Terms
...Tuesday, January 12, 7:18PM EST (UTC-5:00 hours)
...Costco Wholesale Parking Lot
...Washington, DC

Robert Wilton struggled to push his shopping cart through the parking lot sludge. He wasn't that young anymore, that was definitely a contributing factor. Yet he blamed his pained difficulty in getting the groceries to the car on the constant turmoil he had endured since December.

Robert had lived a life above reproach, taking pride in his work ethics and moral standards. Raised by strict parents and influenced by Catholic precepts, Robert had grown to be valued by his friends, coworkers, and family for his wise helpfulness and resourceful mind. Well-suited for global sourcing, his brain processed information on a large scale. Ever since he had discovered the world as a young Army volunteer, he had fostered an intense passion for exploring what the world had to offer.

Robert had been deeply marked by his experience, at only twenty years of age, of being part of the Armed Forces that had ended the Vietnam War. He had taken part in Operation Homecoming. His unit had been instrumental in freeing and repatriating American prisoners of war, and that deeply emotional experience had transformed him. He was empathic, compassionate, and considerate, and the year 1973 had influenced his thinking, general attitude toward people, and the way he understood them. Living in harmony with his demanding conscience was a fundamental requisite of his well-being. There was none of that harmony left in his existence: only anguish, guilt, sorrow, and fear, mixed with gratitude for having Melanie still alive, still a part of his life.

He reached his car and unlocked it. He let go of the cart, looking to open the SUV's cargo door. The cart slipped in the sludge, but Robert managed to stop it before it could ding his side panel. He pushed the cart farther out and tried to open the cargo door again. The wind and cold drizzle were not helping, and the cart started sliding again.

"Let me hold that for you."

Robert turned to look at the helper. Recognizing the wrinkled features of the face haunting his nightmares, he suddenly felt sick. A shockwave of adrenaline flooded his stomach, making it twist into a knot.

"What do you want?" Robert managed a question.

"I wanted to thank you for awarding the contract just like we discussed. My friends and I appreciate your help." Helms had the audacity to smile in

eighteen, she had worked ardently to build a life for herself, worked to put herself through college and to get as far as she could possibly get from the city of her birth, Mt. Angel, Oregon, from her German heritage, and from her parents.

Her reflection caught her eye again, this time not so flattering: her head still bowed, back hunched, as if she were carrying the weight of the world. *Nah, just crappy post-Christmas blues, that's all,* she thought, correcting her posture. Christmas had always been tough, as thoughts of her parents were making her feel her loneliness even more. Yet, when her father gave her one of the two calls he gave her each year, on her birthday and around the holidays, she had nothing left to say. *Being broke was not helping much with the holiday blues.* She giggled at the thought. *But now that's over, so let's enjoy it to the max.* She cheered herself.

Alex took a few moments to immerse herself in the present moment. She was ambitious, driven to the point of becoming consumed, self-sufficient, competent, creative, and adaptable. She had an amazing talent of adapting to any environment and integrating without any problems, a talent she had developed over numerous job changes and moves, looking for a good professional fit for her highly intelligent brain and impetuous personality.

She had found that perfect fit. She had a fascinating, yet dangerous job that rewarded her curiosity and need for excitement and exploration. She still interviewed for jobs, but only to infiltrate organizations where owners or CEOs had suspicions of wrongdoing, and wanted matters investigated with paramount discretion. She had been the director of technology for a drone manufacturing company for a few months, then the vice president of payment processing for a global bank for a few months more.

Alex now had challenge and reward in her professional life beyond her wildest dreams. She had a nice home, a rental though, not very well furnished and still looking like a dorm room, only with much more technology. She had money in the bank, her own money, and that made her feel safe. She didn't need to use The Agency's limitless corporate card anymore to make ends meet. Her job paid really well. She had friends, and she had a new family in Tom Isaac, Claire, and the team. This past Christmas had been the most fun she'd had since she was nine. She was not alone anymore. *Yup, I've done good,* she thought, giving her reflection a wide smile and proceeding to visit Chanel's outlet store.

She looked into the store window at some fantastic bags and was absorbed in fashionable new trends rather than her own reflection. More reflections in the glass caught her eye though. The image of a person wearing a gray, dingy, hooded sweatshirt appeared several feet behind and to the left of her own reflected image. The hood covered his entire head, and large shades covered his face. His or hers, Alex couldn't tell.

The person's figure was tiny, weighing most likely under 120 pounds. Wearing a fully zipped hoodie on such a sunny, warm day was a little bit weird. Pretending to admire a red shoulder bag from the newest collection by Chanel,

Alex focused more on Hoodie's reflection. It was a woman. The jaw line was delicate, the frame too frail for a man. She shrugged it off, blaming Lou and Tom for her recently acquired paranoia. "You must be aware of your surroundings at all times," Tom had said.

"Where is the attack going to come from? If you know, you live," was Lou's version of the same advice. *Must be nothing,* she dismissed, moving on to visit Ann Taylor.

Minutes later, a new shopping bag in her growing collection, she had forgotten everything about Hoodie. Neiman Marcus was right there, and she had never really spent time in it. Just passed through a couple of times in a hurry. Her taste in clothing had improved after having shopped with her Agency colleague and fashion mentor Richard Fergusson, who had taught her how to dress for any occasion with class, while projecting any image she desired. She and Neiman had work to do.

Look at that, Alex thought with excitement, *I must try this out.* Out of habit, she first checked the price tag of the long-sleeve tunic by Donna Karan. *Holy shit! Almost a thousand bucks!* She hesitated and started to turn away, then remembered her new reality. *The hell with it,* she thought, *let's live a little!*

She picked the blouse off the rack and headed for a fitting room. She opened the door to one of the fitting rooms, and just before closing it, caught a glimpse of Hoodie in her peripheral view. Shades still on and fisted hands buried deep into the sweatshirt's belly pockets, the stranger looked even more out of place here, at Neiman Marcus, among lightweight silk gowns, evening cashmere dresses, and fine Italian leather shoes.

Alex pulled the fitting room door closed and locked it. She didn't rush to try on the tunic; her thoughts were stuck on Hoodie and why she kept appearing wherever she went. Was Hoodie following her? She spent a few minutes evaluating options, the thousand-dollar Karan outfit forgotten on its hanger. Leaving it behind with regret, she exited the fitting room, cautiously looking to spot Hoodie. The stranger was nowhere to be seen. Alex let out a long sigh but decided to head home anyway. *Tom and Lou would be proud of me right now, but I am not,* she thought. *Damn, letting some two-bit stranger scare me off my shopping spree.*

Alex headed for the parking garage, carrying shopping bags in each hand. *The day hasn't been completely wasted,* she thought, starting to feel good again. Turning the corner toward her parking section, she felt a painful nudge in her back. She turned and saw Hoodie holding a gun firmly pressed against her ribs.

"Keep going," Hoodie said in a low, menacing tone. "This time I will not hesitate."

This time?

"Who are you?" Alex asked.

"How very fitting of you to ask that question." Hoodie nudged Alex with the gun, causing her to groan.

Hoodie's voice sounded eerily familiar, but Alex couldn't place her. She turned to face her attacker, dropping her shopping bags quietly, and discreetly looking around. No one was there, just parked cars in semi-darkness. It was all up to her.

"Only months after ruining my life, and you forget I ever existed," Hoodie continued.

"Kramer?" Alex suddenly remembered. Her first case, NanoLance, the drone manufacturer. Kramer was the first person to ever hold her at gunpoint. The first person who had tried to kill her. "I thought you were in jail. I remember putting you there." Alex smirked, buying herself time to get grounded. She started moving slightly sideways to have room to move and place Kramer with her back against the concrete wall.

She remembered Lou's instructions. "Feet well-rooted into the ground, knees slightly flexed and springy, arms ready to strike. Think fast, don't hesitate. Maximum prejudice in defense." Yep, this lady deserved the maximum prejudice she was going to get.

"Out on bail with one purpose in life," Kramer said, lifting the gun to Alex's face. "To make you pay."

"Umm...not today, bitch!" Fast as lightning, Alex prepared to deflect Kramer's gun-holding hand away from her face and toward her left. She hit Kramer's right hand with a quick blow of her right palm. Her left hand grabbed the gun and twisted it upward, forcing Kramer to release it. Alex's right palm then came right back and hit Kramer's chin with full force, making her head bounce back and hit the concrete wall behind her. Kramer fell to the ground, out cold.

"Lou would be so proud," Alex muttered, crouching to check the vitals on Kramer. She was still alive. "Lou *will* be so proud," she corrected herself, "and there will be no end in sight to his smugness."

She pulled her cell and speed-dialed Tom's number.

"Hello," the familiar voice answered almost immediately.

"Tom? It's me."

"How's shopping?"

"I've acquired some unwanted merchandise," she answered. "Hey, are the NanoLance bastards out on bail?"

A quick moment of silence, then Tom replied, "I have no idea. Are you all right? What happened?"

"Nothing much, really, didn't even break a fingernail," she said, amusement seeping into her voice. "I ran into Kramer at the shopping mall, and she had a gun again. This lady loves her firepower. She's out cold now, but I'll need someone to come clean up this mess. Can you call our detective friends for me, please?"

"Alex," Tom said, then cleared his throat. Definite sign of concern when that happened. "This is not something to laugh about. I am glad you're OK, but this is serious. I need to make some calls and figure out what's going on. In the meantime, why don't you join Steve in the Virgin Islands for a quick vacation?"

"What? No," Alex said, determined. "I'm not letting this incident scare me away. I will not run. What's my life gonna be like if I run away every time one of these bastards resurfaces? Plus, I enjoyed it. I owed her a good beating from the last time we met. She left me locked in that bunker to die, so she had it a long time coming you know."

"This is not negotiable," Tom said in his I-am-the-boss-and-I-will-act-like-it voice. "You need to give me time to sort this out, and I want to make sure you're safe while I get things figured out."

Silence. Alex did not respond. A few days in the sun wouldn't hurt at all, and she always loved spending time with Steve.

Kramer moaned and started to move, coming about. Alex turned, and with a quick kick in the neck, knocked her out cold again.

"Look, it's Thursday," Tom continued. "Hop on a plane, get down there, spend the weekend. You can come back on Monday if you like, or you can fly back with Steve."

"All right." She caved. There was logic to Tom's request, and the perspective of a weekend in the islands was not an easy offer to decline. "But I'm not scared, and I'm not running, so you know."

"Yes, yes, I know." Tom chuckled. "Head straight for the airport as soon as the cops take Kramer. No packing, no going by the house, no nothing. Buy some new stuff from the airport; it's on me."

...Chapter 26: New Name, Old Habits
...Friday, January 15, 9:17AM Local Time (UTC+3:00 hours)
...The Kremlin
...Moscow, Russia

Russian President Piotr Abramovich greeted Minister of Defense Mikhail Nikolaev Dimitrov with open arms and a full glass of vodka, despite the early morning hour.

"Mishka," Abramovich said, hugging the man in a rare gesture of benevolence, "have one with me. Let's drink to Russia's glory." He handed Dimitrov the glass.

Dimitrov took the glass and inhaled the cold alcohol vapor. "To Russia the great," he cheered and downed the liquor.

"To Russia the great," Abramovich followed.

Dimitrov's senses perked up. Abramovich was unusually friendly, a state of mind just as dangerous as one of his famous rages, because it could change without notice or reason. One wrong step, one uninspired comment, and he could be thrown into the depths of Siberia, never to see his family again. *Damn...*

"Tell me about your plan," Abramovich said. "When can I have my old KGB back?"

He had suggested the idea to Abramovich only a few days earlier. His current friendliness was an indication of how much the president had liked his idea. Now he had to make it happen. Dimitrov truly believed Russia deserved to recover its long-lost glory and restore order, progress, and control within its boundaries. Maybe this was the way to make that happen. And hopefully it would please the unstable alcoholic he had the privilege to work for.

"Yes, of course I have a plan," Dimitrov said, unbuttoning his overcoat. The vodka was heating his blood, making him sweat under the heavy winter astrakhan coat he was wearing.

"Great, I knew you wouldn't let me down," Abramovich said, reaching to fill Dimitrov's glass again. "When do we start operations?"

"We've already started. Vitya is organizing the network for his first assignment. On my end, I'm assembling a joint unit, FSB and SVR, and we're going to name it Joint 7th Division. It will be entirely dedicated to covert operations. Our own black-ops unit. The unit commander will report directly to me, bypassing the heads of the FSB and SVR."

"Why joint?" Abramovich asked. "Why not completely new,

independent?"

"KGB disbanded to form two pieces in 1991; that's how FSB and SVR came to be, you remember. That's where all the talented operatives are, in one or the other of those organizations."

"So we are going to join the two to bring KGB back?"

"No. In that case, everyone would know what we're planning. We're just going to handpick the best of the best operatives from each organization and assign them to the new Joint 7th Division, unseen and unnoticed. FSB and SVR will continue to exist as cover for the real intelligence black ops. Vitya will lead the 7th."

"Good, good," Abramovich said, deep in thought.

"Any concerns? Anything you don't like about this plan?" Dimitrov probed.

"It's the name. Why the 7th Division? What are the other six?"

"They don't exist, gospodin prezident, but everyone will think they do. They'll waste their intelligence resources trying to find them."

"Da! I like that! What are you planning to do next? When will you start making the bastards pay?"

"Soon, gospodin prezident. Our first Joint 7th Division mission is well underway, and it will make you proud."

...Chapter 27: At the Spa
...Friday, January 15, 9:22PM Local Time (UTC+1:00 hours)
...Kurhaus of Baden-Baden
...Baden-Baden, Germany

Vitaliy Kirillovich Myatlev relished in the VIP treatment he was offered every time he visited the majestic Kurhaus Casino and Resort in Baden-Baden. Secular building, famous for two centuries for its fine dining, excellent amenities, and high-roller gambling in discrete, full-service settings, Kurhaus knew how to welcome its regulars. Especially the very rich ones like Myatlev.

Myatlev loved to party, and the state of decay of his fifty-nine-year-old body reflected that fact ruthlessly. Dark circles around his sunken eyes, swollen eyelids, and the reddish hue of the typical alcohol abuser's nose gave him the physiognomy of a Moscow street drunk. The five-day stubble, peppered with gray, did not help improve his appearance. Neither did the relatively short, greasy, and unkempt hair, running in all directions from his receding hairline, despite Myatlev's attempt to get it under control by cutting it often.

His neckline was where all the street drunk resemblance stopped. From the neck down, Myatlev was dressed impeccably in high-end couture, custom-made by some of the finest tailors in Paris and London. Myatlev took trips twice a year to get his wardrobe refreshed, and he placed no limit on what he was willing to spend to achieve the look he wanted.

Kurhaus Baden-Baden was one of Myatlev's favorite stomping grounds. The massive building, featuring neo-classical interiors lushly decorated with elegant chandeliers and exquisite paintings, was very well suited to the image he wanted to present. The Kurhaus staff was efficient to the point of reading his mind, or so he believed. In fact, most staffers were quite good at reading the body language of their clients, and they rushed to satisfy any need, even before Myatlev acknowledged or formulated his desire. Any need whatsoever. The Kurhaus was very accommodating, ensuring each stay was going to fulfill his every wish.

This time Myatlev was there for business, not pleasure. He was there to make the acquaintance of Dave Vaughn, American billionaire from Texas, with interests similar to his in oil, gas, and energy. The encounter had to appear serendipitous to Vaughn, but that was no issue; Myatlev was good at setting such things up, thanks to his KGB upbringing. A well-compensated bellhop had been watching for Vaughn to make a reservation. Once that had happened, Myatlev was on his way too. The same bellhop had texted him that Vaughn was at the blackjack high-roller table, so that's where Myatlev went, directly after his arrival at Kurhaus, without even bothering to check-in.

He headed for the high-roller tables, separated from the rest of the casino by tinted glass windows and lavishly decorated walls. Each high-roller table had its own private room. Minimum bet 500 Euros, no high limit at the table for selected clientele. Dedicated staff for every room, waiters in white shirts and black vests assisted by lovely young ladies, keeping the players nourished, hydrated, and slightly buzzed.

Myatlev toured the high-roller area, looking to pinpoint his target, Vaughn. There he was, in a blackjack high-roller suite, just as his favorite bellhop had said. Right next to Vaughn's table, an empty one waited for him, courtesy of the same bellhop. He took it and was greeted warmly by the room staff, all old acquaintances from his previous trips.

He started playing double-deck blackjack, half-focused on the game while keeping an eye on his next-door neighbor. Catching his eye at the right moment, Myatlev raised his glass toward Vaughn and made an inviting gesture with his hand. The American nodded, accepting the invitation. He entered Myatlev's room with his hand extended.

"Dave Vaughn, nice to meet you," he said, then took a seat at the table.

"Vitya Myatlev, or V for short," the Russian said.

"I think I'll stick with V." Vaughn laughed.

"I think we've crossed paths before around here, yes?"

"Most likely," Vaughn confirmed. "You do look familiar, and we do seem to like the same game."

"Do you want to join forces?"

"Sure, why not?" Vaughn made a hand gesture, indicating the change in play. The dealer added two more decks to the card-shuffling machine.

The American liked his Scotch, and Myatlev kept them coming discreetly, while making sure the vodka martinis he was downing were more and more virgin as the night advanced. He needed to think sharp and be on top of his game. It was time to move in for the kill.

"Ah, I think I have had enough for tonight," Myatlev said, right after Vaughn had scored several hundred thousand in a winning hand. "Want to join me on the terrace for some fresh air and a cigar?

"Absolutely," a happy and tipsy Vaughn replied.

"Excellent game, thank you for joining my table; it was an honor."

"Pleasure was mine, all mine," Vaughn said, slurring a little and lighting his cigar with moderate difficulty.

"It's amazing what we can do if we join forces, isn't it?"

"Right, right." Vaughn puffed some smoke toward the moonlit sky.

"Makes me wonder if we couldn't join our forces outside the blackjack table, what do you think?"

The American did not answer. Myatlev continued his sale.

"We're both in oil and energy, we have common interests; we care about little more than our respective businesses, yet we compete instead of being allies. Can you imagine the things we could do as allies?"

"An alliance with a Russian?" Vaughn blurted out, his typical diplomacy diluted by the Scotch.

"Who cares about that kind of stuff anymore? It's all gone, right?" Myatlev laughed, patting the American on his shoulder.

"What do you have in mind?" Vaughn was trying to focus, the effort to regain use of his thinking brain creasing his forehead in the process.

"We could make more money working together, dividing areas and markets, building new distribution channels and new markets, taking all our competitors by storm."

"Interesting," Vaughn said, thinking hard. "Yes, I guess we could become stronger against Arab oil, suffocate the bastards a little."

"Yes, yes," Myatlev said, "and much more."

"Like what?"

"We could influence things for each other. For example," he said, carefully watching Vaughn's reactions, "you could become the supporter of the democratic candidate for president in the United States."

Vaughn didn't seem bothered by the idea. Good. Maybe not all Texans were republicans. That just made it easier.

"Do you know what that would do for you and me?"

Vaughn did not respond, so Myatlev continued. "The republican candidate will most likely put protectionist sanctions in place, or that's what he said, anyway. That will bring taxes and limitations for you even more than for me. That guy is trouble. Bobby Johnson, on the other hand, is open-minded and malleable, is pro-globalization, and is willing to listen to big business before making policy. He's the man you want in the White House. Trust me, he's the one."

"I know; you're right. I like Johnson. I think he'll be less trouble than the republican, Krassner."

"Right, so go for it, help the guy a little; put your own guy in the White House." Myatlev laughed, patting Vaughn on the shoulder again.

Hopefully, all that Vaughn would remember the following morning would be that he had a good time, made a new friend, won a small fortune at a card game, and decided to support Bobby Johnson's run for president.

...Chapter 28: A Call for Help
...Saturday, January 16, 7:17AM EST (UTC-5:00 hours)
...Robert Wilton's Residence
...Washington, DC

This is pointless, Robert thought, giving up the night-long effort to catch some shuteye in favor of letting Melanie sleep undisturbed. All he'd been able to do this past night was toss and turn, fall asleep for brief periods of time, then wake up startled and start tossing and turning again.

He sat on his side of the bed, careful to not wake her. He looked at her and felt a knot climbing in his throat and his eyes moisten. Her face was shedding the sickly gray complexion bestowed by the congestive heart failure. She was sleeping well, eating well; she was regaining her old energy and passion for life. *It was worth it,* Robert reflected, *she was worth it. Anything.*

Yet his conscience wouldn't let him find his peace. Maybe it was his upbringing, an upbringing that had instilled solid moral values, in a family where right was right and wrong was wrong, with no room for gray areas in the middle. Born to a middle-class, Midwestern family in Iowa, Robert had benefitted from the undivided attention of an intelligent, patient, principled, yet strict mother. A single child, Robert had been encouraged to think before acting and to evaluate the moral value of all decisions.

His mother had taught him to analyze before acting and to refrain from pursuing actions or deeds with a negative moral value. Not from a religious point of view though, despite her Catholic convictions. Although she was a faithful woman, she was not obsessed with religion, but she did find moral guidance in Catholic principles whenever in doubt. She had taught him to analyze actions from a logical perspective, and she had explained the meaning of right and wrong by reason. Her definition of a moral code had been about determining the set of guiding principles that would keep Robert out of trouble with the law, would make him successful in life, would make him feel good, even proud about his actions and how he conducted himself, and would help him find peace with his conscience. There was no peace to be found now. A month had passed since Melanie's surgery, and his conscience bothered him more and more.

His mother had always encouraged him to fix things when they were broken. Robert had lived his entire adult life on these moral principles and had built a remarkable career for himself by doing the right things, fixing what was broken, and taking assertive action when needed. Something was definitely broken now, and Robert knew only one person who could, maybe, be of some help. Or at least offer some advice.

He stood quietly, gathered his cell phone from his nightstand, and left the bedroom, closing the door gently behind him. He got dressed in a hurry, putting on some crumpled jeans, a shirt, and a parka. In a hurry, he scribbled "out shopping" on a sticky note and slapped it on the fridge door, then closed the garage door behind him.

Climbing into his car, he took a deep breath, holding his face in his cold hands. Although new to him, this gesture was becoming more and more common.

"May God help me do the right thing," he murmured and turned the key in the ignition.

Almost an hour later, just an anonymous figure in the crowded Walmart parking lot, Robert unwrapped a burner cell with trembling hands. He verified that it worked properly, then dialed a number, holding his breath.

The phone rang for a while.

"Hello?" a sleepy voice greeted.

"Sam? It's Robert, Robert Wilton. Sorry to call so—"

"Hey, Rob, long time no see," Sam interrupted. "Almost didn't pick up, didn't recognize your new number. How have you been?"

"It's a burn phone," Robert clarified, skipping past pleasantries and jumping into the core of the problem.

Thick silence ensued. Sam Russell, retired CIA operative and lifelong friend of Robert's since their paths had crossed in Vietnam, reacted instantly to the words indicating that his friend was facing some predicament.

Silence broke with some fumbling noises, as if Sam were touching phone keys or attaching hardware to his phone.

"Line is secure now, Rob, you can spill it. What's up?"

Robert unloaded the entire story in one breath, one long phrase that made little sense.

"I'm in serious trouble, Sam. I screwed up," he concluded. "And I don't even know what kind of trouble. People are dead. I need to call the cops, but I need you to protect Melanie."

"OK, slow down. Let's take this one step at a time; let's start over," Sam said in a reassuring tone. "We'll get to the bottom of this. Together. Like old times."

Sam's reference to their shared Vietnam tribulations had a grounding effect on Robert. Sam had been a POW in a camp liberated by Robert's unit at the end of the Vietnam War. Robert's skinny, grimy face had been the first American face Sam had seen in months. Getting to safety had not been easy for the two of them. They'd had no food or water, and Sam had been malnourished and tortured for months. Robert gave him every bit of food he could get and carried him when he couldn't walk anymore. During their endless, exhausting march through the jungle, they had saved each other's lives more than once and had become closer than brothers. They had been through worse and still made it home in one piece. Maybe there was hope.

"Let's start over; let me get the facts," Sam said. "So, they declined Melanie for the heart transplant, right? When was that?"

"Yes, that's right. MedStar Georgetown University Hospital declined her at the beginning of December. They said it was because of her DUI."

"Then this guy approached you? What was his name?"

"Helms, that's what he said. Not sure if it's real."

"Probably not. Then he offered you a transplant in return for your influencing an outsourcing or offshoring decision? That seems like a lot of trouble to get a contract. What kind of money are we talking about with this contract? What's it for?"

"It's the..." Robert hesitated, thinking of the confidentiality he was sworn to maintain. "It's for the e-vote overhaul, Sam."

"Oh, fuck me..." Sam said, letting several seconds of silence say the rest. "Then what happened?"

Sam's voice had dropped to almost a whisper.

"Then two of my employees died—one in a car crash in Nevada, the other from a heart attack here in DC."

"That could be a coincidence, Bobby; have you thought of that?"

"They were the only ones opposing the offshoring of this contract. They were not going to let it go. And I don't know how, but somehow he knew. That guy, Helms, knew."

"Then what happened?"

"Then we awarded the contract to the company Helms was pushing. They were the strongest offshore vendor anyway, so I didn't have to do anything."

"Is that it?"

"No, Helms appeared again, told me I can't pull out of the contract or they'll kill Melanie. He said the contract must run its entire course or she's dead."

"OK, so what do you want to do?" Sam asked.

"I've got to call the cops. They'll throw me in jail, I know, but there's no other way. People are dead, Sam, and e-vote? Out of all the contracts in this world? I have a gut feeling this isn't about money or that Indian CEO's ego. This is about the next president, Sam. It must be."

"Here's what we need to do. You need to give me a couple of days to look into some options."

"No." Robert snapped. "No, we have to call the cops, the feds, or you tell me who to call, who handles stuff like this."

"If you do that, Robert, you go to jail most likely for the rest of your life, Melanie's life is in danger, and whoever is doing this will go underground and will never be caught. They'll strike again, who knows when and how. How is that better?"

Robert couldn't think of an answer. Sam was right.

"What do you want me to do?"

"Hold on to that burn phone. Keep it handy and make sure it has minutes and the battery is charged. I'll be in touch in a day or two with options. And Bobby?"

"Yes," Robert managed to say.

"Hang in there. We'll fix this somehow."

...Chapter 29: Withdrawal
...Saturday, January 16, 10:00AM EST (UTC-5:00 hours)
...Flash Elections: Breaking News
...Nationally Syndicated

Phil Fournier's greeting opened the newscast on a background of red, white, and blue. The background shifted to show the portrait of Vice President Sheridan.

"A surprise announcement came today when Vice President Mark Sheridan revealed that he will not be pursuing his candidacy for the US presidential elections. His decision comes as a shock to everyone, including the Democrats. Everyone was sure that Mark Sheridan would succeed President Mason and continue the democratic top-level presence in the White House. With President Mason by his side when he made the announcement, the vice president claimed health and family reasons for his decision to step down. At the end of his mandate as vice president, he will retire completely from the active political arena."

The background shifted again, displaying the image of Senator Bobby Johnson, Democrat from Illinois and presidential candidate.

"In the wake of VP Sheridan's announcement, the spotlight moves to Senator Bobby Johnson's bid for president. Most likely he will now be granted Democratic support for his candidacy. With VP Sheridan in the run this support would have never been granted. Consequently, his ratings have gone up, but not by a lot. His support is currently at 22.8 percent, and he will need to do a lot better that that to have a chance to enter the White House as our next president. The low support for Johnson is attributed largely to his perceived indecisiveness.

"A moderate with open yet hesitant views of what America's role should be in the world, Johnson is failing to convince the public that he has what it takes to revive the economy, address the burning issues in our immigration legislation, and stabilize healthcare. Johnson appears undecided about how to tackle poverty and illiteracy in our country, while stating he strongly believes the economy will make a comeback, which will address at least some of these issues."

The background image changed again, cueing footage filmed on the streets of New York City.

"Let's hear a few reactions to today's surprise announcement," Phil Fournier announced before the filmed interviews expanded onto the entire screen.

"I am a Democrat at heart, so I don't care whose candidacy they decide to support. I am voting for him," a young man responded, his face partially hidden by the hood of a down parka.

"Johnson's lame, that's what he is. He could bring this country to ruin. This one bends in the wind; that's what he does. No backbone whatsoever," remarked a man in his fifties, bracing the windy New York City winter in a business suit and hurrying to get out of the wind.

"I don't think Johnson's views on immigration will do this country any good," said a woman in her thirties while hailing a cab. "I think we need to think of the welfare of our own children before caring about other countries and their problems. I want a job and a future for my son, first," she finished speaking, slamming the cab door behind her.

"He's a kind man, he is, you know," an elderly man stated, "and we need kind men."

The screen shifted back to the studio.

"Senator Johnson has some strong supporters, and he could get more. The coming months will be critical for his chances to win, and we will keep an eye on things for you. From *Flash Elections*, this is Phil Fournier, wishing you a good rest of the day."

...Chapter 30: Calling a Friend
...Saturday, January 16, 12:13PM EST (UTC-5:00 hours)
...Sam Russell's Residence
...Timberlake, Virginia

Sam paced his snow-covered deck; he was wearing a light jacket on top of a sweat suit, not feeling the cold, not noticing the winter wonderland landscape unfolding behind his home. There were many ways this could go terribly wrong. He'd been out of the spy business for six years now, and yes, some things never change, but this deal that Robert had gotten himself into seemed intricate and treacherous, a real can of worms.

Sam scratched his clean-shaven head, thinking hard. He had options, quite a few, some legal, some not so much. He could call his former boss, still working for the CIA, and hand this case over on a platter and let the experts do whatever they saw fit with it. There were many other alphabet agencies he could call, with the same results, including throwing Robert in jail for a very long time. All these were his lawful options. He was now aware of a crime being committed, and, under the law, he was obligated to report it. *OK, yeah, but screw that,* he thought, moving on to less lawful options.

A smile curled the right corner of his lips. *Do I still have it in me? One more case?* He flexed his left arm, feeling his bicep with his right hand. He stretched his legs and tried a couple boxing moves, made his feet dance, and threw a couple of jabs in the air. *Yep, still alive,* he thought. *But I can't do this on my own, that's for sure. I need a team.*

He went back inside the house, grabbed his encrypted cell, and retrieved a number from the phone's memory. A man's voice answered almost instantly.

"Tom Isaac speaking."

"Hey, ol' buddy, this is Sam Russell; how are ya?"

"Hey! Great, really great, how have you been?"

"All good, retired and all, just getting old and stale, that's all," Sam said jokingly.

"That's bullshit if I ever heard bullshit before. You, old and stale? Never gonna happen!" Tom laughed.

"Hey, listen," Sam's voice turned serious all of a sudden. "Are you in the same line of business?"

"Yes, absolutely. What can I do for you?"

"How soon can you get here? There's someone you need to meet. You're on the West Coast now, right?"

"Yep, that's where I am. Let's see..." Tom paused, checking flight options online. "It's early here, so I can hop on a flight before lunch. How's nine tonight your time? Landing at Reagan National? Fast enough for you?"

"That'll work. Can we meet inside the airport?"

"Sure," Tom responded, his answer delayed by a split-second of hesitation. "Wherever works for you."

"Text me at wheels down."

...Chapter 31: Vacation
...Saturday, January 16, 9:52PM Local Time (UTC-4:00 hours)
...Flamboyant Avenue
...St. Thomas, US Virgin Islands

Alex enjoyed the Caribbean more than she had expected. She didn't care she technically had to run from San Diego because of Kramer and other potentially loose and dangerous ex-NanoLance executives. Her bruised ego healed in exactly five minutes after being in St. Thomas. Steve's impeccable taste in beaches, convertibles, dining, and overall entertainment was helping as well, but Alex enjoyed his presence most of all.

"What are you smiling about, Miss Hoffmann?" Steve interrupted her reverie.

You, she thought, her smile widening. "I'm having a great time; thank you so much for putting up with me," she said instead. "I took over your vacation without notice or invitation, and I appreciate you taking me in."

"Always a pleasure," Steve replied, frowning a little, a shadow coming over his blue eyes.

There were many unspoken things between them, the relationship that could have been but Alex had rejected because of her own insecurities and the complications such a relationship would bring to their work. Steve disagreed with her reasons, but of course he did; he was the shrink. He always disagreed, always challenged her thoughts, her feelings. They had stopped arguing about it though, both valuing their friendship to the greatest degree. It still felt awkward at times though. Deciding not to think about it anymore, Alex lifted her arms, playing with the wind and enjoying the high-speed convertible ride.

"So, tell me, do you have one of these customized cars brought over when you travel?

Steve's frown evaporated.

"This? This is a rental; it's not customized at all. But it was, in all fairness, very difficult to find."

"Why the extra trouble? You can't drive the average rental sedan for a few days?"

"Seriously? How can you ask that? I will always put in the extra effort to ensure I enjoy my ride. It's important to me."

"Food is important to me right now. Beach makes me very hungry." She growled playfully, baring her teeth and contorting her tan face in imitation of a feral predator. "Where are we eating?"

"We're gonna have pizzas at the Pie Whole. It's an excellent place, you'll love the pies."

Seated and waiting for their pizzas, the conversation stalled. Alex broke the silence, not comfortable with it at all.

"Do you come here every year?"

"In the past few I have, yes," Steve replied.

"Cheers." She raised her glass, then downed her Heineken thirstily. Putting it down empty, she beckoned the waitress for another one.

"Go easy on it; it'll get to your head before you know it," Steve warned, playfully waving a finger at her.

"Ah, shut up, buzzkill. I'm thirsty, that's all." She laughed.

"Actually, that's not all," Steve added, turning pedantic. "You're also dehydrated from a full day on the beach, and alcohol will get you intoxicated faster than normal. That's why alcoholic beverages should not be consumed on the beach or in intense heat."

The man loved to teach, that was a sure fact.

"That's why Arabs don't drink alcohol," he continued, undisturbed.

The tidbit of information caught Alex's curious mind.

"What? I thought it was by religious precept that they couldn't drink. Written in the Quran, right?"

"Yes, but like with all forms of religious doctrine, the Quran was developed as a guide to keep people lawful, healthy, and productive during times where law and law enforcement, healthcare and health education, and government infrastructure were altogether absent. The religious books taught people what to eat and what to avoid to live a healthy life. You see, back then 'Thou shalt not kill' was about the only thing keeping people from killing one another. Back then, if anyone decided to commit murder, in the absence of the legal mechanisms we have today, there was little that could be done to catch the killers and hold them accountable."

"Interesting. So that's why alcohol is banned in Islam, because Islam is found in the hot zones of the planet, right?"

"The Islamic faith originated in the very hot areas of the planet; although now you can find some limited Islamic influences in temperate climates, yes. But even the expansion of the Islam happened primarily toward other hot regions, like Africa. One can only speculate that it happened this way because their precepts made more sense to people living in very hot climates."

"I see what you mean," Alex said, thoughtful. "Muslims cannot drink alcohol, but Catholics can, the majority of them living in temperate or cold areas."

"Catholics can and are even encouraged to taste a little red wine, very healthy for people living in temperate or cold climates. Wine is a natural circulatory aid. What other examples can you think of?" Steve asked in his teacher voice, addressing her as he would a student.

"Well, Muslims can't eat pork either. Pork is fat, hard to digest in a hot climate, and spoils easily. What else...Ah, the Catholics and the Orthodox have biannual fasting, which detoxifies your body, if you stop and think about it. But both these religions allow eating of meat, especially at the beginning of winter."

"Why then? Why sacrifice pigs at the start of winter?"

"Because it's cold outside, and, historically, people living thousands of years ago did not have freezers to preserve their meats."

"Yep, that's precisely it," he agreed.

"Why do you like to teach, Steve?"

"Because it changes how people, how *you* look at things. How you think about things. I open your mind to different points of view that you later decide to use or discard. That is very rewarding." He paused, taking a wolf bite out of his pizza. "I also like to hear myself talk," he laughed.

"How long have you worked with Tom and the gang, with The Agency?"

"Almost twelve years now," he replied and took another bite.

"How was it back then? How were the earlier cases?" Alex gulped her second glass of ice-cold beer and gestured for a third.

"Oh, I don't know about the early cases. Tom had started The Agency almost twenty years before he met me. He worked the cases himself; he did everything on his own at first, or with Claire's help. Then we met, and I started working for him."

"Did you work on tough cases like the ones we take now?"

"You've only worked two cases; you're very junior in this job, but yes, both your cases so far were tough, and no, back then they weren't all like that. For example, no one held me at gunpoint or wanted to kill me until several years in."

"So I should be flattered?" She smiled playfully, almost flirtatiously.

"No, you should be concerned and wary and behave like an adult about this." Steve was serious. "I am worried, you know," he softened his voice a little, touching her hand. "I am concerned that you show no sign of trauma after these events. On the surface it's almost like these events did not affect you at all, like you don't care."

"Steve, don't be a shrink with me, please. I'm having a great time. Be a friend," she pleaded, slurring a little, raising her third glass of beer and clinking it against Steve's tall order of sparkling mineral water.

"I *am* your friend, and I am concerned about you. You should feel anger, fear, anxiety, or any mix of these feelings. Instead, it seems to me you don't let yourself feel anything."

"Nope, not true. I feel proud of being able to handle myself well. I felt embarrassment when I didn't. I had my ass handed to me a couple of times in the past, and that was awful. I was afraid I'd get fired for not being able to take care of myself." She chuckled.

"That would never happen, don't worry. Tom will probably give you a hard time and train you some more, but he wouldn't do that."

"Good to know, but I still don't wanna screw it up again, 'cause it was a lousy feeling, to let that biatch Kramer have the upper hand. But see? The tides have turned, and fate gave me the opportunity to even the score with her, so I actually felt happy about it. That's how I felt. And grateful to Lou for spending his Christmas vacation on my self-defense lessons. My butt hurt for days...It had to count for something, and it did. And I am grateful."

"Were you afraid? Talk to me," Steve asked in a soft voice.

"Hell, yeah, and still am sometimes, but I don't wanna talk about it," she said, sadness coloring her voice. She stood up, a little unsteady, then found her balance and sense of humor. "Let's go. I am so done letting you ruin this awesome dinner."

"That's your way of saying you're a little tipsy, exactly like I said you'd be, and you wanna get to the hotel early?" Steve asked mischievously, laughter in his voice.

"Ha! In your dreams, buddy, I am so not drunk! The night's still young!"

"Prove it to me, then," Steve challenged her as they left the restaurant.

"How?"

Steve stepped toward a patch of fresh-mowed lawn next to the Pie Whole. Cut blades of grass covered the lawn, left behind by the mower.

"Well, it's a scientifically proven fact that a person can't sit on their knees, hands behind their back, and lean forward to grab a blade of grass with their teeth, then sit upright again, if they're intoxicated."

"You're on." Alex cheered at the challenge.

She kneeled on the grass and put her hands behind her back. She felt unsteady momentarily. This was going to be hard, but she wasn't going to back down from the challenge. She started leaning forward toward the grass, slowly, barely managing to hold her balance and not fall face down on that lawn. A few passersby were watching, intrigued and entertained, but she didn't care. She grunted a little, leaned in some more, struggling for balance with a lot of effort, and finally reached the grass. She took a couple blades between her teeth, then got back up, cheering loudly.

"See? I told you I'm not drunk!"

"Oh, but you are, my dear," Steve said.

"What? But you said—"

"No sober person would have accepted that challenge." Steve laughed, followed by the chuckles of their impromptu audience.

"You bastard!" Alex laughed, punching him in the chest.

It felt good to be there; it felt safe. It was OK to be a careless kid again.

Steve's cell phone rang, interrupting them. He spoke with the caller briefly, then turned to her, his glee gone.

"That was Tom. We're going back home tomorrow; we have a new client."

...Chapter 32: A Trip to Vegas
...Sunday, January 17, 4:27PM EST (UTC-5:00 hours)
...Robert Wilton's Residence
...Washington, DC

Regardless of what Robert did that day, he did not let the burn phone out of his sight, waiting for a sign from Sam Russell or his friend, Tom Isaac. He had met with Tom at the airport, late the night before, and somehow, without really promising much, that guy had put hope back into his heart.

When the burn cell finally chimed, it startled him. With trembling hands, he flipped the cell open to read the text message.

Find a legit business reason to travel to Las Vegas on Tuesday—meet a vendor for dinner. Check into Aria hotel—reservation already made. While at dinner, you'll get a new text with instructions. Hang in there.

...Chapter 33: Startup
...Monday, January 18, 10:14AM Local Time (UTC+1:00 hours)
...Prague East—Brandýs nad Labem-Stará Boleslav
...Prague, The Czech Republic

Karmal Shah pulled his Audi Q7 into the courtyard. Before parking, he looked around carefully, checking for movement, people, cars, anything out of the ordinary. All was quiet in the backyard of his newly purchased property in East Prague. He had spent 12,000,000 Czech koruny, or almost $470,000, to buy a 7,500-square-foot warehouse with refrigeration capabilities, an office that could accommodate five or six people, and an apartment for his personal use. The building had truck access and a loading dock and could be fitted to house even more industrial-sized refrigerators, if the business were to suddenly pick up. The colors were awful though; the place needed a paint job badly, but there was no time for that.

This location worked great for Shah. It was just a few miles northeast of a small airport, Letiště Praha-Kbely. A small air base that welcomed civilian aircraft traffic for the right amount of money, Kbely was large enough to accommodate his personal plane, a Piaggio Avanti EVO, custom-fitted to carry cargo with minimal reconfiguration. His aircraft turned people's heads and got a lot of attention due to its twin engines mounted in push configuration. A small forward wing made the nine-seater plane look like it had whiskers and made its silhouette unmistakable. It was a great aircraft: fast, reliable, and low cost to fly. Seven million dollars very well spent.

Karmal Shah, a Pashtun from Afghanistan and successful entrepreneur in the gourmet and exotic foods market with rumored yet unconfirmed ties to the Taliban, was very aware that his current commercial flight status could change overnight if the FBI, CIA, or any such organization should decide to add him to the no-fly list. That was probably going to happen anyway, sooner rather than later. Shah was not delusional; he knew that was coming, especially with the new rise in the terrorist activity generated by ISIL and the renewed focus on antiterrorism that ISIL had generated.

Damn fools, ISIL, ISIS, or whatever they wanted to call themselves. They didn't have the refinement or patience to think through or build complex strategies. They were savages, barbarians who liked to scream threats and decapitate hostages on television, getting people and organizations like Shah's under the microscope again. Damn fools. Sometimes Shah wondered whom ISIL really worked for.

Nevertheless, Shah needed to preserve his air mobility, and he needed a private plane for his current needs anyway. The Piaggio was hardly a cargo hauler, but it could take a decent payload. With some careful planning and a few refueling stops along the way, it could even make it to America. A simple stopover would take his plane to Moscow, Eastern Africa, or the Middle East. Great piece of equipment to have, very helpful in his business. The only thing left to do was to register the plane with the Czech Republic Civil Aviation Authority.

Shah liked the location of his new building for many other reasons. The Czechs were happy to grant him business permits and a tax break in exchange for the twenty-five million dollars he was bringing as an investment to their country. Shah was moving his booming online gourmet foods business away from France, where it had operated and grown successfully for years, away from high taxes and overzealous inspectors. All inspectors bothered Shah, whether food, safety, tax, or labor. He simply didn't want them snooping around. The Czechs were willing to be flexible in exchange for such a strong injection of capital into the region. The local authorities had become his best friends for minimal amounts of cash. Great place to do business.

Engine idling, he checked the task list stored on his iPad. Almost ready to operate. He needed people hired, warehouse and office furniture bought and delivered, and the bulk of his gourmet delicacies stock moved on a large cargo plane from France. Then close down the French location, while the Prague location would already be shipping caviar and smoked oysters to customers all over the world. If he started writing some seriously large checks today, maybe he could be operational here within a week. He hated to rush through these things; that's how mistakes happen. This time it wasn't really his choice.

He dialed a number on his mobile.

"Yes, we can do this. We'll be ready."

...Chapter 34: A New Client
...Tuesday, January 19, 8:17PM PST (UTC-8:00 hours)
...Aria Sky Suites
...Las Vegas, Nevada

Alex found the room number indicated in her detailed instructions and unlocked the door with her keycard. The entire team was there. Well, almost; she noticed Richard was absent.

"Come on in, Alex," Tom greeted her. "Let me introduce Sam Russell, an old friend of mine. He's the one who referred our new client to us."

"A pleasure," Alex said, offering her hand. The man, in his early sixties, had a strong handshake and an agreeable smile.

"Alex is our technology executive," Tom continued the introduction. "Sam was a CIA man until he retired a few years ago and started dedicating all his energy and skills to unveiling the secret locations of catfish in his backyard lake."

"I take it catfish are disappearing from your neighborhood?" Alex quipped. Sam intimidated her a little, despite his easy-going manner. She had never met a real spy before. The man didn't look the part, or at least he didn't look like what Alex had imagined a spy would look like. He looked harmless and benevolent. *What were you expecting, guns blazing?* Alex thought and swallowed a chuckle.

"Not in the least, covert catfish are safe with me," Sam replied, his smile widening.

Alex looked around the room, noticing that no one was seated. There was enough seating to accommodate all of them in the luxurious hotel suite, yet everyone preferred to stand. Steve, leaning against a distant wall in his usual style, had a little bit of a frown shadowing his intense gaze. Brian, professional mien and apparently relaxed, was nothing but. Lou was checking messages on his phone and had barely made eye contact with her. Tom was pacing the room slowly. Sam was hovering near the suite door. There was palpable tension in the air.

Alex wondered who the client was responsible for generating such tension before the meeting. They had taken some unprecedented precautionary measures. They had traveled separately, dined separately, and had all been using burn phones for the past two days. *What kind of case are we getting ourselves into? Well, I guess we'll find out soon enough.*

Outside the suite's door, someone tried to open the lock with a keycard, but the lock beeped quietly and stayed locked. Sam opened the door wide.

"Come on in, Robert," he said.

A hesitant man with a haunted look came in, smiling tentatively.

"Mr. Wilton, please let me introduce my team," Tom said, shaking Robert's hand. "This is Alex; she's our technology executive. Steve is our human interaction executive and resident psychologist, and Brian is our business executive and device expert. Lou is our very own hacker and self-defense trainer."

He turned to introduce the visitor. "Robert Wilton is the vice president of Global Sourcing and Engagement for DCBI." Tom saw the micro-reactions in his team the moment he spoke the company name. "Yes, *that* DCBI."

They all sat down on armchairs around a small coffee table, except for Steve, who didn't move and stayed leaning against the wall.

"The case we are discussing today is a bit unusual for us," Tom continued. "We have never before considered engaging a client unless it had the CEO's signature, or the Board of Directors signing off on the engagement with a majority vote. In light of the sensitivity of this case, I wanted you to make that decision," Tom gestured toward the team. "Either accepting or rejecting this case carries immense responsibility. Let's give Mr. Wilton the opportunity to tell us what happened."

Alex listened to Robert speak, going through facts and events in a guilt-ridden voice, his eyes fixated on the elaborate design of the Sky Suite's thick carpeting. The denied transplant. The deal offered by a stranger with the name of Helms. The two employees killed with no apparent foul play or correlation between them. A car crash on ice-covered mountain roads and a heart attack in plain view. Awarding the e-vote contract to the Indian offshoring company ERamSys. The threat to Melanie's life if the deal was cut short. The deal. The deal with the devil. She took some notes, while her brain, in high gear, started correlating the events and speculating as to what could be the reasons and motives behind the facts described by Robert Wilton. *These cases aren't getting any easier with time, that's for sure,* she thought. *Can't even believe we're having this conversation, here, in a Vegas hotel room. This sounds more like a case for the feds or the CIA or something, not for...me.* She shuddered.

Robert Wilton finished his story, and silence took over the room for a few moments.

"Any questions? Opinions, ideas?" Tom asked.

"So, let me get this straight," Alex said, "we're looking at a terrorist attack targeting our elections? Hidden behind an offshore software development contract?"

"Hidden behind it, or linked to it somehow," Tom clarified.

"This goes way beyond corporate conspiracies, our normal cup of tea," she offered. "Way beyond. Terrorism? I don't think we're even remotely equipped to deal with that."

"Terrorists are not that different from the mainstream corporate bad guys we've been tackling," Steve responded. "They all want the same things, follow more or less similar goals, money, or some strong personal or group belief. Terrorists just go about it in a different way, that's all."

"And they're more dangerous," Lou added.

"True. They've crossed the line into illegal activities and have nothing to lose. That makes them very dangerous." Steve agreed. "But the same core psychology still applies. If a crime is being committed, think means, motive, and opportunity. This rule applies to the master plan and its creator. Think strategically about all these moving parts. They are part of a whole, of a blueprint of serious proportions. This whole we don't understand yet. That being said, I still believe we should walk away from this case. It's just way too dangerous. Could get us all killed."

"You have a point, Steve. Why aren't we taking this case to the feds or Homeland Security?" Alex asked.

Sam leaned forward a little before answering.

"There is a strong risk that if the feds or any law enforcement agency is called in, they will simply stop the deal and fail to uncover who is behind this. The conspirators would go underground, and we would never find them, nor will we know when they decide to strike next. Or how."

"Can't the feds go undercover and investigate discreetly, like we would do? Can't they see the big picture?" Alex continued her chain of thought.

"No law enforcement agency directors would gamble with the presidential elections. With their careers at stake, they'd go strictly by procedure. They would just kill e-vote altogether to be safe, and in the wake of that, DCBI would be bankrupted, and Robert would be thrown in jail for the rest of his life."

"I can accept that," Robert said, still staring at the floor.

"You don't know what you're talking about," Sam snapped. "You wouldn't be going down for taking a bribe. You'd go down for treason!"

Silence filled the room: thick, compact, and heavy. Robert's pallor turned grayish.

"Wow," Alex whispered. "That puts things in a very different perspective, right?"

"Yes," Sam acknowledged. "We have to think of the potential ramifications. This deal is most likely not about money. This doesn't sound like it's about helping the Indian vendor get the contract to satisfy his ego. There is some kind of conspiracy behind it. I'd bet on it. Could be terrorism, yes, you're right. Sure feels like terrorism. But it also could be something else we can't even think of right now. We only know for sure that it has to do with the presidential elections coming this November; it's linked with the offshore deal, and it's worth killing for."

"Alex, if we take this case," Tom said in a gentle voice, "it will have your name all over it. You're the only one of us who we can deploy in a technology environment."

"Yeah, I know." She looked at Tom with concern. "And I'm worried I could let everyone down. I could get all of us in serious trouble, even killed, if I make a mistake. This deal is way more serious than our typical corporate investigations. Tom, I am not a spy, and I don't know how to function like one."

"But I am," Sam interjected. "I would work the case with you, with all of you."

"Officially?" Alex asked.

"As in 'with the CIA'? No, unofficially, I am afraid. I'm still retired, and I can't call the company for the same reason we can't call the feds."

"I see," Alex said quietly.

"So you're considering this, Tom?" Steve asked, leaving his wall and stepping toward the center of the room. "This can go wrong in so many ways that I can't even think of a way it can go right! Have you thought about what happens to Alex if she gets caught? What happens to all of us?"

"I have thought about it a lot. That's why I'm asking the team to make the decision. Personally, I can't just shrug this off and walk away from it. Call me a patriotic fool, delusional, or whatever, but it feels to me we have little choice. This is one of those things that once you learn they exist, you can never be the same again; you can't just walk away from it."

"I get it," Steve said angrily, "but think of what you're asking. All of us here could end up in jail for the rest of our lives, not just him." Steve pointed at Robert Wilton.

"I agree, and that's why, again, I am not asking anything of you other than to decide."

"Do you realize we'd go in without support?" Steve continued. "DCBI knows nothing of this, and we would have zero leadership support behind us. We'd be blind, exposed, completely on our own. A bunch of crazy, rogue vigilantes on a truth quest across continents."

"Correct," Tom said, frowning. "No argument here. What else do we need to think about?"

"I hate to be the business head in this discussion, but how will we get paid?" Brian asked. "This operation will be very costly."

"I could raise—" Robert started to say and was interrupted immediately.

"No need for that. I would waive any fees and fund the entire case myself," Tom said. "The financial loss would be mine and mine only." He hesitated a little, then continued. "I feel very strongly about this case. It stirred me up, brought back memories of war, of sacrifice, of just doing the right thing, and the hell with the rest. Of being heroes, no matter how dumb that sounds today. Are we being patriotic here? Or delusional? Or just plain stupid? You need to tell me. If this case stirs you the same way, you'll let me know. Personally, I am willing to take the risk, and I am willing to sacrifice for it. However, regardless of that, if your decision is to say no, I will not think any less of any of you. You have my word."

"You said 'will,' Brian," Alex commented.

"Not sure I understand," Brian responded. "What do you mean?"

"You said 'this operation *will* be very costly,' not 'would.' Are you inclined to say yes?"

"Good catch, Alex." Brian agreed with a frown. "I guess I do. Businesswise it might be a mistake of epic proportions, but it made me think I want to do this because they simply can't get away with it, and I want to make sure of that. Personally. You see, normally we deal with corrupt business people; we fix things, and we right the wrongs. Yes, I can totally see how we bring value and why. It makes me feel good about the work we do. However, in most of the cases we take, the effect of our work is limited to the client corporation. That's what we fix, that's what we help with. But in this case, it's personal. They, whomever *they* might be, are coming after me, after us, our families, our lives maybe. They are targeting our elections somehow. They've crossed a line. They could be planning to bomb the voting precincts, for example, and that's as personal as it can get for me."

"It's probably not going to be explosives." Lou made his voice heard for the first time that evening. "Because the software is what they care about. They said they didn't care about hardware, so probably there won't be bombs inside the devices."

"Sure," Alex said humorously, "and we always believe the bad guys when they give us their word, and there is no such thing as a diversion." She winked in his direction, softening the lesson. Her protégé needed work.

"Yeah, but they said hardware could go anywhere, didn't they?"

"Yes," Alex explained, "but that could very well be because they already had the right hardware vendor in play. How do you know if that isn't the case here?"

"Umm...a confirmed kill," Lou said, smiling bitterly and blushing at the same time. "I better shut up then."

"No, no, not at all," Tom encouraged him. "What do you think about what you heard here tonight?"

"I heard a few very scary things. If the deaths were not random or coincidental, they were executed by a pro, or more than one. Timing a heart attack with this kind of accuracy is top-notch contract work. Expensive. Car crashes are not that hard to get done, but one so clean, on a random rental car and leaving absolutely no evidence behind, that's also scary. The scariest thing remains how they knew who was against awarding the deal to the offshore vendor.

"What do you mean?" Tom asked.

"All these hits had precision. That means there is heavy surveillance deployed in everyone's homes, offices, computers, phones, cars, everything. To get an op like this done you need months to prep. Makes you wonder when it all started, really. How did DCBI get the contract at first? Was someone else blackmailed to get *that contract* assigned? How far up or back does this reach? Is this Electionsgate?"

"Exactly," Sam agreed. "You think like a spy; you've got some serious talent, young man. You know what else we don't know? Is this deal with the offshore company the entire game or just a piece of a bigger strategy?"

"How would we even know?" Lou asked.

"We wouldn't," Sam replied, "not until we find out who the players are behind this and what they're after."

"Tom," Steve asked, "what did Claire say about this? What does she think?"

"She said I'm a crazy old fool, but she'll support me and all of you in whatever we decide to do. Richard said essentially the same. If we choose to take this case, he'll help us all the way."

Alex looked at Robert Wilton. He was sunk into his chair, pale, expressionless, staring into nothingness. She felt a wave of empathy for the man who had started this series of events, only wanting to save his wife's life and ending as a traitor against his country.

"Mr. Wilton, can you—"

"It's Robert, please," he interrupted.

"Robert, yes, will you please tell us how you feel about letting us, a group of strangers, deal with this and hold your life in our hands?"

It was a loaded question. Robert thought a little before answering, his voice unsure and faint.

"You see, Sam brought me here. He saved my life before, many years ago. He said I could trust you with my life and that he's going to trust you with his to get this done. I realized that I did a terrible thing. Even though we don't understand all the implications or what those people want, it's still a dreadful thing I have done. No doubt about that, and I will have to live with that for the rest of my life, no matter what happens. It's not about me anymore. I don't think it ever was. Even more than keeping Melanie safe, I am determined to do whatever it takes to fix this and make it right again. I am not sure we will be able to, but I am definitely hoping you will help me. If anyone can save Melanie, save us, it's all of you."

"Steve, anything else you'd like to add or ask?" Tom probed.

"I am 100 percent in agreement that something needs to be done. Normally I'd say call the feds and let's be done, because this job is just too damn risky for us to attempt on our own. It's too dangerous for Alex to work this case. But if we bow out, whoever's orchestrating this attack will succeed anyway. Not even later, when they'll regroup and figure out their Plan B. They'll win now, when the feds shut down e-vote reform citing security concerns. They will win, because if that happens we will be voting on paper for the rest of our lives. They will steal our progress, our courage to change."

Tom turned toward Robert.

"Robert, we will make a decision tonight. It will probably be a long night. Please allow us time to think though this."

Robert stood up and headed toward the door.

"Whatever you decide, just know that you're a remarkable group of people. Thank you for hearing me out."

"Absolutely. Please go straight to your room and keep in mind every move you make might be monitored. We will be in touch shortly. Try to get some sleep."

As soon as the door closed behind him, Alex stood up and starting pacing angrily.

"Do you guys realize that he might have been set up? To begin with? He doesn't even realize it. How did they know DCBI would have a vulnerable sourcing leader at the right time to go for this deal?"

"Oh, my God," Steve said, "are you saying his wife's heart disease might have been a setup?"

"I am saying it's possible. They definitely know how to give people precisely timed heart attacks."

"Interesting idea, definitely worth looking into," Tom said. "Let's get back to decision making for now. How do we do this, want to take a vote?"

Alex felt the sweat break at the roots of her hair. She was scared, yet very excited at the thought of being part of such a bold operation. *Oh, God...please let this be the right decision.*

"Can't believe I'm crazy enough to say this, but I'm willing to do it. I think if I say no, there will be no one else left to say yes the right way and get to the bottom of this. I'd be abandoning you, this team, Robert, and every single individual who will want to cast a vote this November. But I am not a spy...I will need some serious time with Sam to teach me a few tricks. I will need tons of support."

She spoke with enthusiasm, an enthusiasm she felt with every fiber in her body and could not explain. *I did get stirred up. Tom was right. But I am also certifiable. And scared,* she thought. She took a deep breath, then continued, "I would prefer it if I don't end up dead or in jail. It scares me to even think about that, so I won't. And I will need a very stiff drink as soon as we're done here." She smiled awkwardly. Her hands were trembling, but she felt good about her decision. *Screw the bastards.*

"We're batshit crazy, all of us, but let's do it," Brian said. "Can't believe myself; I have everything a man could dream of, and I'm willing to risk it all because of some patriotically bruised ego by a threat of unknown source and magnitude. Textbook definition of insanity."

"Steve?" Tom asked. Steve was back to leaning against his favorite wall, a look of concern wrinkling his forehead.

"I'm behind you, like I've always been, but I'm fearful that we're getting in over our heads. We're sending Alex to who knows where, while we'll be in the safety and comfort of our California office. That just doesn't seem right."

"I'll be fine," Alex said. He was protective of her, too protective for a rational business decision, but it did make her feel good.

"Lou, how about you?" Tom asked.

"I'm all in. What I wouldn't do for five minutes alone with whoever thought this shit up," he replied without any reluctance.

"OK, then, let's do this," Steve said. "Let's nail whoever's playing with our country and our future. But if I sense the danger levels are beyond acceptable, I'll hit the brakes."

"Fair enough," Tom said. "We're in agreement, then. Let's hope it's the right thing to do. Drinks, anyone?"

They attacked the room's mini-fridge bar in a tight formation, not wasting any time with glasses or ice.

Alex gulped a shot-size bottle of Martini vermouth and said, "Since we're all facing mortal peril with this case, and considering tonight might very well be our last night of freedom and relative tranquility, can we at least make the most of our stay in Vegas?"

...Chapter 35: Krassner's Press Conference
...Wednesday, January 20, 9:01PM EST (UTC-5:00 hours)
...Flash Elections: At a Glance
...Nationally Syndicated

The waving colors of the American flag marked the show's opening credits, then faded out, leaving the studio image of Phil Fournier in its place.

"Good evening, everyone. Republican Senator and presidential candidate Doug Krassner held a press conference today, presenting his platform in more detail and answering questions from the press for an unprecedented marathon of almost three hours.

"Krassner impressed his audience with the very firm stance he holds on many contentious items of general concern, such as immigration reform, healthcare, unemployment, economy, poverty, illiteracy, and defense.

"Some of Krassner's views were quite surprising, considering that traditionally Republicans have been more on the side of big business. Despite incorporating platform ideas that are out of alignment with current big business lobbying efforts, Krassner maintains that this platform is actually going to help big business more, by bringing long-term vision and strategy to the forefront.

"For example, Krassner's views about immigration state clearly that he will not support a relaxation of the immigration laws, leading to more temporary or permanent foreign workers being allowed to enter the workforce, as long as the American workforce is plagued by long-term unemployment. This single point is an exposed nerve for big business, that has been lobbying for an increased number of temporary visas and the relaxation of immigration limitations and criteria in the effort to secure highly qualified labor at lower cost.

"Krassner is very aware of this issue and has promised big businesses that he will work with them to make sure their labor needs are solved without prejudice to their interests and without any further prejudice to 'our wounded and desperate workforce,' as he called it. When prompted by questions from the media, he quoted thoughtful and compelling solutions, such as a government-funded program to relocate unemployed workers to where the jobs are, including housing buy-back and buy-in aids, significant tax breaks for corporations that choose to establish operations in high-unemployment areas, incentives for telecommuting work arrangements, and professional development programs for the unemployed, where corporations would be invited to participate and train their future workers in exchange for tax breaks.

He also proposed tax incentives for corporations that hire young graduates and place them in skill development or apprenticeship programs.

"Krassner said, and I quote, 'the problem is that corporations don't want to spend any time in developing their workers. They expect all new hires to come fully trained for the jobs they are getting. Corporate citizenship has become, for some time, just lip service. A demonstrated, yet often ignored fact remains that a corporation cannot sustain itself long term if the social environment and the health of the community around it are decaying.'"

The studio monitor rotated through pictures taken at the press conference, showing the charismatic Republican engaging with the press. Phil continued his summary, "Krassner proceeded in the same strong-minded manner to expose his views on healthcare reform. Healthcare reform has been an ongoing battle for many years, and Krassner's presentation today dedicated ample time to address it. In his view, healthcare needs to undergo a process of, and I quote again, 'dramatic simplification.'"

The screen shifted to show footage from the press conference. Krassner's voice was bold and determined.

"We have a healthcare law that few people understand, and with a reported twelve-million words on some thirty-thousand pages, even fewer will ever actually read. This is ludicrous. We need to simplify healthcare and build a system that allows people to just get care when they need it. Having developed a piece of legislation the size of a truck was a terrible waste of government money.

"The two things we do need to control in healthcare are simplification and cost. Do we understand why, if I want to have my cholesterol checked and I don't have any insurance, the lab will charge me four hundred dollars? But if I go the next day and present my insurance card, the same test only costs $17.50. What's really going on? How is that acceptable? Wouldn't you want to find out? How much should cholesterol testing cost?"

Krassner paused for a second, loosening his tie, then continued. "I believe in the core values of the Republican doctrine, and, based on these values, I believe that we should preserve the unalienable right of the American people to access a healthcare system free of corruption and self-destructive greed. I believe we should look in the right direction when trying to fix healthcare, poverty, and illiteracy. We should go back to our core precepts, the precepts that have been at the cornerstone of our government's constitution. Because here's what's happening: in the maze of healthcare costs that don't make sense from one patient to the next, and in the wake of a multi-year effort to generate a twelve-million word piece of legislation, we have become weary and unable to remember what we started fighting for. We are defeated."

Applause and cheer erupted in the press room. The image faded, returning to Phil Fournier's studio desk.

"Yes, they liked it a lot. But it remains to be seen if Krassner, who some are already calling a radical, can secure the nomination from the Republican Party and win the presidential election after threatening a few big-business interests.

"After today's press conference, Krassner's ratings spiked to 41.5 percent. Definitely bold and willing to break patterns, Krassner's resolve is aided by his personal wealth, making him less dependent on fundraising for his campaign success and less vulnerable to big business pressure. Speaking of breaking patterns, Krassner might have started his press conference attired in a formal business suit, but he ended up losing the jacket and tie and rolling the sleeves of his white shirt to his elbows. Whether that was intentional or not, I guess we'll never know, but the subliminal message conveyed by his image was loud and clear.

"We will keep you informed of Krassner's ratings as today's message reaches the homes of voting Americans. From *Flash Elections*, this is Phil Fournier, wishing you a good evening."

...Chapter 36: Work Session
...Friday, January 22, 9:27AM PST (UTC-8:00 hours)
...Tom Isaac's Residence
...Laguna Beach, California

Alex had suggested, and they'd all agreed, that the best location to work on their new case was out of Tom's home, not the corporate office. Too much sensitive information was in play to allow janitorial services or the corporate building's administrator to set eyes on any of it. She requested a large corkboard and a whiteboard, and Tom had installed those on the wall of his home office. The chic room had lost in style but gained in functionality, giving up elegant wall art and uncluttered real estate in favor of juxtaposed corkboards, a small meeting table, and enough seating for the team. It made for a crowded workspace, but it was the safest place to have conversations about the new case.

Alex came in carrying colored knitting yarn, a set of dry-erase markers, highlighters, Sharpies, corkboard pins, and sticky notes. She unloaded the supplies on the table and gave a sigh of relief when she noticed the Keurig coffee maker on the small table next to the window. They had everything they needed.

"She's here; let's get started," Steve called from the doorway, then turned and gave Alex a quick hug. "How are you this morning, doing all right?"

"Yeah, I guess. It all started sinking in, what we're about to do, and...yeah, I'm all right. I think I have an idea where to start," she said, unsure how to express her thoughts.

"Good morning," Tom greeted her. "How's your day so far?"

"Busy," she responded, gesturing toward the pile of supplies scattered on the table.

Brian and Sam, houseguests of the Isaacs for the past couple of days, took their seats. Lou, still a little intimidated and uncomfortable in Tom's home, picked the most distant chair to sit on at the back of the room.

"All right, let's hear your approach, Alex. What are your thoughts so far?" Tom invited her to start.

She took a hurried gulp of fresh coffee and walked toward the whiteboard, marker in her hand. She drew a vertical line on the whiteboard, separating the space into two sections of different sizes, and wrote above the left space "Known" and above the right space "Unknown."

"As you can see, we know very few things at this point. We know there's this guy, Helms, keeping busy to set things up." She wrote Helms' name under the Known category. Then she pulled a file folder from her laptop bag and took out a sketched likeness of Helms and pinned it in the higher mid-section of the corkboard. "Steve worked with Robert to get us this sketch. You have talent, Steve," she complimented him, then went back to the whiteboard. "We know they were behind Melanie Wilton's transplant. Facilitating it? Definitely. Causing the need for it? Unknown at this point. Do we know what happened to Melanie's heart? Why did she need a transplant in the first place?"

"She had congestive heart failure," Sam said. "I probed discreetly with Robert; I couldn't bring myself to tell him that he might have been set up before we're absolutely sure of it."

"Yeah, definitely," Tom agreed. Steve nodded his agreement. There was no need to add to the man's internal anguish.

"He said that Melanie started developing heart failure a few months ago, maybe six or seven," Sam continued. "At first she was more and more tired, unable to sustain the slightest physical effort. For a while she just rested, thinking it would eventually go away. Then they saw a cardiologist, who was able to manage it successfully with medication for three or four months. Then she started accumulating blood in her extremities, abdomen, and lungs. That only evolved a month or so before the transplant, so it was fairly new."

"We need to start building a timeline," Alex said and drew a long, horizontal line spanning across the entire lower section of the whiteboard. She marked the right extremity of it with an arrow and a "t," for time. She marked "November" very close to the right end of the time axis. She marked January right about the middle and then went back in time, to the left of the board, and marked "June?" on the axis. Next to June, she drew a line at a sixty-degree angle and wrote on it "Heart failure starts." Then she marked November of the previous year as "Congestive failure," and in December she marked "Transplant."

"OK, I'll continue adding events as we go though the facts. Back to what we know." She wrote "transplant facilitation" under the Known section and "heart disease cause" under the Unknown section.

"I think it's fairly clear they did this," Lou offered. "We could move that to the Knowns."

"I think it's very likely," Alex replied, "but it's not really known or proven yet. We will operate under the assumption that this scenario is very likely, but for now we don't have enough data to confirm it."

"That's a very cautious way to look at things," Brian confirmed. "The hypothesis that they caused Melanie's heart failure is changing the timeline dramatically and turns this into a two-year long conspiracy."

"As a side note," Alex intervened, "I struggle with calling these people 'they' all the time. Can we call them something else? Until we figure out who 'they' are?"

"Let's call them UNSUB," Sam suggested. "Works for law enforcement really well, stands for unknown subject."

"Yeah, I'd say that's very applicable, thanks!" She wrote "UNSUB" on a sticky note and placed it above Helms' sketched likeness on the corkboard. "It could be more than one UNSUB, you know."

"UNSUB can be a person, a group, or an organization. Until you know for sure you cannot assume," Sam clarified.

"Works for me," she confirmed. "OK, so what else do we know? We know it's about the presidential election somehow." She wrote "Elections" under the Known category. "We don't know how they, the UNSUB, are planning to hit the elections. But because it's the elections that the UNSUB is targeting, we have a very valuable piece of information."

She wrote "November 8" in the Known column. "We have a date. We know the when. We don't know the what, the how, or the who, but we can say we're fairly certain about the when, don't you think?"

"I'd say it's a safe assumption," Tom said.

"I agree," Brian said.

"Same here," Lou confirmed.

"We might learn differently as we uncover more facts," Steve said. "Election Day, this date we think we know could be one hell of a red herring, getting all eyes focused on the election process, while the UNSUB could be trying to blow something up elsewhere. The NSA is heavily involved in securing the election software and the actual election data during the voting process. How do we know it's not an attack against the NSA, using the election software or hardware as a Trojan horse?"

A few moments of silence took over the room.

"What a disturbing thought," Alex said.

"Very," Tom agreed.

"All right, let's adapt our strategy, then. Let's brainstorm and speculate on what the UNSUB could be planning. Mild to wild, lazy to crazy ideas, nothing is too much or too little. Let's bring it." She carved a space on the whiteboard by drawing a rectangle on it, taking from the ample space she had reserved for the Unknown.

"I'll be eating crow now and bring back the idea of explosives in the hardware. All or some of the devices could be rigged," Lou said, smiling shyly.

Alex wrote "Bomb(s) / hardware" in the rectangle. "No crow needed for your sustenance, Lou. Tom will share his steaks, you know."

They all chuckled quietly and relaxed just a little bit.

"They could be targeting the NSA," Steve reminded her of his red herring.

"Ah, yes." She added it to the list. "How about if they want to plant a back-door into the software, so they can hack the results?"

"And bypass the NSA security and firewalls?" Sam replied. "I seriously doubt it, but put it on the board."

"What else? Could this be, after all, only about money and ego?" Alex asked, while adding "$" to the board.

"It's farfetched, in my opinion," Brian said, "but I guess it's a possibility.

They spend a few million getting the contract that's worth hundreds of millions. Nice return on investment there."

"Not just worth hundreds of millions, but it affirms this government's commitment to sending work offshore," Tom said, "which could have a political motive."

"Political? For which country? For the States?" Alex asked in rapid fire.

"No, I was thinking for India. For the States, it wouldn't make much of a difference, and although some voices are speaking loudly against globalization in general and outsourcing in particular, these voices remain strangely ineffective in the States. For us, outsourcing has become an accepted status quo, no matter how damaging. But for India it would mean a great deal of political capital to be able to say that even the most American of processes has been handed over to them. It's like having the biggest and best reference or portfolio item in history; huge political capital asset for them."

"OK, adding it," Alex said, then added "India politics" to the list. "Sam, you're more experienced in things like this; what's your theory?"

"I have a theory, and it's not fully fleshed out, but it has to do with terrorism. When I see a heart attack here, a car crash there, arranging a black-market heart transplant in the middle of the modern US medical system, that spells power and money to me. Huge power, lots and lots of money. That's why I'm thinking a terrorist organization, not sure who, but an organization nevertheless, that wants to take the election hostage somehow, maybe in the biggest blackmail in the history of our country. Maybe the biggest concentrated terror attack in history. Something like that," Sam said.

Alex looked at him, puzzled, a frown developing on her forehead.

"Can you please give us more details?" Tom asked.

"If the UNSUB organization gains access to the single nationwide event that puts the majority of all adults in a certain place within a certain time frame, I'd say that's a power play of immense magnitude and potential. By 'gaining access' I mean a lot of things could happen. They could threaten: detonate a few warning charges here and there, make public threats, and cause terror to prevent Americans from voting. They could ask for billions of dollars to allow the voting process to happen peacefully. They could defraud the voting process; although it's hard to say why they'd care, unless there's an American political connection involved somehow. Has some politician outsourced the committing of electoral fraud? That'd be something, wouldn't it?"

They were all staring at Sam in disbelief. Alex felt a wave of anger rising in her throat, choking her. *Oh, my God!* She made an effort to regain her calm, analytical demeanor.

"We should have started with you," Alex said. "Wow...that's a lot to think about. Why do you say organization? Can't a single individual hold the power and the money necessary to make this happen?"

"Not really. From what I am seeing," Sam replied thoughtfully, "this plan is not only large and complex but also elegant. It plays like a symphony, not like a single-instrument tune."

"How do you mean?" Alex asked.

"A single individual wouldn't have had the capacity, mentally and operationally, to lead and execute such a complex plan. A single individual could have *created* the plan, that's true, but he'd need an organization to execute this plan. The facts we know don't seem to be that many, but the precision of execution leads me to believe there are many people behind this plan, deploying and executing surveillance on multiple targets, drawing conclusions, making things happen. That's why I said symphony."

Sam rubbed the back of his neck, thinking hard. "Here's another thought for you. We don't know anything about the money. How the money flows, where it comes from, and how. Getting a black-market heart transplant arranged, that's north of a million dollars, considering it was done in a legitimate clinic, not someone's back room."

"Yep, we don't know much about the money, that's true," Alex said and wrote "Money trail" under Unknown. "Any other thoughts, ideas, scenarios?"

No one offered; they were tapped out.

"I think we're out of any new ideas, especially after Sam's input," Steve said. "The one thing circling in my mind now is that we might have underestimated the complexity of this case, and by complexity, I also mean danger. If we're about to uncover a conspiracy of this magnitude we are facing extreme danger and we should proceed, if we still want to, with extreme caution."

"Oh, we're still proceeding, if you'd like my opinion," Alex said. "Let's figure out how. I'll finish the timeline and the categorization this afternoon and see if any new ideas pop up." She took a couple of gulps from her coffee mug. The coffee had turned cold. She went toward the coffee maker and programmed it to brew a new serving on top of her cold coffee leftovers.

Sam popped a cold Coke from the mini fridge, drinking it with large gulps.

"What are you planning to do?" Tom asked. He stood and started pacing a little, not having much room to do his traditional back and forth. "How would you like to approach this?"

Steve also stood and, grabbing a bottle of water from the small table, went near the window and leaned against the wall. Lou fidgeted, tapping his foot quietly against the floor, but remained seated. Brian was the only one maintaining his relaxed pose, probably because he was used to sitting through very long business meetings. They were ready for a break; the work session had been intense and bothersome.

"I'd approach it the usual way, thinking Robert could get me hired on his team. He does have two openings. Getting me aboard will probably take longer than usual because we don't have DCBI as a client, so there's no senior leadership support for our case. I would have to go through channels and act like any other employee. No fast tracking will happen here. Robert, who most likely is also under complete surveillance in both home and office, has to play this very carefully. We have to get this phase started." She took a sip of fresh coffee. "I'd have to move to DC," she said, a little concern seeping into her voice.

Steve caught on to that and looked straight at her. She smiled and made a quick reassuring gesture. She would be fine, she'd have to be, no matter how scary it felt to think she'd be on her own in a strange new city and most likely under surveillance all the time, just like the rest of Robert's team had been. *That ups the ante a little bit*, she thought, *and if I make a mistake or voice the wrong opinion, I won't even know what hit me. But damn if I'll let them win this, no way in hell I'm backing down now.*

"We can follow three things." She turned and wrote them on the whiteboard. "Tech, heart, and money. It's what we have. We have the two technology contracts, hardware to Taiwan and software to India. We'll follow those as soon as I'm inside DCBI. Until then, we can get started on the heart and the money used to pay for the transplant."

"It's a plan," Tom said. "Brian, what are your next steps?"

"I'll work on the equipment, encryption devices, decoders, locators, anything I can think of, and maybe Sam can help with a few ideas. I will also give Alex a crash course in strategic sourcing, vendor engagement, quality assurance for outsourced contracts, and all that good stuff."

"So we're still a go?" Sam asked.

Alex looked at Tom. He nodded almost imperceptibly.

"Hell, yeah," she responded.

...Chapter 37: The Sign
...Tuesday, January 26, 2:19PM Local Time (UTC+1:00 hours)
...Zur Roten Buche Corporate Center
...Zürich, Switzerland

Ahmad Babak Javadi was about to lose every bit of temper he had left. These handymen were idiots. The task couldn't have been easier, and they were screwing it up. All they had to do was put four holes in the wall, drive screws through them, and hang the damn sign. Centered, level, at the right height.

He let himself drop into a huge leather armchair, one of the two in his office reception area. As soon as he hit the red, sumptuous leather, he let a long sigh escape.

"Did you measure from the sides? It's to the left, not in the middle of the wall," Javadi said, his thick Iranian accent enhanced by frustration.

"Ja, ja, we did," one of the nitwits replied.

"Like hell you did," Javadi said, getting up. He took off his charcoal suit jacket and grabbed the measuring tape. He had to do everything himself it seemed.

Until now, everything had gone quite nicely, according to plan, and with minimal difficulty. He had leased a nice, secluded home for himself, only a few minutes away, yet buried in the hills just off Triemlihalde. Yes, he had the rattling of passing trains bothering him every now and then, but he had the privacy of the thick forest in return. The office space wasn't that bad either, and he was almost done setting things up.

Javadi was used to getting things done his way, precisely his way, when he wanted, how he wanted. Sitting on a considerable fortune invested in a diversified portfolio of household names like eBay, Google, AT&T, and General Electric, he was used to the utmost deference. In his palatial home in Tehran, worthy of the Eram Garden, this measure of ineptitude would have never happened. Now there were six holes in the wall, two of them visible to the left of the sign. He would have to make them cover the holes and repaint the wall and have it ready before the next morning, when his first appointment was scheduled to arrive.

But the damn thing was finally hanging on the wall where it was supposed to, and it looked quite nice. That was if the eye of the beholder chose to ignore the two ugly holes that were soon to be covered and focus on the brushed metal letters spelling out elegantly "Eastern Africa Development Fund."

...Chapter 38: Equipment
...Wednesday, January 27, 1:47PM PST (UTC-8:00 hours)
...Tom Isaac's Residence
...Laguna Beach, California

Tom's home office, once elegant, open, and tastefully decorated with items that were chosen to fit together harmoniously, had been dubbed the war room. *How very appropriate,* Alex thought, entering the semi-disorganized work area and setting up her laptop on the improvised conference table. The corkboard on the wall now showed images and sticky notes with names, events, and concepts pinned up and tied together with colorful knitting yarn, color-coded by meaning. Green yarn symbolized a verified, proven connection between two people or events. Blue signified a suspected and plausible connection. There was red yarn available; it was going to be used for unexpected, surprising connections—if they were going to find any. Red had not been used yet.

The night before she had torn everything down and rebuilt it to incorporate a timeline. It worked better like this, made more sense. They might call this system the Crazy Wall, but it was very helpful. She was going to miss it in DC.

"Admiring your handiwork, huh?" Brian asked, walking through the door with his arms full. He deposited everything he was carrying on the table, and then went straight for the coffee machine.

"Hey, Brian. Yeah, I am," Alex responded. "I was wondering if there's a connection between the hardware vendor and the software vendor, between India and Taiwan, somewhere in the background somehow. Maybe they're owned by the same investors? I think we need some yellow yarn, for untested hypotheses and wild hunches."

"Maybe Lou can dig a little and test your hunch."

"Yeah, I'll ask him," she said, grabbing her coffee mug and going for a refill. "What do you have for me?"

"Lots and lots of toys, you'll see." He sat down and grabbed a boxy device, about the size of a laptop, only a little thicker. "Since you'll be heading into some travel, specifically to Taiwan and India, I wanted to make sure that you can communicate freely with us, regardless of time and location. These devices will also ensure you maintain the confidentiality of all communication, because you won't have to go through your hotel's Wi-Fi, or through the vendor's network."

Alex took the device from Brian, examining it closely.

"Ah, a satellite link," she said, connecting it to the laptop. "I always wanted to try one of these."

"Go ahead, play with it. It's the Inmarsat BGAN terminal from Globalcom. It will give you voice, data, and a WLAN access point to hook up your laptop. It's not very fast, but it will give you data and voice access from anywhere. The data transfer fees are ridiculously large, but feel free to use it as you need."

"Yep, it's slow, but it gets the job done, excellent. What's next?"

Brian grabbed a black object that resembled a phone with a thimble-sized antenna, entirely black and without a screen or keypad.

"For when you can't use the Inmarsat terminal, we have something else. Let me have your cell phone, please," Brain asked. "If you attach this device to your cell it turns it into a satellite phone. You attach it to this case first," he said, picking another object from the pile, one that looked like a typical cell phone holder, "then you attach the sat phone device."

"Really? Sweet deal," Alex said, grinning widely.

"It's called the Thuraya SatSleeve. Once connected to your iPhone, it will instantly give you access via satellite, while using your own number, wherever you are. You can make and receive calls and text messages. The antenna extends like this," he demonstrated. "But the product is sensitive enough to alert you of incoming calls or messages even if the antenna is not extended."

He picked up two smaller devices.

"These are for voice and data encryption: one's for your laptop, the other for your cell. Additionally, we will all have an encryption app installed on our phones, and we will start using that encryption software immediately. If you recall, we're running the risk of getting our communications intercepted very soon. This is how it works. You install the Encrypher app, and it will add an option to your phone dial screen. If you touch this small circle before dialing, the app will look for its counterpart on the recipient's phone and encrypt the call. The encryption will kick in within the first three seconds of the call, so it's fairly fast. When the encryption goes active, both call parties will hear a quiet beep."

"Excellent," Alex said. "I was wondering how we were going to manage communications."

"Also, when you get to either place, you should buy a cellular data access token and subscription. Don't go through anyone else's Wi-Fi with your data transmissions, not even your hotel. You never know who's watching."

"Yeah, I can see why. Cellular data transfers via tokens are actually the safest wireless data transfers available when you travel outside your firewalled home network. They have their own number that doesn't appear anywhere, in any records, so it's fairly hard to even know they exist, not to mention intercept."

"Correct. To the average surveillance team it will appear as if you're not connected to the Internet. If they're watching your screen, they'll figure it out though and start looking for a signal to intercept. Be careful."

"What if the surveillance team is better than average?"

"We're getting there," Brian said, picking up the last remaining item on the table. "This is a bug sweeper, a countersurveillance tool of very high performance. It will detect any active surveillance or tracking devices, such as hidden cameras, mics, GPS trackers, essentially anything that transmits any signal from your location, wired or wireless."

"What did I miss?" Steve asked, barging through the door.

"A bucket load of gizmos," Alex said. "Nothing else."

Steve grabbed a seat across the table.

"Don't stop because of me. I'm here for the next part," he said.

"We'll get to that shortly. Just finishing up with the devices," Brian answered. "OK, so back to countersurveillance."

Alex was listening, fascinated. She had never had the opportunity to learn about these things other than from movies and books.

"The first instinct, when we find a bug, is to rip it apart and flush it down the toilet," Brian continued.

"Totally." She laughed.

"Yeah, but what does that do? That informs whoever's listening that you know you're being bugged, which will increase their level of attention, and, most likely, the caliber of surveillance they're deploying. They'll bring bigger, better, more sophisticated tools that you might not be able to uncover that easily. So what do you do when you find surveillance gear in your space?"

"Nothing?" Alex ventured a guess.

"Not really, no. You start feeding them what you want them to know. Behave as normally as possible, and use the blind spots in their surveillance to do the things you don't want them to know about or see."

"It doesn't sound that easy," Alex said.

"It isn't," Brian confirmed. "Sam will show you how to do this. He'll bug one of the rooms here and walk you through how to handle bug sweeping, because you can't really show up on their cameras with a bug sweeper in your hand, either."

"Oh, OK, that's a good idea. But how am I going to carry all this stuff with me and not have anyone see it? They could search my room when I'm out, go through my luggage."

"Correct. That's why you'll be carrying it all with you in your laptop bag. It's gonna be heavy, I know," Brian said in response to Alex's raised eyebrows. "You'll also have to get into the habit of never letting it out of your sight. If anyone picks up on that just tell them you don't carry a purse and that all your personal stuff's in there, and they'll back off. Remember, you'll have to take the bag with you everywhere you go. Restroom, dinner, meetings, everywhere."

She looked in disbelief at the pile of hardware on the table. Maybe, if carefully organized in the bag, they could all fit. The Inmarsat terminal was the issue. The rest were small enough not to pose problems.

"In case of emergency, if you absolutely have to leave the bag behind, take this with you, in a pocket or something," Brian said, pointing at the SatSleeve. "Make sure you can call us anytime; that's the number one priority."

"Thank you. For all of it." She gestured toward the pile of devices.

"One more thing," Brian said, "do you have the 'Find My iPhone' app installed on your cell?"

"Yes, I do, why?"

"I'll need your Apple ID and password," Brian said. "Using that app and your Apple credentials, we'll be able to see where you are," he continued, causing Alex to raise her eyebrows in disbelief. "Great app to track your stolen or misplaced phone, but also the greatest stalker tool ever invented. Yes, we will be stalking you, a lot."

"All right, I guess." She agreed hesitantly. These were all measures they were taking to ensure her safety, but she also felt like they didn't trust she could do the job. She frowned.

"What's on your mind, Alex?" Steve picked up on her vibes, as he always did.

"Do you have any confidence that I can do the job?" Alex asked.

"If anyone can pull this off, that's you," Brian answered. "But there are others in play we don't trust. These people mean business in a very serious way. They're cold-blooded, calculated killers. We want to be there for you if anything should happen. We want to make sure you're safe."

She nodded slightly, deep in thought. *Yeah, they do have a point,* she thought.

"Speaking of danger," Steve said, "how do you feel about this venture? Still wanna do it?"

"Steve, if it's the last thing I do, I still wanna do this. One hundred percent. At first I was just curious, curious and driven to solve the puzzle, unravel the mystery. Now I'm angry, just like you are, because whatever they're planning to do, it's huge. It's beyond anything that we could live with ourselves if we decided to shrug it off and leave it in someone else's hands. This is our future we're talking about.

"If whatever they're planning to do should succeed, because it targets such a core element of our values, it will create a permanent scar in our identity as a nation. It won't just be a random terrorist attack, big or small, that people could forget in a few years. This will alter our history, will impact the entire American people. It could be another 9/11, or worse. We just can't let that happen. *I* just can't let that happen. So yes, I still very much wanna do this."

"All right, then, let's move on to the business section of our meeting," Brian said. "Steve wanted to sit in and get educated about the principles of outsourcing, offshoring, globalization, and vendor management."

"Good, I have lots of questions," Alex said. She replenished her coffee with a new brew of French vanilla. The flavor filled the room.

"We could spend months and not get to everything there is to say, know, or consider about globalization. So I will keep it very simple, structuring what you'll need to know for this assignment." He stood up, stretched a little, and continued. "I will start with my favorite definition. Globalization is 'the processes by which the peoples of the world are incorporated in a single world society.' This definition was crafted by Martin Albrow, a sociologist. I like this definition because it's simple. Globalization is the overall process through which we become a single nation, if you'd like." He stopped for a long sip of coffee. "A very long and increasingly painful process that has stirred up controversy and has hordes of supporters and opponents, equally passionate."

"Which one are you?" Alex asked. "Are you pro or con?"

"That's not a quick, simple answer. There are several components to globalization. I am absolutely in favor of free trade and the free dissemination of knowledge transcending borders. But I am definitely not a fan of other aspects, like pollution, accelerated resource depletion, and some of the current practices regarding outsourcing of labor. I'll explain more in a little while. Let's go back to our vendors for now. Why do companies outsource?" He looked at his audience, waiting for an answer.

"That's easy," Alex ventured, "to get things done cheaper."

"Precisely so. Our economy is cost-driven, and a corporation's main allegiance is not to its employees, as one might think. Not even to its customers. A corporation's single focus is to make more money. It's that simple. One way to do this is by cutting costs: labor cost, supply chain cost, product cost, any type of cost. That's why, in the past twenty-some years, we have seen manufacturing slowly but surely moving to China and other Asian destinations, such as Taiwan. We've seen services, including software development, moving to India, Pakistan, Latin America, and other emerging markets. Popular brand names have been associated with the labor offshoring controversy as early as the 1970s.

"These companies have struggled for years to shed the sweatshop reputation brought by allegations of forced overtime, child labor, and minimum wage violations in manufacturing plants in Vietnam, Mexico, and China, among others. But they were not the only ones adopting these practices. Even today, the majority of offshore manufacturing practices still leaves much to be desired, despite the public's attention and countless whistle-blowers, Maybe you've heard on the news or read in the papers about the suicides at Chinese electronic assembly facilities in Shenzhen," he said, waiting to see if they knew anything about that.

"I think I remember seeing something," Steve said. "They installed netting, right? To catch the jumpers? I remember struggling with the idea. That's not how you prevent suicide, how you heal people. It can seem helpful at first, but it can't be the only thing you do for the long term."

Alex shuddered. How awful it must be to want to kill yourself rather than go to work another day.

"Correct. So the question is why would such corporations risk bad PR about this? The answer is very simple: for money. Let's use a random example. Let's say Company A used to make TVs in New Hampshire. The cost to make a TV in the United States with US parts and US labor was, say, $80. I'm just making these numbers up, you know. The company then sells the TVs at $100, with a 20 percent margin. The competition is fierce, and the consumers' purchasing decisions are, unfortunately yet predominantly, price-driven. Now Company A has no choice but to take labor offshore, because the competition, an Asian brand, can afford to bring the TVs in at $90 per unit.

"Company A takes its manufacturing offshore, fires the American workers, and suddenly, the cost is only $45 to make one TV. Two things happen at this point. One: Company A will sell the TV for $89, just barely under its competitor's price, and, by doing so, it drives the margins from the 20 percent in the initial phase, to almost 100 percent after offshoring. By doing so, the company accumulates a lot of money that, in many cases, will end up invested offshore as well, in additional manufacturing facilities, instead of injected back into the local economy.

"The pricing wars will continue though, and the margins will erode somewhat over time. The second aspect is that Company A lost a few customers, because the employees who lost their jobs and their families won't be able to afford new TVs anymore. Those employees won't be able to afford many other things, such as cars, furniture, clothing, appliances, and so on. One by one, all these companies, the furniture store and manufacturers, clothing companies, everyone in the community will suffer because those TV manufacturing employees got laid off, and their jobs were sent to China. The local economy is shrinking. Then what happens?"

"More pressure on cost to compete in price-driven purchasing?" Alex ventured.

"Precisely. Soon enough, even if they wouldn't have originally considered it, other manufacturers will be forced to drop their prices further, and the only way to do this will be to outsource some more."

"But wouldn't that ruin the local economy even more?" Alex asked. "It's counterintuitive, and somehow it's the only way they can compete."

"That is exactly what happens. The companies' immediate survivals dictate that more and more of the labor is to be moved offshore, yet this labor export spirals the standard of living further into the ground, taking employment opportunities away from the American labor market. But here's where it gets really interesting. You'll hear reports every quarter stating that the economy had grown one, maybe two percent. The economy is not shrinking. The standard of living is dropping, while the economy still grows, albeit at a very moderate pace."

"Why? How is this possible?" Alex asked.

"Do you remember Pascal's principle of communicating vessels? Early school science class?"

"Yeah, I do," she answered. "What's it got to do with the labor market?"

"Well, you can think of all these countries, including ours, as vessels filled with fluid. The fluid levels in them represent the standard of living, or the purchasing power, if you'd like to call it that. It's the ability to purchase goods and services for the average individual working an average job. Obviously, before the age of outsourcing started, the United States had one of the highest fluid levels in all the world's vessels. Do you agree?"

"Yes, absolutely."

"Then we put our vessel in direct communication with other countries' vessels, like China, India, the Philippines, and now our fluid levels are dropping, and theirs are rising. The fluid leaving our vessel and going into theirs is our wealth, our standard of living, our purchasing power, and our financial security as individuals."

"In Pascal's principle, this drain will not stop until all connected vessels reach the same level."

"Correct. But here's a thought for you: how can the American labor market hope to survive when we are just a hundred million workers or so, and we are seeping resources toward a global market two billion strong? If you look at things strictly from the physics perspective, we will be drained dry, as a people and an economic system, before we manage to raise the levels in those countries to a high enough level to stop draining us. Additionally, in most of these countries, population growth is also a concern, so it's not getting any better with time."

"I still don't think I completely understand. I get that taking jobs offshore is bad for the labor force here, at home. I understand that we are no longer building wealth in our communities. I have lived through it, and I am still living it. But at a larger scale, isn't offshoring good for the economy?" Alex asked.

"You tell me," Brian said, pulling all the devices he had brought into a pile in front of him and adding the dry-erase markers and knitting yarns. "Let's imagine this is our money. Every month we get services and labor provided offshore; we bring consumables in," he said, bringing his coffee mug to the pile, "and we pay for them," he continued, taking away from the pile one of the encryption devices and a marker. "Then we consume the services; we use what we have bought," he added, drinking his coffee, "and next month we need to buy some more."

He moved more objects from his pile and scattered them around the table. "See how our cash flows away? What do we bring back instead? What do we buy? Labor, consumables, services, things that add value but do not last. But our money goes away permanently. What do we sell offshore to bring some of this money back? Do you know?"

"I know we're exporting grain, food products, mostly," Alex said.

"And weapons, we sell a lot of military equipment," Steve added.

"Yeah, all correct. We also export oil, aircraft, equipment, chemicals, and pharmaceuticals."

"So it should balance out, I'd think?"

"Well, ideally it should, but it doesn't," Brian said, bringing back from the scattered objects a yellow marker and placing it in the pile in front of him. "We bring some money back, but only a small percentage of what we send out. This is called a balance of trade deficit, or trade deficit for short, and it has fueled the American national debt to unprecedented levels."

"So why doesn't it stop? This resource and wealth drain?"

"I'd have to say there's no real interest in protecting it. Most corporations prefer to go offshore, because they get more for less, and they think it's the only way to stay competitive. This is a shortsighted point of view, focused on making the next quarter financial results look good and discarding any long-term vision that involves the community or the wealth of the people. People and their purchasing decisions are also a part of this. When we go to Target we normally buy the TV that has the best value, not the Made-in-the-USA TV. Patriotism means sacrifice, and the vast majority of customers would rather not sacrifice whatever they have left of their disappearing standard of living. Even those who strongly believe in this form of patriotism and who would be willing to make the sacrifice are discouraged by how little difference their sacrifice would make."

"I agree, " Steve said. "How many Made-in-the-USA products can you find on the shelves at the store? Almost zero, after thirty years of offshoring."

"Yes, they're all gone," Brian confirmed. "They were eliminated by the fierce cost competition brought by the offshore labor, product, or service."

"So we're doomed?" Alex asked. "As a nation, we're heading into poverty? That's what you're saying?"

"We're already *in* poverty. More than 20 percent of our people live under the poverty line, and millions have given up on their hope to ever get a job. We're definitely heading in the wrong direction, but there is some hope. BMW, for example, manufactures the SUVs for their entire world market in the United States. Other manufacturers have realized the value of having manufacturing done here rather than offshore, here where standards are respected and products have a very high level of quality. Cost-wise, onshore manufacturing has started becoming competitive again, due to wages rising in the offshore markets and a higher cost of transportation. Here and there, the jobs are coming back. It's a start, and a weak one at best, but it's a start."

"The one thing I see as a positive in all this," Steve said, "is the overall benefit that offshoring brings to those markets, to the people living there. I remember reading that offshoring has extended the life expectancy in those areas and has improved the health and mortality rates in those populations. Do you think this is what drives America's commitment to globalization?"

"In my entire business career, sitting in countless board meetings, I promise you I have never heard someone say, 'Let's outsource our manufacturing to China because people are dying or starving.' Instead I have heard numerous times how outsourcing saves the corporation money and how much it saves, all demonstrated in colorful charts and plump cash-flow forecasts. For corporations this is a cost-driven decision.

"However, you do have a point, Steve, and I agree with it. It is important that we actively work, as a nation, to improve the standard of living in other countries, but not beyond the point where we stop being able to maintain our own. If we continue to do that, we will soon lose the ability to help anyone, including ourselves. However, we can improve the standard of living in those areas in many different ways. We could share knowledge, innovation, healthcare advances, and best practices. We could make targeted infusions of capital and investment to the local economies."

"What do you think will happen, long term, with our economy?" Alex asked.

"It's hard to say. A lot is riding on who's going to win the election. The Republican presidential candidate, Krassner, seems to have a good grasp of what could be done to stimulate the recovery of our standard of living. There are many things that could be done, by the government and by the consumers. The government, if it decides to take this path, could deploy taxes and duties to prevent the labor drain. It could also give tax incentives to create homegrown expertise. You see, part of the problem is that now, after more than thirty years of offshoring, you can't even find skilled manufacturing workers anymore. People have abandoned this career path due to obvious reasons."

Brian paused a little, scratching his head. "As for the consumers, well, we'd have to decide that it might be worth it for everyone if we buy fewer quantities but higher quality products. Germany has such a culture, for example. People there do not buy seven pots and pans at a time; they only buy one when they need it. If the product is imported from outside the European Union, that product carries a significant customs duty tax that the government uses to fund development programs for the German workforce. In Germany and other places, offshoring funds their labor development, not ruins it, because it carries significant levels of tax. By having such a high tax applied to any outsourced work, offshoring also loses its low-cost appeal and stops being the Holy Grail of all corporations. It's not worth pursuing anymore, so companies become invested in the local communities. In Germany, unemployment is low, GDP is high, and the country doesn't have that much debt, either. So yes, there are ways to fix our economy; it just needs to become a priority for our political leaders."

"So, going back to our unofficial client, DCBI, offshoring these two contracts was a cost-driven decision, I understand?" Alex asked.

"Robert Wilton's team uses a points system to award contracts, with cost being a key component of their scale. They also look at the financial health of the vendor company, the experience, the clientele, the processes, quality standards, and many other aspects, but cost has a high impact in DCBI scoring."

"I remember he said he didn't have to do anything to promote the selected vendor, that the vendor surfaced as a prime candidate on the points system without his help," Alex said. "That means the vendor is good, right?"

"Yes, that's precisely what that means," Brian confirmed. "The fact that the UNSUB decided to execute such an elaborate plan to ensure that the vendor would be awarded the software contract speaks to the determination and preparedness. It also speaks to the UNSUB's reach; it knew everything about the competitors and filed an aggressive offer."

"OK. What else do I need to know?"

"You'll need to know how to interact with the company employees culturally and how to get ready for your trips."

"This is where I come in," Steve said.

Alex turned in her chair to face Steve.

"All right, let's start with Taiwan." He consulted his tablet. "Taiwan is quite simple. Stay away from large gatherings, don't fall for any advance fees or inheritance scams; this is their local flavor of the Nigerian scam, and they love to try it on Westerners who are new to the country. If you're invited to a meal, wait to be invited to eat, as opposed to just diving in when food is served. Be careful not to lose face and not to cause anyone else to lose face. Losing face is any form of blemishing someone's public image. Criticizing someone will cause him or her to lose face, especially if it's in public. Getting angry and losing your temper in public will cause you to lose face. Umm...what else?...Ah, here. Always travel with your best friend, toilet paper."

Alex burst into laughter.

"Are you serious?"

"Better safe than sorry. Not all restrooms have it, and you might want to be prepared."

"Soon I'll need a dolly to carry what I'm supposed to have with me everywhere I go. All right, got it, I'll make sure I have plenty of TP."

"Remember the Taiwanese are very superstitious. Any mention of death or anything negative is bad luck. For any special situations where you don't know how to behave or what to do, email me or search the Internet. Oh, and if someone laughs nervously, that's because they're uncomfortable with something and not necessarily amused. Think about that when responding."

"Got it," Alex said, taking notes. "What else?"

"I think this is it for Taiwan, for now," Steve said. "Let's move on to India. We're used to the Indian culture because we have a strong Indian presence here in the States. We have colleagues and friends who are from India, and we are quite familiar with their culture, up to a certain point. I'm not worried about that at all. I'm more worried with some other aspects of your travel. Water, for example. You cannot drink any tap water when you get there, or let it get into your nose and eyes. You'll get what's called 'Delhi Belly,' and it's not fun. Of course, there are other deadly pathogens in the Delhi water that can give you cholera, pneumonia, or dysentery."

"Oh, how lovely." Alex scoffed. "Travel all around the world to die on some god-forsaken toilet. Not what I had in plan for this stage of my career."

"Be careful and you won't die." Steve smiled encouragingly. "Just don't touch the water."

"Seriously? How the hell am I gonna brush my teeth, wash my face, and take a shower if it can't get in my eyes, nose, or mouth?"

"Bottled water. Brush your teeth and wash your face with bottled water. I heard that brushing with beer sucks, especially if you use Sensodyne toothpaste," Steve said with a very serious face.

They all burst into laughter. Alex mimicked brushing her teeth and spitting out copious amounts of foam.

"All right, I get it; how about my hair? Washing my hair with bottled water will probably take two hours." She continued her protests.

"It's either that or death on the toilet. Eat well-cooked foods, nothing raw or underdone, and do not eat any vegetables or fruits."

"Seriously? Why?"

"'Cause they're rinsed in the same water. Remember, nothing, nothing at all. No lettuce leaf on your burger. No tomatoes or raw onion next to your steak. No uncooked vegetables, under any circumstance."

"Good thing I like meat, then. I'll just eat steaks."

Brian stifled a laugh. Alex gave him a homicidal gaze.

"Do you think that's funny? Really?"

"Actually, yes," Brian answered. "You aren't focusing much today, or else you might have remembered cows are sacred in India."

"Oh," she said. Brian's laughter was contagious. She snickered. "Then what the hell am I gonna eat?"

"First of all, they prepare chicken and mutton really well; you'll love those." Steve smacked his lips. "Really yummy. The slaughter of cattle is highly restricted, but some restaurants might still put a steak on their menus, especially those with high Westerner traffic. I do recommend you think twice before ordering beef, because you don't know what that meat really is, considering how restricted cattle slaughtering is, and because even if it is beef, it might be processed by people whose deep beliefs are insulted by the idea of having to kill cattle to serve you and people like you."

"What are you saying?" Alex asked. "Will there be something wrong with it?"

"No, not necessarily. Just bad karma, if you'd like to think that way. I, for one, wouldn't like to offend anyone's beliefs with the food I'm ordering if I can avoid it. Stick to chicken and mutton, try some of the vegetarian dishes and see if you like them. There's also McDonalds in Delhi and Domino's Pizza and other alternatives, only don't expect them to taste like they do here. They are heavily spiced to add the local flavor. Just save your steak cravings for when you come home. Tom will grill you a monster one, I promise."

"Oh, I know. It's just a lot to remember and a lot of risk of getting sick." She frowned.

"Let's talk immunizations now," Steve continued, pushing a list in front of her. "You'll need shots for Hepatitis A and B, Japanese encephalitis, polio—but I guess you have that done already. Rabies, typhoid, and yellow fever."

"Huh? All these?"

"Yep, and you need to get started. I'm not sure if your doctor will want all of them done at the same time or staggered to make it easier on your body. Get your appointment set up with him, and make sure you're immunized before leaving. He'll also recommend a malaria prevention therapy, an oral drug like Mefloquine or Cloroquine, that you have to start taking a few weeks before leaving."

"Whoa, hold it just a second," she stopped him. "Isn't this drug responsible for psychotic rages in some veterans or active-duty soldiers? Not sure, but I remember seeing it on TV. There was something wrong with their malaria drugs. Are these the same drugs we're talking about?"

"Largely, yes. Antimalaria drugs have significant side effects, some of which can be neuropsychiatric."

"Can you be more specific, please?" Alex asked in her low, calm-before-the-storm tone of voice.

"Anxiety, paranoia, hallucinations, depression. But not all patients experience these side effects. "

"Just what I need on a covert, high-risk investigation in a foreign, dangerous country. To become paranoid, see things that aren't there, and be more anxious than I already am." She stood abruptly and started pacing the floor. "Let me make it clear for you, Steve. Hell, no! Not taking them, and the hell with it."

"This is not negotiable, Alex. If you get sick with malaria, what will happen then? If you don't get proper treatment you could die," Steve said. "I cannot accept this risk."

"This risk is not yours to accept, Steve," she snapped at him, instantly regretting it. "Look, I'll wear a ton of mosquito spray, and I'll be careful, I promise."

"Let's be practical here." Brian intervened. "Alex's concern with maintaining the integrity of her cognitive processes is a legitimate one."

"Thank you," Alex said, nodding in his direction.

"Let's explore options," Brian continued. "If she gets malaria, what's the treatment?"

"The same drugs, or doxycycline," Steve said.

"I'll take doxy anytime," Alex said.

"You can't take doxy for weeks in a row to prevent it," Steve said.

"Yeah, but I can take it if I get sick. Case closed," she said, not willing to discuss it any further.

Great meeting, she thought bitterly, *just uncovered fifteen million more ways to die.*

...Chapter 39: Inauguration
...Monday, February 1, 1:32PM Local Time (UTC+1:00 hours)
...Overnight Delight Headquarters—Brandýs nad Labem-Stará Boleslav
...Prague, The Czech Republic

Cameras were clicking constantly, targeting the precise moment when the mayor of Prague cut the red ribbon in front of the warehouse doors. It was an honor to have the mayor himself inaugurate a business; Karmal Shah knew that very well. He also knew that not every day a city like Prague gets such a large investment in one of its suburbs.

The mayor cut the ribbon with scissors offered on a silver tray by Shah's new executive assistant, Hana, a slender girl with flowing blonde hair and unforgettable cleavage. By the looks of it, the mayor wouldn't be forgetting her cleavage any time soon. Perfect.

A surge of applause marked the moment the ribbon was cut. The mayor then turned to Shah and shook his hand. They both smiled, posing for the media.

"We are both grateful and excited," the mayor said, "to welcome 'Overnight Delight' and Mr. Karmal Shah to Prague and to our community. Mr. Shah is a successful entrepreneur who has a lot to teach us about building a business in the modern, borderless world. Please join me in wishing Mr. Shah and 'Overnight Delight' the best of luck!"

Another wave of applause. It was his turn now. He stepped in front of the microphones after shaking the mayor's hand again.

"Thank you all for your warm welcome and your incredible hospitality. It was the world-famous Czech hospitality that prompted me to relocate my business interests from France to the Czech Republic. It is friendship I am looking for and a sense of community in a place I can start calling home. Personally, I am looking to put down roots in a welcoming community such as yours. My business, which already employs twenty-two people here, has unlimited growth potential. I am investing millions of dollars to promote our products on Google and other online venues, and I am planning to open a business-to-business catering service. Our website and online marketplace are state of the art, and our customers are exigent connoisseurs with a high degree of loyalty once they find a good product and excellent service. The sky is the limit, and we can reach it together."

He put his hand up to silence the applause that was igniting. "How better to celebrate," he asked, "than by sampling my product while visiting the facility? Please, help yourselves, and don't forget the open bar!"

Now they were free to applaud, and they did, for a long time. The Czech people were impressionable and easy-going. Perfect.

Shah led the way into his building. He stepped into the front office, showing them around.

"This is our office. We have accounting there and order management here. Through that door is my own office. I will be spending a lot of my time here, making sure we get everything organized to service our growing customer base. Online advertising is over there," he said and pointed toward a couple of desks in the back corner. "We'll need to add more space and more resources to this area. Can we do more with online advertising?" Shah asked, then answered the question himself with a lot of poignancy. "Yes, we can. We just need the right resources to get things done. Through here," he said, opening two large doors, "we are entering the main warehouse. The left side of the warehouse is entirely refrigerated, dedicated to perishables. We keep caviar in there: oysters, foie gras, truffles, fine cheeses, smoked salmon, and sturgeon. The rest of the warehouse, as you can see, is climate-controlled, yet not fully refrigerated. In here we maintain a temperature of fifty-seven degrees Fahrenheit, or fourteen degrees Celsius, and less than 50 percent humidity. It's the equivalent of the dark, cold basements from old times. Ideal to store chocolates, fine liquors, olives, and gourmet oils."

He showed the crowd a couple of large tables to the side, covered in fine linens, displaying a generous variety of mouth-watering delicacies. "Please sample to your heart's desire; there's a lot more in the warehouse if we run out."

His guests scattered immediately, scouting the goodies on the tables and getting wine glasses from the improvised bar. It was hard to say who was there for anything other than the rare opportunity to sample all these exotic foods. They were expensive, and the average person rarely, if ever, indulged in real Beluga caviar priced at $115 per ounce, served on the finest crackers, or tasted pâté de foie gras, freshly imported from France and going for $295 a can. They will remember this day for a while. No one would ever suspect Overnight Delight was in anything else but gourmet foods. Perfect.

He was ready for the next phase.

...Chapter 40: New Horizons
...Tuesday, February 9, 10:47AM EST (UTC-5:00 hours)
...New Horizons Cardiology & Transplant Center
...Burlington, Vermont

Alex drove slowly, heading north on Shelburne Road and looking for her turn. Every other minute she checked her rearview mirror, trying to remember all the makes and models of the cars to figure out if anyone was trailing her.

The Agency team members had been more than careful since they'd started working this case. Burn phones with encryption software, regular bug-screenings in their homes, offices, and cars, but so far nothing was found. Yet. Regardless, working the case gave her an uneasy feeling in her gut, and she hated that. She liked being in control as much as possible, and she hated her own fears more than anything. No one can be in any control if they can't control their fears. *Get it together, girl; there's no one there,* she encouraged herself after checking the mirror for the fifteenth time since she had left her hotel. She was expecting them, the UNSUB, to be watching the clinic closely, looking for people who came snooping around. If she were the UNSUB, that's what she'd do. Carefully put surveillance at the clinic, the only location that correlated Robert Wilton with the UNSUB. The starting point of any investigation into this case. Her starting point. Therefore, she'd have to be very creative. That, fortunately, was one of her top strengths.

Alex allowed herself to breathe, while turning onto the street of her destination. There it was, on her right, a three-story, red-brick building with a modern, almost luxurious look. It sat proudly on landscaped acreage covered in the famous Vermont greenery, now winter clad, overlooking Burlington Bay. She circled the massive building, driving slowly and keeping one eye on the rearview mirror until she reached the front entrance again. She took the driveway marked "Patient Parking" and found a spot not very close to the main entrance.

After cutting the engine off, she deliberated a few moments about the best approach to take. Deciding, she dialed a number on her cell, retrieving it with a quick Internet search. A voice picked up the call promptly.

"New Horizons, how may I direct your call?"

"Yeah, hi, I need your help, please," Alex started to say, "I need to make an appointment with a doctor."

"Can I have your name, please?"

"Yes, sure, it's Parker, Jessica Parker," Alex responded, thinking of one of her favorite movie stars.

"Who would you like to see?"

"Well, I'm not sure. I was hoping you could tell me. You see, I'm here for my mom. She needs a heart transplant, and I need to understand what's at stake and how to proceed, how to deal with this. Can you help me?"

"Absolutely, Miss Parker. We can have you come in for a consultation with Dr. Kanellis; he's the director of our Transplant Center. He can answer all your questions. When are you looking to come in?"

"As soon as possible, of course. This is urgent; my mother is very sick."

"I understand. How's tomorrow morning at nine-thirty? Will that work?"

"Absolutely, many thanks!"

Alex hung up with a bitter chuckle, her ruse taking her back to the last day she had seen her mother, when she had told Alex she could never come back home again. Her mother's heart had definitely not been working properly back then. With an effort, she pulled herself back into the present reality. The opening move was executed; the game was on.

...Chapter 41: The Campaign Manager
...Tuesday, February 9, 3:49PM CST (UTC-6:00 hours)
...Johnson Campaign Headquarters
...Chicago, Illinois

"Focus, for Chrissake, just focus, will ya?" Anthony Fischer, campaign manager to potentially the future democratic holder of the highest office in the United States, was losing it again. *I'm too old for this shit*, he thought, rubbing his forehead in search of some hard-to-find patience. *Damn...this man is ignorant beyond belief! But if he gets to the Oval Office, what a masterpiece! What a retirement gift!*

"All right, all right, I will," Bobby Johnson said, pouring himself another stiff one. "Want another shot?"

"No, and you should take it easy, otherwise you won't remember anything by tomorrow. Let's start over." He passed his fingers through his hair, pulling it hard toward the back of his head. The consistent abuse of his signature gesture of exasperation had probably contributed to his receding hairline. His hair was simply giving up on him, just like he felt he should do with this candidate. The man was mostly a moron, at least half the time, yet Fischer never could say no to such a challenge. He took a deep breath and started all over again.

"So, tomorrow you're going on prime time television to answer questions about what?"

"Umm...my platform, views on economy, healthcare reform, war on terror, and immigration."

"OK, great! What's the one-liner for your platform?"

"Umm...America needs peace, stability, and time to heal and grow back into greatness."

"Drop the umms," Fischer said. "They make you look indecisive and unprepared. You cannot ask people to follow you, if you aren't even sure where you're leading them. Got it?"

Senator Bobby Johnson let out a long sigh. "All right, I got it."

"OK. Your views on the economy?"

"Yes. We need to strengthen the working class and stabilize the job market, ensuring that our children have gainful employment opportunities available for them after graduation. We need to provide viable alternatives for unemployed skilled workers to reintegrate them into the productive labor force. We will focus on strengthening the middle class, currently under pressures brought by recession, unemployment, and an increasing debt balance."

For a few seconds, Fischer felt his confidence rise. When Johnson focused and was still sober, he was articulate and had solid principles. Well, for the most part.

"Your views on healthcare reform?"

"That's a tricky one," Senator Johnson responded hesitantly.

Nope, still a moron, Fischer thought.

"Keep it simple and general; stick to core principles, such as universal access to healthcare, affordability, and simplification. You're a Democrat, for Chrissake. Just think what the people would like to have, what *you* would like to have for yourself and your family when it comes to healthcare. Got it?"

"Got it." Johnson started to reach for the bottle but stopped in his tracks when he met Fischer's disapproving look.

"How many did you have today, Bobby?"

"Umm...just one? Two, maybe?"

"Bobby, I told you before, and I'm not going to repeat myself forever. Stop drinking, or I am out of here. One a day, plus a nightcap when you're between toothbrush and bed and no one can hear you speak anymore. That clear?"

"Crystal."

"Hope so. War on terror, go!"

"With the wars in Iraq and Afghanistan ending, we're assisting the peoples of the respective countries in their transitions to peace. We're dismantling and annihilating any terrorist organizations, whether al-Qaeda, ISIL, or any other new emerging threat. We are committed to maintaining the strongest military force in the world. We will engage to protect, secure, and maintain peace for us and our allies."

"This is great, Bobby; you did great! You said the right words with the right attitude. Remember that for tomorrow. How come you're so strong on terror and not really on healthcare? What's the difference?"

"It's Dan's writing; he's so much better and clearer than Janie. She wrote all my healthcare talking points, and I can't even remember a single one. But Dan is structured."

"Is he still here now?"

"Yeah, I guess." Johnson stood up from the leather couch and opened the door to his front campaign office. "Hey, Danny boy, come on over here!"

A young man, not a day older than twenty-five, came in. "Yes, sir?"

"Did you write the senator's talking points for the war on terror?" Fischer asked.

"Yes, I did. Anything wrong?"

"No, quite the opposite," Fischer answered. "Can you slap something together for healthcare too? What's your background?"

"Sure I can," he said, displaying exceptionally white teeth in a very wide smile. "I'm pure public relations, sir. I graduated magna cum laude with a PR major. I can write anything about anything, sir."

"Perfect, go get it done; we need it in an hour," Fischer said, patting the young man on his shoulder.

"Consider it done," he said, then closed the door gently on his way out.

"You have a nugget of gold in this boy, Bobby; make sure you keep him happy, you hear me?"

"Don't I know it?" Johnson answered, resuming his place on the couch.

"Not sure you do. Immigration?"

"My platform calls for the relaxation of immigration rules, allowing a higher number of highly qualified professionals to enter the American job market and build our economy strong."

"How about unemployment? How about protecting the American laborers? How about the permanent pressure on American salaries due to the constant import of cheap labor from overseas? How would you handle these objections?"

"Well, America was built on immigration. The biggest, strongest economy of the world was built and thrives on immigration. Today, almost 30 percent of all patents filed are authored by new immigrants or H-1B visa holders. We need to bring this innovation to strengthen our economy."

"Who wrote this for you?"

"Janie."

"Okay, it's not as bad as healthcare, but if Dan has the time he should brush this up too." Fischer ran his hand through his hair yet again. "There are at least two areas where the public can crucify you. One is healthcare, and the other is immigration. Both are slippery slopes, so refrain from diving in too deep or getting pulled into the weeds."

"Got it."

"Then anything involving the current or historical geopolitical environment you should avoid like the leper, unless you're willing to really take this seriously, study, and understand it well. Until you do that, just try to back out of any geopolitically loaded question you can't grasp. Elevate the issue, or bring the topic back to something you're comfortable with, like the war on terror."

"Got it."

"Are you ready to do this, Bobby? Will you make me proud tomorrow?"

"Yes, I'm ready. I am the next president. I know it. I can feel it in my heart," he said, his voice sounding full of unwavering faith.

Maybe there was hope. Fischer stood, ready to leave.

"Oh, almost forgot. You'll be meeting your new best friend, Dave Vaughn, the Texas oil billionaire. I'm bringing him over in a day or two."

"I don't know the guy," Johnson protested, unconvinced.

"That's irrelevant; you will know him once you two meet. He wants to throw his money behind your campaign, so we'll be here, ready to accept gracefully and become the best of friends. He's your age, so you'll find something in common to talk about. He's a nice guy."

"Yeah, but what does he want? Why is he supporting me?"

Involuntarily, Fischer's hand passed through the remaining strands of thinning hair, pulling forcefully.

"Bobby, listen to me and listen good," Fischer said in almost a menacing tone.

The senator nodded quietly.

"You need all the help you can get," Fischer continued, his anger on the rise. "Do you understand me? All. The. Help. You. Can. Get. And for that help, you'll do whatever it takes, are we clear?" Fischer's question was faced with silence. He asked it in a different way. "Bobby, what are you willing to do to become the next president?"

"Oh, anything, anything at all, I promise."

"Good. Then remember that when you meet with Dave Vaughn."

...Chapter 42: Mother's Problems
...Wednesday, February 10, 9:35AM EST (UTC-5:00 hours)
...New Horizons Cardiology & Transplant Center, Office of Dr. Kanellis
...Burlington, Vermont

Alex entered the posh office, following the assistant who held the door for her with a professional smile. A distinguished-looking man, wearing scrubs and the typical buzz cut popular with male medical practitioners beyond a certain age, stood up to greet her.

"Dr. Kanellis? Good morning," Alex said, "and thank you for seeing me on such short notice."

"Absolutely, no problem." The doctor shook her hand. "Take a seat. What can I do for you?"

Why do doctors always have warm, dry hands? Alex found herself wondering for a second, then refocused on the conversation at hand.

"It's about my mother," she started to say hesitantly. "She needs a transplant, or so we have been told. I'm afraid I don't know much of what this entails or how to proceed." She handed Kanellis the file folder she had brought, where the combined talents of Sam and Lou had carefully constructed her mother's medical record based on Melanie Wilton's case parameters.

Kanellis started reviewing, making the occasional uh-huh and aah sounds quietly.

"I'm afraid you are correct, Miss Parker; your mother does need a transplant and without much delay. The severity of fluid accumulation due to her congestive heart failure is what dictates the urgency. Her heart has lost the ability to do its job. We can try managing it with medication until a heart becomes available, but we have to act fast."

"So what do I need to do?"

"We can start by admitting her here, to the Transplant Center, where I can evaluate her and prepare her case for the transplant committee to review."

"How hard is it to get approved by the committee?"

Kanellis delayed his answer by a few seconds, dropping his tone from neutral and professional to almost parental.

"I'm not going to lie to you, Miss Parker. Getting a heart is tricky. There aren't nearly enough available organs for transplant to address the growing needs of our patients. People live longer, healthier lives, so the likelihood of someone needing a transplant during their natural life span has increased tenfold. Despite the growing number of donor card carriers, there are simply not enough hearts to help everyone."

"What are you saying?" Alex asked. "That she won't get a heart?"

"I am saying that the transplant committee can decide either way, or even if they do add your mother's name to the list, her priority on the waiting list might change. For example, if a younger patient is accepted before she gets a heart, she might be bumped down on the waiting list. But let's worry about getting her name on the waiting list first. What can you tell me about her lifestyle?"

"Well, like everyone else, I guess, less than perfect. A few years back she had a DUI, but she's not an alcoholic. It was just a mishap, when she and Dad were coming back from a party. Will that disqualify her?"

"I don't see why it should, especially if it wasn't recent."

Alex's head was spinning. *What? DUI is not a disqualifier? I was right...Robert was set up. Bastards!*

"How about substance abuse or smoking?" Dr. Kanellis asked.

She had to invent something, so she picked at random.

"She is a smoker, I'm afraid. Will that damage her chances?"

"Definitely, I'm afraid," Dr. Kanellis replied. "Our center requires that patients are smoke free for at least six months before they can be placed on a transplant waiting list."

"What if she quits now?"

"Based on what I see here," he tapped gently on the file folder containing the medical records, "I'm afraid she doesn't have six months left to live."

"But there must be something we can do," she pleaded, almost whimpering. The more she entered into her character, the more she felt sympathy for Robert Wilton and what he must have been through. "You can't tell me there's nothing that can be done." She sniffled, then continued. "We have money. We can raise significant amounts. There's nothing we won't do for my mother."

Dr. Kanellis quietly rejected her argument, raising his hand with his palm facing outward, as if to push her away.

"I'm afraid that money won't make a difference here, Miss Parker. This selection process and the transplant committee were created specifically to prevent the allocation of organs to be dictated by personal wealth, as opposed to medical reasons and individual merit. The heart should go to the patient who has the best chance of survival, the greatest lifespan ahead of them, the cleanest and healthiest lifestyle. Money doesn't come into play at any point in this process."

She let him finish, watching him with pleading eyes.

"The only way money makes a difference," Kanellis said, "is if you try medical tourism. There are agencies that can send you and your mother abroad, to China most likely, where you can get a heart for a very large sum of money, a couple hundred thousand at least. You also have to not mind where the heart comes from. I personally struggle even mentioning this alternative to you."

"What do you mean?"

"Well, where do you think these organs come from, in such places? Executed prisoners, most likely. You would buy somebody else's life."

She shuddered hearing him explain. *Good thing I don't really have this dilemma. It's a shitty one to have*, she thought.

"Do you think she can make the trip, though? She's very weak."

"Most likely, no. Looking at her file, I wouldn't advise her to be out of bed more than fifteen minutes per day. A flight to China is twenty hours long. It would completely exhaust her and risk her life. Even if she makes it, she'd be entering the procedure weakened and exhausted, diminishing her chances to survive and accept the organ."

"Then what other options do I have? How about the black market for organs, here in the United States?"

"We're not having this conversation, Miss Parker," Kanellis said firmly. "Organ trafficking is illegal, plus it's almost exclusively about kidneys, not hearts."

"So there's nothing I can do? There's no hope? I can raise a lot of cash that no one has to know about," she pleaded.

"Because you're under a lot of personal hardship I will forget you mentioned that, but I'm afraid our conversation is over, Miss Parker." He stood up frowning, visibly offended by her blatant bribe offer.

She left quietly, thinking he was a little too offended by an offer he must receive every now and then, considering what he did for a living.

Damn. Back to square one.

In her car, she grabbed her encrypted cell and speed-dialed a number.

"Hey, Lou, how's it going?"

"Hey, partner, we were just talking about you. How are things?"

"Not impressive, I'm afraid. Need your help."

"Shoot."

"See if you can't snoop around in the New Horizon systems a little. I couldn't get anything from this Kanellis guy; he just wouldn't budge. But I'm sure there's something to be found. Use Melanie's admission date to help you find the info."

"All right, I'll get to it. What are you up to while I work?"

"I'm gonna cruise the local watering holes, see where these surgeons like to have their dinners and drinks. Might be useful for later."

"Sounds like a plan. Please be careful," Lou said, all serious.

"I will," she replied.

I most surely will, Alex thought, starting her engine and checking her surroundings for the tenth time. No one was following her; she hadn't noticed any familiar cars, faces, or anything. Yet her gut was telling her to be on full alert.

...Chapter 43: Helms Calls
...Wednesday, February 10, 10:12AM EST (UTC-5:00 hours)
...New Horizons Cardiology & Transplant Center, Office of Dr. Kanellis
...Burlington, Vermont

Dr. Kanellis resumed his morning activities after the frustrating Miss Parker had just left. *It wasn't her fault.* He softened a little. It's hard for people to walk the line when their loved ones are dying.

His cell rang, disrupting his thoughts. One look at the cell's display, and his stomach tied into a knot. It was him again, the man that a twisted fate had brought into his life, the man by the name of Helms.

"Hello?" He picked up the call in an almost normal voice.

"Who was that?"

"Who was who?" Kanellis asked, confused.

"The woman who just left your office."

"Umm...nobody. Just a patient's daughter looking for an exception."

"What was the issue?"

"Patient's a smoker, won't qualify. I sent them to China. I probably won't see her again."

"Very good."

"Listen, you said you were going to leave me alone. It's been months! How much longer are you going to be lurking around?" Kanellis was getting angry.

"We're going to leave you alone when we decide you can keep your end of the deal and your mouth shut."

The caller hung up, leaving Kanellis boiling with frustration. It had been months since he had made the biggest mistake of his career, and it just seemed like it would never go away.

...Chapter 44: Phase One Complete
...Wednesday, February 10, 9:09PM Local Time (UTC+1:00 hours)
...Millennium Ballroom, Zurich Marriott Hotel
...Zurich, Switzerland

The last of the guests were leaving slowly, smiling and chatting left and right. They had enjoyed themselves very much, and their generous donations to the Eastern Africa Development Fund were statements to the caliber of parties Ahmad Javadi could throw. The venue was classy and well-serviced by armies of waiters with impeccable manners. The music was soft, not too loud, yet encouraging his guests to dance if they liked. The hors-d'oeuvres were the best in all of Europe, freshly imported from exotic destinations and complementing a selection of the most exquisite wine collection. The custom fireworks at the end of the evening, a splendid show of light and color, caused everyone to gasp when the last round of bursts wrote *EADF* above the Zurich skyline.

His guests—bankers, businessmen, and high-ranking officials—deserved the best in food and drink but also in company. Javadi's negotiating abilities had secured for the evening the presence and endorsement of famous musicians, entertainers, and movie stars. Even last year's Wimbledon champion had spoken on behalf of EADF. The evening, carefully planned by one of the greatest fundraising minds of the time, had been a complete success, one that would be mentioned in newspapers for weeks to come. Almost ten million dollars in donations in one evening. That was impressive, even by Javadi's standards.

All his rushed efforts to set things up had paid off. Javadi was happy. Satisfied, he headed out onto the terrace, where just an hour earlier everyone applauded his fireworks show in the brisk Swiss mountain air. He lit a cigar, then extended the antenna on his sat phone. When the other end of the line picked up, he only said three words:

"Phase one complete."

...Chapter 45: Tracking Doctors
...Wednesday, February 10, 3:15PM EST (UTC-5:00 hours)
...Starbucks, Burlington Town Center
...Burlington, Vermont

"Thank you," Alex said gratefully, grabbing the grande coffee from the barista with both her frozen hands. Winter was serious business anywhere else but California.

She sat at a small table in the corner of the coffee shop and started sipping the hot liquid, savoring the heat and inhaling the strong scent of fresh-brewed house blend. Her encrypted cell buzzed, displaying Lou's mischievous smile on the LCD screen.

"Shoot," she said.

"Yep, got what you asked for, with some limitations though," he blurted at machine-gun speed.

"Meaning?"

"I found the procedure in the New Horizon system, but the details are sketchy. Most of the surgical staff is identified by initials, not by full names. There's no patient registration information, just a note saying that the patient had been transferred from Municipal to recover post-surgery; although there are entries that confirm the surgery took place at the Transplant Center."

"Huh," Alex said, "so there's a discrepancy, right there."

"Spot on, partner. There's more. The patient is marked in their system as a VIP, with instructions to provide special care, whatever that means, and to keep isolated. Restricted access, even from the center's personnel."

"Very interesting. What else?"

"There are obviously no insurance claims filed for this and no insurance information on file, yet the account shows paid in full. Probably a cash transaction."

"OK, I was expecting that."

"Probably you weren't expecting that most of the initials marked on the case file in the system don't match any of their current surgical employees."

"What? So where were they coming from?"

"No idea," Lou said. "Her discharge date matches what Robert gave us, but there's no surgery date and time like there should be. The drug regimen is documented in detail, but again, no insurance claims attached to that one either."

"Text me the initials found on her record, and tell me which ones match with any of the existing staff."

"Will do. There's one very positive match: initials GWH matching a Dr. Gary William Hager, cardiothoracic surgeon and transplant specialist. I don't think this is a coincidence; I think this is him, the surgeon who operated on Melanie. I'll text you his mug."

"OK, thanks much, Lou. You're a lifesaver."

"Speaking of which...watch your back! These guys are pros, and I'm not there."

"Speaking of which...were you careful snooping around?"

"What do you think?"

Alex hung up, immersed in scenarios playing wildly in her head. One thought bothered her. *If these guys are such pros, why is this patient record still available in the Transplant Center's computer system? It should have been deleted long ago, erasing all evidence that anything had ever happened. What am I missing?*

...Chapter 46: Vote Secrecy
...Wednesday, February 10, 9:01PM EST (UTC-5:00 hours)
...News of the Hour Special Edition Report
...Nationally Syndicated

"Good evening, ladies and gentlemen." Stephanie Wainwright's smile filled the screen. "We're revisiting today the controversial issue of vote secrecy in the light of the e-vote overhaul. This issue has been increasingly visible, with strong opponents rallying support and lobbying Congress for an injunction. With us in studio to help us understand what's at stake is California Senator Sidney Mulligan, pioneer of the e-vote reform, the man who started it all. Welcome, senator."

The senator appeared on the screen. The camera zoomed out, showing two armchairs in a studio setting, very common when Stephanie had a high-profile guest.

"Thank you for inviting me," the senator answered. The relaxed demeanor and friendly attitude were a constant with Senator Mulligan, no matter how heated the debates became.

"Senator, what do you think this concern for vote secrecy could do to your initiative? Is it a serious concern?"

"Any concern with the integrity of a constitutional right is a serious concern. We are taking the concern very seriously. We have launched a campaign of educational videos to demonstrate how the voters' identities will never be correlated with the actual vote inputs into the system at any given point in the voting process. This will simply not happen. I am hoping that the people will learn to understand how e-vote really works, and when doing so, also learn to trust us."

"I have seen the videos you're referencing; they are quite informative, engaging, and well done."

"Thank you, Stephanie, you are very kind."

"Senator, the voices in the streets are getting louder by the minute, despite these educational efforts. Let's watch together some snapshots our crew took yesterday in the heart of New York City, at the corner of Bowery and Canal."

The screen switched to show the hustle of a busy New York City street corner, countless people hurrying through a cold, slushy, windy winter morning. The reporter, almost unrecognizable under his heavy parka hood, was asking the same question over and over again.

"How concerned are you with your constitutional right to voter secrecy and why?"

"Ha! That's a good one. No one has any secrecy anymore, no privacy, nothing. Rights? Pfft...This is the land of Big Brother. Where do you think you are? Ha!" jeered a man in his late thirties, battling the street slush in light shoes.

"I'm very concerned. I'm not even sure I want to vote anymore, if that's the case. I am scared," remarked a middle-aged woman who avoided making eye contact with the camera and didn't stop to deliver her response. She just kept going, making the reporter chase her with the microphone.

"Are you for real? No comment!" yelled a man wearing high-end business attire and holding an expensive leather briefcase.

"You seen them videos, my man? What do they want us to do, trust the government? I ain't stupid, dawg," said an African American man in his twenties, bundled up and wearing a colorful knitted scarf.

"I...I...no vote," an elderly Chinese woman managed to articulate.

"It's all a big conspiracy. I know it is. I am sure of it. You see, they already know everything about us. They have these big databases buried under mountains. I know they do. I read about it. Seen it on TV. They listen to our calls and read our emails. They know everything. What we eat. What we buy. What we say. What we see on the Internet. But so far, they don't know what we think. So this is the last step, I am telling you, to figure out what we think. And then, what do you think is gonna happen, huh? Whoever doesn't think the way they want, suddenly loses their jobs, or has accidents, or gets Ebola, or something. That's the only thing they're missing: how we think. Then the conspiracy wins. We never win." The cabbie's diatribe was interrupted by brutal honking and swearing from the cars behind his battered cab. The stoplight had turned green about halfway through his speech.

The screen returned to Stephanie and the senator in studio.

"So, what do you think, senator?"

"It's obvious and disheartening that the majority of our citizens do not trust us with safeguarding their constitutional right to vote secrecy. This is a fact that cannot be denied. I also strongly believe," the senator continued, wearing the same kind, reassuring smile, "that our government has lost the confidence of our people. We need to own that. We have made many mistakes, and our government's reputation, although in shambles, is of our own doing. I also believe that sometimes you have to push for progress despite resistance to change. Change is hard, change is scary, especially when you have a strong underlying issue of trust. What have we done, as a government, to gain the confidence of our citizens? We have burst into people's homes in the dead of the night with SWAT teams, to execute simple search warrants, or for no reason at all. Even better, one time SWAT had the wrong address to begin with but ended up charging the man of the house for pulling a gun in self-defense.

Police officers are discharging weapons at minivans full of children for speeding. The same police force steers clear of high-crime zones and prefers to waste time setting up speed traps on deserted highways, where the officers can be safe and do as little as possible to curb real crime, such as drug trafficking, home invasions, assaults, or homicides. How do you think our citizens feel when we distribute military-grade weapons and vehicles to the same police force? How about illegal wire-tapping, surveillance, and all sorts of invasions of privacy that we have subjected our constituents to over and over again? And now we expect them to trust us, and we're surprised and disappointed when they don't? I'm sorry, but this is hardly a surprise. Yes, it is disheartening, but it's not a surprise. We need to own that before we can start fixing it."

"Then how do you see the future of e-vote in the face of the growing anxiety about voter secrecy?"

"We can only hope that our education campaign bears fruit and reduces the anxiety levels over time. We definitely don't want these concerns to impact voter participation. I strongly encourage all citizens to exercise their right to vote. To me, this is more than a right; it's a duty. I am also hoping that what we're seeing now is the initial response, when people react emotionally. With time, education, dialogue, and increased visibility about the e-vote process, I'm hoping this anxiety level will be dulled, enough for citizens to exercise their right to vote with sufficient confidence that their constitutional right to voter secrecy will be safeguarded at all times and at all costs. This is my personal promise. If I had any concern about how voter data is stored and manipulated, I would be the first one to pull the plug on e-vote reform."

"Senator, in conclusion, you're hoping that this widespread fear will blow over, and you're essentially asking the citizens of America to trust you?"

"I am confident that we will be able to gain some level of confidence over time, with continued communication, dialogue, and understanding on both sides. We are still a few months away from November. And I promise you, Stephanie, and everyone else that the way the system is designed and built doesn't permit the type of privacy issues that the citizens fear. You have my word."

"Thank you, senator, we wish you all the best in achieving this ambitious goal."

"Thank you, Stephanie, always a pleasure."

The camera zoomed in, showcasing Stephanie's portrait.

"That was Senator Sidney Mulligan, the pioneer of electronic voting, responding to the growing concerns about voter secrecy. Live from our studio, this is Stephanie Wainwright, with *News of the Hour*."

...Chapter 47: The Harbormaster
...Thursday, February 11, 11:07AM EST (UTC-5:00 hours)
...Fort Lauderdale Marina, Harbormaster's Office
...Fort Lauderdale, Florida

Muhammad Sadiq moved with difficulty along the building, holding the cane tightly and limping visibly. His right leg, still unable to support his body weight after the recent hip replacement, was causing him to cringe at every step. A native of Pakistan, Sadiq had lived in the United States for many years, enjoying the benefits of his wealth, while increasing it at the same time. His wealth had been built in textiles and commerce, driven by the ambitious, relentless vision of a shepherd's son. Now almost seventy years old, Sadiq still couldn't deal with the consequences of his age. In the depths of his mind, even if irrational, the thought that wealth should help one bypass the miseries of old age was a well-rooted concept. In all fairness, it was half-true. He had bought himself the hip replacement, done by the best surgeons that money could buy, and had enjoyed post-surgery recovery in a top-notch private clinic. What his money couldn't do, no matter how much of it he was willing to spend, was to cut his recovery time from weeks to days.

Yet he couldn't postpone this visit any longer. He was on a tight schedule. Entering the harbormaster's office, he gestured between labored breaths to the chair in front of the man's desk and sat heavily, stretching his right leg.

"What can I do for you?" the harbormaster asked. Middle-aged and chubby, he looked supportive, almost friendly. His perceptive eyes scanned Sadiq from head to toe from behind thick-rimmed glasses.

"I'd like to lease or buy a slip for my boat. They will be delivering it shortly, and I need a place to park it on the water." Sadiq spoke with little accent, his English well-articulated.

"Absolutely," the man said, displaying a helpful, professional smile. "That's what we're here for. What kind of boat are we talking about?"

"Forty-seven," Sadiq said without skipping a beat.

"Oh, wow, nice," the man commented. "New? What are you getting?"

"Brand new, a Sea Ray 470 Sundancer."

"Wow, that's a million-dollar boat. Congratulations! It's not every day we get one of those; although we do have quite a few vessels here. We'd be happy to accommodate your new boat. For a yacht that size, we offer fueling by truck."

"Can I ask, please, if you could give me a spot closer to the parking lot and easy to maneuver on the water? As you can see," Sadiq gestured to his right leg, "I am not exactly able to move around as I used to. Not anymore."

"Sure, let's see." He pulled out a map of the marina and showed it to Sadiq. "We can accommodate forty-seven footers here, here, and here," he said, pointing at the available slots with the tip of his pen. "How often are you planning to take this beauty out?"

"Umm...maybe a couple of times per month, maybe more often once my leg gets better."

"Are you planning to live on board?"

"What? No, I am not." Sadiq smiled. "I have a house here in Lauderdale."

"You could, you know, it's beautiful. In any case, I would recommend this spot for you. Only seventy-five feet or so from the parking lot and just a couple of maneuvers to get it aligned with the pier. Leaving is even easier, see?"

"Perfect," Sadiq confirmed. "Is it possible for me to reserve a parking spot for my car?"

"No, I'm afraid that is not something we offer."

"What if I signed a lease for the slip for a year, would that change things maybe?"

The harbormaster thought for a few seconds. The man seemed harmless enough, despite his Arabic name. He was old and in obvious pain and getting him a reserved spot would almost be an act of kindness. Definitely it wouldn't be a security risk for the marina, and it could be an additional income stream. The only question was how much he could charge for it. By the looks of it, however much he wanted.

"It could," he said. "It requires me to generate a lot of paperwork in support of your request and to order a custom sign and permit number."

"I understand," Sadiq said, "and I appreciate you bending the rules for me. Money is not an object."

"Let's see...The boat slip for a year comes to $1.55 per foot per day, or $2,185 per month. Let's say...$2,900, parking included? And you get to pick your spot," he offered.

Sadiq nodded his approval, placing his right hand on his heart. "Thank you."

He allowed a discreet sigh of relief to slip between his parched lips. He was ready.

...Chapter 48: Luck
...Thursday, February 11, 6:14PM EST (UTC-5:00 hours)
...Randy Turner's Residence
...New York, New York

"Oh, no, no, no, no! Fuck! I am so dead!" Randy stared at his computer screen in disbelief. "He is so gonna kill me. Can't believe this!"

When he had taken the quick job from the wrinkled stranger with scary-cold blue eyes, he had thought he had just hit the jackpot. Five thousand dollars for what appeared to be a whim, five large ones to just keep an eye on some clinic's system and see if someone hacks into it. Then five grand more when he'd report the hack, as soon as it happened. The man had been adamant, almost threatening. He had to report the hack the moment it happened.

Of course he'd taken the five grand, never really expecting he'd get the rest of the dough. He was smart enough to know this was not legit. Legit people concerned with systems security buy firewalls, not the services from nineteen year olds with expunged records for computer hacking. Nope, dead sure not legit.

So he'd taken the money, hadn't thought twice about it, and had written a piece of code, a small intrusion detection application that watched for any unauthorized entry into the transplant clinic's systems. Easy-peasy. He'd dusted off an old laptop he wasn't using anymore and had it monitor the application. For weeks, nothing. He stopped believing anyone would ever hack in there, and why would they? He also stopped believing he'd ever see the other five large ones; although his client had called every now and then to check the status.

Then one day, the only time he'd taken off with his new girl and spent a cool afternoon and a hot night at her place, in the absence of her parents, it had to happen. Of course, he hadn't been there to see it happen, and now more than twenty-four hours had passed since the attack. *Goddamn shitty luck... He is so gonna kill me!*

He stood there, staring at the screen displaying information about the intrusion and weighing his options. Of course, he could just pretend nothing happened and never see his other five grand. Such a waste of some really decent payday, and those were hard to find. Then he could, of course, run the risk that his client would still find out about it, a case in which his life wouldn't be worth much. The man, who'd said his name was Helms, had made that very clear. The other option was to call him and give him as little information as possible, covering his screw-up. Maybe, just maybe he'd get his other five grand.

With trembling hands, he picked up the cell phone the stranger had left with him and recalled the only number stored in the phone's memory, chanting in his mind *no TMI, no TMI, God, help me, no TMI.* He had this character flaw, always giving people too much information and talking too much. Way too much. Well, on this call, he'd better stick to his *no TMI* strategy.

"Helms here," the stranger answered.

"Y–yeah, hi, it's Randy," he stuttered almost.

"Randy, what do you have for me?"

"You were right, someone did hack into the clinic system. So my job is done," he blurted, awaiting his prize.

"When?"

Oh, shit! He decided to lie a little, probably it would hurt way less than the truth.

"Just a few hours ago," he said hesitantly.

"Precisely when?" Helms insisted in a deathly cold voice.

"Um...at precisely 1:17PM Eastern," he said, conveniently omitting to add the date to this information. He was hoping the man would assume it had been today, not yesterday, and not probe any further. At least the 1:17PM Eastern was accurate.

"Why did you take so long to let me know?"

Tell the truth? Lie? Randy envisioned what the man would do if he heard the real reason for this delay. *Lie, definitely lie.*

"I wanted to track where the attack was coming from, and that wasn't easy. It was done by pros," he said, spitting out one lie after another and getting more and more comfortable in the web of lies he was creating. "The attack was bounced around from China to Singapore, then to Russia, and so on. It took me hours to decrypt it."

"Do you have the source? Where did it come from?"

Randy hit a few keys and said, "Yes, it came from San Diego. But I can't tell you more than that. It came from behind an excellent firewall, government grade or something. When do I get my money?"

"Soon," the man said, then hung up.

"Whew, you son of a bitch, that was close," Randy said out loud, allowing himself to slide down onto the couch.

...Chapter 49: Dr. Hager
...Thursday, February 11, 6:49PM EST (UTC-5:00 hours)
...Hen of the Wood Restaurant
...Burlington, Vermont

Alex walked through the restaurant's double wooden doors, grateful to feel some warm air against her flushed, tingly face. The local weather was fairly brutal, and the snow seemed to keep on falling, continuously, with no end in sight.

She stomped her feet near the entrance to shake the snow off her boots. She unzipped her parka and took out her cell. Checking the image on her phone one more time, she consolidated in her mind the key information about the man she was looking for. Dr. Gary William Hager, thirty-nine, light brown hair, green eyes, relatively handsome.

She looked around the restaurant, ignoring the hostess who was trying to seat her.

"Just a second," Alex said, "I'm looking for a friend."

There he was, seated at the chef's counter. Not a very favorable location for a private conversation. Dr. Hager was seated between two other men, but they didn't seem to know each other. Alex noticed the empty shot glass in front of him. Good.

She waited a little, stalling, thinking of ways to approach him. She fumbled with her gloves, took off her parka and spent forever hanging it on the coat rack in the corner. She checked the restaurant for other familiar faces and the windowed doors behind her for anyone who might have followed her here. There was no one.

The man sitting at Dr. Hager's left paid his tab and made for the exit. Alex took the opportunity and headed for the empty seat, no clear strategy in mind. She sat next to Hager and smiled.

"Hi," she started cautiously, "I hope you don't mind."

"No, you're fine," Hager said and turned slightly away from her, giving her a clear signal he wanted to be left alone. He seemed tired and preoccupied.

"I'm new to town, just passing through," she said with a light chuckle, "and I was thinking you could recommend a few places to go."

Hager turned her way and checked her out real quick.

"Listen, I mean no disrespect, but I would rather be by myself."

"I understand. I also understand you think I might be hitting on you right now," she said, dropping her voice to almost a whisper and gently touching the man's forearm, "but I'm not. However, it is in your best interest to behave like I *am* actually hitting on you and like you are very much into it and share a table. That is if you want to hear what I have to say in private. For me, it will work either way."

Hager checked her out again, this time with a deep frown above his intense green eyes. He decided to follow her lead and stood.

"There's a table right there." He pointed to an empty one in the far corner of the restaurant.

"Perfect," Alex said, grabbing his arm and flashing her power smile.

"So, what's this about?" Hager asked as soon as they were seated. "Are you a patient?"

"No, but I'm here about a patient. I need some information about a case you operated on last December. The patient's name is Melanie Wilton."

Alex watched him intently as she said Melanie's name. Blood ran from his face, and his pupils dilated, giving away the pang of fear he must have felt.

"I can't discuss anything. All patient information is confidential; I'm sure you know that much. You're wasting your time and mine."

"Not so fast," Alex said, smiling and touching Hager's hand lightly. From a distance, they appeared to be a new couple enjoying their time together. "I have specific questions regarding that procedure, and they're not about Melanie Wilton's cholesterol levels. However, I'm prepared to ask my questions with the authorities present. Are you?"

Hager swallowed hard but didn't say a word.

"Listen," Alex insisted, "there are many ways this can end terribly wrong for you and only one way it could end well. I suggest you make the right choice."

He nodded, giving up. His shoulders hunched, and his head hung. He clasped his palms together. "Ask away."

"All right then, I'll make this as quick and painless as I can. Who paid for her surgery?"

"I have no idea. It was paid in cash and lots of it. Some for the clinic, some for me personally. I'm sure the surgical team was nicely compensated too. I received a package at my house with my fee, all cash, used twenty bills."

He was very cooperative, holding nothing back. She continued. "Where did you get the heart?"

"I didn't. I'm not aware of where the heart came from. It was delivered in the middle of the night by an unmarked chopper. The chopper landed right in the clinic's backyard, left the container, and took off within minutes. The heart we received was strong, viable, the right donor match and everything, ready to be transplanted. It was delivered on order. We were told to start prepping her even before we had the heart, and we did. We knew the heart would come at a certain time and date, which almost never really happens."

"How was it packaged?"

"Perfectly packaged, by the book, cold crystalloid ischemic storage with all legal organ transplants, minus the paperwork. Cooler was unmarked. No logos on anything. There was no paperwork and no documented origin for the organ. No source."

"If you were to venture a guess as to where the heart came from, what would you say?"

"I wouldn't. It's really hard to tell. A heart can only survive four to six hours after harvesting, so it had to be close, or relatively close, two-hour chopper flight range, tops. Someone, somewhere, spent a lot of cash to make that heart appear."

"How about the surgical team?" Alex asked.

"They were strangers to me. I had never met them before. They came in that night, all traveling together in a large SUV, a GMC Yukon, I think. They showed up, they scrubbed, they did an excellent job, and they left before dawn. They were a good surgical team. They seemed to know one another and had experience working together."

"Any names you can remember?"

"They didn't say any names."

"What time was the surgery?"

"It started after midnight and lasted a few hours."

"Is this normal?"

"It can happen, because the harvested heart can't survive for too long. Our normal staff wasn't recalled on duty, like normally happens when surgeries are scheduled. That was strange. There was minimal staff only, the typical core crew for a night without any OR bookings."

"Where did Melanie come from?"

"Her paperwork said she had transferred from Municipal to recover post-surgery. That's obviously not true. Somewhere between Municipal and the clinic, the paperwork got fixed. That's if she ever set foot in Municipal."

"Why did you do it? Who approached you and offered you the cash?"

Hager hesitated a little. "My boss."

"Dr. Kanellis?"

"Yes."

"Did he explain why?"

"He said it was a personal favor to him, of utmost importance to keep quiet; our licenses were at stake, and so on. He was very insistent. I couldn't say no. After all, we did save a life. Maybe not the right one, or the right priority one, but nevertheless, a life."

"Did Kanellis mention any names?"

Hager frowned as he was trying to remember.

"At some point, in a related conversation regarding the procedure and the drug regimen to follow, he had a slip of the tongue and mentioned a name. Hems, Helms, Holmes, maybe? Does this mean anything?"

Alex didn't respond. That Helms guy again. He was everywhere.

"Do you know where I could find the man Kanellis mentioned?"

"No idea."

"One more question. If this procedure was so hush-hush, why are there records of it in the system?"

"I often ask myself the same thing, even asked Kanellis about it. It was by his decision that we entered anything in the system, but we didn't enter much. Nothing relevant, anyway. No names, no insurance information, not even Mrs. Wilton's social. In retrospect, I think we shouldn't have entered anything. What purpose does that system entry serve?"

Excellent question, Dr. Hager, Alex thought.

"If someone wanted to delete that record, would they be able to?"

"I'm sure they would, no doubt. We've had duplicate entries and errors in the system cleaned up before."

"OK, that's all I needed from you, Dr. Hager. Thank you for your cooperation."

"What's gonna happen to me?" Hager asked, looking up for the first time since she'd started asking her questions.

"Hopefully, nothing. Keep this conversation a secret, and I promise I'll do the same."

"Who are you?"

"Just someone you won't ever see again, Dr. Hager. And now, just in case someone was watching us have this little talk, I will be providing you with a good cover story. Just remember I hit on you at first," Alex said and winked. She stood up abruptly, slapped Hager across the face, and yelled, "You bastard!"

Then she rushed toward the exit, grabbed her parka on the way out, and was gone in seconds.

To anyone watching, Dr. Hager must have said something very wrong to this young lady. His chances were not looking too good with her. A couple of patrons commented on the event, stifling their laughs.

...Chapter 50: Payday
...Friday, February 12, 11:02AM EST (UTC-5:00 hours)
...Randy Turner's Residence
...New York, New York

A rapid tap on the door woke him. He groaned, the typical groan of a nineteen year old when he has to wake up before noon. He turned on the other side and mumbled.

"Who is it?"

The tap reoccurred. Randy tried harder this time, getting out of bed and dragging his feet to the door.

"Yeah?"

A voice from behind the door said quietly, "I have your money."

Randy took the door chain off in a second and welcomed the man in.

"Come on in, man, I am so happy to see you."

Helms walked in, looking around.

Randy grabbed a pile of clothing scattered on the old, beat-down couch and made room for his guest. The air was stale and smelled of dirty laundry, but Randy didn't smell that anymore. However, any time his friends dropped by, they bitched about it, so Randy opened the sliding window to let in some fresh air. The frazzled window sheers waved in the brisk winter breeze.

"Here, sit down. Shit, man, am I glad to see you!"

Helms continued to stand. He patted the kid on his back. Helms looked scary, just as scary as the day he had met him. He was smiling, but the smile didn't reach his eyes. Cold as ice, the man's blue eyes gave him the willies. He hated how this guy skeezed him out.

"Where can we speak privately?"

Randy hesitated for a second, confused by a question with an obvious answer.

"Right here. There's no one else here."

"Good. You did good on the assignment, kid, show me."

"Show you what?"

"Show me how you saw the intrusion. Can you figure out what that person saw in the system?"

Randy went to his old laptop and demonstrated, flipping through screens fast, so that Helms wouldn't catch the date on the intrusion report.

"Yeah. See? This is the app I'm running; it shows the hack alert here, on this screen." He displayed the report screen for half a second. "Then in here you see what he saw."

"He looked at multiple records?"

"Yeah, the dude checked a few of them out. Checked this one fairly thoroughly, then looked around some more."

"Which one did he check first?"

"This one, umm...Melanie Wilton. But there ain't any info that makes any sense in there. The other records have info in them, see? They have dates, names, activity, socials, stuff like that. This one has nothing, just a name and some codes and acronyms."

"Good, good," the man said, grabbing Randy by the back of his head, gently, as if to pet him like a parent would stroke a child. "You did really good."

"Great, so I get my money now?" Randy asked, turning around to look at Helms.

Suddenly, the grip on his neck became forceful, not allowing him to turn his head any farther. He kicked around, flailed his arms, tried to grab something, but he was almost paralyzed.

"What...? The fuck...?" Randy managed to say as the grip turned to steel.

"Yes," the man said, "you did good."

With a rapid twist of his right hand, he gripped Randy's neck rendering him helpless. His left hand then grabbed his chin and executed a sudden right-to-left movement. Randy's legs turned to jelly as loud cracks marked the multiple fractures in his cervical spine. Before glossing over, Randy's eyes continued to express the utmost disbelief.

Helms dropped the body to the floor gently to avoid making too much noise. He closed the window after looking around and checking for any unusual activity. He grabbed the laptop, slid it under his overcoat, and left, closing the door behind him without a sound.

...Chapter 51: The Replacement
...Monday, February 15, 10:14AM EST (UTC-5:00 hours)
...DCBI Headquarters, Sixth Floor Conference Room
...Washington, DC

Robert fidgeted before settling down at his conference room table. He was about to enter a new phase of this madness, a phase in which he had to involve his team. To some extent. They'd be ignorant players, manipulated into taking certain actions by a man they had learned to trust. The thought made him sick to the stomach; he hated lying to his people, or to anyone for that matter. Making things even worse was knowing that someone was watching his every move and listening to every word being said, waiting for the tiniest misspoken word or hint of betrayal to kill Melanie. It was a very fine line to walk, but he felt determination replacing his anxiety. They were going to pay for everything they had done. Soon. He was working on it, and he was no longer alone.

The conference room seemed too big without Laura and Jimmy; it was just Ellen, Eddie, and Brad now. But today was not the right time to think of those departed. Today was the day to start focusing on fixing things, on finding out who had killed two members of his team. Focus on preventing a disaster of immense proportions.

He finally settled into his chair and opened his portfolio, extracting some papers from it.

His team followed his lead and took their usual seats. Ellen sipped some of the steaming coffee in her mug, holding it with both hands. Eddie looked a little absent, lost in his thoughts. Brad, his normal professional and focused self, waited for him to start the weekly staff meeting.

"All right, guys, it's time we get going on finding replacements. I know how painful this is, believe me, I know. I sometimes feel like no one else can ever take their places, like we're betraying their memories if we replace them so soon." He paused, checking their expressions. All of them nodded in approval, sadness written on their faces. "But it's time to move on, because we have a contract of historical importance to handle, and we must handle it well." He handed them each a copy of a three-page stapled document. "This is the résumé of a highly qualified contractor, currently working for our number one competitor, Innovatix Consulting in Texas. Her name is Alex Hoffmann. We could employ her for the right amount of money of course. Please take a look and let me know what you think."

They read through the résumé quietly for a while.

"I like that she has a lot of experience in quality," Brad opened. "And she did some offshoring too. In technology. I think she'd be a great fit, very solid."

"I like her too," Ellen offered. "You're right; it's hard to think of bringing someone new on board, but we have to. Currently, there's almost no time or resources available for vendor performance management. My guys generate the reports, but we don't have the capabilities to spend enough time studying progress and performance and to act on that data. I say let's move on with this; let's give her a shot."

"She'd be a contractor," Eddie said, "that means we have very low risk bringing her in, and we get to bypass certain delays that normally happen with fulltime employees. Yeah, let's go for it. We need someone onsite at this level."

"She'd need to relo, right?" Brad asked. "How long would that take?"

"Yeah, she'd need to relocate, but with contractors you know how it works," Robert said. "We can offer her assisted temporary living, get her a furnished apartment or a long-term hotel room, and we're there. She'd be working offshore for the majority of the time anyway, so there's no reason to actually mover her at this time. Not with the time pressures we're currently under."

"Sounds a bit insensitive," Ellen said.

"Yeah, it does." Robert agreed. "We can always ask her if that poses a problem and manage from there. But if you like her profile I'll hand it over to HR to start the process and schedule our interviews."

"Yep, let's get started," Brad said, "we can't afford to wait any longer."

Robert smiled faintly. Brad's statement held true from many different perspectives.

...Chapter 52: A Terrific Interview
...Wednesday, March 2, 9:01PM EST (UTC-5:00 hours)
...Flash Elections: At a Glance
...Nationally Syndicated

The colorful opening credits faded, leaving only the smiling, charismatic image of Phil Fournier to fill the screen.

"Well, he's done it again! Doug Krassner had a terrific interview late last night, answering tough questions with completely unexpected answers and somehow managing to hit homeruns every time. Let's watch together."

The screen shifted to show Krassner in a heated conversation with the one of the top political show hosts, Al Bernstein.

"Senator," Bernstein asked, "your opponent, Bobby Johnson, stated that almost 30 percent of all new patents filed are authored by new immigrants or H-1B visa holders and that we should open the gates wider to capture more innovation. If you're looking to limit immigration to protect the American labor force, wouldn't your proposed measure jeopardize progress and innovation?"

"That is a very good question, Al. I'm happy you asked. Before answering, I have to ask another fundamental question: why aren't Americans bringing innovations on their own? Why aren't they authoring more patents, making breakthrough discoveries, and pushing the boundaries of science and technology? Well, the answer is a sad yet simple one. Let's take software development, for example. Let's say my kid is about to choose a career. If he chooses a college program that prepares him to be a top-notch software developer, he'd leave school with roughly $150,000, maybe even $200,000 in student debt. When he graduates, he would get job offers that have the pay levels set by the constant wave of immigrants bringing the same top-notch skills for only about $60,000 a year. That would mean a lifetime of fighting debt, not having much of a future, and always running the risk of having his job snatched from underneath him by some new offshoring program, or by the cheapest H-1B worker of the day.

"Then what does he do? He chooses a different career, where he has a chance to have a decent, stable future. That career won't be in software development. It will be in business, medicine, finance, or anything else we haven't figured out how to offshore or H-1B yet. What does that mean, besides his broken dreams to pursue software development? That he, and others like him, won't be bringing innovation to the American world of technology. The

H-1Bs will. So my answer to you, Al, is that we have to create the possibility for Americans to innovate and win in the highly competitive global knowledge market. We have taken that opportunity away, and now we have to bring it back. We have to decide whether we'd like to invest in our future as a people, make a commitment, and then execute."

"Senator, you're essentially saying we're suffocating our own innovation ourselves?"

"That's exactly what I'm saying. In business, America's innovation is second to none in the entire world. But there aren't any H-1B business immigrants who jeopardize the career choices of our kids by limiting their income potentials. Same with medicine. Our healthcare competes with top healthcare in the world and wins almost every time, for the same reasons. In medicine, there are researchers who come as H-1Bs or permanent immigrants, and so are in business or finance. They help us gain an edge in those fields. But they don't compete with the college grads or bring job instability to their fields. They are the brains we want to have among us, to teach us what we haven't figured out on our own and to develop our graduates into inspired, knowledgeable professionals who can do research and innovate. That's why I'm not saying we should eliminate immigration, not at all. I'm saying that we should restructure our immigration programs to bring more of the researchers, the thought leaders who can teach our kids, instead of bringing a competing workforce that replaces them for a cheaper labor cost. If we change our approach to immigration, we all win and win big."

"Senator, you've got a lot of people talking, I can tell you that."

Krassner smiled and nodded gently as an unspoken thank you to Bernstein's compliment.

"Change of topic, senator, if you will."

"Sure, fire away, Al," Krassner responded in his naturally calm manner.

"Despite numerous talk shows and campaign speeches you have given, the electorate has little understanding of your views on abortion. Where do you stand on this controversial issue that has brought serious media attention to numerous Republicans? As you well know, abortion remains a heated controversy across the country, transcending party lines and genders lines equally."

"I don't consider it a priority in my platform and here's why: at any given time, roughly 3.4 percent of all American women of childbearing age of our country are pregnant. That means abortion is an issue for less than 1.2 percent of the population overall, including women, men, and children of all ages. Considering that abortion is an issue only during the first trimester of the pregnancy, that number goes even lower. Keeping those numbers in mind, I have decided to focus my platform on issues that affect more significant percentages of the population. Poverty claims 22 percent of the population. Uninsured Americans who need access to healthcare they can actually afford is higher than 10 percent. Unemployment, in some areas, exceeds 10 percent as well. Childhood poverty scores a whopping and highly disturbing 27.5 percent.

So yes, I have made a strategic decision to focus on issues that have a bigger impact on the country's well-being and stop wasting time and resources on abortion. For now."

"Interesting point of view, senator. Where do you personally stand on the issue of abortion?"

"Abortion is a side effect of poverty and hopelessness, in my opinion. If we want to curb abortion, we should fix the reasons why women are desperate enough to act against their own beliefs and instincts and terminate their pregnancies. We should tackle the real reasons behind their difficult decisions."

The screen shifted to the in-studio view, centered on Phil Fournier's portrait.

"Yes, homeruns every time, in my opinion and in the electorate's as well," Phil commented excitedly. "Krassner's ratings picked up another seven percentage points in the polls after last night's show, bringing his ratings to almost 50 percent. While elections are still eight months away, and technically anything can still happen, many are already calling Krassner our future president. We will continue to keep you informed with any news and reactions to Krassner's soaring campaign. From *Flash Elections*, this is Phil Fournier, wishing you a good evening."

...Chapter 53: Deployment
...Tuesday, March 8, 3:31PM PST (UTC-8:00 hours)
...Tom Isaac's Residence
...Laguna Beach, California

The war room was getting more and more cluttered every day, and yet there was a feeling of comfort about it that helped Alex think clearly. Maybe it was the timeline wall, a web of colored yarn, sticky notes, and pictures. Maybe it was the essence of Tom's spirit that had impregnated the room with feelings of security, confidence, and courage. Maybe it was the fresh smell of French vanilla coffee, just dripped into her mug by the Keurig machine.

She took a sip of fresh coffee without taking her eyes off the wall, where the notes and images related to the Vermont transplant clinic were connected with colorful yarn. She needed to adjust a couple of things, add a few notes and pictures. Doctors Hager and Kanellis were not yet represented on that wall.

Chatter disrupted her thoughts.

"Nope, that's not true," Steve said, walking through the door. "You cannot assume either alternative is true without verifying it, without getting some kind of proof."

"All I'm saying is we need to conduct a side-by-side study before we conclude, to that I can agree," Brian argued. "I'm not maintaining that one method is absolutely better than the other. I just have my preference, that's all. A very strong preference."

Tom chuckled but didn't say anything.

"But if you do both studies at the same time, you'll contaminate the test samples," Steve continued supporting his point.

"What's this about?" Alex asked Tom.

"Steak marinades," he replied. "Specifically, the effect of onions on the steak marinade." Tom's eyes were filled with laughter, despite his serious answer. "Kids these days, they don't trust our wisdom. They want to verify everything."

"OK, guys," Alex said, "let's work through our agenda for today, and then we'll conduct as many experiments as you'd like. I *am* getting hungry."

"Yes, ma'am," Brian answered and sat down. Steve took his normal place, leaning against the wall by the window.

"Main topic, deployment," Alex said. "Robert has completed his task, and I have an interview scheduled for next week. It's a phone interview, the initial phase with the DCBI Human Resources person. I'm not overly concerned, but

I am painfully aware we don't have CEO support on this, so I have to be extra careful. Claire did an awesome job on my résumé, and I've learned it by heart. I am ready."

"Would you like me to sit in with you when you interview?" Brian asked. "I could help you in real time if they throw you a curveball."

"Always appreciated, but I don't think it's necessary. Thank you, nevertheless. I have a high level of confidence at this point."

"After the HR interview, what's next?" Tom asked.

"Robert made them agree to go straight into team interviews and the final interview with him, all in one day at their HQ in DC. Very typical for relocating executives."

"Do you know your future title yet?" Steve asked.

"Yeah. I'll be replacing Jimmy Doherty, the one who died of a heart attack," Alex replied, walking toward the timeline wall and pointing toward a picture lined up underneath an area titled DCBI. The man in the picture was serious and grim, his eyes revealing internal turmoil and high levels of stress. "I will be the director of Vendor Quality." She took another sip of coffee. "That means I'm looking at a start date a month or so away from today, followed by another month spent on orientation, training, and all kinds of corporate crap we have literally no time for. We are cutting it very close from a timing perspective. By the time I'll be able to start my deployment onsite at the first vendor it will be summer already. Way, way late."

"I agree," Tom said. "It will put our backs against the wall from a timing perspective. What can we do to crash this schedule?"

"Nothing, really," Alex replied. "One of the issues is that DCBI is not officially a client. We don't have the full support of the CEO. Then there's the fact that the office is under intense, nonstop surveillance. The UNSUB is watching every move, every change. If we push the matter, someone will comment on it, and the UNSUB will be on to us immediately. We cannot create any ripple effects or rock the boat in any way. Everything has to seem normal."

"It's very tight," Brian said. "Let's see if we can do any preliminary work before that."

"Like what?" Alex asked.

"Like deep background checks on the vendor companies, their senior executives, their financials, their former clients. Anything we can gather as preliminary intelligence would help." Brian checked his Breitling watch impatiently.

"Don't lose your patience, I'm here," Sam said, entering the room. "Lou's right behind me, parking the car."

"Hey, good to see you," Alex said, enjoying his bear hug. Sam had been a great asset for their small team, and for her personally. She was learning a lot from this guy. Between Lou, with his endless Krav Maga and target practice sessions, and Sam, with his CIA 101 special training, as she liked to think of it, she was learning a lot of new things. How to sweep a room for bugs discreetly, so no one would be the wiser. How to figure out if she's being followed. How to "lose that tail," by Sam's own definition. How to enter a character's story without getting confused about details and risk making mistakes. How to use her cover story as a second skin, feeling natural and appearing natural. How to not hesitate, no matter what she had to do. She was still learning that part; she wasn't there yet, not 100 percent. That was still work in progress, her kind nature posing issues for her at times.

However, she hadn't expected she'd love spy training so much. She had enjoyed her work with The Agency since day one. It was stimulating, mentally rewarding, and kept her highly intelligent brain from getting bored. Puzzles to solve, people to figure out, scenarios to be constructed, validated, and played out. But with Sam's CIA 101 she felt supercharged. She was aware she had barely scratched the surface of what the man could teach her, and she was constantly looking to get more, absorbing everything like a sponge, dreading the day their roads would part.

"Hello, everyone," Lou said and headed straight for the coffee maker.

"Now that we're all here," Brian said, "let's bring you two up to speed." He gestured toward Sam and Lou. "We were saying that we have a couple of months of process time, with Alex's interview schedule, background check, and onboarding, before we can even get started with the actual investigation. This is a concern to us because of the little remaining time to investigate and figure things out in the field before November. I was suggesting we use this time to get as much info about these vendor companies as possible, do a full background on them, and gather any intel we can."

"Yep, I'll work with Lou on that," Sam offered.

"Alex," Tom said, "did you have time to decide how you would deploy?"

"Yeah. I'm thinking of going to Taiwan first. One of the reasons is that hardware has an earlier due date than software. The other reason is that the UNSUB didn't seem to care about the hardware, which could mean there's nothing wrong with it. I should be able to confirm that quite easily. If that's not the case, no matter how hard I try, I can't think of ways to sabotage or booby-trap tablet-type devices other than by loading them with explosives. And that's relatively easy to detect."

"What if they have software on them?" Lou asked. "Software that wasn't in the spec?"

"That should be fairly easy to check, because they're supposed to be clean, only loaded with an operating system, networking drivers, and protocols. We can check every single one of them when they get delivered in the central warehouse in Utah for software installation. Just reminding everyone, they are expected to be delivered to InfraTech's warehouse in Utah by August, leaving me very little time to inspect both vendor locations. That's why I want to start with Taiwan. I'm not expecting to need more than a week there."

"Got you a new toy," Brian said.

"Oh, no." Alex protested. "Look at this pile here," she said, pointing at the devices still stacked on the table. "Where am I supposed to fit all that, plus generous amounts of toilet paper?"

Sam nodded with large movements, underlining the importance of toilet paper.

"And this thing," she pointed at the Inmarsat, "weighs a ton!"

"This one's not so big, neither is it heavy," Brian said. "It's a bomb-sniffing handheld device. It goes with this," he said, putting a pack of Oxy pads on the table.

"Acne treatment?" Alex laughed quizzically.

"Not really, but it looks like it. You take a pad out," he demonstrated, "wipe the object of interest, and then place the pad in here."

The bomb-sniffing device was disguised as a small electronic alarm clock, complete with a functioning green display and snooze button. Brian opened the device's battery compartment and placed the pad inside. He closed the battery compartment, then pressed the snooze button. The digits showing the time flashed once and remained green.

"If these digits were to turn red that would indicate the presence of explosives. It recognizes trace amounts of chemicals that are used when handling explosives."

Sam whistled in appreciation. "Where do you get your devices? I would love to shop there."

"This one's special order to my specs."

"Nice job, Brian," Tom said.

"Thanks so much, that will come in handy," Alex said, studying the device up close.

"Done with hardware already? Boys and their toys..." Steve said. "How are you doing with your immunizations?"

A flicker of guilt showed on Alex's face for a millisecond, but Steve caught it. His initial scowl turned into an expression of sadness and disappointment. Alex reacted to that.

"I'm sorry. I got caught up with other things, but I promise you I'll get right to it. I swear."

"The sooner you get those done the better. Your immunity will be stronger. Don't delay anymore," Steve insisted.

"Nope, I promise. I'll get them scheduled next week."

"This week," Steve insisted.

"This week," Alex confirmed sheepishly.

Silence took over the room for a few seconds. Alex stood and started pacing slowly in front of the timeline wall, back and forth, a frown on her forehead.

"What's on your mind?" Tom asked.

"Umm..." Alex started to say hesitantly, clearing her throat. "There might be something else we need to discuss." She stopped, thinking how best to present the facts to the guys. "I've been back from Vermont for a while and spent a lot of time exploring scenarios, possibilities, and options. There is one big question mark, and that is the transplant clinic's system record for Melanie

Wilton."

"What do you mean by that?" Tom asked. "We discussed the details when you came back from there. Any new developments?"

"No, no new developments, just thoughts about it, that's all. There are a few things that don't add up." She took a deep breath, then continued, "It's just that there's no logic to that record existing in the clinic's system in the first place, that's all. If you had performed an illegal heart transplant in the middle of the night, paid for it in cash, would you have put a record in the system to show everyone something was not entirely kosher about that patient's procedure? No matter how hard I think about it I can't find any logical explanation."

"You're right; it makes no sense at all." Tom agreed.

Steve's gaze was intense, anticipating more to it and not all good.

"Unless," Alex started to say, but Lou took over.

"I'm thinking booby trap, or a silent alarm of sorts," he said.

"Exactly," Alex said, "in which case we stepped in it and we got made."

"Would anyone care to explain for the rest of us?" Steve asked.

"Let's think for a minute. What would be the easiest way for UNSUB to know if anyone was looking to pick up the trail at the only point they could, Melanie's transplant clinic? That's where the trail starts, right? That's why we started there."

"You mean they put the record in the system on purpose to track us?" Sam asked.

"Precisely. Either by having some intrusion detection software watching that particular record or some other type of silent alarm deployed on that system. It's my belief this trick gave them the heads-up as soon as we started snooping around. From that point forward, they could have been on to us with accuracy, while putting in a minimal surveillance effort to catch us. I think we've been made."

"Hell... I miss the old days of real covert work, gun in hand, moving in the shadows," Sam said bitterly. "I don't understand half of what you're talking about. We haven't even started our op, and you're telling me we've been discovered?"

"I think the UNSUB is definitely aware someone's looking. There's no other logical reason to have that record that I could find. Now, if the UNSUB is on to us, specifically, that's a question for Lou. How careful were you?"

"Very. I connected from behind the University of California San Diego firewall, so worst-case scenario, they have a general location for the source, such as La Jolla, San Diego, or even the university. That'll throw them off for a while."

"Throw them off? They have our goddamn location!" Steve raised his voice, which rarely ever happened. "I'm pulling the plug on this, right now."

"And I'm not letting you," Alex said, turning to him, amped up and ready to fight. She was not a kid anymore, and she wasn't about to let anyone treat her as such, regardless of how well intended they were. This decision was hers and hers alone.

"Alex," Steve continued in a soothing tone, "I remember we agreed that if the situation got too dangerous, we'd pull out of this."

"Yes, we did, but it's not too dangerous. Not yet. What do they have? A city? How would they even know that means anything? How would they know this is where we are? Lou could have logged in from New York, and it wouldn't have meant more. You're overreacting, Steve. I'm fine. We're fine; we're good to go."

"I'm not overreacting. These bastards are always a step or more ahead of everything we do. And we have Robert to think of. If someone looked at Melanie's record, that could put her and Robert in danger. We're gambling with their lives. Tom, please talk some sense into Alex."

Tom started to say something, but Alex cut in, not letting him utter a syllable.

"Talk some sense into me? Now I'm mad, Steve; you're crossing the line. I know what I signed up for, and we all knew it wasn't gonna be easy. But this is my call and my call only. God damn it..." She leaned against the side table, almost tipping over the coffee machine. "All I have done in my life was for me, rarely for others. The core reason for anything I have ever done until now was to survive. Pay some bills, another month's rent, eat a little bit better, get new shoes. This is my shot at doing something really important, that has meaning, that will add meaning to my entire existence. If everything I end up doing in this life is fight for my daily survival, how the heck am I different from an amoeba?

"Don't get me wrong, I am not the generous kind. I will never volunteer at some church or anywhere else for that matter. To me, that seems too small, and I know this sounds arrogant, but I can do way more than just organize bake sales. This is my shot to do something really worthwhile with my life. And yes, I am scared shitless. I know we're walking on thin ice, and if that ice should break, I probably won't survive. That, in the grand scheme of things, doesn't really matter, by comparison with what we're trying to achieve.

"We are fighting an unseen enemy who has tremendous resources and will stop at nothing to organize what could very well be the largest terrorist attack in our history. We are fighting to maintain our most important constitutional right, the right to vote safely, securely, in peace, without any fear. Families will go to the voting precincts together, Steve, families, taking their children along. This is not about preventing some localized attack that would harm one or two innocent bystanders. We could be looking at thousands of victims, maybe many more. This is the one time where almost every citizen of the United States will have to be at a certain location within a certain time frame. Can you see the proportions of that? Can you see the monstrosity of their plan?

"The American people could be looking at never voting the same way again. Did you know people still don't want to fly on 9/11? Each year, during the week of 9/11, airline ticket sales drop significantly. We are fighting to prevent that kind of scar on our nation's identity, that kind of terror in our collective lives. We don't know what the attack is gonna be about, or what it will look like, but we will find out. We will, I can guarantee you that. That's why I'm not stopping now. I'm not pulling any plug, so Steve, I'm sorry to say but you're either behind me one hundred percent, or you get out of the way."

Silence took over the room. Alex saw mixed emotions on Steve's face. Hurt, concern, and admiration. She swallowed hard, tears coming to her eyes.

"And that, my friends, is called courage," Sam said.

"Hear, hear," Tom said. Brian smiled, looking at her slightly different than he normally did. Lou gave her a military salute, executed by the book, with a very serious expression on his face.

"Good. Then we're set. By the way," she continued, "I don't think Robert or Melanie's lives are at risk at this point. I don't think the UNSUB would touch them while the contract's still in progress."

"I'd say that makes sense," Sam said, "we can count on that logic for a while, but let's not trip the alarms again."

...Chapter 54: A Beautiful Plane
...Thursday, May 19, 8:57AM Local Time (UTC+2:00 hours)
...Letiště Praha-Kbely Airport—Air Traffic Control, Prague East
...Prague, The Czech Republic

Jaro Zelezny rubbed his eyes for the tenth time since he had started his shift, less than an hour before. His back hurt, his abs and buttocks were sore, and he had slept less than two hours for the third night in a row. At this rate, his new girlfriend was going to kill him soon. But she was hot. She was hotter than he'd thought he'd ever find, and a total sex addict too. Jaro was still young, not even thirty-five yet, but he was feeling exhausted, worn out, and horny at the same time. There was no ending in sight. She was too damn hot. Her full breasts, her blonde, wavy hair, and those long, slender legs that wrapped tightly around him until he couldn't breathe...He was getting an erection just thinking about her. How to say no to a girl like that?

Jaro poured himself another cup of coffee, extra-dark brew and the third one in the last hour. He spent a few minutes considering the drugs he could take to keep up with her desires. No need for Viagra, not yet, anyway. Some vitamins wouldn't hurt and a nap between flights. It didn't seem like a busy day today, so it might be a good time to get caught up on some shuteye. He pulled a file folder in front of him, thinking he'd better deal with flight-plan approvals before napping so the phone wouldn't wake him.

A quiet day, indeed. Only one flight plan filed, for the new Piaggio Avanti EVO owned by that deli mogul or whatever he was. Jaro couldn't get enough of that plane. He liked to watch it taxi, take off, and land. The elegance of its silhouette, the unusual wing design, the speed, and climb rate. He was in love. With a woman and with a plane. He already had the woman; he hoped one day he'd have the plane, or at least fly in it. His daydreams, when not filled with images of Helenka's naked body, were populated by the Piaggio.

The flight plan was more complicated than usual. He concentrated with difficulty, trying to follow what the plane was scheduled to do. Fly out of Prague-Kbely Airport, LKKB, home base, and into Aden Adde International, Mogadishu, Somalia, airport code MGQ, with a quick refueling stop in Turkey. Refuel in MGQ and pick up, umm...three cases of coconut oil, one case of sesame oil, and two cases of camel meat. Who eats that crap? Very rich people, apparently.

Then the Piaggio would land here at home base, refuel, drop the sesame oil, pick up three cases of smoked oysters and four cases of various caviar assortments, and take off, heading to final destination BXM, Brunswick Executive Airport in Maine, United States. Of course, the Piaggio had to stop and refuel a couple of times before making it to Maine. But wasn't it wonderful that it could cross the ocean all the way to America?

Jaro slammed the stamp down, marking the flight plan "Approved" with red ink, then started toward the fax machine. Dialing the number indicated on the flight plan, he wondered if he could use the Piaggio's stopover on its way back from Somalia to check it out on the inside, pretending to inspect the cargo. He just wanted to smell that fine leather, feel the softness of it, and see the cockpit with all the electronic displays. It seemed like a good idea.

...Chapter 55: A Bonding
...Friday, July 8, 5:12PM CDT (UTC-5:00 hours)
...Bobby Johnson's Hunting Lodge
...Fox Lake, Illinois

Anthony Fischer allowed himself to relax a little and took a taste of single malt Scotch. The lodge was beautiful, its large windows overlooking the lake and forested areas around it. A large deck surrounded three quarters of the lodge, equipped with long chairs and small tables. The summer air was mild and carried the scents of forest and wildlife, the sounds of birds chirping and insects buzzing. Peaceful.

His protégé was a charismatic host, making Dave Vaughn feel welcome and appreciated, just like he should. The two of them were hitting it off nicely and had a good chance to forge an enduring partnership, maybe even a friendship. Vaughn's endless resources and determined support were priceless at this stage in Johnson's campaign. Vaughn's presence at Fox Lake was a testimony that he was prepared to make a long-term commitment to Johnson's presidential campaign.

They were both smoking cigars and sipping some of the most expensive single malt that money could buy, a gift from Vaughn. The man knew how to make an instant friend out of Johnson, who could never resist the lure of a good bottle. Good thing Bobby Johnson was taking it slow, keeping things under control and focusing on his guest.

At a small table near the window, Danny, Johnson's ridiculously young PR expert, was playing a Texas hold 'em game with Vaughn's assistant. Money was piling up on their table, and by the looks of it, Danny was winning big.

Their conversation was heating up, catching Fischer's attention.

"Absolutely," Johnson was saying, "it makes perfect sense to relax our policies and increase the collaboration with foreign energy players. We have to examine how it would best work for our interests and take action, make it happen."

"Maybe I can offer some guidance, Mr. President?" Vaughn asked.

The man was smooth, Fischer had to admit. Johnson was purring like a kitten every time Vaughn called him Mr. President.

"I am counting on your guidance, Dave. I am counting on it! What would you do?"

"I would increase oil production, especially home oil production. Global warming has come and almost gone, and, yes, we must be aware of the risks and put control measures in place, but this is not the time to limit oil production here at home. Do we want to reduce our dependency of foreign oil? Yes, we absolutely have to. But we have to achieve that goal by drilling a little bit more, giving researchers time to come up with viable, truly viable alternate solutions for energy."

"Uh-huh, I see," Johnson said. "What would need to happen?"

"Change policy a little. Let's make drilling permits easier to get and faster, for both inland and offshore drilling. That will allow us an increase in oil production that will achieve this goal for you, the independence from foreign oil."

"That's not going to be hard," Johnson said.

"Not hard at all, but it could give you some unwanted media attention. It will just come and go, nothing really damaging. After all, everyone wants their cars more than they want global warming policy. And then, then we take it one step further."

"How? What do you mean?"

"Then we invest. With the right permits and legislation in place, people like me can acquire oil fields in other countries, invest in pipelines and tanker distribution, and slowly get to control more and more of the black gold, globally. Of course, I'd need a little bit of help with satellite surveys," Vaughn said, taking a long drag from his cigar.

"Of course." Johnson agreed.

"Would that be a problem, you think?"

"No, I don't see why it would."

"Excellent. That would give me the upper hand in locating the ripest oil fields that money can buy, to consolidate America's independence from foreign oil."

They both stopped talking for a while, enjoying their cigars and single malt, eyes lost on the horizon and dreams of the future.

Fischer approached the two, engaging them in small talk.

"I see your boy is taking a beating, Mr. Vaughn," Fischer said.

"Well, he didn't come here to win," Vaughn replied and winked. The other men laughed wholeheartedly. Vaughn had class. He had found a way to make a sizeable donation to the campaign without getting things too complicated for any of them.

"Tell me, please," Vaughn asked Johnson, "what can I do for you, Mr. President?"

"Your support is highly appreciated, from all perspectives," Johnson replied. "The fact that I can count on you as a friend and supporter in my campaign is priceless for me. From what I can see, our interests align perfectly, and that can be the basis of a long-term partnership that will be very rewarding for both of us."

"Cheers!" Vaughn raised his glass to meet Johnson's.

"Cheers!" Johnson said, raising his.

"Is there something, anything at all, you need right now? How can I make myself useful to you now, Mr. President?"

Johnson hesitated, giving the question some thought. Fischer held his breath. They had not discussed any immediate engagement strategy. He had no idea how Johnson would handle this.

"Well, there is a small problem you might be able to offer some advice on," he started to say.

"Shoot," Vaughn encouraged him.

"Many years ago, when I was still in college, I got a girl pregnant."

Fischer's hand went straight to his forehead, grabbing the thinning remnants of hair still clinging to his ever-higher forehead, and pulling them back vigorously. *Damn. Damn it to bloody hell!*

"It can happen," Vaughn smiled encouragingly.

"Well, back then I dealt with it." He stopped, gathering courage. There was not a trace of judgment in Vaughn's kind eyes. "I...I paid for her abortion. She was fine with it. We were both young students; we didn't want a kid. She was fine. Back then, she was fine. But she called me yesterday, just asking how I was."

Just asking for a big payday, that's what she was asking for, you preposterous idiot, Fischer thought bitterly. He froze, wondering if Vaughn could indeed be trusted at this level. What on earth brought Johnson to tell this guy about the girl and not discuss it with him first? The man was a wild card.

"Well, Mr. President, consider the matter handled," Vaughn answered. "We'll make sure she is very well taken care of, so well that she can retire at a destination of her choice, where her newly acquired financial comfort will be the reward for her absolute discretion."

Holy shit, this might work out after all, Fischer said to himself. *They have bonded.*

...Chapter 56: Response
...Thursday, July 14, 10:01PM EDT (UTC-4:00 hours)
...Evening News at Ten
...Nationally Syndicated

The anchor's face was somber, not a trace of a smile. He was grim.

"We start our newscast tonight with President John Mason's remarks in response to the brutal attack on the cruise ship *Alabaster Light* that took place yesterday near the Ukrainian port Sevastopol. The ship, carrying 2,271 passengers and 218 crew members, was sunk by a surface-to-surface missile, launched by unknown forces operating in Ukraine, most likely Russian separatist rebels. Very few survivors were rescued, making this attack the most brutal and costly terrorist attack in recent history, with a total of 2,137 people dead and many of the survivors injured."

The screen showed President Mason standing in front of the very familiar lectern in the White House briefing room, addressing the press. He spoke slowly, showing resolve with every word.

"We stand here today, joined in grief for the lives lost and appalled at the viciousness of this attack. The ship, sailing under the flag of a country that is not at war with Russia, was sunk in an act of defiance, of pure terrorism. Forty-seven American lives were lost on the *Alabaster Light* yesterday."

He paused slightly to allow a moment of silence for the victims; then he resumed his address in a stern tone of voice. "My message to President Abramovich is clear: please work with us and the other peaceful nations of Earth to establish and maintain a state of equilibrium in Ukraine, prevent such disasters from happening, and eliminate terrorism at all costs."

Mason cleared his throat quietly before continuing. "The American people are committed to spare no effort in reestablishing democratic values in the countries where these values have been put in danger. We are offering our support to any leader who wishes to maintain peace, civil liberties, and democracy."

The screen shifted back to the news anchor.

"A strong message that left many wondering if it could be interpreted as a declaration of war by Russian President Abramovich."

The screen shifted again to show the evening's next news title.

...Chapter 57: A Visit to Taiwan
...Tuesday, July 19, 6:38AM Local Time (UTC+8:00 hours)
...Taiwan Taoyuan Airport—International Arrivals
...Taipei, Taiwan

Alex dragged her wheelie luggage on the endless corridors of the international airport, surprised to see how little it differed from any modern, high-traffic American airport. If it weren't for the Chinese lettering on every sign and every advertisement, it was hard to imagine she had flown around the world to Taiwan.

It felt good to stretch her legs after the long flight. She had flown nonstop from Los Angeles for fourteen hours, and despite flying Delta Business Elite and having her own personal private space where she could lie horizontally and rest or sit comfortably and work on her laptop, she hadn't slept or gotten much work done. She kept going over the details of her planned visit and spent generous amounts of time thinking, speculating, and analyzing the very limited data she had to work with. She knew the hardware and software specifications by heart. How the devices should look, how many, how they should work, when they were scheduled to be ready and delivered, how quality control would happen, and so on. But that was all she knew.

All resemblance with an airport from back home stopped abruptly when she exited the terminal. A wave of impossibly humid and hot air hit her as soon as the sliding doors of the terminal opened. She felt sweat beads form instantly on her face, at the roots of her hair, and on her back. She struggled to breathe for a minute or so until she adjusted. *Damn, this place is hot*, she thought.

She walked out of the terminal with her wheelie, laptop bag on it, and suitcase now in tow. A cab pulled up, and she climbed in, holding onto her heavy laptop bag and letting the driver deal with the rest of her luggage. She gave him the hotel address, and they started driving on a highway at first, then on narrow streets filled with motorcycles, bicycles, and pedestrians. Everything was in Chinese. Every storefront in the low-rise buildings, every sign, every street name. *This is gonna be tough,* she thought. When the cab turned a corner, she saw a Starbucks coffee shop and sighed with relief. There was at least one familiar place she could go.

The Okura Prestige Taipei hotel was impressive. Situated at the heart of Taipei, on the busy Nanjing Road East, the hotel was another one of the surprising places that could easily be taken for a five-star hotel on American soil. She entered, relieved to be breathing conditioned air again, and got checked in fast by a beautiful young receptionist. The hotel was a pleasure to explore. Marble floors featuring intricate designs, vaulted ceilings illuminated by exquisite crystal chandeliers shining thousands of miniature bulbs, thick carpeting in the dining areas, and a croissant smell to die for in the breakfast restaurant.

Finally in her room, Alex started her stay by running the bug sweeper across every corner, discreetly, just like Sam had taught her. The room was clean. Relieved, she kicked off her shoes and went for the shower, promising herself a croissant breakfast immediately afterward.

She had a day to explore the city a little and get over the jet lag. The next morning she would head to the manufacturing plant and start her investigation. She could hardly wait, feeling the intense time pressure. They had less than four months left until Election Day and less than six weeks until everything had to be ready for deployment, both hardware and software.

But no matter how she tried to rationalize it, she couldn't head straight to the plant today. No other regular business traveler in her place did that, jumping straight to work after a fourteen-hour flight, so she couldn't do that either. If she did, she'd raise the suspicions of anyone who paid any attention. She was forced to sacrifice yet another precious day to keep her cover intact. She just hoped she'd finally be able to find some answers. Soon.

...Chapter 58: Cargo Inspection
...Friday, July 22, 10:26AM Local Time (UTC+2:00 hours)
...Letiště Praha-Kbely Airport Tarmac, Prague East
...Prague, The Czech Republic

Karmal Shah loved flying his new plane, but too much of anything can become a bit of a pain before you know it. He opted to stretch his legs on the tarmac and maybe get a coffee from somewhere, while waiting for the Piaggio to be refueled and loaded. His pilot would stay with the plane, making sure everything was in order for their scheduled departure to the United States.

He stood from the pilot seat with a groan. His back was killing him. A little overweight and carrying a potbelly that he blamed not only on his age but also on the constant temptations offered by Overnight Delight's product stock, his back hurt quite often. He looked outside the window and noticed the tanker was approaching, right on schedule. It might have been difficult to get this small converted air base to accept him and his plane, but it was totally worth it. The place was quiet, there was hardly any activity, and the staff was complacent, leaving him alone and undisturbed, just the way he liked it.

He made his way toward the plane's door, careful not to trip on the cases they had picked up in Somalia, his departure point for this trip. The back of the plane had been configured for cargo, and neatly laid out cases of merchandise were hooked to the sides of the plane, immobilized in place.

He unlocked and pushed the plane's door open.

"Good morning, sir," a young man holding a clipboard greeted him.

Shah frowned.

"Good morning. What can I do for you?"

"My name is Jaroslav Zelezny, Air Traffic Control. I am asking your permission to inspect the cargo."

The man's English was grammatically correct, yet his heavy accent made it hard to follow. Why was ATC looking at his cargo? If anyone would look, it would be Customs.

"We're a small air base; sometimes we do it all," the man responded with a crooked, almost embarrassed smile, as if reading his mind. "May I come aboard?"

Shah clenched his jaws, his right hand instinctively reaching for the gun he was carrying at his back, tucked in his belt.

"All right," Shah invited him coldly, stepping aside to make room. The man climbed up almost happily, or so it seemed. At least he was easy going, not your typical customs officer.

"I need to check your cargo against the cargo manifest you filed with your flight plan. What are you bringing in today? Are you unloading any cargo here today?"

"Yes, I am dropping a case of sesame oil, that one," Shah said, pointing at the case closest to the plane's door. The ATC man approached the case and lifted the lid. Neatly packaged bottles, surrounded by straw to prevent breakage during transport. He picked up one of the thin bottles and held it in the light.

"Interesting," he said. "Is this good?"

"It is. It's healthy too."

The man put the bottle back in its case and moved on, touching the wall as he walked toward the front of the plane.

"Are you picking anything up today?" He checked his paperwork.

"Yes, I am loading four cases of caviar and three cases of oysters," Shah replied. He was starting to lose his patience.

The man kept walking slowly toward the front of the plane, carefully looking at everything. He reached the two cases nearest to the cockpit and stopped. Shah's right hand went behind his back, grabbing the handle of his pistol.

"What do you have here?"

"More oil, I am afraid," he said. "There are many rich people who will pay a fortune for these oils," he continued. He hoped he wouldn't have to kill the guy. It would be one hell of a mess to clean up, from all perspectives. Maybe he wanted money, a bribe or something.

The man reached and touched the lid of the case next to him. Shah pulled his gun from his belt and brought his arm alongside his body, ready to fire.

"Nice," the man said, touching the case lid without opening it. "And in here?" He stepped toward the cockpit. "Any cargo in here?"

"Of course not," Shah replied.

The man checked out the cockpit thoroughly. Shah's pilot was still in his seat, flipping switches and preparing the Piaggio for the next leg of the trip. He turned and smiled at the ATC man.

"Would you like to sit in the pilot seat for a moment?"

The man's face lit up. Shah sighed, tucking the semi-automatic SIG Pro in his belt. This plane of his turned more heads than a Paris Pigalle hooker at the prime of her career. His pilot deserved a bonus. The ATC man thoroughly enjoyed a few minutes of examining the plane's glass cockpit, controls, and chatting with the pilot. The cargo wasn't brought up again. Then he stood up and left, excited and thankful, not looking once in the direction of any crate as he made his way out of the plane.

...Chapter 59: Hardware
...Friday, July 22, 8:17AM Local Time (UTC+8:00 hours)
...Taiwan Electronics Manufacturing Co.
...Taipei, Taiwan

On her third day visiting the manufacturing plant in Taiwan, Alex saw no difference from the other two days she had spent there looking for any clue, any indication about what the election day attack was planned to be. At the end of two long and frustrating days, she literally had nothing.

Initially, she had been discrete and extremely cautious in her investigation, not wanting to potentially alert the UNSUB to her real agenda. But everywhere she looked, across thousands of square feet of workstations staffed by people wearing white coveralls, facial masks, and hairnets, the story was the same. The workers continued their work undisturbed by her presence, rarely acknowledging her or looking up from the work in front of them. Whenever they looked at her they smiled, a smile only visible in their eyes, as white masks covered their mouths and noses. The sterile and antistatic environment was maintained to the highest standards, not allowing a speck of dust or a single personal item to make it near the production line. Even Alex had to wear white coveralls to enter the assembly floor and special shoes that prevented static electricity from accumulating as she walked. A static discharge, no matter how small, could fry the exposed circuitry of open voting tablets, rendering them useless.

Even the plant managers, just as disciplined as the workers and just as polite, showed no concern for her being there. Smiling and accommodating, they took care of everything she asked for immediately, with the only roadblock being the language barrier. Yes, English was not very common on this factory floor, and when someone did speak a little English, it was broken and very hard to follow and understand. Of course, everyone spoke Chinese, but that didn't help Alex much.

The day before, she had collected a few pads to test for explosives. She had swiped a few open tablets, even swiped discreetly over a counter and across a production line. Then she swiped the conveyor belt toward the end of the packaging process line. Back at her hotel, she tested all the swabs to find that none carried even the tiniest amount of trace chemicals indicative of the presence of explosives. This was a dead end.

People's calm reactions were also an indication of a dead end. No matter how hard she pushed it, she wasn't able to generate one reaction of fear or anger in any of the plant managers. She made them uncomfortable; they seemed confused as to what she was expecting of them and a little flustered, but that was all.

She decided to take it one step further and be bolder, grabbing partially assembled devices from assembly consoles and walking away with them. The workers, unperturbed, just jotted something down on a notepad and picked the next tablet in line, starting the assembly process again. It was obvious these people had nothing to hide.

She gave the factory floor one last look, filled with disbelief and admiration at the same time. Countless rows of people working quietly in perfect discipline and alignment, moving in harmony and following tight procedures, their synchronized performance yielding hundreds of e-voting tablets per hour. It was her first opportunity to observe closely the famous Asian worker discipline and manufacturing principles that had made Japan a famous leader in the field several decades ago.

That observation aside, she decided to cut her Taiwan visit short. There was nothing more she could do here, and her gut told her the action, the real threat was at the other vendor's location in New Delhi.

Alex thanked the floor manager profusely, bowed a little to show her respect as she had observed others do, and left the plant carrying four assembled tablets. Making a stop at a DHL service location after making sure no one was following her, she shipped two of the units to Tom's address, expedited air.

Back in her hotel room, she screened the room for bugs one last time, then pulled out her encrypted sat phone and called Tom.

"Alex, good to hear from you," Tom greeted her, recognizing her number. "What's up?"

"Well, nothing. I mean literally absolutely nothing. This place is squeaky clean, so I'll book myself on the next flight to New Delhi and leave ASAP. Oh, and I sent you two devices; you should get them in a couple of days. They're completed devices, picked at random from the packaging line. I swabbed them and everything else at the plant for that matter, and they're clear."

"Got it. We'll do a more thorough inspection once we get them over here. "

"Some things for the lab to consider. We didn't think of biological threats embedded in the devices, and we didn't think of toxic chemicals, slowly released as the devices warm up due to prolonged use."

There was a second silence at the end of the line. Then Tom's voice said gravely, "I understand."

"There's another possible theory," Alex continued. "Even if the plant is clean, there could be something planned to happen to the physical devices while in transit to get on the ship. These days, entire manufacturing processes take place on ships, en route to the continental United States. Please arrange 100 percent unit testing to be conducted at the receiving warehouse in Utah, and have the staff there on high alert."

"That's a good idea," Tom acknowledged. "What else?"

"That's it; that's all I got. I'm booking my flight now. Hopefully, I'll be in Delhi by tomorrow morning. That's where my gut tells me I should be. Please let Robert know. He should tell them to expect me on Monday first thing."

"Keep us posted with every step, Alex, and be very careful."

"I will, I promise," Alex said, then hung up. She had every intention to keep that promise.

...Chapter 60: Secrecy Amendment
...Friday, July 22, 10:01PM EDT (UTC-4:00 hours)
...Evening News at Ten
...Nationally Syndicated

Phil Fournier cleared his throat quietly before announcing.

"Good evening, ladies and gentlemen. In a highly anticipated decision today, the proposed amendment to the e-vote reform, known as the secrecy amendment, was passed into law. The amendment, proposed by several members of the Senate concerned with preserving the constitutional right to voter secrecy as part of e-vote reform, is eliminating the scanning of the voter registration cards by the electronic voting machines. This single component of the upcoming electronic vote reform has caused numerous concerns to be voiced and an overall increase in people's distrust in our government, as shown by polls and interviews.

"The amendment passed today is aiming to restore voters' confidence that their constitutional rights will be respected in the same degree or higher with the e-voting system as they have been with the traditional, paper-based voting process."

The screen showed a clip demonstrating how electronic voting worked.

"Upon arrival at the voting precincts, voters will present their registration cards at the front desk, where support personnel will check the validity of their registration cards and check the voters' names off a list. No personal information will be extracted from the voter registration card, and the cards will not be scanned or processed in any other way. This part of the voting process will remain entirely unchanged from previous years. Once the voter has been validated at the front desk, he or she will be invited to proceed to a booth, where they will be using the new e-voting devices to cast their ballots.

After entering the private booth, they will touch the screen to start, then be walked through a series of screens, one for each ballot. The voters will be prompted to select their preferred option for each question by touching it. The voter's option will then be highlighted in green, and another screen will prompt the voter to confirm the entry. After receiving the confirmation by another tap on the screen, where it says 'Confirm,' the voter will be taken to the next ballot, until the entire set is completed and the process is concluded."

The image refocused on Phil Fournier's in-studio desk.

"As you can see, with the new amendment there will be absolutely no possibility to correlate the voting data captured by the e-voting devices with the voter registration cards, as it was feared in the initial process. The passing of the secrecy amendment into law today was cheered enthusiastically by demonstrators, rallied in support in front of the Capitol. This measure will restore the badly bruised voter confidence, leading to higher participation rates during the November elections.

"From *Flash Elections* reporting for the *Evening News at Ten,* this is Phil Fournier."

...Chapter 61: Welcome to New Delhi
...Saturday, July 23, 1:07PM Local Time (UTC+5:30 hours)
...Indira Gandhi International Airport
...New Delhi, India

Alex dragged her wheelie over the gap between the aircraft's door and the jetway, feeling a sudden burst of incredibly hot air as she crossed between the two climate-controlled spaces. Happy to be finally leaving the aircraft where she had spent the past eleven hours, she didn't pay much attention to that sensation of intense, scorching humid heat, blaming it on the brisk air conditioning she had enjoyed throughout her flight.

She passed through Immigration and found ground transportation with ease. Her car and driver were supposed to pick her up there. Walking through the long corridor leading to the exit, she smelled musty air mixed with some menthol or camphor-based air fresheners. As she approached the exit, she started looking for her expected pickup, and there he was, holding a piece of cardboard with her name, misspelled, but still her name. She approached the man and introduced herself.

"Hi, I'm Alex Hoffmann," she said, then pointed at the sign when the man didn't respond the way she'd been anticipating.

"Oh, yes, ma'am, yes, ma'am," the man said as soon as he understood. He grabbed her suitcase and started toward the exit in a hurry. She followed him, and as she stepped through the sliding doors of the airport exit, she had to stop, dizzy and shocked. It was hot. A humid and fierce kind of hot, reminding her of the rare times when she'd opened the oven to baste a roast. The wave of heat coming from that oven was very similar to what she was feeling just outside the airport terminal. She leaned against the wall, struggling to breathe. There was no way anyone could breathe in this. Instant sweat covered her from head to toe, her clothing sticking to her skin in a very unpleasant way. She felt her skin burning wherever the fabric touched her. *Oh my God,* she thought, *what the hell am I gonna do?*

"Welcome to Delhi," her driver said in very badly accented English, smiling widely and showing several missing teeth under a moustache-covered upper lip. He was either being very nice with her, or he was just sarcastic and entertained by her reaction to the Delhi mid-summer heat. It was hard to tell when she couldn't breathe; her brain refused to process any information.

She looked at her watch and noticed sadly that the glass had cracked, most likely from the temperature shock when exiting the airplane's climate-controlled environment. It was still working though, and she had to settle for that for now.

She started walking slowly, adjusting to the air she struggled to inhale and following her very alert driver. He led her to an SUV bearing the Toyota logo, but it wasn't a model she had seen before. As he was loading her luggage, she went toward the right side of the car and opened the front door. *Not gonna work,* she thought as she saw the steering wheel on the right side. She went around the front and opened the left front door but delayed climbing in. Inside the car, although it seemed impossible to imagine, it was even hotter.

The drive to her hotel was long and interesting. Her driver, with the name of Pranav if she had understood him correctly, had very little concern with red lights. He seemed to take a red light as a personal challenge to see how he could pass through the intersection as the fastest and loudest of all cars. Alex was embarrassed to find herself screaming and covering her face a couple of times, until she finally acknowledged that Pranav had some serious driving skills. However, following traffic law didn't seem to be one of them. The streets were a disorganized mess of small cars, SUVs, even some very expensive luxury vehicles from time to time, and some three-wheeled green and yellow contraptions built on the frames of motorcycles and meant to carry two passengers in the back.

"Red light," Alex pointed out, "why aren't we stopping?"

"No need, ma'am," Pranav said, very amused by her question.

"What are these things?" Alex asked, pointing at one of the green contraptions on wheels. It carried five young men where two would have been the maximum load she thought they'd be able to take. The five young men were crammed together, a couple of them hanging from the sides almost entirely outside the vehicle, smiling widely as if this were great fun.

"Tuk-tuk, ma'am," Pranav said.

Such a tuk-tuk had stopped at a traffic light, holding the Toyota behind it; although there was no one in front of that exotic vehicle. To Alex's surprise, Pranav pushed the tuk-tuk with the Toyota's bull bar, gently yet firmly enough to make room for their car to bolt and pass through yet another intersection, against red lights and cross traffic honking something terrible.

Finally at her hotel, she found herself thankful she had survived the drive and wondering if she should ask for a new driver. She chuckled, thinking that the drive had been so scary she had completely forgotten the mind-numbing heat. She entered through the front door of the Taj Palace, and, within seconds, the strong jets of air conditioning brought her back to a world of normality, with the faint smell of mildew being the only reminder of the humid hell outside.

Her room was one of the most elegant hotel rooms she had ever seen. Thick, plush, dark red carpeting covered it wall to wall. A wide, arched window, dressed with assorted thick velvet drapery and matching sheers, and a king-sized bed covered in top grade sheets and a feather-light comforter. The room was decorated with exquisite style, and her hosts had placed flowers and fruit in the small reading corner, where several armchairs were placed around a coffee table, with wall lighting above it. The bathroom was amazing, all done in marble, sparkling clean, and decorated with impeccable taste. She noticed with amusement a phone installed right next to the toilet, on the wall. *Maybe it's for the really bad Delhi Belly cases*, she thought.

She pulled out her bug detector and started scanning the room, discreetly, wall to wall, making it appear as if she were texting on her cell phone while absently walking. A faint beep and a red dot on the device's screen indicated the first audio bug, near her nightstand somewhere, probably in the phone. *Crap*, she nearly said out loud. She paced some more, making a huge effort to refrain from looking right at the offending nightstand. A few steps more toward the window, and a different beep indicated a video bug. *This is disgusting*, she thought, *damn assholes.*

She completed her walkthrough with the bathroom and found another audio bug. She took a deep breath, and, remembering what Sam had taught her, started to mentally organize her life as she wanted it to appear on the UNSUB's surveillance. She'd have to change in the bathroom, where there was no video. She'd have to drop the AC settings a couple degrees, so she'd keep her comforter on while she slept. She didn't want to put on an involuntary show for these perverts. She shouldn't be too proper though, or display too much restraint. She had to be seen doing things people normally do when they're completely on their own, like yawn without covering their mouths, belch loudly, go to the toilet without closing the door, scratch, swear, and so on.

She let herself fall on her bed, face up and arms spread to her sides, as if to enjoy the comfort of the mattress and fresh sheets. This was the way Sam had taught her to look discreetly for the video bug, because usually these were housed somewhere on the ceiling, in some fixture or vent. There were no fixtures, but there was an AC vent toward the window, and there it was, almost imperceptible. She braced herself, happy she was on to them, and hoping they were not on to her.

...Chapter 62: The Secret Vice
...Saturday, July 23, 9:52AM EDT (UTC-4:00 hours)
...Fort Lauderdale Marina Parking Lot
...Fort Lauderdale, Florida

Muhammad Sadiq opened the trunk of his white Lexus LX 570 and took out a large cooler, putting it down on the heated asphalt of the parking lot with a groan. He was fully recovered after his hip replacement earlier in the year, but he wasn't young anymore, and he felt that with every step. He stopped, straightened his back after putting down the heavy cooler, and wiped his sweaty brow with a napkin he took out of his pocket. He looked at the crystal blue sky and inhaled the salty sea air, enjoying the morning of what would be a gorgeous, yet very hot summer day. A great day to be on the water.

He took the rest of his luggage from the Lexus: a couple of telescopic fishing rods, a net and a gaff, both with telescopic handles, and a bucket of fresh bait. From the back seat of his car, he took a small duffel bag with personal items for his journey: sunscreen, a couple of fresh towels, things he didn't already have on his boat.

He started pushing and pulling all his cargo toward the Sea Ray, struggling at every step and straining from the effort. His strife didn't go unnoticed, as he dragged his paraphernalia at a painfully slow speed right under the Harbor Administration Office window. The office door opened, and the familiar face of the harbormaster greeted him joyfully.

"Good morning, Mr. Sadiq, going out today?"

"Yes, yes, if I can make it to my boat."

"Let me help you," he offered, grabbing the handle of the cooler. "Whoa, this is heavy," he commented.

"There's no need. I can pull this on my own eventually," Sadiq answered.

"It's not a problem, Mr. Sadiq; it's my pleasure to help you. But it is heavy. What do you have in there?" The harbormaster's curiosity overcame his manners, a glint of suspicion lighting his eyes from behind the thick-rimmed glasses.

"I can tell you," Sadiq answered between labored breaths, "but you have to promise me you won't say a word to anyone."

"I promise," the harbormaster said. He wasn't smiling anymore.

"Well, you see, I am a Muslim," Sadiq started to say. "By the holy letter of the Quran, this," he pointed to the cooler, "is the mother of evil."

The harbormaster's eyebrows raised in surprise. They had made it to the

Sea Ray, and Sadiq took his fishing gear onboard, then came back to the cooler. He lifted the lid and extracted a can of Bud Light from the ice inside, offering it to the harbormaster.

"Beer?"

"My sin, for which Islam fanatics would have me killed. Please do not tell a soul," Sadiq said pleadingly.

"Don't worry, Mr. Sadiq," the harbormaster said, relieved, popping the can open and taking a long, thirsty gulp. "Your secret is safe with me."

Judging by the harbormaster's demeanor, he seemed to like him better once he had learned of his sin. It was a helpful cover to have. His plan had worked quite well; he was pleased.

Finally aboard the Sea Ray, engines running smoothly, Sadiq pushed the throttle gently, leaving the harbor at no wake speed. Once outside the harbor, he programmed his GPS to take him to the Bahamas and pushed the throttle almost 80 percent in. The Sea Ray cut the waves majestically, leaving the shore behind, and within minutes, Sadiq was far enough from the shore to lose sight of it completely.

He put the throttle in neutral and cut the engines. He then dragged the cooler toward the edge of the boat, opened it, and started opening cans of beer and spilling the contents into the ocean. After emptying a few, he crushed them somewhat, just as a beer drinker would when finishing one. He set the crushed cans next to the cooler. Then threw overboard the rest of the unopened cans and all the remaining ice. He wiped the cooler dry, carefully with one of the towels he had brought onboard. He closed the cooler lid, and then resumed his high-speed trip to the Bahamas. He would make it there on time, he thought, after checking his watch. The bank would still be open, even if it was a Saturday.

...Chapter 63: The Office
...Monday, July 25, 9:12AM Local Time (UTC+5:30 hours)
...ERamSys Headquarters
...New Delhi, India

Pranav had somehow managed to drive Alex to her destination without having them both killed, and she was grateful for that. She wasn't very sure his English included more than a few words, because his reaction to her firm demands to slow down was to hit the gas, smiling widely and repeating, "Yes, ma'am, yes, ma'am."

She looked at the building before entering, the morning air still hot and humid, yet somehow more bearable than it had been the day before. The building was modern, six stories of metal and glass structures built as two separate sections and united by a central tower that went up eight stories high. All three sections of the building had some activity happening on their flat roofs, people walking, looking down, using them as terraces to sit and relax, or places where they could smoke. The central section seemed to have trees planted on the roof.

There wasn't much green in New Delhi. Vegetation was rare, and trees were scarce, at least in the areas where she had traveled. Everything was concrete and asphalt, radiating in the scorching heat. The sun was there, but then again, it wasn't. A layer of thick yellow smog covered every inch of the sky even when it was clear, and the sun appeared as a dim yellow disc that she could look straight into without even squinting. She extended her arm and looked at the pavement. No, there was no real shadow in this dimmed sunlight, just a trace of it. She suddenly felt better about having to take her car for smog checks every two years.

She entered the building, the strong AC in the lobby making her dizzy for a few seconds until she adjusted. She was getting used to these shocks, coming indoors from the intense heat and going through a fifty-degree drop in temperature just by opening a door.

In the lobby was a small blackboard displaying, "Welcome, Alex Hoffmann" written in green chalk. She asked the receptionist for directions, and she learned that DCBI had its own floor, in Building A on the fifth floor, reserved for its project only, with high-security access cards limiting the access to the project team and executive leadership only. Her own security access card was ready for her.

Alex got off the elevator on the fifth floor and accessed the secure door.

Entering the floor, she noticed the open concept layout, with numerous cubicles lined up, with tens of workers typing on their computers quietly. The separation walls between the cubicles were low, making it possible for floor supervisors to see all across the floor. It was vast, clean, and well organized. On each side of the floor were podiums, where several other cubicles had a higher position, allowing supervisors good vantage points across the floor without having to leave their desks. Along the walls there were several offices, most of them with their doors closed.

"Hey, welcome," a man said, touching her shoulder gently. "I'm Brent Rieker. I work for Eddie Swanson at DCBI. Scott, our on-site analyst, and I are the only American faces you're gonna see on this floor. Scott reports to Ellen Butler."

"Ah, I see, thanks." She shook his hand enthusiastically. "Good to meet you."

"So, how do you like it so far?"

"I haven't had time to like or dislike anything yet, just got here. Where can I put my gear?"

"You have your own office," he said, showing her to one of the offices with closed doors. She dropped her laptop bag in there, glad to see the office had a glass wall, so she could keep her eye on the bag.

"When can I see the software? I want to get to work as soon as possible. Do you or Scott have access to the modules in the staging environment?"

"Well, it's not that simple, or hasn't been so far," Brent said. "We see demos of several components on a sprint schedule every two weeks. Scott can run reports for productivity, hours worked, progress made, and so on. But neither of us is charged with inspecting the code per se. We're not qualified; we're not programmers. Scott is an analyst whose job is to generate reports and interpret them and hold the vendor accountable against the SLA. I'm in charge of the vendor engagement. I answer all their questions, point them in the right direction if they need more info, and make sure they don't misunderstand anything, that kind of stuff. But we were not told we needed access to the actual product."

"We'll have to gain that access ASAP; this is what I'm here for. I can't sign off on the quality of the software without getting my hands on it and in it," she said, smiling casually.

Her smile froze when she encountered the gaze of a man staring at her from across the floor. The man, wearing a white cap she later learned was called a *taqiyah*, was looking at her with immense contempt. His beard was very short and neatly trimmed, making him appear unshaven rather than wearing an actual beard. His mouth, slightly open, showed pearly white teeth, quite uncommon for India. He wasn't smiling though. It was more like a snarl. The man's eyes were vicious and sharp, making Alex feel their stark gaze like knives stabbing her. She repressed a shudder.

"Who is that?" Alex whispered, nodding discreetly with a head movement toward the man.

"Oh, that is Abid Bal, a ray of sunshine, no less," Brent answered. "He's the leader of the DCBI project for ERamSys. Everything you need and do goes through him."

"Oh, fantastic," Alex said with a sigh.

Bal continued to stare, his contempt even more visible, tangible, like she was a leper or something. She decided to deal with the issue immediately. She stepped courageously toward Bal, controlling her posture and gait to project self-confidence and authority, a self-confidence she didn't really feel.

"Hi, I am Alex Hoffmann from DCBI," she said, extending her hand to greet Bal.

"I know who you are," he said harshly, taking her hand and shaking it briefly, only the tip of his fingers touching hers. The contempt in his gaze did not go away as he looked at her from up close. "Tell me if there is anything you need."

"Yes, there is," she answered promptly. She was regaining her assertiveness, almost defiant in the face of his contempt. "I would like to gain access to the software modules as soon as possible to begin my quality assessment. If we do this immediately I can sign off on the product faster, literally days after you finish with the last module."

The man frowned, his contempt mixed with anger, his jaws clenched. She looked into his eyes and saw the violence Bal was capable of.

"We will set some appointments up for you. In the meantime, you have some materials to review in your office about the quality standards of ERamSys, our practices, our people, our mission. Please review and tell me if you have questions."

He abruptly turned away and left, not waiting for her reply.

This wasn't going to be easy, but at least she knew she was on to something. Finally, she had a lead she could follow. Regardless of how intimidating or dangerous Bal proved to be, there was something in those software modules she needed to find.

...Chapter 64: In the Aquarium
...Thursday, July 28, 8:32PM Local Time (UTC+3:00 hours)
...CANWE Headquarters
...Undisclosed Location, Greece

The Aquarium, well-lit, had welcomed its guests for the evening. The five of them, with Vitaliy Myatlev sitting at the head of the table, had just arrived, his chopper delivering them on the well-lit heliport. Outside the Aquarium, Myatlev's security surrounded the transparent conference room on all sides, guarding all doors. When the last guest had been seated, the Aquarium walls polarized and turned opaque, protecting the secrecy of their meeting.

"Thank you all for coming," Myatlev said, "and thank you for all your hard work in the past few months. We have made tremendous progress together." He bowed slightly toward Mastaan Singh. "Mr. Singh has raised awareness across all of Europe for the humanitarian cause of Eastern Africa Development Fund, making fundraising easier. That doesn't diminish the value of Mr. Javadi, whose fundraising abilities have been very fruitful. Mr. Shah has ensured we can move funds and materials freely across all of Europe and America by plane or by courier under a very ingenious cover, and Mr. Sadiq ensured we have a clear, direct connection to access our cash in the Bahamas and bring it into the continental United States without much trouble. This is a remarkable accomplishment. Gentlemen, we have achieved everything we had planned to achieve in the six months since we started our work. These activities must continue, at an accelerated pace, because they are the lifeline behind our operations."

The four men nodded their approval.

"But I didn't invite you all the way here today just to thank you," Myatlev continued in his flawless English. "In only three months' time, America will be electing a new president. We need to examine and agree which candidate will make the most sense for us to support. I am strongly inclined to say Bobby Johnson will be the most favorable candidate for our common cause. What do you think?"

"I am very disappointed, Mr. Myatlev, no offense," Muhammad Sadiq said. "I thought this council was about more than just lobbying for one candidate versus the other. I thought we were going to make a difference, take bold action to establish the new world equity. That was the goal we all embraced when we joined your council, wasn't it?"

Javadi and Shah voiced their support to Sadiq's point. Singh remained immobile, impenetrable, with a trace of an enigmatic smile on his lips.

"We have done everything you asked us to do," Sadiq continued. "We have built the infrastructure you said we needed to execute the plan. Yet the plan continues to disappoint. We can move explosives, but are we moving them? We can fund military action, mercenaries if we want to, but what are we funding? Nothing, at this point. I thought we were going to take over America, not just talk nonsense and politics. Who cares who wins the elections? Not much difference to me, it's still going to be an American in the White House, right? I don't see much difference at all."

Shah started laughing quietly. Everyone looked at him. He cleared his throat a little before speaking. "There are many ways to accomplish our goal. For example, India is already taking over America. I've always admired your country for its slow yet certain invasion," he said, bowing his head a little in the direction of a puzzled Mastaan Singh. "While other countries train soldiers and spend billions to arm and prepare them for an invasion, your country sends tens of thousands to America each year as workers, and Americans even pay for it! Brilliant, I have to say," he said, laughing with admiration. "See? Even a peaceful solution can help you reach the same goal, but differently."

"Pfft." Singh dismissed Shah's comment with a wave of his hand. "You don't know what you're talking about, Mr. Shah. This is ridiculous."

"Let's stick to the issue at hand," Sadiq interrupted. "Mr. Myatlev, where is the action we were promised; when will it start happening? I am eager to see some results."

"The action is happening already," Myatlev answered, causing his audience to shift in their seats and look at him with raised eyebrows. "Despite what you might be thinking or how much you would like to see bombs go off, we have a lot more to gain if we place a certain individual in the White House, Johnson to be precise. We have ways to influence Johnson's decisions. No, better said, we have ways to *control* Johnson's policy. Just think what that could mean. Shifting trade policy to favor our respective countries. If we need a war someplace, we can make that happen. We could just send the Americans to fight it for us. You want more Indian workers to be accepted in the States each year, Mr. Singh? Johnson can make that happen for us. We need weapons at preferred pricing? We can make that happen. We need America to leave us to our own devices in Crimea, for example? Just tug on the American's leash, and he'll back off. Now think of that and tell me it's not a worthy plan, bound to get us the new world equity we all want."

No one spoke for a while. Shah broke the silence eventually.

"I don't know if you are brilliant or delusional. How strong is your grip on Johnson?"

"Very. The moment he steps into the White House he belongs to us."

"Personally, I am deeply bothered by something, Mr. Myatlev," Javadi said. "Since we have joined your council, you have not fully trusted us with your strategy. I feel like a pawn in your game, not like a partner. This grip you say you have on Johnson, this is not something that you gained overnight, or since we last met."

"I agree," Sadiq said. "You're asking us all to trust you and work with you, but you don't trust us."

"Gentlemen, this is not an issue of trust," Myatlev said. "This grip we have on Johnson was the work of many months of work that could have failed many times. While it didn't happen overnight, it did achieve an important milestone very recently. There are a lot of moving parts in this plan and some I had to execute on my own because of the high risk involved with them. Just to give you an example of such a high-risk maneuver and a demonstration of my trust in you, I can tell you that Johnson wouldn't have had a shot to run for president if the current vice president, Mark Sheridan, hadn't stepped down. And that, my friends, was just one of the many moving parts. He was a favorite for this year's elections, and, with him in the running, the Democrats would have never thrown their support behind Johnson. Against Sheridan, Johnson wouldn't have had a chance in hell."

"How did you get Sheridan to back off?" Javadi asked.

"Let's say that everyone has something they're never willing to sacrifice, no matter what the prize is," Myatlev responded.

The looks of disappointment Myatlev had faced earlier were replaced by looks of respect, admiration even.

"Let's remind ourselves why we are here," Myatlev continued. "For my country, American interference with our internal affairs, especially in Crimea, is a very sore point. However, on a personal level, I have a lot to gain if the right policy is in place in America, favoring my oil, gas, and energy interests and allowing me to build a stronger infrastructure of energy distribution. You all have interests, personal, as well as national for the countries you represent, interests that would have a lot to gain from a favorable American President.

"Mr. Singh would surely like a higher number of Indians to be able to immigrate to America each year, and he'd like to make sure there aren't any protectionist measures against the outsourcing of labor to India. This is probably, at this point, one of the biggest revenue sources for his country and for him personally, if not the biggest one. Furthermore, India would prefer to have no American interference in its military and economic policy and would like its diplomats treated with more respect.

"Mr. Sadiq would go home a hero if he could promise Pakistan a sky clear of American drones. Mr. Shah has infrastructure interests in his native Afghanistan that are hindered by the American forces still meddling with the way things are done and putting their own people in the government. Afghanistan is ready, and has been for a long time, to get rid of the last remaining American forces in the area and to bring peace and restore the rights of the Afghan people, whether Taliban or not. Finally, Mr. Javadi, for himself personally and for Iran, would like the self-determination and true values of Islam to be restored to the Iranian people, without fear of American intervention. Am I right?"

They approved silently.

"All right, then let's figure out how to put Johnson in the White House."

...Chapter 65: Democratic Nomination
...Friday, July 29, 10:01PM EDT (UTC-4:00 hours)
...Flash Elections: Breaking News
...Nationally Syndicated

The familiar credits faded to allow a wide-smiling, slightly excited Phil Fournier to announce the political happenings of the day.

"We saw this coming, especially in the wake of Vice President Sheridan's decision to not run for president in the upcoming elections. Today, the Democratic Party presidential primaries concluded its vote, and now it's official. Senator Bobby Johnson, Illinois, has secured his party's nomination by an undisputed majority. Initially seen as the underdog in the Democratic Party race for nomination, holding little hope if he were to compete against Sheridan, Bobby Johnson has been riding the tidal wave of Sheridan's retirement announcement and has gained increasing momentum and public support, even though at modest rates.

"His key opponent this coming November, Douglas Krassner, holds a higher share of the people's support, as captured by recent polls. The latest surveys shows support for Krassner at 51 percent, while Johnson's trailing quite a ways behind at 28 percent. While significantly behind Krassner, Johnson's numbers are steadily increasing and will most likely continue to climb, considering today's nomination.

:The one question clouding the celebratory spirit at Johnson's campaign headquarters today is how do they reverse the poll results and capture the majority. From here on for Johnson, campaigning will be a head-on battle against Krassner. We will watch every minute of that battle and report back to you the most quintessential moments of what promises to be a fiery game of all-or-nothing. From *Flash Elections,* this is Phil Fournier, wishing you a good evening."

...Chapter 66: PowerPoint Woes
...Thursday, August 4, 10:53AM Local Time (UTC+5:30 hours)
...ERamSys Headquarters
...New Delhi, India

Alex repressed a sigh, sneaking a peek at her watch. Another PowerPoint slide and she would scream. During the past few days, all requests she had made to gain access to the software's source code, no matter how high up the power chain she went, were passive-aggressively deterred and answered with semi-mandatory invitations to attend yet another presentation. She had absorbed, one after the other, hundreds of slides illustrating just how good the quality practices were, how talented and educated the people were, all kinds of testimonials and references from ERamSys' long portfolio of household brand-name clients, and there was no end in sight. No end in sight for the bullshit PowerPointology, and not a single minute of access to see the actual code she was supposed to sign off on.

She had even tried to hack into a server that she thought the code might be stored on. She'd gotten caught in less than fifteen minutes. Someone just barged through her office door and invited her to yet another three-hour lunch she couldn't refuse. She missed Lou badly. She had asked him for support, but he couldn't hack in from the outside. They'd be on to him in no time, and that put both her life and her mission at risk.

Well, the mission is already at risk—at risk of not being accomplished due to the biggest stonewalling conspiracy ever, she thought bitterly. *Gotta do something about it, and if they don't like it, well tough luck.* She felt bad for the enthusiastic young woman walking her through the impeccable work conditions offered by ERamSys, but she had to interrupt.

"Priya," she said, "please don't take offense, but I have to go. This was very interesting, but I do have some other things I need to look into right away." She stood up and gathered her things, but before she could leave the room, the door opened and Bal stepped right through it, wearing his signature frown and clenched teeth. He waved Priya away without a word, and the girl disappeared in a hurry, avoiding eye contact the whole time.

How does he know when to come in? Alex wondered for a split second before remembering that everything was under strict video and audio surveillance. They knew everything and heard everything.

"Sit down, Ms. Hoffmann," Bal said as he took a seat.

"I prefer to stand," Alex responded almost defiantly, "I have some serious work to do, so I'm a little pressed for time. I hope you understand."

"What is your mandate here, Ms. Hoffmann?"

"Oh? I thought you knew," Alex answered, surprised by the question. "I am responsible for software quality and scope validation. Before DCBI can close the contract, I need to sign off on the software from a quality and scope perspective. I will evaluate the software to make sure it meets all the specs and does exactly what it's supposed to do, and that it is bug free and working smoothly. That's what my mandate is," she said, still standing and ready to leave.

"We didn't manage to make you gain any confidence in our company's ability to deliver the highest quality software, after all you have seen?" Bal asked, his eyes drilling into hers angrily.

"You have absolutely succeeded in that goal, Mr. Bal, because otherwise you wouldn't have been awarded this contract in the first place. You see, having me see these presentations is a waste of my time and not what I came here to do."

Bal stood and started walking slowly, approaching her. When he was within inches of her face, close enough that she could smell his sweat, he said, "India is very different from America, Ms. Hoffmann. Many things in India are dangerous to Americans coming here. They could eat the wrong thing, be in the wrong part of town, say the wrong thing, and any such thing can kill them within minutes. Our commitment was to show you not only how trustworthy we are, but also how to keep you safe and out of trouble. We would hate to have to ship you home in one of those metallic caskets. It has happened before, you know...Cholera here is rampant. I hope you understand," he finished speaking so close to her face that she felt his breath touch her skin. That made her sick, sicker than the actual threat.

"Are you threatening me, Mr. Bal?" Alex asked, holding his dominating gaze staring her down with contempt.

"I am warning you, that is all. Warning you of the many dangers of India, Ms. Hoffmann."

"Well, consider me warned. Now, when can I get access to the code?"

Bal turned around angrily and left the room without responding. Alex felt a slight moment of pride for not being the one to break eye contact first, securing a small victory for her ego. Then reality overwhelmed her. *Holy shit! What am I gonna do? He's gonna kill me!*

She wanted to sit down badly, to steady her trembling knees and shaking hands. She remembered the video surveillance and decided not to give the viewer the satisfaction. She took her things and went straight for the elevator, heading for the roof, for a breath of hot, humid air and a place where she could call Tom.

There weren't many people on the roof yet; lunch break had not yet started. She took her cell phone equipped with the SatSleeve and dialed Tom's number from memory.

"Well, hello stranger," he picked up immediately, although it was late at night in sunny California.

"Hey," she whispered and felt tears burning her eyes when she heard his voice.

"What's wrong?" Tom asked. He had an uncanny way of knowing immediately when something was bothering her, no matter how far away she was.

"I'm not getting anything done," she said, getting a grip on her emotions. "I've been here how long, and I haven't even seen a line of code. All they do is stonewall me, and, more recently, threaten me."

"What did they say?"

"Just your typical threats, not even very creative. India is dangerous, people die here, and all that crap. I'm not overly impressed; we knew that was coming. I'm just frustrated I can't break through and see any lines of that damn code."

"I understand," Tom said quietly. "What do you want to do?"

"Well, after today's threats, I think diplomacy has failed, don't you agree? I will crank this up a notch, see what happens. Let's rattle the cages, see what snakes crawl out."

He didn't say anything for a while. "Be very careful, Alex. I don't need to repeat that, do I?"

"No, you don't. I will, I promise."

She hung up, a tear-filled knot still in her throat. She swallowed hard and headed for the roof access door, regaining control of her emotions. *Damn these assholes!*

...Chapter 67: Strategy Session
...Sunday, August 7, 3:38PM Local Time (UTC+3:00 hours)
...CANWE Headquarters
...Undisclosed Location, Greece

The Aquarium lit up and filled with people for the second time in less than two weeks. Things were heating up, and Myatlev wanted to make sure his council members' support stayed active and focused.

As soon as the last of his guests took a seat, Myatlev polarized the glass walls, turning them an impenetrable milky white that reflected the strong lights within the Aquarium.

"Thank you all for taking yet another Sunday away from your families to meet with me," Myatlev said. He had a gift for addressing people, making it standard to thank everyone for their time. After all, time spent you can never recover; it's the most precious gift someone can give. He continued, "As you might have heard, we have made an important step forward in our plans. Our preferred candidate for president of America has been nominated by his party, which means we are now on our final stretch."

Myatlev looked at everyone at the table. They were watching him intently but were very guarded and neutral. Singh was the only one whose body language showed some openness and support. It was normal; after all, he knew a little bit more than anyone else. They needed a show of trust.

"Because we have reached this milestone in our plan, I wanted to share with you our progress."

"Mr. Myatlev, if you please," Javadi interrupted, "I would appreciate it if you wouldn't call it 'our plan,' considering how little we all know about it. It's insulting. It is your plan, and you only feed us crumbs of it when you see fit. I personally find it harder and harder to believe in it. I find it humiliating to be treated like children, when we have put our lives and fortunes at stake for this plan of yours."

"I see," Myatlev answered, unperturbed. "I understand how this secrecy must make you feel, and I sincerely apologize. But today is the day of revelations, so I am hoping you will have more confidence in the plan by the time we finish."

Myatlev touched the console in front of him, and the Aquarium walls turned transparent again. They saw a man being screened by Myatlev's security, just as everyone else had been on their arrival. As soon as the man was cleared, he joined them inside the Aquarium, and Myatlev instantly polarized the walls back to full opacity.

"Gentlemen, please let me introduce Mr. Warren Helms," Myatlev said. The stranger bowed slightly and continued to stand, ignoring the open seat at the table. Singh started to extend his hand, but Myatlev stopped him.

"No further introductions will be necessary, for our own security. Mr. Helms understands and will not be offended."

Helms nodded to confirm.

"Mr. Helms has been helping us for a while," Myatlev said. "He has been making things happen in the United States. Things, such as getting the right people in the right places, making sure we stay informed with decisions made in political and business circles, orchestrating any actions that needed to be taken."

"Could you be any more vague, Myatlev? This is ludicrous!" Javadi said angrily, slamming his palm down on the table.

"All right, I will then translate for you," Myatlev answered. "Mr. Helms made sure the current vice president, Mark Sheridan, will want to retire after his mandate expires. He ensured that Bobby Johnson has the best campaign manager on the market. He has placed our ears and eyes inside DCBI, the company that owns the contract to deploy the new e-voting system in America this November. Need I say more?"

Javadi pursed his lips for a second.

"No. I get the picture."

The other members of the council seemed impressed as well, except for Singh, who just continued to look smug.

"But isn't DCBI outsourcing the contract to India?" Sadiq asked. "Do we have a finger in that?"

"No," Myatlev answered very seriously, "we have our whole hand. Thanks to Mr. Singh, we have control over the facility where the software is being developed. Losing access to the voter database was a blow, but the plan is still viable. If you recall, there was an amendment, recently ratified, to eliminate the scanning of voter registration cards using the devices, which would have placed a database of almost all American citizens, their personal information, and their political preferences in our hands. We lost access to that; it couldn't be helped. Nevertheless, we are, from all other perspectives, in control of the American presidential elections coming this November, to the point where I can promise you, gentlemen, Bobby Johnson is the new American president. And we own him."

He paused for a while, looking around the table to see the effect of his words on the audience. "We, the five of us here, own the future president of the United States of America. I hope this qualifies as a good plan for this council. I hope you will agree and continue to support it as the initiative that will help this council reach its goal."

Javadi was the first to offer his support.

"OK, I am convinced. Still don't know why you didn't trust us with the details earlier, but this strategy and the way we are executing it seems to be working."

Sadiq nodded, while Singh remained impassible.

"I would have preferred to be aware of the details sooner," Shah said, still bothered. His ego suffered, most likely. He had been excluded from knowing all the details, and he probably found that offensive, demeaning, and humiliating. Shah knew how to keep secrets, and he had hoped he would be fully trusted, as a real partner would be. That hadn't been the case, and it still bothered him quite visibly. Inside every powerful man lies a powerful ego. Shah was no exception.

"I understand that some of you might be offended by my choice to play this very close, and I have to apologize for that," Myatlev stated. "I am hoping that what we are going to achieve will help you overcome that. I recognize we haven't been full partners in the early stages of the plan, but I can promise you right now," he said firmly, while solemnly placing his right hand on his chest, "we will be full partners in reaping the results of this plan and building the strategic blueprint of tomorrow's distribution of power in the world. I promise you that."

No one spoke for a few seconds; Helms continued to stand quietly.

"Why is Mr. Helms joining us today?" Singh asked.

"I will let him explain," Myatlev said. "Mr. Helms?"

"There's something you need to be aware of," he started to say. "We have only three months left until Election Day, and there is a big difference in the polls between the two leading candidates. Krassner, the Republican, has the lead in the polls at 51 percent, while Johnson, the Democrat, only has 28 percent. The rest is spread across other candidates at much lower values."

"Your point? We all know that," Singh said.

"We need to be more aggressive in demolishing Krassner's support. So far, we have focused on building up Johnson, and we didn't touch Krassner. I need you to authorize the level at which I can intervene."

"What are you saying?" Shah asked.

"We could do many things. Discredit him, play dirty but still engage almost entirely lawful actions, or at the other end of the spectrum, we could eliminate him altogether. Mr. Myatlev had suggested I ask for the council's guidance before choosing a method."

"We can't kill him," Javadi said, "That's for sure."

"Why the hell not?" Sadiq pushed back. "I'd say time is too damn short to do anything else. Only three months left until November."

"We'd generate a shit storm of unprecedented proportions and unforeseeable consequences," Javadi said. "If this plan of ours is subjected to an unpredictable tornado of reactions, it's going to fail. We'll lose control of it."

"He could also have a car accident or a stroke," Helms offered. "With a little bit of work he can have that accident in full daylight, witnesses present, and no room for any doubt."

Silence engulfed the room as everyone considered the option.

"Mr. Helms, I am glad you are on our side," Singh said after a while. "But can you get near him?"

"It will take some work. He's very well guarded; he just received his own Secret Service detail. This only makes it hard, not impossible."

"Huh," Singh said thoughtfully.

"I am in favor of an accident," Sadiq said.

"I have no doubt," Javadi responded sarcastically.

"Gentlemen," Myatlev said, "I'd like to propose a compromise. Why don't we allow Mr. Helms to work his magic and discredit Krassner to the best of his abilities, lawfully or not. We can offer him a month, maybe six weeks at the most. If that fails, we can always get him to step down, which I think would be better than killing him."

"You are soft, Myatlev, very soft," Sadiq said, contempt filling his voice.

"And you are nothing but a small-minded butcher," Singh said. "You are in such a hurry to kill one man, when you could be wise and wait."

"I agree," Javadi offered. "Myatlev's approach makes sense to me."

"He's got my support as well. It's just a good business decision, that's all," Shah said.

"Then we're set?" Singh asked.

"Yes," Myatlev confirmed. "Mr. Helms, you have your orders."

Helms nodded and left the room without delay.

"One thing bothers me," Sadiq said. "You had the opportunity to gain access to the devices, and you forfeited that in favor of some software deal and stealing a database? Why?" Sadiq asked. "Just think of what you could have done with the devices! Load them with C4, detonate all of them at the same time in a majestic attack of unprecedented greatness and effectiveness, and kill millions! How could you not see that opportunity, Myatlev? How could you give up access to the devices?"

"I never said I gave that up. Yes, we also control the devices, and at some point in the future, the plan will include them. I promise you will be satisfied, Mr. Sadiq."

...Chapter 68: Blocked Access
...Wednesday, August 10, 10:03AM Local Time (UTC+5:30 hours)
...ERamSys Headquarters
...New Delhi, India

Alex opened the main entrance door, bracing for the temperature shock from the intense air conditioning. On her way to the elevator, a lovely receptionist greeted her with a charming smile. She found harder and harder to see value in her presence in the New Delhi office of ERamSys, but she couldn't leave either. This is where the secret was. This is where she could uncover the conspiracy, or at least a solid lead to it. Yet, her entire plan to rattle their cages had proven very ineffective. Every day she had been more demanding, more insisting, yet she had gained access to precisely nothing. She had been almost rude sometimes, provoking Bal and his team, and had gotten nothing but passive-aggressive bullshit, more PowerPoint presentations on the benefits of India outsourcing and the high quality of their work, and more lies. In short, she had made zero progress. Even Scott and Brent, the other two DCBI representatives onsite, had been unable to offer any useful advice. They were performing their work well, without any hindrances. But then again, their work did not touch the actual code. That simple fact, in itself, was a clue.

Then she changed tactics. She had approached the issue indirectly, trying to engage in conversations with the smokers on the roof, but everyone turned suspiciously silent at any mention of the code. She had found a sort of a friend in Priya, but even she wouldn't disclose anything, or couldn't. Her laptop continued to operate on a network completely isolated from the development environment, and any attempt she made to gain access to the rest of the network raised Bal immediately, no matter what time of day she attempted to penetrate the security. He even showed up immediately if she spent any extent of time behind one of the developers on the floor when they were working, or when she chatted with any of them. She was effectively locked out, and Bal seemed to be on premises 24/7, needing no sleep.

She looked across the software development floor, wondering what else she could try. While evaluating her options, she let her eyes wander. She continued to be surprised at the differences between genders in India. Men dressed almost like Americans, in shirts and slacks, sometimes wearing suits and ties. Women had preserved the traditional attire almost intact, opting for one of the two main styles, the sari, with its ample draping of colorful, shiny fabric, and the shalwar kameez, with its pajama-like pants that had to be very comfortable to wear in the brutal heat.

Since she had landed in Delhi, she had learned to appreciate the local clothing wisdom, especially the strict preference for cotton fabrics. In the humid heat, cotton kept her cooler and drier than any Western polyester fiber mix. Smart. Women here were very smart, she had observed, focused more on practical things, while their men were absorbed by their immense egos and illusions of superiority. One time, she had asked Priya why such intelligent, apt women resigned themselves to allow these men to treat them as if they were inferior beings, many times like servants. Priya had been confused by the question at first, but then she had said it was their custom, the way they had been raised. They loved their culture and their men as they were. They knew no other way.

Alex opened the door to her office and sat down in front of her desk phone. An idea was starting to form in her mind. What would an employee in her situation do? The answer was simple. Call her boss.

She dialed Robert's number from her desk phone, as anyone in her position would do. She hoped Robert would notice the call coming in on his business cell instead of the encrypted phone and be careful with what he said.

"Wilton here," he answered.

"Good evening, Robert, sorry to bother you at this hour," she said.

"No bother, how's it going?"

"Well, that's what I'm calling about. I can't gain access to see the actual code, and I don't know how I can do my job like this."

"You still haven't seen the code?"

"Nope, still haven't. They've been showing me a mountain of PowerPoints but not a single snippet of code. You must help me find a way to get them to show me the code. How can I sign off on it like this?"

"I understand," Robert said. "Are you sure you're not having communication issues? Scott's been sending us reports every week; he seems to be doing just fine."

"Yes, I'm sure. I could have not been any clearer about it. And I hope you do understand, I cannot sign off on the quality of the code without seeing it or testing it myself. This is how this job is done, and you know that very well, Robert. This is too important to let it slide."

"Yes, yes, I know," Robert said in a pacifying tone. "You seem to be a little overwhelmed by this; why don't I send you a quality analyst who can help?"

This call was not going as she had hoped. An analyst? How the hell was an analyst gonna help? There was no code to analyze! How the hell was she going to be able to do anything with yet another person watching her every move? Had the UNSUB got to Robert again? Bal had threatened her life, but nothing had happened to her yet, despite her relentless pressures. They must have done something to Robert instead.

"Robert, listen, I really don't need an analyst. I'm fine on my own. The only thing I need is access to the code."

"Alex, please don't argue. The team was discussing it this past Monday. This project is too big for a single individual to be asked to sign off on its quality. The burden is too big. The analyst is arriving tomorrow, and we're not discussing this further, please."

"But what's he going to do without access to the code? He's just going to sit in the same damn PowerPoint meetings as I do, until the deadline comes, and we're screwed. What's he going to do that I can't?"

"He's a very experienced DCBI quality analyst; give him a chance, Alex. You'll still be running the show. He's just going to be there to help you."

"All right," she said and hung up, so preoccupied she didn't even remember to say goodbye.

She stood and went to the window, looking outside at the New Delhi city landscape against the permanently yellow sky. *What the hell am I gonna do?* Alex thought, leaning her forehead against the window and hiding her face from the omnipresent cameras. *Now I am really screwed.*

...Chapter 69: A Tax Issue
...Monday, December 14, 9:02PM EDT (UTC-4:00 hours)
...News of the Hour Special Edition Report
...Nationally Syndicated

The anchor's charismatic smile had a trace of excitement in it, making her look eager to share the day's top news story with her audience.

"Good evening, ladies and gentlemen," Stephanie opened. "After Doug Krassner's ratings had reached more than 50 percent support in electorate polls, today they took a hit, and for a reason that caught everyone by surprise, Democrats and Republicans equally."

The screen showed images from an old interview with Krassner, back then significantly younger, speaking with a reporter on a busy city street and pointing his hand in the direction of a billboard with an advertisement for a Baptist Church. His voice, young, yet just as charismatic then as it was now, was saying, "I honestly think some of these churches should pay taxes."

The image shifted back to Stephanie's in-studio layout.

"This single phrase, that I am sure Mr. Krassner regrets, has already cost him thirteen percentage points in the polls, leaving him at 38 percent. His main opponent, Bobby Johnson, picked up a good 7 percent of the fallout. Now at 35 percent, Johnson is following closely behind Krassner and could overtake his position in the polls as Krassner's comment continue to penetrate the audience. Doug Krassner has been unavailable for comment. He is currently on a business trip to Europe. We will keep you posted with his response to this revelation."

Stephanie's smile widened a little before her end-of-show greeting. "Live from our studio, this is Stephanie Wainwright, with *News of the Hour.*"

...Chapter 70: New Colleague
...Friday, August 12, 9:23AM Local Time (UTC+5:30 hours)
...ERamSys Headquarters
...New Delhi, India

Priya opened the office door just wide enough to stick her pretty face through the opening.

"Alex? Your new colleague is here," she said.

"All right, bring him in," she answered, trying to hide the discouragement she felt.

Priya opened the door fully and let the man in.

"Miss Hoffmann?" A familiar voice with a hint of ill-disguised humor. She looked up in disbelief, then covered her mouth briefly so she wouldn't scream with joy.

"I'm Lou Bailey, your new analyst," he said, shaking her hand warmly.

Alex grabbed her laptop bag and said, "Grab your stuff and follow me."

She led him to the elevator and from there to the roof of the side building. The roof was deserted; it was too early for anyone to be on a cigarette break yet. She led him behind the elevator equipment tower on the roof. In that spot, they were hidden from anyone looking at the rooftop from the main tower's terrace, rising two stories above them. Once they reached that blind spot, she bear-hugged him.

"Lou, I'm so happy you're here," she said. "How did you guys pull it off?"

"Tom figured out a plan with Sam and Robert. They fudged some paperwork, and now I am a tenured QA analyst with DCBI, been with them for years."

"Great! Maybe you can figure out how to get to the damn code," she said, not letting go of his arm.

"Well, guess why I'm here," he said and winked.

"I'm telling you, there must be something with the code. I'm sure of it. They protect it big time, and they're very determined not to let anyone near it. They've threatened me, but so far nothing has happened." She was excited to have someone she could trust. "How do they expect to continue to control our interaction with that code when they eventually have to deliver the software to DCBI? How does any of this make any sense?"

"Not sure yet. How do you want to attack this?"

"You have to get to the code; that's really all there is to it," she said with a shrug.

"Not quite. First, we must get rid of your driver," Lou said. "Sam said that Pranav might become a risk fairly soon."

"Great, just great," she muttered.

"How about you and I start to date? For cover, I mean," he clarified, seeing how confused she looked.

"Absolutely, would love to," she replied. "We'll start dating today at lunch, or is that too soon for you, sir?" She fluttered her eyelids in a mock flirting gesture.

"Nope, that will work. And I'll take the role of driving you around."

"You can drive in this?" She gestured in the direction of the street filled with chaotically moving vehicles in a concert of honks, several stories below them. Something caught her eye. "I wonder who that is and why he's visiting," she said, pointing at a car below.

His eyes followed her hand gesture.

"Who's that?" Lou asked.

He looked down and saw a huge black limo pulling in front of the building. A man, wearing a dark suit and a burgundy turban, had the car door opened for him as he climbed out of the limo and entered the building.

"No idea, but it could be our first break in this damn case," she said and pulled her SatSleeve phone. She speed-dialed Sam's encrypted cell.

"Hey, kiddo," he greeted her.

"Hey, do you have someone on the ground here in Delhi?" Alex half-whispered her question, while Lou kept guard, watching for anyone who could wander onto the roof for a cigarette break.

"I might, what's up?"

"A limo just pulled up here; I'd love to know who the passenger is," she whispered. "You need to confirm, 'cause otherwise I need to tail him myself."

"Got it. Give me a minute."

They chatted for a few minutes, putting their plan together and watching the limo to make sure it didn't leave before Sam's confirmation. They planned how to travel around, where to go, where to eat, when and how to get to the code.

The familiar chime of a new text message got her attention. Sam's message read, "My friend already in position at your location."

...Chapter 71: Celebration
...Monday, August 15, 6:47PM CDT (UTC-5:00 hours)
...Johnson Campaign Headquarters
...Chicago, Illinois

Anthony Fischer was willing to let his presidential candidate, Bobby Johnson, celebrate a little. Fischer had been stern and hadn't even allowed him to celebrate when he had received the nomination, concerned with the media attention. However, today's news was worth something to both of them, so he decided to let it be. By the looks of it, Johnson had already started celebrating on his own, probably as soon as one of his young interns brought the recorded newscast for him to view.

He was sprawled on the couch, his white shirt wrinkled, stained with sweat, and partially hanging out of his pants. Jacket and tie were on the floor, and Fischer had to pay attention not to step on them, or on the shoes, scattered randomly where Johnson had kicked them off. The level of remaining Scotch in the cut crystal bottle was less than half, and he knew for a fact that Johnson's crew topped that bottle full every morning, like a ritual. Johnson hated seeing half-empty bottles. *But of course he did*, Fischer thought, almost chuckling when he saw that Johnson had replaced the original cut crystal glasses (that had come with the bottle as a set) with plain ones, only much larger. That was Johnson's response to Fischer's strict rule of only one glass per day before going home. Maybe he was cut out to be the next president after all. This type of response was very appropriate for many different crises, not just for his personal alcohol restriction.

Johnson held the TV remote in one hand and the Scotch glass in the other. He smiled jovially when Fischer approached.

"You've seen it?" Johnson asked, not even slurring that badly.

"Sure I have, Bobby, sure I have." Fischer briefly ran his hand against his forehead and sat in an armchair next to his client.

"OK, but let's watch it again, will ya? I just wanna watch it again," he pleaded and pushed the button on the remote without waiting for Fischer's consent. The TV played the recording of a prime-time political news show, *Flash Elections*, with the familiar voice of the anchor, Phil Fournier, opening the evening's program.

"Is our strongest presidential candidate a Godless man?" Fournier opened. "The recently found recording, dated more than two decades ago, has Senator and presidential candidate Doug Krassner declaring that he'd prefer to see churches pay taxes. This strong stance has gained Krassner significant media and electorate attention of the kind he probably didn't want at this time in his campaign. His ratings lost thirteen percentage points in the first day the recording came out, then lost additional points more gradually, placing him a little behind Bobby Johnson. This is the first time Krassner has ranked behind Johnson in the polls since the campaign started. Separated by only a percentage point, Johnson has the lead in the race for now, but he wasn't able to capture all the losses Krassner incurred.

"Senator Krassner held a press conference today, the most heated one in recent history. It took a few minutes to get the press calm enough to ask questions in an organized fashion, and Krassner remained imperturbable while organizing a system that allowed him to have a productive session with the media. Here are the highlights from this session," Phil announced, as the screen transitioned to a recording from the earlier press conference.

Johnson poured Fischer a stiff drink and handed him the glass. They both took long gulps, eyes glued to the TV.

"Senator, when's the last time you went to church?" A young reporter with short, golden hair and elaborate makeup asked.

"I think that was in 2004, if I'm not mistaken, when I attended my best friend's wedding," Krassner replied with his usual charismatic smile, as if unaware of the storm his answer was going to generate.

The press fell silent for a second, the calm before the storm. Then everyone started talking at the same time, louder and louder, trying to cover one another's voices in the tumult. A man from the back of the media room yelled, "Are you an atheist, senator? Do you believe in God?"

"Yes, I do believe in God," he replied.

"But you're not going to church? Would you care to explain?" the same man continued.

"I believe in God, not in one church or the other. I exercise my faith in the privacy of my home. That is where I pray, that is where I observe my faith. I guess I could say I am a faithful man, not a religious one. There's a big difference, you know."

The room fermented for a few seconds, and then a voice rose above the rest, "Our nation has as an official motto, 'In God We Trust.' Keeping this aspect in mind, how do you see yourself, when you haven't set foot in church since 2004, fit to lead this nation?"

Krassner smiled before answering, as if secretly entertained.

"Our motto is, precisely as you said, 'In God We Trust.' It has never been, 'To Church We All Go.' I am drawing your attention to this key difference. I see myself fit to lead our proud nation because I am a faithful man, and I do believe in God. This fact, if you think about it, has very little to do with attendance at a certain church. I happen to think I don't need intermediaries to pray, confess, or talk to God. I can do that on my own."

"Do you hate churches, senator? Do you hate pastors and priests?"

"No, absolutely not. I simply don't need churches or ministers to observe my faith. I pray at home, I confess at home—to God, and I light candles at home. Nowhere in any scripture has this choice of observance been deemed any less worthy than churchgoing."

"Senator, why would you have churches pay taxes? Do you still believe that?"

"Yes, I still believe that, for some churches, not for all of them. Let me explain why. Some of them advertise. If you recall the recording that started all the media attention regarding my beliefs, I was pointing to a billboard when I made that statement, many years ago. That billboard held an advertising piece for a church that, unfortunately, was not entirely captured in that video, only partially. Therefore, I can't speak about that particular billboard message. But I can show you these billboards still exist today, and I can show you what they look like today."

He clicked a small remote, and on the screen behind his lectern, some slides started showing, each holding for a couple of seconds. One read, "If you die today, where will you go? Heaven or Hell? For the truth dial 1-888-555-5555." Another one read, "Judgment Day Is Coming," and had another toll-free number posted. A third one said, "Anti-God is Anti-American. Anti-American is Treason." The fourth and last one remained displayed on the screen, making an impression on the media. It read, "You *will* burn in hell. To save yourself call this number."

Krassner allowed the media to absorb the images for a few seconds, and when whispers started to rise, he resumed, "A business that advertises to get more sales, a business that spends tens of thousands of dollars in advertising every year should be taxed. That's the letter and the spirit of our tax law. But most of all what really gets to me is that these organizations are supposed to bring relief and comfort, not anxiety, fear, and guilt. These are the churches that I'd like to see pay taxes. They operate like reckless insurance companies, instilling fear and then offering relief for a price. What price, you might ask? Well, the majority of them charge or ask you to donate 10 percent of your income for being a member. That is precisely how a business operates. That's a business that should pay taxes, in my opinion."

Another reporter raised his hand to ask a question.

"I have another point to make, if you don't mind, and then I will answer your question," Krassner announced. The reporter lowered his hand. "My final point is that a church should be a place of healing and tolerance and should not promote hate, not under any circumstances. *Hate* is anti-American, not atheists. Our constitution guarantees our right to freedom of religion, and that includes having a different religion than the billboard is trying to sell, or having none, as an atheist or an agnostic. That's why I still strongly believe that churches that demonstrate corporate greed or intolerance should be taxed, because they are in violation of their declared mandate, and they operate as corporations."

He took a quick sip of water from the glass next to him and continued, pointing at the man whose hand was raised just a minute before. "Yes, sir, now your question, if you please?"

"Umm, you just answered it, senator. I have no more questions."

Johnson clicked his remote and the TV went dark.

"He is so gonna burn over this," he said, leaning toward Fischer and clicking his glass against Fischer's. "Cheers! I am the new president of the United States, thank you, Mr. Krassner," he said, raising his glass toward the TV and then taking another gulp.

"Maybe," Fischer said thoughtfully. "It's a possibility. He did make logical sense, you know, and I hate to admit it. I'm sure the religious fanatics will drop him anyway, but I'd be curious to see his ratings in a few days."

"I did get lucky, didn't I?"

Fischer considered the question before answering it. Either he was lucky or he had some very strong supporters who had started getting involved more. He knew Johnson came with a lot of strong support from some very powerful people, who chose to remain anonymous. Fischer was well aware of that support; although he still didn't know who was behind it. That strong financial support had motivated him to come out of retirement and help Johnson ascend to power, persuaded by the generous, yet anonymous deal they had offered. It had taken a lot of money to get him engaged, but now it didn't seem like enough. Even with all the experience he had putting people in the White House, Johnson had proven to be a hard case, making Fischer fear his career would end in shame rather than glory. After today though, he felt there was some serious hope, especially if Johnson's unseen friends continued their campaign.

His entire reasoning was too much for Johnson to handle, even if he were sober.

"Yes, you did, Bobby. You did get lucky, and so did I."

...Chapter 72: Routine
...Tuesday, August 16, 6:07PM Local Time (UTC+5:30 hours)
...Taj Palace Hotel
...New Delhi, India

They had their routine down. In the mornings, Alex and Lou would go to the office, get involved for a while, ask to see the code, put some useless pressure on the local project managers, run into Bal every now and then and exchange some more pleasantries, then head out for a long lunch, from about 11AM 'til about 2:30PM. Then they'd waltz right back into corporate HQ, holding hands, smiling, and looking at each other, causing most women to snicker and men to frown. They'd kill some more time at the office, but at about 4PM or so they'd be out of there. Then they'd head to their hotel, the Taj, where surveillance would place them near the pool, mostly tanning in the pollution-filtered sunlight or hanging out in the hotel lobby. Later on they'd head out to dinner, always in one of two places, either the Bukhara, famous for its fantastic mutton, or the Masala Art, right inside the Taj. Finally, as darkness fell, they'd hit the road and get lost in the vast city.

That was when the real work started. Pranav, Alex's driver, was history, and Lou did a fairly good job driving the streets of New Delhi and losing their surveillance. They'd drive around for at least half an hour, making sure no one was following them, then stop somewhere remote and safe to run the bug finder on their car, clothes, laptop bags, everything. Then they would resume their drive and choose, on the spur of the moment, a hotel they liked. They'd enter the hotel's parking structure, making sure yet again they were not followed. Lou would check-in under a well-documented alias, provided by Sam, with fake passport, fake credit cards, and the whole nine yards. Alex, waiting for the check-in to be complete, would sip a cup of coffee in the lobby and watch for anyone who showed too much interest in Lou's midnight check-in. Then they'd go up to the room, and their work would finally start.

At first, Lou wrote some code that allowed him to discreetly map the network security parameters and figure out ways to get in. The heavy and bulky Inmarsat device had proven invaluable. It made it possible for them to deploy the sniffer code and figure out a way in from the Leela Palace in central Delhi. Then they grabbed their first modules of code, hacking into precise locations within the ERamSys network, from inside the Dusit Devarana, via encrypted satellite connection. They were finally making some progress.

Back at their own Taj Palace, by the pool, Alex was reading a book on her iPad, while Lou, with his laptop open, scrutinized every line of code. He frowned and slapped the laptop lid shut, then turned to her.

"Come on, baby, let's grab an early dinner," he said, grabbing her hand and pulling her up from the lounge chair. Immediately, young poolside personnel approached them with towels and trays with fresh lemonade. The service at the Taj was impeccable, but Alex's focus remained on the lines on Lou's forehead. She grabbed her things.

After enduring a long dinner, dying to ask questions she couldn't ask until much later, they had finally made it though their daily routine. Once they were safely in an exquisite suite at the Shangri-La, she got to look at the code.

"What am I looking at?" Alex asked impatiently.

"This module seems fine, but it has some routines that shouldn't be there. You see," he pointed, "this routine calculates the results by state every five minutes. There's no entry in the specification document that requires any such calculation. Seems redundant but doesn't do any harm whatsoever. Then this other section of code shouldn't exist either. It evaluates the state in which the vote is captured, and, based on the set of rules outlined here, it returns a value. That value could be called at some point into a different module to generate actions that might differ by state. Again, no harm done in this module, only a lot of useless coding. Nothing in the specs calls for processing by state or state type."

"What actions?"

"Unknown. There isn't anything in these modules that would explain that or call this variable. But keep in mind I couldn't get everything. I just got a few modules, that's it."

"Then hack away, my man, hack away," she said, stretching out on the luxurious bed and immediately falling asleep.

...Chapter 73: Republican Nomination
...Wednesday, August 17, 10:02PM EDT (UTC-4:00 hours)
...Flash Elections: Breaking News
...Nationally Syndicated

Phil Fournier's smiling face came on the screen immediately after the opening credits faded.

"Well, it was not a given that the Republican Party would still support Senator Douglas Krassner in his run for president in the upcoming elections. It was not a given, especially after the recent turmoil in the media regarding Krassner's views on religion, faith, and church—turmoil that happened at the precise time when people were casting their votes in the primaries. However, earlier today the Republican Party announced the results of the Republican National Convention, placing its support behind Krassner's candidacy with a very strong majority.

"The announcement gained Krassner six percentage points within hours, putting him back in the lead at 42 percent and leaving democratic presidential candidate Bobby Johnson behind yet again by several percentage points. Johnson, now at 34 percent, has some catching up to do and only two-and-a-half months left until Election Day. We will continue keeping you informed with details and numbers as the presidential race heats up. From *Flash Elections*, this is Phil Fournier, wishing you a good evening."

...Chapter 74: The Terrorism Link
...Thursday, August 18, 9:17AM EDT (UTC-4:00 hours)
...Sam Russell's Residence
...Timberlake, Virginia

Sam sat on his deck, ignoring the early morning sunshine bringing up the colors in the landscape spread behind his home. He was reading an encrypted email for the fifth time since he had received it less than ten minutes before. He checked the time. It was still very early in California, but it didn't matter. He pressed a few buttons to make a call.

"Hello," the man answered immediately.

"Tom, it's me, Sam. Sorry to wake you."

"You didn't. What's up?"

"If you recall, Alex had us follow a limo in New Delhi last Friday to see who was visiting the vendor's CEO."

"Yes, I remember." Tom confirmed.

"The intel came back just now, and it's trouble. Big trouble. The man we followed that day is Mastaan Eshwar Singh, sixty-four years old, very rich, self-made businessman with interests in steel and manufacturing. But that's not where the trouble is."

"I'm listening," Tom whispered.

"He's a terrorist, Tom, a terrorist who hasn't made it yet on the FBI's most wanted list, but definitely belongs there. He is on Mossad's list though. He's got known ties with Kashmir terrorist networks and is thought to be responsible for the New Delhi bombings in 2005 that killed or injured more than 250 people. He's also believed to be the force behind the attack on the Parliament of India in 2001, but he wasn't charged. He's a self-declared anti-American, and it was his people who instigated the burning of American flags in New Delhi in 2012."

"Oh, my God," Tom whispered. "What are they stepping into?"

"Whatever it is, they're already in the middle of it."

...Chapter 75: No Coincidences
...Thursday, August 18, 10:09PM PDT (UTC-7:00 hours)
...Hilton San Diego Bayfront
...San Diego, California

Warren Helms looked out the window of his seventh-story hotel room, which overlooked the bay. The blue water reminded him of Panama; although the bay waters were a dark blue, not the Caribbean bluish-green he still recalled after so many years.

Only in his mid-twenties back then, he had deployed as a well-trained and enthusiastic Green Beret in Operation Just Cause, along with some twenty thousand other US troops on a mission to overthrow Panama dictator Manuel Noriega and install the democratically elected Guillermo Endara. Should have been easy, and it had been, for the vast majority of the troops, heavily supported by hundreds of aircraft. It was the conflagration the United States had won with the least casualties, losing only 23 men and taking home 324 wounded.

Him, they had left behind, wounded within an inch of his life, in the aftermath of one of the very few altercations with the Panamanian Defense Forces, where Americans had actually been wounded. His lieutenant made the call to leave him behind, not even bothering to check to see if he was still alive. He'd taken a bullet in the abdomen and another one in the leg, causing him to drop face down in the sand, suffocating with pain. He wasn't able to call out. He saw them leaving him there, and he couldn't call out. He heard his lieutenant give the order and say, "Let's move out; he's probably gone." Every time he closed his eyes, he could still hear him give that fateful order.

He had somehow survived. A family, so poor he felt guilty every time he ate, nursed him to health. They had no medical supplies, no money, and no means of any kind. They knew a retired doctor who gave them some advice, and he found some support in a hospital so decrepit and fetid he had considered dying rather than going inside. The hospital was able to stop his infection and patch him up, then returned him to the family who had no food to spare, but somehow managed to feed him every day.

As soon as he was strong enough, he made his way to the American Embassy. It was a long and exhausting walk through dirty, endless city streets, hours of agony spent enduring the pain of putting one foot in front of the other. Three days later he was home, coming back a hero, and getting the medical attention he needed. Six days after that, he was dishonorably discharged for punching his former lieutenant several times and putting him in a coma. Then he was charged with assault.

Then Helms fell off the grid, turning toward the mercenaries in search for a place where he could belong and make a living. With his record permanently damaged by the dishonorable discharge and the suspended sentence for assault and battery, he had little choice to find a way to earn a lawful living. He didn't regret it though. In Panama, fighting for his life in the poorest of environments, he had learned the value of money. When his lieutenant had turned his back on him, leaving him for dead, he had learned the value of loyalty.

Since then, everything he did he did for money, and there was no line drawn anywhere. There wasn't anything he wouldn't do for the right amount of cash. He was smart and merciless, and his conscience never bothered him. He had left it in Panama. He was an efficient and competent killer, trained by the best Fort Bragg had to offer, and had real combat experience. He was a sought-after commodity in today's shady market for contractors and mercenaries, and he was never out of work.

Helms moved away from the window and grabbed his phone. He had interesting news to break to his current employer, a Russian he had only recently met face to face. Helms didn't care whom he worked for, as long as they paid on time and generously and could keep their mouth shut.

"Da?" His employer answered in a raspy, sleepy voice.

"This is Helms," he identified himself.

"Da?" The man repeated.

"Your Indian friend might have a problem. Two of the people DCBI sent to New Delhi are originally from San Diego."

"So? Why does that matter?"

"The hacker who looked into the transplant clinic's database was traced back there, to San Diego. In my line of work there are no coincidences."

"*Blyad*!" the Russian exclaimed in his mother tongue, all sleepiness gone. "If your suspicions are confirmed, figure out control measures on your end. I will deal with my end."

"Understood," Helms confirmed.

...Chapter 76: The Insider Plan
...Thursday, August 25, 11:14PM Local Time (UTC+5:30 hours)
...The Lalit Hotel
...New Delhi, India

Alex still screened the temporary hotel rooms for bugs, almost religiously; although it made little sense. No matter how intense the surveillance, the UNSUB wouldn't have time to bug a room that fast. Alex and Lou picked their hotels spontaneously, and from the reception desk, where they would get the key card in a matter of minutes, they would go straight to their room to work. No one was that fast. No one was powerful enough to bug all the hotels in Delhi, just in case the two of them decided to show up. Nevertheless, she still swept them, carefully, methodically, just to be sure.

Satisfied, she put the bug sweeper back into her laptop bag and sat next to Lou at the small desk.

"Shoot," she said, looking at his screen.

"I downloaded a few more modules. I still don't have everything; I'm missing a few more. I don't know where they are, haven't found them yet. They're supposed to all be together on this staging server, but at least one module is definitely missing."

"Did you find anything interesting in these?"

"Somewhat," he answered, scratching his forehead. "Not sure if it's intentional or just a leftover, but I found a randomizer sub-module in the code. It just generates random numbers if called, that's all it does."

"So, nothing to worry about?"

"Not by itself, no. But we keep finding these sequences of code that are not in the spec and shouldn't exist."

"Sometimes these software companies reuse code they wrote for some other client without cleaning it up. They mix and match blocks of code from previous projects to maximize their profits. I struggle with this idea though, because I don't think they'd normally get a lot of projects involving voting. These are fairly rare. If our project were a dashboard, for example, this scenario would make more sense."

"You know what else doesn't make sense? If doing sloppy coding work is what they're trying to hide, do you think that's worth killing for? I don't think so," Lou said firmly. "I just don't. Here's what I want to do. I want us to go see Bal tomorrow and show him what we found, call him on it and watch what he has to say."

"Bad idea," Alex replied, shaking her head. "Bad, really bad."

"Why?"

"Do you think this is a situation where you can play fair, in the open? First, you said you don't have all the code yet. Second, you're dealing with a man who threatened me, personally and unequivocally. Something tells me he'll take the news that you hacked their systems and downloaded their code badly, as in pull out a gun and shoot us both. And finally, Sam said the man who visited a few days ago in that huge limo is a known terrorist. Need I say more? You can't confront them, not now, not later."

He blushed a little and stood and turned toward the window to hide it.

"Embarrassing," he said. "Sometimes I wonder if I have what it takes to do this job."

"Sure you do, you just need a little more experience, and sometimes you just have to forget you're an ex-SEAL. Not all fights are open and fair, clean hand-to-hand combat, or your Krav Maga. Most of them aren't. You still have a misconception that corporate environments are open, honest, and encourage direct communication. Maybe some do, but we're not usually investigating those. I am sure your SEAL trainers taught you to be covert and think like the enemy. How would this enemy think? What would they do?"

"Well, considering how they keep on stonewalling us, I'd say they're delaying the moment when we see the code, if we're ever gonna see it. I'd say they might even present us with a couple of devices with the software already loaded on it, for us to test and sign off on, when it's already too late to object or ask for anything else. They're already behind schedule on delivering the software, and that's what I think they're planning. That's why I thought we could approach Bal and make him face the music."

"Remember why we're here," Alex said, sounding almost maternal, which made her smile. "We wanna catch all the bastards, not just Bal and his boss. They didn't start this on their own; they didn't think this plan up. Until we know everything there is to know about that code we cannot draw attention to ourselves. They have to believe they had us fooled and that we're too busy romancing in Delhi to even care. They think Americans are idiots, so let's just play right to their ideas. Steve could have given you a great speech on using someone's preconceived notions against themselves. That's exactly what we're doing here. And most likely, keeping Robert and Melanie's safety in mind, we will sign off on that software, no matter what's in it, and pretend everything's fine, then control the situation as best as we can stateside. They'll still have to hand over that software at some point, right? That's the plan, my man," she ended her speech, punching him in his arm.

"So what do you need me to do next?"

She thought for a little while before answering.

"It feels like we're playing a chess game with the devil. It's the devil's move next, and we can't figure out what it's going to be. But until we do, we can't win."

"The devil's move? I didn't take you for religious," Lou remarked.

"I'm not, not really. Nevertheless, there's someone brilliant and evil behind all of this, and I couldn't think of any better moniker to give the man who's leading this game. Bal and his CEO, Ramachandran, are just his pawns, and so is that other guy, Helms." She stood and walked to the window, where the yellow lights of the Delhi cityscape were spreading into the horizon. "We need to be able to anticipate his next move, that's for sure. Can you grab the rest of the code and be sure you grabbed it all?"

"Sure can," he answered confidently.

"How can you be so sure? What kept you from grabbing it already?"

"I have to spend more time within the ERamSys network, from inside the domain and behind the firewalls, and you know how complicated that can get. Even if I run my sniffer code, I still have to be physically inside the building, logged onto the network, without any cameras facing my laptop's screen. There are cameras everywhere, and my quiet work time is very limited. They keep badgering us with those damn presentations and all kinds of useless activities. As soon as I figure out where the rest of the modules are housed, I can download them from the hotels, remotely, without any issues."

"They're not useless activities, you know."

"Huh?" He looked confused.

"They're not useless to them. They keep us busy, stuck in this muck we can't get out of. They control us, or they think they do. If they stop believing they're in control, our lives won't be worth much. They'll eliminate us without any hesitation."

...Chapter 77: Work Direction
...Friday, August 26, 9:54AM Local Time (UTC+5:30 hours)
...ERamSys Headquarters—Jeevan Ramachandran's Office
...New Delhi, India

Abid Bal let ten minutes pass after Ramachandran's car had pulled in front of the building, then started his way to his office on the top floor of the central tower. He hated how weak this man was. Ramachandran's vast fortune irritated Bal, because it had been achieved by a weak man, a nonbeliever with no sacred goals. This man didn't believe in anything else but his own money and a life of luxury and sin, nothing else. He had not embraced Islam, and that made him a lesser person in Bal's eyes.

Bal's commitment to the values of Islam was absolute, and living his life surrounded by blasphemers was a trying experience for him. His frustration suffocated him. He knew what he had to do to make things right, but he was never allowed to. Especially with that American woman. Bal hated all Americans. He saw them as sinful, menial creatures that should be put in their places, especially their women.

His younger brother, Raazi, had lost his way and had become one of them, abandoning his Islam beliefs and marrying an American woman. His own brother had betrayed them and allowed himself to become intoxicated by the vile sin those people lived in, enough to forget his heritage.

The two brothers, Abid and Raazi Bal had been raised together in strict Islamic creed by devout parents and had shared every aspect of their lives until their mid-twenties. Then, one day, his younger brother plainly announced to everyone that he had obtained his visa and was leaving for America to work for a large technology company in the damned Silicon Valley. Bal held his own during his brother's announcement, even through his mother's endless tears and sobs. His father had left the room the moment Raazi finished speaking; he had nothing left to say to such a betrayer of their way of life. Later that night, long after everyone had finally fallen asleep, Bal allowed himself to shed bitter tears for his soon-to-be-lost brother.

A few years later Raazi had called and announced with excitement that he had received his green card, allowing him to stay permanently in America. All hope was lost for the Bal family to see their youngest member come back to their hearth. Two years after that, Raazi sent them an invitation to his wedding. He was marrying an American, and an infidel on top of that, a *shlokeh* who wouldn't embrace Islam. His brother had become lost forever, deciding to live the rest of his life in mortal sin, surrounded by blasphemers. No one from the Bal family traveled to Raazi's wedding; they had spent that day in prayer for his soul.

Then another year or so later, Raazi had come home to visit, bringing his new wife, Christine. Raazi wanted to reconcile the two parts of his family, and he had hoped that his brother and parents would be able to accept Christine and his new chosen life. But that would have been blasphemy. Bal remembered the woman. Nothing but a whore, showing the skin of her arms and her flowing hair shamelessly, laughing, joking, considering herself the equal of everyone. Displaying no respect. Arrogant, loud, obnoxious, not knowing her place. She had the audacity to ask Raazi to get her things, do things for her, as if she were the man of the house. Bal would have given anything to teach that whore a lesson. When he thought of what he'd do to her, he felt an erection taking over his body's senses and mind's focus. It was the strongest erection he'd had in years. That was sinful. That day he saved himself by praying, locked in his small room. The next morning his sinful brother and infidel sister in law were gone. Forever gone, never to be heard from again.

Bal knew his personal history was at risk to cloud his judgment where these Americans were involved. Yet the facts were the facts, and he needed to take action, even if his weak leader was too limp to acknowledge them.

He entered the office after a polite knock and an invitation from his boss. He bowed his head in a respectful greeting that Ramachandran barely bothered to acknowledge. Then the CEO looked straight at him.

"What is it?"

"It is the DCBI woman," Bal answered, "I am sure there is something wrong with her. Her eyes are lying."

"We have surveillance on every move they make. What does surveillance say? Have they said anything, seen anything?"

"Nothing yet. She is doing what she is supposed to do, actually not even that. She is busy whoring with that man, Bailey. But almost every night we lose them in the city. That cannot be by accident."

"Lose them? How?"

"Traffic is heavy, you know, and that man, Bailey, drives the car himself now, so there are some nights when we do not know where they go. Our people lost them a few times."

Ramachandran frowned and muttered some swear words under his breath.

"Incompetents. Idiots. Your people should hang for this. When they do not lose them, where do they go and what do they do?"

"They take very long dinners, then visit the city, spend time in bars, clubs, eat some more, then they go back to their hotel rooms. Just wasteful, sinful, whoring behavior."

"Do they sleep together?"

"Not yet, but that will soon happen."

"So, what do you want from me?"

"I want a couple of hours with the woman, in a room. I will find out what she is up to."

"No. We have less than a month before we deliver. I will not screw this up on your hunch."

"But, sir, I strongly believe—"

"And I do not want to hear it. I am telling you what to do, and you will do it. We were supposed to deliver the software by now. We are already late, and it could pose problems, even if we are late on purpose. You have three weeks left until delivery. All you have to do is make sure she continues to visit the city, or whatever else she does, and your people do not lose her anymore. Then everyone goes back to where they came from without any incident. How do you think I could justify the interrogation of a client's representative? You would have to kill her."

"I would not mind that at all," Bal said, unable to restrain a sadistic smile and feeling a twitch below his waist. "I would actually prefer it. I would get to the truth faster."

"You would cause a lot of suspicion. Do you want DCBI to raise hell and hit the brakes? One American woman dies here and it is in every damn newspaper and TV channel newscast in the whole world. Do not be an idiot. Do as I say. And if your people lose her again I expect to hear about how they died, slowly and painfully."

"Yes, sir."

There was nothing else left to say. Bal swallowed his frustration and exited the CEO's office, walking backward for a few steps. Such a shame he couldn't have his way with that *sharmuta*, at least not for now.

...Chapter 78: Delivering America
...Monday, August 29, 10:32AM Local Time (UTC+3:00 hours)
...CANWE Headquarters
...Undisclosed Location, Greece

Vitaliy Myatlev's hangover had started to subside, enough to make him want to get out of bed and go outside, with his eyes covered by dark shades. A beautiful summer day, and he had a lot of plans for it. He looked over his shoulder at the naked young woman sleeping in his bed. *Khorosho, otlichno devushka*...She was a good girl, excellent. Didn't speak a word of Russian, this girl, and he didn't speak a word of Greek. But it didn't matter; she wasn't there for the conversation. He didn't remember much of his performance from the previous night, his memory faded in the fumes of first-grade vodka, yet he felt really good this morning. The sex must have been great.

The morning hangover was almost a given these days, and he knew just how to deal with it. His staff knew too. One of his bodyguards, Ivan, approached him with a tall glass of spicy tomato juice, generously christened with Stolichnaya, and an aspirin bottle.

"Spasibo," Myatlev said, swallowing the pills with the Bloody Mary, "thank you, Ivan."

He sat on the lounge chair in the shade of the big oak trees and dozed off for a minute.

His encrypted cell startled him, but he answered immediately when he recognized the name on the caller ID.

"Misha," he greeted the caller, "how are you? How is Russia?"

"Vitya, like you care," the caller answered.

"I do care, Misha, I care deeply. And I am working hard on our business arrangement," he stated, shifting on the lounge chair to find a more comfortable position.

"I hope that's true. We have a lot riding on your word, and Abramovich is losing his patience. He's not a very patient man, our president, you know that very well."

"I need a little bit more time," Myatlev replied, rubbing the headache away from his forehead. "I am very close to delivering an amazing gift to you both. I just need more time."

"How much more time, Vitya? We've been waiting for months to see something happen, and we have nothing other than your promises."

"I need precisely two-and-a-half months," he pleaded. "Ten weeks, that's all I'm asking."

"Ten weeks to deliver what, Vitya? You never bothered to tell us and make a commitment. Right now, I am not sure I can continue to trust you. It is my head if you disappoint the man. Maybe yours too, but I care about mine a lot more."

Myatlev considered his options. The caller, his lifelong friend Mikhail Dimitrov, sounded less like his friend and more like Russia's minister of defense. A very powerful and dangerous person to have worried about his ability to deliver. Myatlev had a sound respect for anyone who could throw him into the depths of Siberia and forget him there. He decided to trust him a little more than he had planned.

"Misha, what if I tell you that in ten weeks I will deliver America?"

There was no answer for a couple of seconds.

"America? How can you deliver America, Vitya?"

"In ten weeks, our mutual friend, President Piotr Abramovich, will have America under his control. That is my promise to the both of you."

...Chapter 79: An Invitation to Lunch
...Tuesday, August 30, 11:02AM Local Time (UTC+5:30 hours)
...ERamSys Headquarters—Fifth Floor Conference Room
...New Delhi, India

They were almost done enduring another PowerPoint presentation. Priya had talent, and her engagement and style of presenting made it almost enjoyable. The topic was "Steps in Scope Validation and User Acceptance," instructing the DCBI team what to expect in closing the contract with ERamSys. All DCBI representatives were attending, including Scott and Brent, while Bal supervised from the most distant corner of the room without saying a word.

The contract was late in delivery. They should have taken ownership of the software by now and be long gone, back to their homes stateside. They were all eager to leave, yet they were told that at least two more weeks of testing and bug fixing were necessary. Very disappointing news. They all wanted to be gone, and Alex more than anyone wanted to get her hands on that software once and for all, to get to the bottom of whatever the hell was wrong with it. This constant delay, stonewalling, and passive-aggressive responses to everything they were asking for was driving her crazy. She wanted to scream. Instead, she topped her coffee cup from the machine, smiled toward Priya, and said, "Very interesting."

Lou gave her a quick look, as to say "Really? At least don't encourage them!" She smiled at him briefly and sat back in her chair, purposely ignoring Bal's hateful gaze. *Damn that guy*, Alex thought, *I am looking forward to the day I never see him again. And maybe, just maybe, he'll end up in a very dark and forsaken place. Just maybe...A girl can dream, can't she?* Lost in her thoughts, she had let her eyes wander toward Bal, smiling widely, deep in her fantasy of never having to see him again because he was doing hard time in some horrible Indian prison somewhere. Bal grimaced in anger, and she turned her eyes away promptly. *Now that was stupid*, she admonished herself, *a little self-control would do you a world of good.*

Scott's voice brought her back to reality.

"But my reports don't indicate that," he was saying. "Compilation time is off for software this size. It should be at least 50 percent lower."

"Based on what?" Bal asked.

"Based on what software with this type of specification is supposed to do, if it runs in a stable environment, without issues writing on the database. It's just taking too long to complete the step. I think we need to examine the software modules. Alex, can you help with that?" Scott asked, turning toward her.

"I'd be more than happy to," she replied, "as soon as Mr. Bal's team gives us access to the code."

Bal's jaws clenched.

"The software is not ready yet. We're still working our quality assurance and bug fixing. We cannot open access for you while the software is still being worked on," he answered.

"What if you wrote us a copy of the complete software package on a separate server, so we can test it without stepping on your toes, would that work?" Alex asked. It wasn't the first time she was asking for access. But if they could be passive aggressive, so could she. At some point in time, no matter how badly they were trying to avoid it, they had to hand over the software anyway. They were running out of time and options. They needed to find out what was hidden in it as soon as possible.

"That would be perfect," Scott intervened. "That's exactly how we were instructed to proceed and why Alex and Lou are here. They need to inspect the software line by line before we can sign off on it."

"I understand," Bal answered, "and I will make sure the DCBI team receives all needed support to be able to sign off on the code per your company's procedures. Right now, we are simply not ready yet. Our reputation as one of the best software houses in the world is at stake here, I hope you understand." Bal looked at Scott firmly, yet friendlier than how he usually looked at her.

Scott held Bal's gaze, shrugging apologetically.

"I do, but I have to do my job. I have no choice."

"Scott, it is almost lunchtime," Bal said, sounding almost friendly, "will you do me the favor of joining me for lunch? I want to introduce you to the tastes of Dakshin, one of the best restaurants in our city." He turned toward Alex and said, "I understand you two prefer to dine on your own?"

"Yes, we do," Lou said, "thank you."

...Chapter 80: Man Down
...Tuesday, August 30, 1:57PM Local Time (UTC+5:30 hours)
...ERamSys Headquarters—Main Entrance
...New Delhi, India

Alex and Lou arrived at the office building to find an ambulance pulled in front of the main entrance. The marked van had its back doors open, and the crew was exiting the building carrying someone on a stretcher. Alex jumped from the car before it had reached a complete stop and ran to the stretcher. She barely recognized the man writhing in pain, tied to the stretcher with crossties.

"Oh, my God, Scott, what happened?" She reached for his hand and held it tightly.

He gasped and tried to say something intelligible, but he couldn't articulate. He moaned with pain, holding his belly; he wanted to curl up, but the ties wouldn't let him. He mumbled some words she couldn't understand. She turned to the crew.

"What's wrong with him? What happened?"

"Seems to be a violent attack of cholera," the young paramedic replied. "It can be very painful, but we've administered something for the pain, and we're hydrating him. He's got hemorrhagic diarrhea. We're taking him to the hospital."

Scott's grip on her hand turned tighter, and she leaned over, trying to understand what he was saying.

"Arghhh...don't...let...me...die...here," he managed to say before passing out.

"I promise," she whispered, holding his hand for a few more seconds. "I promise."

"Please, ma'am, we have to go now," the paramedic said in heavy-accented English.

"Where are you taking him?" Lou asked.

"To the Sir Ganga Ram Hospital," he answered. "It's the best in New Delhi," he added, seeing how the hospital name didn't mean much to them.

She let go of Scott's hand.

"Go ahead," she said. "We'll be right behind you."

They jumped into their Toyota and followed the ambulance through the busy city streets. The ambulance had the siren on, but no one cared. When they finally arrived at the hospital, almost an hour later, Alex was already at the van's back doors as they opened. The same paramedic didn't seem in a hurry anymore. She grabbed his forearm, feeling her stomach sink.

"I'm sorry, ma'am," he uttered sadly, "there was nothing we could do. Your friend died ten minutes ago."

Alex let go of his arm; she was paralyzed in shock. She turned slowly toward Lou and saw Bal's car pull right behind theirs. Before Lou could stop her, she went straight to Bal, grabbed him by the collar of his shirt, and shoved him hard against his car door.

"You killed him!" Alex yelled. "You killed him, you son of a bitch, and if it's the last thing I do, I will make you pay for it!"

Bal pushed her away, straightening his clothes. He was livid with anger.

"Know your place, woman," he growled.

"Know *my* place? You arrogant piece of shit! How about *your* place?"

"Enough," Lou intervened, grabbing her and leading her away from Bal. "Enough," he whispered. "Remember why we're here. You can't go after him like that. You taught me that."

She struggled to calm down. She was panting angrily, hands shaking and tears flowing freely on her face.

"They killed him," she whispered into Lou's shoulder as he continued to hold her. "Please tell me you know that."

"Yes, I do know that, and we'll make them pay, but not like this, not here, not today."

...Chapter 81: The Code
...Tuesday, August 30, 11:45PM Local Time (UTC+5:30 hours)
...Hotel Le Meridien
...New Delhi, India

As soon as the hotel room door closed behind them, Alex dropped the laptop bag on the floor and started pacing the room like a caged animal.

"I am sick and tired of this goddamn place. Sick of its smells and stupid heat. Sick of these assholes and their stonewalling. Sick of it all," she said, struggling to control her tears. "They killed a man like he was nothing, Lou. Bal didn't even flinch. I remember looking at him when he decided to take Scott for lunch. It was routine for him; it was nothing!"

Lou hooked up the Inmarsat to his laptop, getting ready to download the remaining module. He had found it, running his sniffer algorithm discreetly during the morning's PowerPoint presentation, right under Bal's eyes. The man's all-consuming contempt for Alex made him focus solely on her, while Lou was able to execute the program sequences unnoticed.

"You need to calm down, boss," he reminded her for the tenth time. "You can't think straight like this. Why don't you run the bug sweeper? Just to be sure?"

That gave her something to do to get her brain back into logical thinking. She sighed.

"Yep, I need to do that. How much longer with that code?"

"Just a couple of minutes, that's all," he said. "Then we'll know."

There were no bugs in this room, either.

"I got it, all of it," Lou said, disconnecting the Inmarsat modem. "Let's take a look." She scrolled fast through the lines of code, looking for things that didn't belong. "There's something here. I almost missed it. This override component, here, you see?"

Alex looked at the code, trying to decipher how it would compile.

"I see it overrides the voter's entry," she said, "but under certain conditions and rules. What are the conditions? Which other modules do these conditions invoke?"

"Let's see," he said, starting to take notes on the notepad provided by the hotel. "The first condition calls the module that calculates the results every five minutes, by state. The second one, here, looks up the state where the vote is entered and returns a set of values. I need to open the module that does the state lookup."

He browsed a little through the modules and found the one he was looking for.

"Ah, here it is. It's got multiple lookups. One is a 'type' lookup, returning one of two values, 'all,' or 'exception.' The other one is defined as a 'direction' lookup, and returns 'left,' 'right,' and 'center.' Any idea what these might be?"

"Oh, yes," she replied without hesitation. "The first one identifies 'all-or-nothing' states, where all electoral votes go where the majority of the popular votes go, and the other one identifies states by their political orientation, as in democratic, republican, and swing, or undecided. Interesting, keep going."

Lou scribbled some notes on the notepad, then went back into the most recent module.

"OK, here we go. Then after getting the state lookup values, the module calculates a quantifier, like an adjustment factor. The calculation returns a numeric value between one and three, that gets applied to...Hmm...Not sure yet. Then here, it calls the randomizer module. Remember the one we found a few days ago and thought it was a leftover from other code? Nope, not a leftover, it's called right here in two places."

"Let me see," Alex said, "OK, I think I got it. Let's walk through it; let's tell the story in the code. First, the malware module calculates the result by state, every five minutes. If democrat, the malware does exactly nothing, see?"

"Yeah, you're right."

"If republican, then the weirdness begins. It checks to see what kind of state the voter is in. If the voter's in an all-or-nothing state, the malware knows it has to reach a certain majority. Then it looks up to see if the republican majority is happening in a republican state, then it can do one of three things. If it's a strong republican state, the malware again does nothing. If it's a swing state, it generates a multiplier. If it's a democratic state, it generates another multiplier, slightly larger and influenced by the results it calculates every five minutes. That multiplier is a correction factor. The bigger the gap it has to correct, the larger the multiplier. Huh..."

She frowned, thinking hard and mumbling to herself unintelligible words, following the logic embedded in the code.

"Let's see what it does with the correction factor," Lou whispered, not taking his eyes off the screen.

"OK, I think I got it. See? Here it invokes the randomizer, which essentially says, 'override these republican votes, as many as the multiplier indicates, randomly chosen by the randomizer, and turn them democratic, for the next five minutes. Then run routine again.' Huh...The result of the malware would be a democratic win, but a very inconspicuous one, that respects political color by state and makes only the needed changes to discreetly steal the vote."

"What are you saying?"

"You see? Technically, if the vote happens to be democratic on its own, the module does exactly nothing." She stood and started pacing the room, rubbing her forehead. "Lou, this is the biggest electoral fraud in our history, in anyone's history."

"Fuck me...they're stealing our elections," he muttered in disbelief. "I mean, we knew there was something wrong with this code, some form of hacking or electoral fraud, but I didn't expect this."

"I didn't see it, either. It's a nationwide, orchestrated, discrete electoral fraud, that's what it is. It's a failsafe, in case Johnson can't win on his own. It's brilliant."

"Holy shit!" Lou exclaimed. "That explains a lot of things."

She continued pacing the room, agitated, rubbing her hands against each other.

"It explains some things, yes, but it raises a lot more questions. By the way," she added, "just to verify, check the databases and see if the data in them confirms my theory. You should see the states in there, two tables. One should have Maine and Nebraska listed as the exception to the all-or-nothing rule. The other table should have, say, Texas, Oklahoma, and Nebraska listed as republican. See if the tables have the data columns named in clear."

"Nope, they don't. They're secretive about it, but you're right, the data supports your theory. I think we got it. Now what?"

She sat on the bed, thinking. Her heart was pounding, adrenaline rushing through her blood. Now they knew what they had come here to find out. They knew what the attack was about, but it made absolutely no sense. She tried to calm herself and think rationally. This was bigger than they had anticipated.

"Let's think through this a little. It's all clear now; they're stealing our elections. That was indeed worth killing for. It all adds up." Deep in thought and frowning, she continued, absentmindedly twisting the cap from her empty water bottle, "Let's just validate my theory. Why would a software company from India give a rat's ass who the next American president is? Malware or not, the president is still an American, right? In that case, is Ramachandran the UNSUB's pawn? Or the orchestrator of this entire plan?"

"There are huge financial gains for India if the future president is pro outsourcing and pro Indian immigration. Billions of dollars worth of American labor goes offshore every year, and India grabs a lot of that dough." He smiled when he saw her surprised gaze. "Just read an article about it, and I paid attention when Brian was explaining these things to us. So yes, I'd say a major Indian software company could have reasons to give more than a rat's ass about who wins our presidential elections."

"Hmm...You might be right, but let's just assume there's someone else behind this plan, just like we had initially suspected. I have no proof. It's just my gut. It feels more logical to me. This is a fairly complex plan to have been orchestrated by a software CEO. You know how many of these software CEOs are in India? So why would this one be different? It just doesn't feel right to believe that. Let's focus on who the UNSUB could really be. This is one area where we've made very little progress and have zero leads to follow. Short of grabbing Ramachandran and torturing him, we have no way of finding out who's behind this."

"We could do that, if we really must," Lou offered hesitantly.

"Ah, hell no," Alex replied. "I'm hoping to live my entire life without having to torture someone, anyone, no matter how badly I want to sometimes. No matter how badly he deserves it. Nope, torture's off the table. Pfft..." She turned her head away, disgusted at the thought. "Sam said the guy in the limo was a known terrorist, right? So maybe there's a terrorism connection behind this, and that's it. That would actually make more sense, because we still don't understand why terrorists would have political preferences strong enough to justify this type of action. It's simply unheard of. There has to be a connection with interests back home." She stood and went back to the computer, looking at the code some more. "You have no idea how much I hate being unable to anticipate this guy's next move. Drives me nuts!"

"You think it's just one guy? Behind all this?"

"Yep, that's what I think. The plan has a certain elegance to it, a harmony, something you rarely see coming out of collective work. This is someone's masterpiece, his vision, but we might not know all of it yet. It just doesn't seem like Ramachandran is that man. He's just too...superficial."

"You still don't want to confront Ramachandran?"

"Absolutely not. We play the game just as we did so far, pretending that we're just minding our business. Then we sign off on the software and go home. But, in the meantime, we need to get the team up to speed and talk action and damage control. You do realize we can't let this software be used on Election Day, and we have very limited alternatives. Not to mention limited time. We only have two more months, and these assholes are gonna stall us for another two or three weeks."

"I still think it's a mistake, not talking to Ramachandran directly, just to see what he has to say."

She raised her eyebrow at him, and he caved instantly.

"What do you want to do?"

"I want us to spend Labor Day weekend in the Maldives," she replied and winked at him. "You could tell Ramachandran that we want to explore the beauty of the region, blah, blah, whatever, and we would like to leave on Thursday, the day after tomorrow, and be back the next Wednesday. Ask him to cover for us; he'll be entertained and less suspicious. Something tells me he won't mind. Then we meet with the team in the Maldives. We need help. This is too big for you and me, buddy. We have too many questions and too few answers."

"Are we done for tonight, then?"

"Yep, grab our stuff. I'll make the call to Tom; tell them to pack their bags."

They left the hotel room feeling optimistic for the first time in weeks. After all, they had finally made some progress. They had all the code, and they knew what was wrong with it. They had one more piece of the puzzle left to find and a lot of damage control to think about.

Just a couple minutes later, a man entered the room quietly and started looking around. He took a picture of the undisturbed bed and went through the trashcans, looking for any trace of evidence left behind. Finally, he approached the desk and looked at the notepad. The pages Lou had scribbled on were gone, but indentations remained on the notepad, still visible in the desk lamp's light. Satisfied, he put the notepad in his pocket and left, just as quietly as he had arrived.

...Chapter 82: Failed Setup
...Friday, September 2, 10:01AM EDT (UTC-4:00 hours)
...Flash Elections: Breaking News
...Nationally Syndicated

"Good morning and welcome to *Flash Elections*," Phil Fournier greeted his audience. "We're opening the headlines this morning with the latest smear campaign against Senator Douglas Krassner, the favorite in this year's presidential races."

The image showed a middle-aged, balding man, an average Joe Anyone, speaking with a reporter somewhere in downtown DC, in the blazing summer heat. Little sweat beads were forming on the man's forehead, and he was wiping them off every minute or so.

"I am surprised, no, I am appalled to learn that a man like Krassner, who is very rich, and who keeps saying how he cares about the country's well-being and all that, has only donated $250 to charity in his entire life. His entire life! Now, what kind of man can sit on such a considerable fortune without finding a single cause worthy of a more substantial donation? Who are we bringing into the White House? The most selfish man who ever lived?"

Phil's smiling face returned to the screen. "Now let's hear what Senator Krassner had to say in response."

The charismatic persona of Doug Krassner appeared, dialoguing with Phil Fournier in a cozy, dim-lit studio.

"Senator," Phil asked, "what do you think about the recording we just watched? Is it true you've only donated $250 to charity in the past years?"

"Yes, it is," Krassner answered without hesitation. "It is also true that I have significant charitable initiatives that I prefer to manage myself, or through my trusted appointees, rather than just donate cash to get tax deductions."

"Can you give us an example?"

"Absolutely. Our family built and endowed the Dallas Medical Haven, a 180-bed hospital and a walk-in clinic, that covers any out-of-pocket medical expenses for families making less than $40,000 a year, regardless of whether they're insured or not. Last year, we added a dental practice to the Medical Haven, with 23 staff dentists. Same rules, no out of pocket for any patient."

"That's amazing, senator. I bet there are long lines in front of the Dallas Medical Haven, aren't there?"

"There are, that's true, and we've noticed that. People travel from other cities to gain access to our care. Consequently, the Houston Medical Haven is scheduled to open its facilities next April."

"Any other initiative you might want to share with us today, senator?"

"My wife is the architect and sponsor of the Smart Girls Center for Development, where girls with an IQ in the 95th percentile receive support to access suitable levels of education, regardless of family income, all the way through college. We all win when smart people are well educated and can lead the nation in business, economics, or medicine."

"Thank you, senator."

The screen shifted again to Phil's in-studio setting. His smile was almost sarcastic.

"Krassner's support gained another four percentage points after this interview was released yesterday. Now at 46 percent, Krassner is leaving his main opponent, Bobby Johnson, a little further behind. If those who started the most recent smear campaign had done a better job researching the facts, they might have chosen not to consolidate Krassner's ratings any further. Johnson's ratings also picked up a couple percentage points, due to his strong religious beliefs, now at 37 percent in popular support. From *Flash Elections,* this is Phil Fournier, wishing you a great Labor Day weekend!"

...Chapter 83: A Reunion
...Friday, September 2, 6:18PM Local Time (UTC+5:00 hours)
...Royal Island Resort and Spa
...The Maldives

"Jeez, Alex, you stink," Steve said, hugging her tight and rocking her left and right.

She laughed.

"I guess I do, but I can't smell it anymore. The nose protects itself. It's the curry that's in everything. Can't help it. Although a long bath wouldn't hurt," she said with an embarrassed smile.

She moved away from Steve and gave Tom a hug.

"Steve's right, you know," Tom added, "you do carry a bit of exotic flavor. How have you been?"

"Curryfied, I guess, considering how you all say I smell. And mad as hell. I wasted a month and a half of my life down there and got very little in return. I feel defeated."

"I disagree," Sam said. "I don't think you are defeated, or any of us, for that matter. We know what they're up to, at least partially, and that's more than we did before you came here."

"Where do we go from here?" Alex asked. "That's what keeps me up at night. What options do we still have?"

"Before attempting to answer your question," Tom said, "let me tell you what we've learned about the heart."

She looked confused for a split second, until she remembered Melanie Wilton's transplant. So many things had happened since then, it seemed like eons had passed.

"We are confident the heart came from a homeless Army veteran in Nebraska. We were unable to find any gray-market connections with respect to this transplant, so Brian had an idea, to search for any homicide victims around that timeframe who were missing organs. The only match was this poor vet in Nebraska. The heart was harvested under anesthesia, perfect surgical conditions, and then the body was dumped in the Platte River, west of Omaha. It was found a few days later, but the coroner was unable to determine the precise time of death."

"Was this vet missing any other organs? Or just the heart?" Steve asked.

"He was only missing his heart, leading us to believe this was a targeted hit, rather than an organ smuggling ring of sorts. Brian's assumption was that they must have hacked the VA database, looking for people who were a perfect donor match and had no family to miss them," Tom clarified.

Silence engulfed the hotel room, which overlooked the paradisiacal view of the Maldives: white sands, lush forests, and green waters. No one paid any attention to the blissful scene right outside their hotel; they were all troubled by the same thoughts.

"All right," Alex broke the silence, "let's talk next steps. We know they're stealing our elections and we know how. Is this the extent of their attack? Or are we missing something? That's my first question. Then, second, how do we contain this mess? What's our damage control strategy?"

"I think it's time to call the feds," Steve suggested.

"Absolutely not," Alex snapped. "Nothing changed from the last time we argued about this subject; what the hell? Robert would still go to jail forever, Melanie's life would be in danger, and the government would pull back on the e-vote reform. Let's say all of that is acceptable, although it isn't, but I'm not even sure we have all the details of what the attack is going to be. More important for me, we cannot let these bastards get away with it. If we call the feds now, the UNSUB will go underground and disappear. Don't know about you, but I want to nail these bastards. They just can't get away with it, not while I'm still alive."

Tom nodded quietly. Steve's expression was impenetrable, but Alex knew he was hurt. She had no choice. This was not about her safety. It had never been.

"Additionally, I would personally prefer," she continued in a more subdued voice, trying to appease Steve's feelings, "if I, and all the people in the world I care about," she gestured toward all of them, "would not have to be imprisoned for the rest of our lives. If we call the feds, don't kid yourselves...that's exactly what's going to happen. Or worse. And the devil, whoever he might be, wins the game."

No one said a word for a while. There was nothing left to say after her disturbing reminder of what their reality looked like.

"What if we rewrite the software?" Lou asked. "Without the malware?"

"We can't possibly rewrite in a few days what tens of programmers took weeks to code," Alex protested. "I haven't written a line of code in years, don't count on me."

"I wasn't," Lou stated. "I'm a hacker, you know. We, hackers, know people."

"What? You're saying you could get the software fixed? Rewritten?"

"Yes, ma'am," he replied, giving a military salute. "I'm fairly confident I can."

"If you can pull it off, Lou, then we're good on the software side," Alex replied. "We give the signoff to the Indian vendor and swap the software without them even knowing. That would work really well. That would be so cool!"

"How about the hardware?" Sam asked. "How confident are we that the hardware is clear? If I were a terrorist, I wouldn't let that opportunity go to waste. I'd rig a few to explode or something."

"Yeah, but wouldn't that jeopardize what they've worked so hard to achieve in the software?" Steve asked. "The democratic win?"

"You got a point," Lou said.

"I'm confident that Taiwan was clear," Alex said. "Not confident for any of the subsequent processes the devices go through after delivery from Taiwan. Where are the devices now?"

"The NSA vendor in Utah, InfraTech, took ownership and is holding them at its warehouse," Tom replied. "The hardware is ready to install the software via cloud as soon as the vendor's ready and DCBI has signed off. It has test stations equipped to check the tablets for malware. InfraTech, and everyone else for that matter, is freaking out because the software is not ready yet. It should have been signed off on last month."

"Wow, Tom, look at you," Alex commented, "using words like cloud and software installation. That's awesome!" She felt the exhilarating joy only hope brings, especially at the end of a trying time.

"You see these new gray hairs?" Tom pointed at his head, almost entirely gray. "These gray hairs are all because of technology," he laughed.

He looked just as Alex had remembered him from a few weeks before. Nothing had changed, other than a few neologisms added to his vocabulary.

"OK, so how do we contain the hardware risk? Even if it makes no sense to think it's rigged to blow up?" Alex asked. "Sam, if you were the terrorist, what would you do?"

"Oh, God, let me think. So Taiwan's out, that leaves transit and InfraTech. Transit is done already; the devices are there. We cannot control transit anymore. If we are to assume the devices came in clean from Taiwan, then it must be InfraTech. Because it's a big-shot vendor for the NSA, I can't think of the company being the culprit. More likely a rogue employee, who could place C4 and timers in a few tablets at random."

"So, if you were the terrorist, you'd rig a few to explode, huh?" Alex asked.

"Yep, that's what I'd do."

"Even if you had a bigger agenda?"

"Hmm...Maybe, because I'm a terrorist, I can't think straight unless I think explosives. It's in my blood. I just couldn't let the opportunity pass."

"Dogs could sniff that in a second." Alex pushed back.

"Yeah, sure, but dogs inspected the cargo upon delivery. Afterward, no one will think to check it again. A rogue employee makes the most sense."

"And it fits the UNSUB's preferred methods," Tom added. "The plan always had these precise targets, these precise interventions. He always went sharpshooting, not carpet-bombing. It fits."

"So what do we do?" Alex asked.

"I'll handle that," Sam said. "I'll get a good friend of mine from the NSA to recommend the replacement of all InfraTech staff with NSA personnel until the devices and the software are deployed."

"How would you prevent the UNSUB from learning that?"

"I can't. We don't know who that rogue employee is, so we can't control the communication," Sam said, "but the NSA has procedures for clean, contained takeovers."

"It's a risk we'll have to take," Tom said.

"I'm not really worried about that," Sam concluded.

"Just wait for me to get back from Delhi, will ya?" Alex asked.

"You're not going back, are you?" Steve asked.

"Yes, I am. I have to sign off on the bloody software, don't I? Maintain our cover?"

"Alex, I can't go back with you. I have to work on getting the software rewritten. I can't do that under their surveillance," Lou said.

"It's all right, Lou, I'll be fine."

"Please reconsider," Steve pleaded. "That guy, Bal, threatened you. It's not safe for you there, Alex."

"It never was, Steve, yet here I am. Please trust me. Trust me that I can do this. Please." She gazed into his blue eyes for seconds, silently. "I'll be fine, I promise. I have no choice, really. If neither of us goes back, our cover is blown, and everything we tried to do goes straight to hell. So, lovely curry, here I come." She joked, trying to lighten the atmosphere.

No one laughed; no one even cracked a smile. They were a tough crowd, these guys.

"The problem remains," she resumed in a serious tone, "that we still don't know who these bastards really are. For that, I see very few options. Any ideas, gentlemen?"

"I could reach out to some old contacts in the CIA," Sam offered, "see if they picked up on any chatter recently, or have any clues of any kind. Ask them if they know anything more about the Indian terrorist, Singh. Maybe his association with the software company CEO would give us something. I've already asked here and there and gotten nothing. No one knows what that bastard's up to these days."

"By the way," Lou asked, "who followed him that day?"

Sam hesitated a little before answering. "Mossad," he finally said.

Lou whistled. "Good to know you have friends, Sam."

"Mossad's got him on their known terrorist list, but they don't have any intel that could help us in our case. I'll check some more, see what's out there."

"What time is it in California right now?" Alex asked.

"We're precisely twelve hours ahead of them, so it's 8:42 in the morning in California," Steve answered. "Why?"

"Friday or Saturday?" Alex asked.

"Friday."

"OK, there's some hope. I see no other option than to do what you men can never do, no matter how high the stakes and how lost you are."

"What's that?" Tom asked, intrigued.

"Ask for help."

...Chapter 84: Calling a Friend
...Friday, September 2, 8:44PM Local Time (UTC+5:00 hours)
...Royal Island Resort and Spa
...The Maldives

She pulled the SatSleeve from her bag and fitted it to her cell phone. Everyone watched quietly, curious to see her next move. She dialed a number and a professional female voice answered on the first ring.

"This is Mr. Bernard's assistant, how can I help you?"

"Good eve...morning," Alex corrected herself, "may I please speak with Mr. Bernard?"

"I am sorry; he is unavailable at the moment." Bernard's assistant had that polite, yet assertive and cold demeanor very common to executive assistants, trained in rejecting all kind of unwanted callers, day in and day out.

"When is the earliest I can reach him?" Alex insisted.

"May I ask who's calling?"

"Yes, this is Alex Hoffmann, an acquaintance of his."

A split second of hesitation, then the executive assistant's voice came back on, much softer and more helpful.

"Miss Hoffmann, if you could kindly hold the line for a second, I will put you right through to Mr. Bernard."

Alex smiled, thinking her name was still worth something with her former client, the CEO of one of the biggest banks in the world.

"Alex, what an unexpected pleasure," Blake Bernard answered. "Glad to see you still remember me."

"Mr. Bernard, of course—"

"Blake, please."

"Blake, yes, how are you? I hope you're well," Alex said, very uncomfortable with such pleasantries. Her direct style didn't value the typical icebreakers other people used, and she struggled with them every time.

"I'm good, very good, Alex. I do remember you quite well, and I know you wouldn't be calling me just to check on me, no matter how depressing that feels. What can I do for you?"

She cleared her throat a little.

"I'm working on a case, and I need your help."

"Shoot," Blake said, getting ready to jot things down on a paper pad.

"I need your jet in the Maldives, ASAP. And no, it's not for personal enjoyment."

"Even if it were, that's not an issue. The jet will be on its way within the hour. What else?"

"I need access to your anti-money laundering team, software, terminals, and to Clarence."

Clarence was one of the best anti-money laundering analysts in the industry, a friend of Alex's since she had worked on Blake Bernard's case.

"He'll have to cancel his Labor Day plans," he said.

"I have no other way," Alex said apologetically.

"That's fine, he'll understand. What are you up to these days?" Bernard asked. "I know you can't really tell me, but—"

"I'm chasing a terrorist, Blake, and don't ask me how that happened, 'cause I don't really know. I just know I have to catch this man, and I need your help. Badly."

"You got it. What else do you need?"

"One more thing, please. Your pilots should be ready to sign our NDA."

He chuckled.

"Consider it done."

...Chapter 85: Help
...Sunday, September 4, 2:23AM Local Time (UTC+5:00 hours)
...Royal Island Resort and Spa
...The Maldives

Lou entered his hacker username, *SealBreaker*, and password and gained instant access to an encrypted chat room where he knew he'd find at least one of his buddies hanging out.

He typed, "Salutations, white hats in there," and waited. A chime soon followed.

TheMoon: Hey, SealBreaker, haven't seen you in a while. What have you been damaging lately, bro?

SealBreaker: All damage has been done already, and it wasn't me. But we can fix with a little sweat and get mega bragging rights.

Another hacker joined their chat.

MissMeNow: Long time no see, Seal, baby, what's new? Any decent hackification lately?

Lou laughed out loud as he typed his reply.

SealBreaker: Turned all cool and nice now, just playing around with some really neat stuff.

TheMoon: What's the gig about?

SealBreaker: Interested?

TheMoon: No spec, no statement.

SealBreaker: Right on. How would you like to prove that we can code in days what offshoring did in months, charging millions for it, and their code still sucked?

TheMoon: How much?

SealBreaker: Coding? Or dough?

MissMeNow: Funny...both, baby, both.

SealBreaker: Code not that much, money unsure, maybe nada. Count on generic bragging rights, 'cause you won't be disclosing what the code is about.

MissMeNow: Sounds like total exploitation to me, baby Seal.

Lou frowned.

TheMoon: Sounds like government fuckup Seal's trying to cover, that's what. What's the code for?

SealBreaker: Code of silence compiles?

MissMeNow: Error free.

TheMoon: Same on this machine.

SealBreaker: It's the e-vote, hats. That's what I need you to write.

TheMoon: Wait a sequence...R U 4 real? WTF, man?

SealBreaker: 100 percent, no rounding up.

MissMeNow: Alpha will want in, and we want Alpha bad for this. I'll get him. Maybe even Hyde&Seek.

A chime announced another participant.

Alpha: Just heard. One Q before I start coding. Why us?

SealBreaker: 'Cause we need the best security ever. You're the best.

Alpha: Have a spec?

SealBreaker: And a good one.

TheMoon: How do we do this?

SealBreaker: I'll coordinate if you like. The functionality ain't much to code. Security is big. Offshore already malwared it. That's why I'm asking you.

Alpha: Bastards.

TheMoon: When do you need it? Next week ok?

SealBreaker: Super.

Alpha: Shoot that spec over and we'll get busy.

MissMeNow: Baby Seal, we shall shine again. There's winnitude in this project. Me excited.

Lou let the air exit his lungs in a long sigh. They were the best American white hat hacking had to offer, despite the fact that some had criminal records, and others were barely of legal drinking age. They were the good guys coming to the rescue. He had more than hope; he had a solution in place.

...Chapter 86: Return to Delhi
...Tuesday, September 6, 9:41AM Local Time (UTC+5:00 hours)
...Ibrahim Nasir International Airport
...The Maldives

Alex was trying to hear over the noise of Blake Bernard's jet, parked nearby with its engines idling. The Phenom 300, relatively silent for a jet its size, still caused their goodbyes to be awkward, covered by the constant whirring of its engines.

"Will you be OK?" Tom asked.

"Yeah, I will," Alex said. "I'll just tell them Lou dumped me and went home. I'll have an excuse to look sad and stay locked in my office all day long."

"Ah, thank you much," Lou said, "make me the asshole."

"If the shoe fits." Alex laughed.

"Bye, kiddo, we're right behind you, one phone call away," Sam said. "I'm not leaving the area. Just paying some friends a visit, then I'll be in New Delhi, very close by in case you need me."

"Who's your friend?" Alex asked.

"Just an old Russian spook, mad at life and willing to have a glass of vodka with me. He knows people, things, stuff like that. Who knows? Might be worth the travel time."

She looked at them, feeling tears coming to her eyes. Steve was quiet, dark, his forehead lined with worry. Sam was confident and encouraging, his normal self. Lou was preoccupied, studying the tarmac's asphalt. *He must be thinking about the software, the burden is on him now*, Alex thought. Tom looked proud; Alex couldn't figure out why. There was nothing to be proud of. Not yet, anyway.

"All right, you guys, go ahead, you're gonna miss your flight," she said, half-jokingly. They climbed the Phenom's ladder and soon were out of sight. The Phenom's door closed and locked, and then the jet started to taxi away. She looked at it until she couldn't see it anymore. Minutes later, she saw it take off on her left.

She watched it disappear, and then she went back inside the terminal, waiting for her commercial flight to New Delhi to start boarding.

...Chapter 87: Controversial
...Tuesday, September 6, 10:07PM EDT(UTC-4:00 hours)
...Flash Elections
...Nationally Syndicated

"If Doug Krassner proves to be as controversial a president as he is a candidate, we're in for an exciting four years," Phil Fournier opened his news insert. "His ratings remained stable during the past few days, high enough to have us believe he's the next president, but low enough to add excitement to this race. The wheel might turn at any moment.

"In Krassner's case, the electoral campaign has been a roller coaster of controversial statements, scandals, revelations, and surprises, out of which, for the most part, he came out shining even brighter than before.

"However, the country stands divided on Krassner, and divided passionately. The issues separating his supporters from his opponents are powerful issues, leading to heated debates and strong emotions. These emotions now transcend the political party lines, becoming more and more personal for both sides. Even long-standing democrats are won over by Krassner's views on the economy. Even hardcore republicans are repelled by his liberal, non-committal stance on religion and abortions.

"After last week's debate, Krassner's rating still holds at 46 percent. While he looks like he might be our next president, that's not entirely sure. Bobby Johnson's ratings rise slowly but surely, and Johnson might yet prove to be the proverbial tortoise that wins the race.

"From *Flash Elections*, this is Phil Fournier, wishing you a good night."

...Chapter 88: New Code
...Tuesday, September 13, 1:08AM PDT (UTC-7:00 hours)
...Lou Bailey's Residence
...San Diego, California

He had spent the past week or so glued to his living room. His laptop was logged into the encrypted chat room he and his white-hat friends normally used. It announced with a chime whenever any of them had questions. A week of eating canned food and delivery pizza, dozing off now and then on the sofa, and keeping track of Alex's whereabouts via her cell phone's tracking app. He was counting the minutes until she'd be able to get out of New Delhi and come back to safety. He was counting the minutes until the voting software they had dubbed e-vote 2.0 would be ready to deliver.

A familiar chime got him to jump off the sofa and grab his laptop. There was activity in their chat room; people were logging on.

MissMeNow: Hey, baby Seal, you up still?

SealBreaker: Always.

TheMoon: Yo, Sealie, what's up?

Alpha: May the Force be with y'all.

SealBreaker: Greetings, hats. Speak.

Alpha: We done.

SealBreaker: For real?

MissMeNow: Real as it gets. Very done.

TheMoon: We've been done since yesterday, but Alpha wanted v 2.0 to be delivered on the 13th.

SealBreaker: LOL. And I've been waiting...

Alpha: Wish it were Friday the 13th.

SealBreaker: Tested?

MissMeNow: Yup.

TheMoon: Test some more, U got time.

SealBreaker: Will do. Encryption?

Alpha: Solidest I've seen. All hats coded that padlock.

SealBreaker: Rewrite/modify/clean? Or new?

Alpha: Entirely new. Offshore modules pure junk.

TheMoon: Pure barf.

MissMeNow: Barf + poison.

SealBreaker: Cool hats, you rock!

Alpha: You just acquired that value?

SealBreaker: Yep. The Force was with you on this.

Alpha: And with you. What next?

SealBreaker: Code transfer, shower, sleep. U?

Alpha: Same.

MissMeNow: Baby Seal, we shine, we rule, we deliver. Who needs running water over that? Just beer and zzz...

Alpha: ROFL.

SealBreaker: Can't thank you enough, hats. *Console.WriteLine ("thank you," 1000000000).*

That line of code, if compiled, would return the words "thank you" one billion times, running down the screen in endless, streaming rows of text.

MissMeNow: Compiles.

TheMoon: Be well, brother. Stay unhacked.

SealBreaker: Will execute. Signing off...

They had the replacement software, clean, secure, and election-ready. But that was only a part of the challenge.

...Chapter 89: Money Trails
...Wednesday, September 14, 7:19PM Local Time (UTC+5:30 hours)
...Bukhara Restaurant
...New Delhi, India

Alex waited for her Tandoori mutton, one of the few Indian cuisine dishes her palate savored. Having dinner alone was not easy, especially in New Delhi, but she didn't want to let herself be intimidated into ordering room service. A woman dining alone was insulting to many, but she willfully ignored any disapproving looks and managed to enjoy her dinners to some extent, evening after endless evening, reading from her iPad or browsing through a magazine. She missed having those lengthy dinner conversations with Lou, but she was still in Delhi for a precise reason, and he wasn't, for another precise reason. The software was almost ready for sign-off, which meant she could soon go home.

Home. The word had a very different meaning now, sitting alone in the Bukhara and ignoring the gazes of countless strangers who thought she didn't belong. More than that, she hated the inaction; there was little she could do other than wait for the damn thing to be finally ready. Every day she thought of hopping on a plane and just going home, the hell with it all, and every day she talked herself out of it, considering the huge risk her departure would pose to their plan, to Robert and Melanie Wilton's lives, to their overall mission.

Her phone rang, scattering her dark thoughts. She didn't recognize the caller ID.

"Hello," she answered neutrally.

"Alex, this is Blake Bernard. Can you talk?"

"Not really," she replied, aware she continued to be under surveillance.

"Can you at least listen?" Blake asked.

She verified the encryption status on the phone. It was working.

"Yes, that I can do."

"Clarence came back with some findings. There are several others names associated with the name you gave us, Mastaan Singh. Clarence ran some database searches looking for anyone traveling at the same times and same places as Singh, for several of his travels. He matched credit card charges, hotel stays, and wherever available, any type of aviation activity, whether commercial or private."

"Great news, please go on," she said enthusiastically.

"We were able to ascertain that there is, in fact, a network of sorts that you have uncovered. They're organized as moneymakers and money movers. The moneymakers are Singh and one other man by the name of Ahmad Babak Javadi. These two have organized a network of charity organizations across Europe, operating as Eastern Africa Development Fund, for which they continuously fundraise. They do it right, and they have access to celebrities and influential people, being able to raise significant amounts of money at events throughout Europe. They receive corporate donations in the hundreds of thousands, even millions. Each event raises several million dollars. Clarence and I can only speculate as to the reasons why some corporations donate so generously, but we have nothing solid yet."

"Very interesting," she said, careful with her words, in case her followers were dining within earshot of her. "I wonder about that too."

"We're still investigating that angle. Money movers, now. The movers we found are Karmal Shah and Muhammad Sadiq. Shah has a prosperous deli business operating out of Prague and operates a Piaggio turboprop airplane that can take him anywhere with significant cargo onboard. The other mover, Sadiq, has a Sea Ray 470, and his favorite destination is the Bahamas."

"So how does this work?" Alex asked.

"From what we've seen, the two moneymakers raise funds and send them legally to Somalia, in Mogadishu. All seemingly legit so far. From here on it turns interesting. Cash is withdrawn and just disappears, but the dates coincide with Shah's Piaggio's shopping visits to the area. His business conveniently imports delicacies from Africa, among other places. In other cases we have seen cash going to a bank in Bahamas, from where it disappears again, dates coinciding with the voyages of Sadiq's Sea Ray. We are assuming that the purpose is to get the cash into the continental United States, untraceable, and this is how they do it."

"Fascinating," she said, "and very useful." She took notes discreetly on a sticky pad she had in her laptop bag.

"A couple more interesting things to note," Blake continued. "They are very discreet, these people. They cover their tracks well. We almost missed the money movers completely. They made only one mistake, allowing us to connect the movers with the makers. The moneymakers, when they organized a fundraiser in Zurich, used Shah's deli business in Prague as a supplier. They ordered caviar and truffles from Overnight Delight and had it shipped to their location, on ice, the next day. Big mistake, sloppy work, but we were grateful for it. Another note, looking at these people's accounts, they're not your typical person of interest for terrorism, Alex. They are all powerful, wealthy business people. I cannot comprehend why someone like that would get involved in terrorism and what they could be planning. Their status is probably the best cover a terrorist could hope for. No one expects it; no one sees it coming. Clarence was thinking that those corporate donations we can't explain might very well be their own companies' network of vendors, being encouraged to donate. We're still exploring that angle."

"Are we missing anyone? From this party?"

"Not sure. Clarence said he'll keep looking. The more they travel and use their credit cards, their passports, or their identities anywhere in the world, we can narrow down other associations. You remember how the association search worked, right? With each move, it eliminates coincidental travelers and pinpoints those people who always happen to be in the same place at the same time as our targets. It becomes very precise after a certain number of iterations. We just need more time."

"I cannot thank you enough," Alex said, "this is extremely helpful for me."

"You're very welcome," Blake replied. "Call anytime, for anything at all. Clarence will keep looking. Good luck!"

She thought for a few seconds about what to do, ignoring the Tandoori mutton that was getting cold in front of her. She grabbed her cell again, this time sending an encrypted text to Sam: "Need to see you now. Say where."

A minute later, his reply came. "Sheraton New Delhi, room 306."

She took a couple of bites from her food, signaled for the check, and programmed her phone to get driving directions. She realized she had to lose Pranav, her driver, and drive herself through New Delhi. She had no other option.

She reached the Toyota and Pranav hopped out from behind the wheel to open her door.

"Pranav, you need to take a cab and get yourself home, do you understand?" She gave him forty dollars in small bills, a small fortune for New Delhi. He looked confused.

"Ma'am, I drive you," he said.

"Not tonight you're not, sorry. May I have the keys, please?" she asked, extending her hand.

He held the keys, looking even more confused.

She sighed and just snatched the keys from his hand. She hopped into the Toyota and drove away slowly, getting used to the car's right-side steering wheel and the streets with left-side driving. *This is gonna hurt*, she thought.

In the rearview mirror, she saw Pranav speaking to the driver of a black SUV, some local brand she didn't recognize, but that SUV looked very much like a Jeep. Now she knew what her followers were driving.

She hit the gas and entered traffic in the screams of horns from the heavy traffic. She held the wheel tight, her knuckles white from effort and her palms sweating. She followed the GPS directions with difficulty for a while, until she got the hang of driving on the left side of the road. It was weird, and the crazy, unpredictable traffic made it even worse. She stopped at a red light, making the cars behind her honk furiously, but she didn't budge.

She checked her rearview mirror and saw the black Jeep knock-off right there behind her, third car back. She took a quick breath and turned left, on the red, pedal to the metal. Then she turned left again into a small alley, instantly killing the engine and lights. She saw the Jeep pass on the street behind her. She waited a few minutes, then drove away from the alley, resuming GPS instructions.

She drove for a few minutes, checking her surroundings all the time. Suddenly, the Jeep was back, on the lane to her left, a little behind her. She hit the gas; there was no other way. She sped by a farmers' market, managing not to hit much; although she did run too close to a clothing rack, her bumper and wiper getting entangled in a couple items. She dragged those along for a while, until they finally became loose. The Jeep was following her aggressively now, giving up all attempts to stay inconspicuous.

She took a sudden right turn into an alley in the market, making her tires squeal and some pedestrians run scared. The Jeep still followed, hitting a bunch of grain buckets and spreading their contents onto the sidewalk. People screamed and ran as she drove by; she honked almost constantly. She came close to hitting an old man, but managed to maneuver out of the way and just hit a small wooden cart instead. Melons scattered everywhere, the Jeep smashing them as they came. She took another tight turn onto a small bridge, squealing her tires some more and scraping the side rails.

The Jeep still followed, hitting a snake charmer's basket and throwing it into the air, snakes falling from it onto the ground as the crowds shrieked and ran. The fake Jeep's turn radius must have been a little too wide, or the driver not very skilled. It missed the tight turn onto the bridge and hit the end rail straight on, making it do a side flip through the air and land in a muddy river.

Alex slowed and watched the black Jeep as it sunk slowly into the muddy waters of the river, while the two men in the vehicle were making their escape. They were going to be just fine. She hit the gas happily, resuming the instructions on her phone's GPS and following the directions it gave.

She arrived at the Sheraton, hands still trembling a little from the effort and the adrenaline of the chase. She went straight to room 306, and after giving Sam a quick hug, she went straight for the mini bar.

"That bad, huh?" Sam probed.

"Wasn't easy," she said, wearing a smile of satisfaction on her lips. She had pulled it off, on her own, and she felt proud.

"Did anyone follow you?"

"Nope," she smiled.

"How come? I thought they were on you 24/7."

"They've gone fishing. In the river. Or canal, or whatever. Really filthy. Cheers!"

"Huh?"

"They took their vehicle into the river too," she winked.

Sam burst out laughing.

"Nice going, kiddo!" He extended a high-five, and she slammed her palm into his with enthusiasm. She took another gulp of Martini vermouth, finishing off the small bottle, then took the sticky pad from her laptop bag and started writing names on the notes, sticking them to the hotel room wall.

"Blake Bernard just called, gave me four names, well, just three we didn't already know, and some money trails."

She explained to Sam what Blake had uncovered, and as she did, she pointed at the names on the wall, connecting them using other sticky notes with arrows drawn on them. The four names were lined up horizontally, under two separate sections, titled "$ Makers" and "$ Movers."

"Do you see what we're missing, Sam?"

"Yep, we don't have their leader," he replied, confirming her conclusion.

She took another note, wrote "X" on it, and placed it on the wall above everyone else.

"Blake seemed confident that the software would identify X at some point in time. I'm thinking X might be too smart for that. If he didn't make a single mistake in so long, more than a year is what Blake said, it's possible the bank's anti-money laundering software will never catch him."

"If he's this good, he'd be using private jets with fake flight plans, cash, or use his staffers' credit cards to pay for stuff, rotate through them often enough. It's a possibility we won't catch him," Sam said.

"Until we know who X is and what he's after, we can't assume we're done, or that this threat has been averted or controlled. So far, no one even knows he exists, and he was able to plan the biggest electoral fraud in our history and get powerful business people to execute it. Our Mr. X is scary good at his game."

"I agree."

"What next, then?"

"I'll make a couple of calls and see if these names ring any bells with my Mossad friends."

...Chapter 90: A Goodbye
...Wednesday, September 21, 7:23AM EDT (UTC-4:00 hours)
...Robert Wilton's Residence
...Washington, DC

Robert Wilton dressed himself carefully that morning. White dress shirt, charcoal suit, silver gray tie. He was getting ready for what could turn into a day of unexpected outcomes. The Agency team had provided a solution, and they were working on tying up loose ends now, which meant the time had come for him to come clean. That could mean he might be arrested that day, minutes after having a conversation with his boss, Campbell. That could not be helped, and it didn't matter.

What mattered was Melanie. Alex and The Agency team had told him she was safe. As soon as he accepted the software from the Indian software vendor and released the final payment owed to them, Melanie's life would stop being under threat. Alex reassured him that the UNSUB was going to have what she had called "bigger concerns" right after that contract ended. He definitely hoped so.

He steadied himself, looking at his image in the mirror. His hands were shaking just a little bit. Quite understandable. He was pale, and dark circles marred his tired, troubled blue eyes. Also understandable.

He took a sealed envelope addressed simply "Melanie" from his dressing room drawer and put it in the breast pocket of his suit jacket. He didn't want Melanie to hear he had been arrested and understand nothing of it. He quietly opened the door to their bedroom and stood there, watching her sleep. Her skin had returned to the pink color of a healthy woman. She slept soundly, an arm thrown over his pillow, her hair covering her face. Robert felt tears coming to his eyes. Missing her, that was going to be the hardest part of what he had to do. Nonetheless, he still had to do it.

He approached the bed and kissed her gently on her hair. She woke up slightly and mumbled in her sleep. "What's up, baby?"

"Nothing, just saying goodbye. Go back to sleep."

He kissed her again and left, closing the bedroom door quietly behind him. He went straight to his home office and placed the envelope by his desk phone. Then took his briefcase and car keys and left.

In his DCBI office, on the sixth floor, Robert watched the early morning sky and recapped the day's agenda. First, he would sign off on the offshore software, marking the end of this contract. Then he would release the payment to the Indian offshoring company and send them the confirmation. The Agency had insisted this step had to be taken; there was no way around it. The thought of paying them still made him very angry, considering everything they had done. But it just had to be done, so he would do it. Then he would swap the Indian software received by FTP from ERamSys with the one Lou Bailey had sent him on a DVD. Very easy.

He'd load the DVD onto the lab's machine and transfer the software onto an encrypted hard disc, which he would then send to InfraTech using the NSA-appointed courier. A senior NSA agent was scheduled to pick up the encrypted HDD and then head out to Utah where he would take things over. He would replace all employees with NSA agents for the few days remaining and ensure all hardware was clean. Everything made sense and everything was doable. He could be done with all this by lunch.

Robert picked up his office phone and dialed an internal extension.

"Campbell," a man answered in seconds.

"Robert Wilton, here. I think you should cancel your afternoon agenda and see me right after lunch. This is important."

...Chapter 91: A Different Approach
...Wednesday, September 21, 10:09AM EDT (UTC-4:00 hours)
...Capitol Skyline Hotel
...Washington, DC

Warren Helms liked open views and elevated vantage points. They made him feel in control. His top-floor room overlooked the city landmarks and the distant noises were barely noticeable. He was irritated this morning, bothered by his inability to deliver on his task, which had never happened before. He had been given a month to bring Doug Krassner's ratings lower than Bobby Johnson's. A month and a half later, he had to admit he had failed.

This acknowledgment bruised his ego and put a blemish on his spotless record of achievement as a private contractor. In his line of business, failure was not an option. Failure could be lethal. His clients weren't exactly forgiving, understanding people. But he was much better at eliminating unwanted people than he was at discrediting them in the eyes of the public; that was a fact. He was not a PR specialist; he was a contractor. The best there was. He should be allowed to do his job, the job he was good at.

Helms grabbed his encrypted cell phone and called his client. It was early afternoon in Greece; the Russian should be awake, his hangover well dissipated by now.

"Yes?" The familiar raspy voice picked up.

"This is Helms."

"Yes...The man who will not give me results, right? The man who is putting our entire operation at risk, da?"

"Sir, I recommend a different approach. This one is not working. No matter what I try, he manages to fix it." He swallowed hard and continued. "Sir, this is not what I do, not what I'm good at. Let's try a different approach, one that would have the guaranteed results you're looking for. It's time he stops being a problem. There's only a month and a half left."

The Russian was silent. Not a good sign. Finally, he spoke. "Yes, not much time left, that is true. OK, do it, but be very careful. He cannot be a martyr, or linked to us in any way. No Russian connection. No Islamic connection, either. The circumstances must be above any suspicion. It needs to be clean, natural, and in the public eye. Can you do that?"

"Absolutely," Helms answered, relieved.

"Good. Make sure it happens just a few days before Election Day, you understand? I do not want them to have time to regroup. And do not fail me again."

"I won't."

"You better not," the Russian answered and hung up.

It was going to be challenging. It wasn't that easy to get anywhere near the presidential candidates, when their Secret Service detail was already in place watching their every move. A precisely timed heart attack, his signature hit, would work best for the annoying Mr. Krassner. It required unrestricted access to what his target ingested, and that wasn't so easy to get. Maybe a carefully placed substance or biological contaminant? He could place it somewhere he would touch, inhale, or brush against.

His plan still needed work.

...Chapter 92: On the Run
...Thursday, September 22, 10:23AM Local Time (UTC+5:30 hours)
...ERamSys Headquarters
...New Delhi, India

Alex felt like singing. She was finally going home. She had checked out of her hotel, wearing her megawatt smile, and had brought her suitcase with her to the office. She had some paperwork left to wrap up, after DCBI had finalized the payment and the contract was closed. That shouldn't take her more than half an hour or so, and then she'd be on her way to the airport.

Pranav helped her with the suitcase, bringing it to the fifth floor conference room. She wanted all remaining documents to travel in her suitcase, not her extra heavy laptop bag. Priya brought her a file folder and a cup of coffee. She drank absently, while reviewing the contract closure, scope validation, and financial transactions documentation, signing off on everything. She waited for Priya to make copies and then shoved all the paperwork into the exterior pocket of her suitcase. She was ready to go home.

She grabbed the laptop bag, put it on her shoulder, and started toward the door. Startling her, Bal appeared out of nowhere.

"Ah, Miss Hoffmann. Can I please have a word with you before you leave?"

He stood in the doorway, inviting her back in with a gesture of his hand. She looked at him briefly. He had a faint trace of a smile on his lips, barely visible, and the coldest eyes Alex had ever seen. She felt goose bumps and a tingling in the back of her head. Adrenaline flushed her stomach, hitting her like a fist. Then, in a split second, she remembered Steve's words, from her first week with The Agency.

"Many times," Steve had said during one of their early training sessions, "the only warning sign we have in the presence of a sociopath is given by our ancestral instincts. Sudden and unexplained fear, tingling in your stomach, indicative of a sudden release of adrenaline, your hackles standing up, that's all you will get. If you just met someone and you feel all that in their presence, walk away, or be very, very wary. If you had met the sociopath before, and your instincts rile up now, just run. Don't look back, don't analyze, just run for your life. The sociopath is about to strike. How do we know? Pure survival instinct, perfected over millennia, triggered by signs our subconscious mind perceives."

Somehow, she managed to smile.

"Sure, but I need to use the restroom real quick. Too much coffee," she laughed, pointing at the empty mug on the table where she had sat.

She slipped right by Bal, not waiting for him to answer, heading to the women's restroom. As she opened the restroom door, she sneaked a peek behind her. He had turned away, not watching her anymore. She turned on her heels and ran for the staircase. She made it through the staircase door and ran down five flights of stairs as fast as she could. Once on the ground floor, she had no other option than to cross the big lobby. She did so in a running pace, but stopped briefly in front of the reception desk, where the beautiful receptionist greeted her with a smile. As usual, she wore a very decorative shalwar kameez ensemble, a very dark blue, decorated lavishly with gold embroidery and fringes.

"Hey," Alex said breathlessly, "can I borrow your scarf?"

"My scarf...My dupatta? Sure..." She took off the long piece of fine cotton and handed it to her. Alex grabbed it, thanked her in a hurry, and stormed out the main door.

Outside, she saw Pranav sitting in the driver's seat of the Toyota. It would take too much time to get rid of him. She stepped into the traffic and hailed for a cab. A tuk-tuk stopped, and she hopped in.

"Drive," she told the driver. "Just go!"

The three-wheeler tuk-tuk started. She sat down in the small cabin, grateful for the side semi-wall that could hide her somewhat. She wrapped the dark blue dupatta around her head, neck, and shoulders, hiding her light brown hair.

"Take me to the airport," she said, still breathless from her run. "As fast as you can."

"Yes, *memsahib*," the driver answered.

As the tuk-tuk turned right at the next stop, Alex peeked her head just enough to see the front door of the ERamSys building. Bal ran out through the main doors, followed closely by two other men, his head on a swivel looking for her. He was gesticulating wildly, but he had not seen her. Probably the receptionist had told him she had left the building.

She sat back against the vehicle's hard seat and called Sam.

"Yeah, kiddo, what's up?"

"Sam, they're after me. I'm in trouble, serious trouble. Bal's coming after me," she unloaded with one breath.

"OK, calm down, where are you?"

"In one of the slowest goddamn vehicles invented, heading for the airport," she said angrily.

Her driver turned briefly to look at her, smiling. *He must understand English fairly well*, Alex thought, as he cranked up the gas on the small vehicle, making it go faster and moving in a zigzag pattern through screaming traffic at what seemed to be about fifty miles per hour.

"All right, kiddo, go straight to the airport, and from there, straight to your gate. Do not stop under any circumstances; don't use the restroom, just make your way to your gate."

"He's gonna catch up to me. He'll figure out I'm headed for the airport; it'll make sense. He'll be looking for me there."

"I know, but he won't be able to snatch you with so many people watching. Just trust me, will ya?"

She closed her eyes. "All right. I got it." She hung up the phone and promised herself she wouldn't go down without a serious fight.

Minutes later, she saw Bal's car passing them on the right side of the road, but they didn't recognize her. She was barely visible, tucked in the corner of the three-wheeler's dirty cabin and wrapped in eight feet of dark blue fabric.

Finally at the airport, she shoved a hundred-dollar bill in the driver's hand, making him cheer. Keeping her head down, covered by the scarf, she made her way almost running to the security screening point. A long line formed there, and she had no alternative but to wait.

Someone touched Alex on her shoulder, startling her.

"You're wearing this wrong," a young Indian woman was saying. "It's an Indian dupatta, and you're wearing it like an Iranian shayla."

Alex struggled to understand what she wanted. Her first thought was to tell her to leave her alone, but then reconsidered it.

"Show me," she encouraged the stranger.

The girl reached out and wanted to bring the fabric down from her head.

"No," Alex said, pushing back her hand.

"Oh." The stranger's expression changed. "I see. If you need to hide your face, then tuck the ends of the dupatta in your shirt. The gold embroidery and fringes will draw attention. If you tuck them in like this, it looks modest. It works best if you're walking with your head down, just like a modest Muslim woman would."

Alex looked at her reflection in a glass wall. She barely recognized herself. She thanked the stranger by gently squeezing her hand.

She passed through security, looking down almost the entire time. On occasions, she checked her surroundings briefly, but there wasn't a trace of Bal and his men anywhere. She made it to the gate and approached the gate attendant, walking slowly through the dense crowd.

"Hi. My name is Alex Hoffmann, and I need your help to get safely on the plane," she said.

A commotion behind her drew her attention. Bal and his men were shouting, trying to get the crowd to move away as they ran toward the gate.

"Yes, ma'am, your plane is waiting," the attendant said and led her through a side gate. Two armed men in black uniforms showed up and flanked her, leading her to the tarmac. Behind her, in the crowded gate area, Bal was making headway fast.

"Stop!" he yelled. "Get out of my way!" he snapped at an older man, shoving him brutally to the side. He approached the side gate that led to the tarmac, but two uniformed men wearing the letters CISF (indicating Central Industrial Security Force) on their backs and sleeve patches stood in his path. They were militarized airport security, people who could not be easily intimidated.

"This gate is for private jet access only. I am afraid I can't let you through."

"Aaargh!" Bal yelled, out of his mind with anger, clenching his fists tightly.

Hearing Bal's scream she turned, and, almost paralyzed, saw him pull a gun and shoot in her direction. The bullet hit one of the CISF men in the shoulder. The other CISF hit Bal in the head with his gun handle, knocking him down.

She resumed her brisk walk onto the tarmac escorted by the two uniformed men carrying automatic weapons. As soon as she turned the corner around the terminal building, Blake's Phenom 300 came into sight. The familiar whirring of its engines was the sweetest sound she'd ever heard. Relieved, she climbed the five steps.

"Welcome aboard," Blake's pilot greeted her, turning his head toward her. He was clicking buttons and checking readouts. "We are ready for departure; we will be taking off shortly, please take your seat."

"Whew, thanks!"

She took her seat, expecting the plane to start moving immediately. She waited for another couple of minutes, but the plane still sat there, door open. She moved forward in the small cabin to speak with the pilot.

"Any idea why we're not leaving yet? It's kind of an intense situation I have going on here," she tried to explain.

"I hope you weren't planning to leave me here," she heard a familiar voice behind her.

"Sam!" she exclaimed and ran to him.

"What happened to *no man left behind*?" Sam asked, hugging her.

"I'm a civilian," she laughed.

"Go," he instructed the pilot.

The plane's door closed with a thump. Minutes later, the Phenom was taking off, soaring toward the permanently yellow sky.

...Chapter 93: Hardware Issues
...Monday, September 26, 10:04AM MDT (UTC-6:00 hours)
... Outside InfraTech Headquarters—NSA / Homeland Security Joint Task Force—Mobile Intervention Unit
...Provo, Utah

Special Agent Lance Huntley fastened his Kevlar vest carefully, checking to see if it was secured in place.

He looked briefly at the geo-location screen, one of the many digital terminals in the Mobile Command Center. The screen showed blue dots corresponding to the respective locations of the team's mobile units and red dots for any unregistered geo-locating devices picked up by the sensors. Blue for friendly, red for unknown or foe. All the blues were exactly where they were supposed to be. There was a cluster of red dots, immobile, centered on the InfraTech warehouse.

Huntley frowned, then dismissed his concern, attributing it to some active geo-locating devices that InfraTech might have had in stock. *Who knows what else they got in there*, he thought. Not giving the red dot cluster another second of attention, he picked up the radio.

"All teams, this is Command. Team Charlie, Team Delta, get ready. Confirm. Over."

He looked at the young technician working on a laptop next to him.

"OK, start cell signal jamming now, five-mile radius. I want it dead quiet. God himself shouldn't be able to make a call."

"Yes, sir," the young man answered and started entering commands on his computer.

"Team Delta in position, over."

"Team Charlie in position, over."

"All signal is down, sir, all is quiet."

"Cut their landlines too."

"They're cut."

"All teams, this is Command. All phone lines are down. Proceed at will."

The MRAP (mine-resistant ambush protected) vehicles, marked "Homeland Security—Special Response Team," took strategic positions around the building. The blue dots on his geo screen reflected their new placement, showing them as a circle made of triangular blue tags enclosing the building, covering all angles and all exits.

Armed to the teeth and in full tactical gear, the two teams fanned out, surrounding the entire InfraTech warehouse and office building. Team Delta moved toward the back of the building, watching every exit. Team Charlie stayed at the front of the building, two of the agents blocking the parking lot exit. Five agents moved toward the main entrance to the building. Special Agent Huntley caught up with them and entered the lobby.

A startled, pale receptionist stood up, unsure what to say.

"Please call Mr. Weston for me," Huntley asked.

"Y–yes, sir, right away."

A few minutes later, Mr. Weston entered the lobby area.

"Good morning. How can I help you?"

"Good morning, sir. I'm Special Agent Lance Huntley with the NSA / Homeland Security joint task force. We have reason to believe the security at your facility has been compromised."

"Oh?" Weston asked, surprised. He must have had many years as the leader of a government contractor, yet he seemed taken aback by the size of the task force. Just as an innocent man would react.

"We cannot go into details at this time. We are here to take over operations until the critical cargo leaves your facility. Please notify your staff they have to vacate the premises immediately."

One by one, employees exited the building, heading toward a cordoned area in the parking lot. The task force was not letting anyone leave yet; the agents needed to know they had everyone's information; everyone had to be accounted for.

Inside the Mobile Command Center, ignored by everyone, the geo-locating screen showed a smaller cluster of red dots in motion, away from the warehouse, where the majority of the red dots remained immobile.

Straying a little to the left, a man, dressed in blue coveralls and wearing steel-toe boots, slid unseen along the side of the building, walking faster as he approached the back. He was almost running when he turned the corner, only to meet the business end of a Heckler & Koch MP7.

"On the ground, now," the agent holding the gun said. "Hands behind your back."

Hands immobilized with quick cuffs, the man was escorted to the Mobile Command Center.

The agent slammed him onto a chair, not even looking at him or asking any questions. Then he swabbed the palms of his hands, his sleeves, and the inside of his pockets, and put the pad into a testing device, waiting for results. One beep indicated the result was negative.

"Command, Command, this is Delta Three, over."

"Go for Command."

"Command, I have one in custody. He swabbed negative for C4, but he was running. Over."

"On my way," Command answered.

A few minutes later, Special Agent Huntley climbed inside the Mobile Command Center. The geo-locating screen caught his attention. There were two red clusters now, and Homeland's blue tag circle was no longer perfect. A red cluster of geo dots superimposed over one of the blue tags. Theirs. Whatever the red dots were, they were there, inside the MCC.

Huntley called the agent guarding the prisoner.

"Ben, empty his pockets."

"Yes, sir," the agent acknowledged. He pulled the man to his feet and started going through the pockets of his coveralls. From one of the side pockets he took out a handful of small screws. From one of his chest pockets, another handful of screws. He placed them on the table, in two separate lumps.

"Screws, smokes, and a lighter, sir; that's it."

Huntley studied the tiny screws attentively, looking at one from each pile. They were slightly different.

"What's your name?"

"Chris Cohen," the man muttered, showing more fear than attitude.

"What are these for?"

"They're screws, for assembly. I work in assembly."

"Why keep them in your pockets?"

"Bad habit, that's all. It's easier to grab them from where you can't drop them on the floor, that's all."

Huntley turned his gaze to the geo-screen and lingered there for a while, thinking. Then he took a screw from each pile and went to the MCC door. He opened it and threw a screw out as far as he could. He looked over his shoulder to the geo-screen. Nothing had changed. Then he threw the other screw. A tiny red dot now showed outside the main cluster centered on top of the MCC, just a few yards away.

He took a chair and sat in front of Cohen, staring at him calmly for a few endless seconds.

"Let me tell you how this is gonna work," he started to say. "I have some questions, and I need answers. I'll only ask once."

The man nodded anxiously.

"Have you heard of Gitmo?"

"I...I...thought it was closed," the man whispered, turning pale and shaking.

"Ha, ha," Huntley laughed. "Don't believe everything you hear on TV. Gitmo's still there. Do you wanna visit?"

"N...no, please, I didn't do anything, I swear." His chin was trembling wildly, signaling he was about to start crying.

"Then tell me, who gave you the screws?"

"It's just screws for assembly, no one, just...I pick them from assembly trays, that's all, I swear...You gotta believe me."

"OK, then, Gitmo it is," Huntley said, then stood up and turned away, ready to leave. "Ben, get a transport ready."

"No, no, please," Cohen pleaded. "I'll tell you everything you wanna know, please..."

Huntley turned around slowly.

"I am not sitting down again unless I hear a reason to in the next three seconds. One," he started counting.

"The screws, the screws, you see, I have to change them," Cohen blurted out.

"What do you mean change them?"

"My line inspects the devices for explosives. I'm at the end of the reassembly line, where we put the device covers back together again. Instead of putting the same screw back again, the one from the battery cover, I pocket it, you see, and then I replace it with one of those," he said, pointing at the pile of screws that generated red dots on the geo-screen.

"That it?"

"Yes, I swear," Cohen pleaded.

"Who gave you the screws? Who put you up to it?"

Cohen turned silent for many seconds, looking at his feet.

Impassible, Huntley shrugged, turned toward Ben, and asked, "Gitmo transport here soon?"

"Just a few minutes out, sir," Ben responded.

"No, no, I'll tell you," Cohen broke his silence. "It was this man; he gave me money."

"Name?"

"He didn't say. I swear he didn't."

Huntley waved dismissively and turned to leave. Cohen started sobbing.

"I swear I don't know, I really don't."

"How much money?"

"Twenty grand, that's all. And twenty more when the job was done. Please...I work a whole year to make that much money...I didn't see anything wrong with it, really. A screw is a screw...they're not explosive, these screws, I checked. Oh, God...I thought it was gonna be OK. What's a screw gonna do?"

...Chapter 94: Off the Books
...Tuesday, October 11, 11:43PM Local Time (UTC+3:00 hours)
...IDF 68 Operational Training Camp
...East of Tel Aviv, Israel

It was hard to get Daniel Krumholz tired, but this came fairly close to what he would call squeezed dry. He had just finished an exhausting weeklong training program with the Special Operations Aviation Group. He had managed to catch almost four hours of sleep before a phone call woke him and recalled him for another assignment. He returned immediately to the Operational Training Camp, this time as an instructor.

He rubbed his forehead in an effort to alleviate his debilitating fatigue and focus on the young agents lined up in front of him in the brisk night air. They deserved better than his exhaustion, no matter how justifiable. He took a deep, sharp breath and focused on his trainees. He saw in their eyes determination, passion, loyalty, and commitment. A good team.

Daniel remembered himself at that stage in life, when he had left his battalion and had chosen to embrace Mossad's demanding career path. He had never looked back since that day. He had chosen to lead a life of service to his country, continuous, devoted, all-sacrificing service to his native Israel. He was proud of each minute spent doing his duty. This heartfelt choice and his talent as a Mossad operative had brought him recognition and advancement in the ranks of the toughest intelligence agency in the world. The speed and effectiveness he demonstrated in delivering his assigned missions had positioned him to be selected for the ranks of Kidon, Mossad's elite, ultra-secret group of operatives. Shortly after that, he was leading his own Kidon team. That was a challenging responsibility, considering how the global environment was evolving. The pressure was on all Mossad agents to be at their very best, increase their activity levels, and join the rest of the world in a joint effort to maintain peace and combat terrorism.

His radio came to life, some static preceding the communication.

"Base to Tango 4, Base to Tango 4, do you read?"

He unclipped the radio from his belt.

"Read you clear, Base, go ahead."

"Base to Tango 4, please confirm position. Over."

"Base, this is Tango 4. At the kill house, over."

"Base to Tango 4. Courier en route. Meet at the Barracks in five, over."

"Base, this is Tango 4. On my way. Over."

This was beyond strange. Confirmation of position during a night shooting drill was an unlikely event, and a courier at this hour was completely unheard of. Such things just didn't happen. Curious about the identity and the urgent message of this unprecedented midnight courier, he started on his way toward the Barracks, code name for the command post mockup.

He needed about three and a half minutes to reach the Barracks; he was good on time. He stopped briefly near a tree, took out a cigarette, and put it in his mouth. He didn't light it though. Although he was safe in the middle of the training camp, he instinctively followed combat rules and preferred to preserve his night vision and stealth instead of lighting up. It was the way he operated; wait in the shadows—unseen, unheard—and be ready.

After a short wait in the complete darkness surrounding the Barracks, two sets of headlights started tearing through the blackness. Two Sand Cat light-armored vehicles approached fast, in close formation, wearing no insignia and no distinctive markings. The way the two drivers moved their vehicles on the unfriendly terrain, the way they stopped after sharp turns in opposite directions, to offer each other maximum cover and be able to leave the area on a dime, told Daniel these men were not regular Army. Nope, not even close. Mossad, maybe, or top-notch executive protection. *Impressive*, Daniel thought. *I'd welcome any of these men on my logistics support team.*

The passenger of the first vehicle came forward into the low light, enough for Daniel to recognize Major Dayan, the deputy base commander. He took the unlit cigarette from his mouth and hid it in his pocket before saluting regulation style.

"Daniel," he greeted him, "our guest wants to speak with you."

"Yes, sir," Daniel answered, intrigued.

Major Dayan moved to the side and stood at attention.

Four soldiers in fatigues, keeping their fingers on the triggers of their automated weapons, came out of the vehicles. They took positions to secure the perimeter. The VIP they were escorting appeared right behind them, moving just as fluidly as his men did, maybe a tad slower. Surprised, Daniel recognized Eli Weismann, the prime minister of Israel.

Most Israeli political leaders had military backgrounds; Weismann was no exception. He had served as an armored brigade officer before he'd moved to paratrooper and later to Mossad. That explained the prime minister's gait and familiarity with the training facility. He was one of them.

"Prime minister, sir." Daniel saluted the visitor by the book.

"Good evening, son," the prime minister replied, exchanging a firm and friendly handshake with Daniel.

"Sir, it's an honor," Daniel said.

"Walk with me if you'd like; let's stretch our legs." The prime minister's voice was calm and kind, despite the obvious urgency of the matter bringing him in the dead of the night to their isolated training facility. "Daniel, where are you from?"

"From Haifa, sir."

"At ease, son. We're not at war, not tonight, anyway."

"Yes, sir, but we are ready, sir," Daniel answered.

"I have no doubt. You know, I was with the 35th Paratrooper Brigade back in the day. I put in my share of sweat with Sa'ar Armored Brigade, but my heart will always be with the institute. By the way, do you still have Mr. Benowitz at the library?"

"Yes, sir, but he's close to retirement."

"Sounds about right." Weismann laughed. "Before getting behind that library desk, he was the best tank gunner I served with in all Sa'ar."

"I didn't know that, sir," Daniel said.

They walked silently for a few seconds, escorted closely by Weismann's protection detail.

"I have heard great things about you, things that encourage me to trust you with a mission of critical importance, highly confidential."

"Whatever you need, sir," Daniel answered.

Weismann cleared his throat before speaking.

"A friend of mine, a long-time friend of Israel, needs our help. You will report directly to me and only me. This mission is off the books." He took a smart phone from his pocket and handed it to Daniel. "There's a single contact saved on this phone—one of my direct numbers. There's also an email with instructions. You'll find the details of this assignment in there. Ask for anything and anyone you need, and you got it. Only one thing you can't ask for: time to prepare."

Daniel looked at the prime minister with curiosity.

"Sir?"

"Can you leave tonight?"

"Yes, sir."

"Make me proud, son. Good luck!"

Eli Weismann smiled and shook his hand before climbing back into one of the Sand Cats and disappearing in a cloud of dust.

On the recently acquired phone, Daniel opened the only email message stored in the Inbox and found a list of targets, with their countries of origin and whereabouts.

1. Mastaan Eshwar Singh, 64, India, Barcelona
2. Muhammad Sadiq, 69, Pakistan, Fort Lauderdale / Bahamas
3. Karmal Shah, 61, Afghanistan, Prague
4. Ahmad Babak Javadi, 57, Iran, Zurich
5. Jeevan Ramachandran, 42, India, New Delhi
6. Warren Helms, 52, USA, Unknown
7. Unknown, presumed Russia, Unknown, leader of the above group—identify

Timeframe: 48 hrs. Confirmation req'd on all targets.

He wiped the sweat accumulating on his upper lip with a quick swipe of the back of his right hand. He woke his team with the preset alert message; they'd all be on their flights by sunrise. He assigned most of the names on the list to his team, keeping Sadiq, Helms, and the unknown subject to himself.

Back at his apartment, Daniel pulled the bed from the wall, exposing a small safe. He punched in the code and then sifted through multiple passports and ID cards. He chose a set, then locked everything back up, and pushed the bed back into place. He threw a few clothing items in a small duffel bag and left, turning off the lights and locking the door carefully behind him.

...Chapter 95: Two Objectives
...Monday, October 17, 10:47AM PDT (UTC-7:00 hours)
...Tom Isaac's Residence
...Laguna Beach, California

Alex entered Tom's den, which had turned into a war room for the past year, and smiled at the sight of the crazy wall, where pictures and notes had been pinned and tied together with colorful yarn. The wall wasn't up to date anymore; she needed to fix that. Maybe even tear it down altogether; they were done. From a different perspective though, they weren't done yet.

"Hey, kiddo," Sam greeted her. He sat at the large table, sipping coffee and going through his email.

"Hey," she answered, making her move toward the Keurig machine. She hesitated a bit, then chose hazelnut coffee for her brew.

Tom entered the room, closing the door behind him, and sat right down.

"Next steps?" he asked.

Alex shrugged, frustration showing on her face.

"Technically, we're done." She paced the room, slowly, deep in thought. "It's frustrating to me...this case, the lack of closure. We're done with everything we can do, yet some things are still up in the air. Maybe this damn case has been so complicated that we forgot what we were trying to achieve, and we just need to remind ourselves."

She looked at the two men; they were listening, a little concern showing on Tom's face and an encouraging smile on Sam's.

"We had two main objectives," she continued. "We wanted to ensure that Election Day would take place safely, and, if possible, save Robert Wilton and his wife, get them out of harm's way. I am confident in saying that the Wiltons are safe. We took every precaution, covered every base. But how sure are we with Election Day? We have the software angle covered, and we have the devices secured and cleared. Nothing will blow up on Election Day, and the people will get to choose their next president in peace. So, technically, we should be fine. I just struggle with the lack of certainty, I guess, because we have not identified who was the author of this terror plan, and we have no control over the rest of the people Blake and Clarence identified. Until we control the terrorist and his network, we cannot call ourselves done. That's what bothers me."

"My friends are going to take care of the people we know about," Sam offered.

"Who? Mossad?" Alex asked.

"Yep," Sam confirmed.

"When?" Tom intervened.

"Umm...today, tomorrow, soon, anyway. They're working on that as we speak. They said they were going to handle everyone over the next few days."

The small room fell silent. Everyone knew what that meant when Mossad was involved.

"Can I ask how come we're working with Mossad on this?" Alex asked hesitantly. "We're not CIA; we're not agents of any official government agency. I understood at first, when I assumed you were just asking old friends for small favors, but now?"

"Your assumption is correct," Sam answered. "That's exactly what I'm doing, asking old friends for favors. They're very perceptive people; they understood immediately that an American president controlled by pro-Islamists would not be a friend of Israel. That, and I also believe that Mossad has no interest to put us in jail. Quite the opposite," he said, winking and smiling, satisfied with the solution he had found.

"Brilliant, and reassuring, I guess...But we still don't know who the UNSUB leader is," Alex insisted. "Clarence, Blake Bernard's AML analyst, said he might be Russian. The lower level associations around the known names and locations indicate a Russian connection, but it's someone different almost every time. We might never find out who that Russian is. To me, that only means one thing: he'll try again, who knows where and how, and we'll be clueless, sitting ducks. That can't happen, simply can't. What do we do? What can we do? If we call the feds, all of us here go straight to jail. That hasn't changed."

No one had a clear answer to that question, regardless of how many sleepless nights they had spent thinking about it.

"Sometimes these things aren't as clear cut as we want them to be," Sam said. "Sometimes it takes years to get one of these people off the grid. This is not corporate, where you walk in at the end of the case and fire the bad guys, 'cause they're all right there, with social security numbers on file, addresses, and everything. This is intelligence work, and it could take years before we can really close this case."

"Yeah, I know, we'll all just keep searching," Alex answered her own question. "Mossad will do the same, and someday soon, we'll nail that bastard. I just don't know how we'll be able to feel safe until that happens."

"We won't," Tom confirmed grimly. "We just won't."

...Chapter 96: Tears
...Monday, October 17, 8:14PM Local Time (UTC+2:00 hours)
...Letiště Praha-Kbely Airport—Air Traffic Control, Prague East
...Prague, The Czech Republic

Jaro's shift had ended some fifteen minutes before, but he didn't budge. His favorite plane, the Piaggio, was scheduled to depart in just a little while. Jaro watched through binoculars how the pilots and Mr. Shah were loading some crates, getting ready for departure. He focused entirely on the plane's beautiful shape, its flickering lights in the dark twilight, and the sweet sound of its idling engines, completely missing the man standing on the side of the tarmac, watching closely the very same aircraft.

A little while later, he saw the Piaggio taxi for a minute, then take off elegantly, quickly disappearing into the dark sky, strobes marking its ascending path. A minute later, it exploded in a blaze of fire, sending pieces of burning debris in all directions, like fireworks.

The man on the side of the tarmac took a couple of pictures, then disappeared, unseen and unheard. Jaro's eyes were not seeing clearly, blurred by tears.

...Chapter 97: Early Dinner
...Monday October 17, 5:08PM Local Time (UTC+2:00 hours)
...Hotel Arts Barcelona—Espiritu del Mar Restaurant
...Barcelona, Spain

She watched discreetly as the waiter, dressed in black pants, a white shirt, vest, and white gloves, brought the appetizer tray and started placing the small plates in front of his guest, a few tables in front of her own. The luminous atmosphere of the restaurant, its white furniture complementing the sparkling table linens, brought forward by an entire wall of glass letting in the gentle October light, made Espiritu del Mar a dining place of choice for the hotel's guests. The doors to the patio were open, letting in a gentle breeze, bringing in salty Mediterranean air to spice up the smell of white truffle sauce and raviolis de langosta.

"Will there be anything else, sir?" The waiter chose to phrase his question in English. His guest, one of only two at that early dinnertime, was definitely not Spanish. His dark blue turban suggested he was an Indian Sikh.

"No, I am fine for the moment," the guest responded.

"How about something to drink? Iced tea, sparkling water? A glass of wine?"

"Pellegrino is fine, thank you."

"Right away, sir."

The waiter brought the bottled water and a chilled glass. He opened the bottle in front of his guest and filled his glass three quarters.

"Thank you," the guest said.

The waiter bowed his head in acknowledgment and stepped away, leaving the Indian to enjoy his food. He didn't go far though, moving to attend to her, the only other dinner guest for the early hour.

She was a stunning young woman, very aware of the effect she had on men. She had waves of undulating, shiny, ash brown hair, and she struggled to keep strands away from her beautiful face. Her delicate fingers tucked rebel strands behind her left ear, and she tilted her head slightly every time she did that.

She was dressed in an evening gown, shimmering burgundy silk falling heavy and enhancing every curve of her body. The gown generously revealed her perfect back and showed impressive cleavage, the plunging neckline stopped only an inch above her waistline. Expensive jewelry completed her attire, and her diamond-encrusted envelope purse matched the dark burgundy shade of her dress and the leather of her high-heeled Louboutins.

She didn't need the waiter's services; she waved him away. He disappeared behind the kitchen door, but she didn't pay much attention to that. Instead, she focused on the turban-wearing man having dinner a few tables away, seated with his back toward her.

She checked her surroundings quickly; there was no one else in the cozy dining room. She stood, and the generous thigh slit of her gown revealed her perfect leg, exposed within millimeters of where her panty line should have been. She grabbed her purse and cell and walked toward the ladies room, choosing to pass right by the Indian's table. She texted as she walked, apparently paying little attention to her surroundings.

She bumped into the Indian's right shoulder, causing him to drop his fork on the floor, as her cell took the same route.

"Oh, I am so sorry," she apologized, touching the man's shoulder with feather-light fingers and slightly flexing her left knee. The thigh slit in her gown opened a little, revealing more.

"It's OK," the man said, the flashes of anger sparkling in his eyes disappearing as he took in the beauty of the woman in front of him.

He pushed his chair from the table and leaned down to pick her phone up off the floor. As he started leaning, the woman flexed her knee a little more, right when the man's eyes were inches away from her skin.

He took his time leaning down and grabbing the phone, absorbed by the view. Time enough for her to drop a minuscule pill into his Pellegrino water. The pill dissolved almost instantly.

Phone back in her hand, she gave him a grateful smile, apologized again, and continued her trip to the ladies room. On her way back to her table, she stopped briefly near the Indian, whose head hung, chin against his chest. She snapped a quick picture with her phone's camera. The picture showed Mastaan Singh's face contorted in pain and frozen in death.

...Chapter 98: Conversation
...Tuesday October 18, 10:23AM Local Time (UTC-4:00 hours)
...Bahamas Territorial Waters
...Bahamas

The Sea Ray moved slowly at no wake speed, leaving the Harbour Bay Marina and heading toward the open waters. It had just passed under the Atlantis Bridge, leaving the marina behind and Paradise Island to the right. Then it turned the corner around Paradise Beach and headed north, gently increasing speed. When it was about a mile away from the shore, the Sea Ray stopped and started drifting in the calm currents.

Daniel Krumholz left the steering wheel of the Sea Ray and went below deck. The boat's owner, Muhammad Sadiq, grunted unhappily when he saw Daniel, his grunts barely audible under the duct tape covering his mouth. His hands and feet were tied with white plastic cable ties. He was trying to worm his way toward the door, moving awkwardly without much success.

Daniel kicked him in the shin.

"Stay there," he said. Sadiq fell silent and stopped moving, watching Daniel with fearful eyes.

Daniel opened a small pouch attached to his belt and extracted a short-bladed scalpel. He held it close to Sadiq's face.

"I have a few questions, and you will answer them. If I'm not happy with your answers, I will cut you."

Sadiq nodded. Sweat was beading on his face, and he breathed with difficulty.

"What's with all this money?" Daniel asked, ripping the duct tape off Sadiq's mouth with a quick move and pointing at an open beer cooler loaded to the brim with hundred-dollar bills.

Sadiq didn't answer. He was panting, struggling to catch his breath.

Swiftly, Daniel ran his blade against Sadiq's left arm, leaving a bleeding gash right above the cable ties immobilizing his hands. Sadiq yelped.

"The money? Where's it coming from?"

"Bahamas bank," Sadiq articulated.

"Whose is it?" Daniel asked calmly.

"Mine...all mine," he whispered between shattered breaths. "I am rich...I can make you rich...just say how much," he continued, and then suddenly screamed. Another gash opened right above the first one. He watched with terror in his eyes while his blood flowed freely and dripped into a pool on the floor.

"Whose is it?" Daniel asked again, using the same calm tone of voice.

Sadiq gasped for air a couple of times.

"The council...we all contribute, raise the money."

"Where do you meet?"

"I...I..." Sadiq stuttered, breathing heavily.

Another cut came immediately.

"Aarghh...Greece," he managed to articulate, "we meet in Greece."

"Where in Greece?"

"I don't know...No! Don't! I really don't know; he picks us up by chopper," Sadiq said, not taking his eyes off the scalpel in Daniel's hand.

"Who? Who leads the council?"

"I...I don't know," Sadiq whispered. He screamed again, a long wailing sound of pain and desperation, as Daniel's blade cut deep into his thigh, right above his left knee.

"Who leads the council?" Daniel repeated. He was starting to lose his temper; this was taking too long, especially for a frail man in his seventies.

"V..." the man tried to articulate, gasping for air and choking. "Vi..." he tried again, taking his tied hands to his chest and grasping at the collar of his shirt, as if it were choking him. He gasped one more time, a hoarse, gurgling noise, as his eyes glossed over. His head fell to his chest, and he didn't move anymore.

Daniel checked for the man's pulse. He was dead, gone, taking his secrets with him.

"*Fakakta drek*," he swore in his native language, taking a picture with his cell.

He climbed above deck wearing swim trunks and splashed into the clear waters, executing a nice dive from the Sea Ray's rear platform. He swam all the way back to shore, coming out of the water right next to the Nassau Harbour lighthouse.

A scooter waited for him there. He took a towel out of the scooter's small trunk and wiped his face and hands with it. Reaching inside the trunk again, he found a flip phone and speed-dialed a number without looking. His eyes were on the horizon line, where the Sea Ray's silhouette was barely visible against the hazy sky.

The yacht exploded as Daniel watched. Satisfied, he hopped on the scooter and started toward the city.

Only scattered debris and hundred-dollar bills remained on the water where the Sea Ray had floated, dispersing slowly on the wavy ocean surface.

...Chapter 99: Dangerous Slopes
...Tuesday October 18, 2:41PM Local Time (UTC+2:00 hours)
...Brunni-Alpthal Ski Resort
...Zurich, Switzerland

Ahmad Javadi was not willing to accept age as a reality of life. In fact, he used every opportunity to defy it, to battle it at all cost, hoping to stay and feel young for as long as possible. Although fifty-seven, he had recently rediscovered his long-forgotten passion for skiing. In his youth, he had been addicted to the buzz of high-speed descents on the slopes of Dizin and Alvarez, in his native Iran. With his current business interests placing him in Switzerland for a while, he was making the most of his stay on the slopes, spending at least one day a week taking ski lifts up to the peaks of Dietikon, Genossenschaft Steig-Baretswil, or Brunni, and then gliding on the sparkling snow all the way down to the base.

On a beautiful day for skiing, with clear blue skies bringing pale violet shades to the fresh fallen snow on the peaks and valleys of the Alps, Javadi was already enjoying his third ski lift ride. Flushed from the exertion and adrenaline, fresh air, and chilly temperatures, Javadi hopped off the ski lift chair and headed straight to the slope. He wanted one more run before having to head back to the city, and he didn't have much time left. He went for the long Brunni slope, not the short one, adding a couple hundred meters to the eleven-hundred meters straight Brunni had. He enjoyed taking the side slope: the landscape to his right completely undisturbed, virgin, just mountain ravines and fir trees covered in snow. The difficulty of the slope was also satisfying for the experienced skier, giving him the opportunity for high-speed turns and a little more excitement.

Javadi started his descent without delay, pushing hard into his poles to gain momentum fast. He soon left the crowds behind as he took to the right, leaving the main slope and taking the side one. Behind him, unseen and unheard, another skier was catching up fast. The skier, dressed in a white ski suit, was very hard to see against the fresh snow.

Once close enough to Javadi, the skier controlled his speed of descent, giving Javadi the time to get near the curve of the slope, where the descending ski trail came within a foot of the deep ravine. This risky portion of descent was the reason why the long Brunni was marked a triple black diamond, the highest difficulty rating for ski slopes. The three diamonds meant the slope was narrow at times, fast descending, and presented hazardous challenges. The long

Brunni challenged its daring skiers with trees, side winds, and the deep crevasse Javadi was preparing to approach. His turn had to be perfect, or else he'd run into a tree on his left, or dive into the chasm opening at his right.

Focused on calculating his turn, Javadi didn't notice the other skier catching up with him on the inside. When almost parallel with him, the skier shoved Javadi toward the crevasse with a quick push against his upper arm. Javadi flailed, tried to recover his lost balance, and then went over the edge screaming. The mountains generously returned his screams in echoes, multiplied, amplified, screeching against the serene silence only disturbed by the wind whooshing against majestic fir trees.

The skier in white stopped and looked down into the chasm opening next to him. Splayed at the bottom, Javadi was not moving, and a pool of blood stained the snow near his head, spreading rapidly. The skier took a picture with his phone and then resumed his rapid descent. If he hurried, he could still make the 6:15PM flight back home.

...Chapter 100: A Snake
...Wednesday, October 19, 8:51AM Local Time (UTC+5:30 hours)
...Jeevan Ramachandran's Residence
...New Delhi, India

Jeevan Ramachandran was running late. It was one of those mornings where he couldn't find anything he looked for. He wasted a few more minutes trying to find his car keys, then finally left his house, slamming the door behind him. He was running twenty or so minutes later than he had intended, although he was rarely pressed for time. As CEO of ERamSys, he could very well come and go as he pleased, but the signing of a software outsourcing contract worth millions with a new American client was one of the very few occasions that demanded timeliness.

He climbed behind the wheel of his black Cadillac Escalade, parked right outside his house. He started the engine without wasting any more time, and shortly he was driving on the freeway, heading for the office. He pushed the pedal to the metal, trying to compensate for the delay in his departure, honking and swerving constantly around slower traffic.

Concentrated on his demanding maneuvers, he didn't hear anything. He only felt a slight tickle on his right ankle, and when he looked down to see what it was, the sight froze the blood in his veins. A large king cobra slithered on the car floor around his legs, holding its terrifying head slightly elevated.

He didn't think; he just reacted. He slammed on the brakes, but the large snake interpreted his sudden move as a sign of aggression. The cobra elevated its head farther, expanded its hood, and attacked, sinking its teeth deep into Ramachandran's right thigh. He screamed, swerved erratically, and came to a full stop after hitting a pole.

The pain he felt in his thigh spread quickly as the neurotoxin in the snake's venom made its way through his blood stream. Soon he was paralyzed, in agonizing pain yet without being able to move or make a sound.

A man on a motorcycle slowed as he drove by, taking a good couple of seconds to look at the victim through the car's window. He took a picture and then accelerated and disappeared into the heavy morning traffic.

...Chapter 101: Unfinished
...Friday, October 28, 6:09PM PDT (UTC-7:00 hours)
...Tom Isaac's Residence
...Laguna Beach, California

They ate quietly, the only noises being the clinking of cutlery on plates, the occasional request to pass the salt, or the filling of a glass.

"We're awfully quiet today," Alex stated the obvious. "Normally I'd blame it on the excellent food, but this time it feels different."

"Oh, are you saying the food is not that great?" Tom asked.

"Oh, no, quite the opposite," Alex reassured him. "It just feels different. When we get together to celebrate the end of a case we're more lively than this," she explained, turning toward Robert Wilton and Sam, both attending such dinner celebrations for the first time.

"I think this is great," Robert commented, pointing at his half-emptied plate.

The skirt steak, grilled with buttered Portabella mushrooms and served with Claire's signature mashed potatoes, was excellent.

"Absolutely agree," Sam said, raising his bottle of beer toward Tom.

Steve observed quietly, not interrupting the dialogue. Brian, at his side, was finishing his steak. Lou had finished his meal altogether, after wolfing down the steak in a few large bites.

"Alex, can I get you anything else to drink?" Claire asked. "I see you're holding an empty glass."

"Yes, Claire, please. I would love another angry mojito. They're really good."

"I'll make that," Tom offered. "Always leave work assignments to the highest qualified workforce, right?" Everyone chuckled. "What else can I bring you? Robert, another beer?"

"Sure, why not?"

"Me too," Sam said.

"Me three," Brian joked.

"All right, full round of drinks coming right up."

He came back shortly, as everyone was finishing up.

"I think I know what it is," Alex said, "with our silence. The case we're celebrating, it's closed but not quite, and I think this bothers you all just as much as it bothers me."

"You have a point there, kiddo," Sam said. "But we have, in fact, fulfilled our mission."

Steve lit a cigar and leaned back more comfortably in his chair.

"Have we, really?" Alex asked. "Yes, we prevented a disaster of immense proportions by thwarting a plan to steal our elections. Never before has a terrorist organization planned to decide our next American president somewhere outside our borders. Yes, we countered that plan. We have achieved that. We have also prevented the multi-point terrorist attacks scheduled to happen at some point in the future. We, all of us here, have restored the integrity and safety of our Election Day and election process. And your friends," she said, pointing at Sam, "took care of the bad guys. Even better, none of us are in jail. Yet."

She paused, allowing time for anyone who wanted to interject, but no one did. "This is all the good stuff. But I still don't know who X is. We still don't know who the leader, the architect of this plan was. You have to give it to him; it was a great plan. It almost worked. It took Robert's solid conscience combined with sheer luck to get us to find out this much about them and reclaim the integrity of our elections process." She stopped talking, deep in thought, her fork stuck in mid-air.

"We got lucky this time, but let's face it," she continued, "this X has thought up a plan that has greatness in it, boldness. He has some serious cojones, this guy. X is smart, calculated, a brilliant orchestrator able to forge a global game of immense reach with laser precision. It bothers me that he's still out there, planning his next move. We think we won, but in fact, the devil's move is next. The game is still on, and it will be on until we catch X, or whatever we want to call him. And what exactly do we know about him?"

"We do know a little more than before. We know for sure he's Russian, and his nickname is V, or that's his initial. We know last time the group met in Greece, somewhere within a half hour by chopper from Thessaloniki. That's the extent of what we know, unfortunately," Sam said.

"Not nearly enough to call the case done," Alex said bitterly. "I know you said that some of these cases take a long time to really close, but I'm not a spy, Sam, I don't have your patience. I want the bastard to hang now. I wanna know who he is. I wanna look him straight in the eye while we take him down."

"Spies aren't patient by choice, kiddo. They're patient by need. This is the game we have to play. It's covert, all smoke and mirrors, and you have to wait, wait like a spider who weaves its web and waits. Sooner or later it will work if the web is woven well. We're working on that, right, kiddo? So take it easy, 'cause this anger I sense brewing inside you will only get you to screw up. Only a cool-headed agent is able to interpret information accurately. A hot-headed, frustrated one will get emotional and then get killed."

"I'm not an agent," Alex said, and to her own surprise, with sadness in her voice. "I am not spy material."

"Yes, you are," Sam countered, "and a darn good one. If I weren't retired I'd try to recruit you for the CIA right now."

"Don't you dare," Tom said, "she's all mine."

Steve chuckled.

"Sorry, Sam," Alex joked. "Tom pays way better than the government."

They all burst into laughter.

"Alex," Robert said as soon as the laughter subsided a little, "you might not be happy with the outcome of this case, but you protected us, my wife and me, and we're both very grateful to all of you. You and your terrific team saved our lives."

Alex nodded, accepting the compliment, but her bitterness remained. "Helms is still out there, chased by the Israelis. Your lives might still be at risk. Robert, be very careful. Helms is still in the wind, so even that's not closed yet. And we might still go to jail over this, at some point in our lives, you know."

"Sure, but something tells me we won't," Sam reassured her. "This is not how such things are handled. No one wants this kind of story to make it out to the public, so they wouldn't risk it at this point, even if they somehow learned about it. It would make the responsible agencies seem like they're asleep at the wheel, right? No one has any interest whatsoever in blowing this thing wide open now, or at any time in the future. Plus, we did nail us some fairly big terrorists, right? That should buy us some slack with law enforcement agencies."

Lou nodded vigorously. "Yep, yep," he whispered.

"I agree," Steve said, his first words in the entire evening.

"Well, I might have to disagree, unfortunately," Robert said. "I had to inform my boss, the main shareholder of DCBI. A few days ago, I brought him up to speed and offered my resignation. He wants me to stay until after Election Day and fully oversee this engagement, but afterward I'm out. Early retirement I would call it, if everything else were OK. However, at that time Campbell might want to hold me accountable for what I have done. I could go to prison for the rest of my life, or be executed for treason. God only knows."

Alex looked at Tom, who nodded almost imperceptibly.

"Umm...not really," she said. "During the course of our investigation we have ascertained that Melanie's heart failure was induced through prolonged and carefully timed exposure to certain drug mixes. She was poisoned. Her heart failure was induced, Robert. Not to mention a DUI doesn't automatically disqualify heart transplant candidates. We've checked. You were set up. You are not a traitor; you are a victim. Melanie is a victim too." Alex looked at everyone around the table. "And we're willing to testify to that."

"Yep," Sam confirmed.

Tom raised his glass toward Robert and smiled with kindness.

Tears flowed freely on Robert's cheeks. He covered his mouth with his hands, trying to control his emotions.

"Oh, my God," he whispered, swallowing his sobs. "Oh, my God."

Steve put his hand on Robert's shoulder, comforting him. "It will all be OK, you'll see. Everything will turn out just fine," he said in a soft, reassuring voice.

Robert wiped his tears with his hands and cleared his throat. "Umm...by the way, Campbell gave me this," he said, taking an envelope from his pocket and handing it to Tom, "to give to you, the leader of the organization that helped DCBI and me. I didn't tell him anything more, not your name, not anything."

Tom took the envelope and studied it silently, with a frown on his forehead.

"Maybe this is where he tells us we have ten days to run to a non-extradition country, or else we're gonna get canned," Brian joked.

"Ah, shut up, you," Tom laughed. "Let's see." He opened the envelope and took out the contents. "OK, so there's a note that says, quite cryptically, 'Thank you. You know what for,' and there's a money order for one-million dollars. See? All good stuff!"

They cheered, a welcome wave of relief inundating them.

Steve's laughter covered everyone else's.

"There goes our opportunity," he said, "our once-in-a-lifetime opportunity to be heroes, true patriots, people who sacrifice, risk, and endure for their country. We're back to being mercenaries again, just like we normally are."

Silence dropped heavy among them. Tom looked at everyone carefully, silently asking for their approval. Somehow, they all knew what he intended, and they all agreed.

"Nope, it doesn't," Tom replied. "Lou, why don't you take this and compensate your...umm...hacker friends, the ones who wrote the new software for us?"

"Sir, that's a lot of coin for a week's worth of work," Lou said.

"It's the value that should be rewarded, not the time," Tom pushed back. "And Lou?"

"Yes, sir?"

"Stop calling me sir, already!"

...Chapter 102: Retirement
...Friday, October 28, 10:17PM EDT (UTC-4:00 hours)
...Evening News at Ten
...Nationally Syndicated

"In other news tonight," the anchor said, starting the final segment of the newscast, "Russian President Piotr Abramovich has announced in a Kremlin press conference today the retirement of Minister of Defense Mikhail Nikolaev Dimitrov. Dimitrov has led the Russian office for almost seven years, and he was considered a moderate, appreciated for his balanced, non-military approach to resolving crises. Dimitrov is also a long-time personal friend of Abramovich, dating to their early careers in the KGB, where they served together in the same foreign intelligence unit. This could maybe explain why the Russian president himself held the press conference to announce Dimitrov's resignation. President Abramovich stated that Dimitrov resigned for personal and health reasons and wished him all the best in his retirement."

The anchor paused a little and changed his pitch slightly as he continued.

"Analysts are saying that being a moderate and the recent frictions between him and the president are the real reasons behind the defense minister's resignation. A successor has not yet been named, but it is expected to be one of the old guard generals, more aligned with President Abramovich's hard-line policy toward the West."

The anchor set down his papers, then continued. "Moving on to coast-to-coast weather, with our very own meteorologist, Dylan McPherson."

...Chapter 103: House Guest
...Friday, October 28, 10:48PM PDT (UTC-7:00 hours)
...Alex Hoffmann's Residence
...San Diego, California

She unlocked the door, happy to be home and looking forward to a nightcap at the end of a long, emotionally draining day. Yes, a martini straight up would do it; the strong taste of undiluted vermouth on ice would definitely help her sort through her mixed thoughts.

She kicked her shoes off and entered her living room. She turned on the light and froze. A man was sitting on her couch, a handgun on the coffee table in front of him. He looked somewhat familiar. At first, she couldn't figure out who the stranger was; then she remembered the sketch she had seen.

"Miss Hoffmann, I presume?"

"Helms...You're Warren Helms, right?"

"I prefer Mr. Helms, if that's all right with you," the man said politely, as if they were just introduced in a social situation.

"Sure, I apologize," she reacted. The slight buzz from her earlier mojitos was all gone, her brain in high gear. How the hell was Mossad looking for this guy, when he was right there, installed comfortably in her living room? How the hell did they miss it?

"Ah, polite...That is refreshing," Helms said.

Alex stood a few feet away from the coffee table, not sure what to do. Her phone was in her pocket, but she doubted Helms would allow her to use it. She decided to engage him, ignoring her trembling knees that were urging her to run.

"What can I do for you, Mr. Helms?"

"You can tell me who you are, Miss Hoffmann. Who are you? How did you get involved in this?"

"I don't understand what you mean," she tried to deflect.

"You know, we're both going to die, Miss Hoffmann. You will die here, today, by my hand. That is a fact. I will probably follow at some time in the future, although I intend to postpone that event as long as I can. Therefore, you can tell me. Who are you?"

"Just someone who can't take your kind of bullshit and be indifferent, I guess," she answered, regaining her self-confidence. *The hell with it*, she thought. "I'm actually happy you found me, relieved to be exact. I knew you were coming, and I was getting tired of looking over my shoulder."

"Happy to oblige," Helms said coldly. "I am glad to finally make your acquaintance. You see, there are only two people in this world who caused me grief in the past few months. You are one of them, and we're going to end that today. The other one is Krassner, and I'll deal with him next week. But let's get back to you. I am glad you saw me coming. You have clear expectations, I take it."

She stood quietly, holding his gaze.

"This is good," Helms continued. "Who pays you?"

"I'll be happy to answer that if you tell me who pays *you*."

Fast and unexpected, Helms rose from the couch and slapped her hard across the face, throwing her off balance. She hit the side of the coffee table with her left shoulder and landed hard on the carpet, face down. Her head throbbed, and tears burned her eyes.

"This is not how this works," Helms said quietly, sitting back down on the couch. His voice was a whisper, almost soft, conveying a level-toned sequence of short phrases, separated by silence in between. It had a silent staccato rhythm, underlying his point. The effect was threatening. "I ask. You answer. Or you get hurt. A lot. Before you die."

He watched her trying to pick herself up from the floor, using just her right arm for support. "The die part is a fact we cannot change, but it can come slowly or quickly. It's entirely up to you. Please don't get to the point where you have to beg for your death. It's just such a bad experience."

She groaned and started crawling on the floor, approaching the coffee table. She turned slightly to her left and leaned on the coffee table with her left hand, grabbing the edge for support and letting out inarticulate whimpers of pain. She watched Helms waiting for her to get up, but she let herself fall back on the floor instead, almost on her back, in parallel with the coffee table. Unseen, her right had reached under it and grabbed the small pistol she had taped under there. Without hesitation and without squinting she pulled the trigger twice. The bullets hit Helms in the chest, tightly grouped. She watched Helms as life left his body, still pointing the gun at him.

"Bang means the bad guy is down. Yes, I want to see that happening," she mumbled, picking herself up from the floor.

She took her encrypted cell out of her pocket and called Tom.

"Hey, sorry to call so late, but I found Helms."

"Where is he?" Tom asked.

"In my living room, staining my damn carpet. The couch is a write-off too."

...Chapter 104: Voting Day
...Tuesday, November 8, 8:07AM PST (UTC-8:00 hours)
...Carmel Valley Recreational Center—Polling Precinct
...San Diego, California

Alex entered the polling precinct and went straight for the registration desk, presenting her driver's license and voter registration card. An absent-minded woman in her fifties checked her ID and let her go through to the booths. She waited for a minute or so for one to become available, a strong sense of excitement making her smile widely. The Agency had made this Election Day possible.

Alex entered the booth and closed the curtain behind her. She touched the upper left corner of the voting tablet, holding her finger in place for a few seconds. A screen prompting for a username and password opened up. Lou's hacker friends had built a backdoor into the software, to allow access to the admin level, control panel, where they could see the statistics. She entered her credentials to gain access and checked the application's performance. Stats were great; the application was running smoothly, not a trace of malware, external attack, or anything of that nature. Satisfied, she exited the admin control panel and cast her vote.

A few minutes later, she exited the polling precinct, smiling just as widely as she had on her way in. Steve was waiting for her, leaning against a side wall. She grabbed his arm in a side-hug and kissed his cheek.

"So, who do you think is gonna win?" Steve asked.

"I don't know, but it's gonna be whoever *they* choose," Alex said, gesturing toward the people coming in and out of the polling precinct. "And *that* just makes it all worthwhile, wouldn't you agree?"

"Absolutely agree," he replied, not letting go of her as they walked toward his car. "What next?"

She looked straight into his blue eyes and considered her options for a second. It was time for a leap of faith.

"How's St. Thomas this time of year?" she asked.

"Always perfect," Steve answered, unable to hide the surprise in his voice.

"Wanna keep me company?"

"I'll book us on the earliest flight."

"Ahh...don't bother," she laughed, as she opened the door to his matte black M6. "I happen to have a good friend with a private jet. I might as well take advantage, don't you think? We can leave as soon as you're ready."

"I'm ready anytime you like," Steve said, "but we won't be able to stay too long. We have to be back by Sunday evening. We should probably fly straight to New York City when we come back."

"Why's that?" Alex pouted.

"We have a new client. You do, to be precise. We're meeting with the Board of Directors on Monday morning, 9AM, on Wall Street."

~~~ The End ~~~

Read on for an excerpt from

THE BACKUP ASSET

Alex Hoffmann Series Book Three

\~\~\~\~\~\~\~\~

Thank You!

A big, heartfelt thank you for choosing to read my book. If you enjoyed it, please take a moment to leave me a five-star review; I would be very grateful. It doesn't need to be more than a couple of words, and it makes a huge difference. This is your shortcut: http://bit.ly/DevilsMoveReview

Did you enjoy Alex Hoffmann and her team? Your thoughts and feedback are very valuable to me. Please contact me directly through one of the channels listed below. Email works best: LW@WolfeNovels.com.

Connect with Me

- Email: LW@WolfeNovels.com
- Twitter: @WolfeNovels
- Facebook: https://www.facebook.com/wolfenovels
- LinkedIn: https://www.linkedin.com/in/wolfenovels
- Web: www.WolfeNovels.com

BOOKS BY LESLIE WOLFE

SELF-STANDING NOVELS

Las Vegas Girl
Stories Untold

TESS WINNETT SERIES

Dawn Girl
The Watson Girl
Glimpse of Death

ALEX HOFFMANN SERIES

Executive
Devil's Move
The Backup Asset
The Ghost Pattern
Operation Sunset

The Backup Asset

LESLIE WOLFE

***** PREVIEW *****

...Chapter 1: Ready
...Undisclosed Date, 4:39PM EST (UTC-5:00 hours)
...Undisclosed Location
...Norfolk, Virginia

He stared at the back of his hands in disbelief. They were shaking so hard it made for a difficult task to get another taste of coffee. Using both hands, he grabbed the mug and took a sip of steaming liquid, warming his frozen hands on contact with the white glazed ceramic. He smiled a little, as his eyes focused in passing on the message written in red lettering on the side of the mug. A gift from his coworkers, it read, "I do math well, what's your excuse?" How appropriate, he thought, I don't do this very well, and I need to get better at it. Grow a pair, for Christ's sake, he admonished himself, giving his trembling hands another disgusted glance.

He made an effort to set the mug on his desk without spilling any coffee, but that didn't work as planned. His hands were shaking too much. A few droplets stained the scattered papers on his desk, most of which bore the stamp TOP SECRET.

"Shit," he muttered, under his breath, and rushed to get some Kleenex.

He patted the papers dry, cleared his desk of everything else, and spread the top-secret files on the glossy surface, carefully going through every piece of paper. He finished sorting through each piece of documentation; then paced his office anxiously for a couple of minutes, clasping his hands together, trying to steady himself. Can't back down now, he thought, and I wouldn't even if I could.

He looked up at the digital weather station hanging on his office wall. His rank within the organization gave him the privilege of a private office, decorated to his taste. Hanging close to the large window overlooking Norfolk Harbor, the device told the time and the weather. It displayed the forecast, showing the high and low temperatures expected, indoor temperature, humidity, and also showed barometric pressure as a yellow chart. In the middle section of its display, a small graphic depicted the sun peeking from behind some clouds, all drawn in blue. It was going to be a nice day, with partly cloudy skies, barometric pressure steady, and reasonable temperatures for the season. None of that mattered, though. He had less than three hours to make the drop, and he wasn't ready yet.

He refocused and wiped his sweaty hands nervously against his suit pants.

"Let's get this done and over with," he mumbled, removing all papers from his desk except a single pile he had just put together. He spread out the contents of the pile and started organizing the documents in order, placing them facedown in an unmarked manila folder.

The first document was an evaluation memorandum regarding the compatibility and readiness status for laser cannon installation aboard USS Fletcher, DDG1005, a Zumwalt-class destroyer. Marked TOP SECRET. It was several pages long, and he made sure he had them all and in the right order.

The second document was a capabilities assessment for Zumwalt-class destroyers, complete with technical specifications, class overview, and general characteristics, including weapons array, sensing technology, and vessel performance. Marked SECRET. Nine pages long.

The third document was a performance and capabilities assessment for the laser cannon itself, the most recent and groundbreaking technology developed for the US Navy, the successful and eagerly awaited result of seven years and $570 million worth of research and development. Marked COMPARTMENTED—ABOVE TOP SECRET.

Satisfied, he turned the carefully constructed pile of documents face up and closed the folder.

He was ready for the drop.

...Chapter 2: The Report
...Tuesday, February 16, 10:23AM EST (UTC-5:00 hours)
...Central Intelligence Agency (CIA) Headquarters, Director Seiden's Office
...Langley, Virginia

Henrietta Marino came a few minutes early for her 10.30AM appointment with Director Seiden. His assistant, a sharp-looking young man in his thirties, barely made eye contact with her before asking her to take a seat and wait.

She didn't follow that invitation. She stood, pacing slowly, feeling uneasy and awkward in her professional attire, and checking her image in the pale reflection of the stainless steel door leading to the restricted communications area. She straightened her back, trying to project the confidence expected of an analyst if she wanted anyone to take her seriously. There was no way she could improve her average, almost plain looks, her dark brown hair tied in a ponytail, or her freckled complexion, but at least she could project some confidence.

Henrietta Marino, Henri for short, was a senior analyst with the CIA's Directorate of Intelligence—Russian and European Analysis. Thirty-five years old, she held a master's degree in political science, and had a twelve-year record of accomplishment as an analyst for the CIA.

For the past eight years, her work had focused on Russia, Russian affairs, and the repositioning of Russia on the world power scale. She understood the Russians really well, or at least she hoped she did.

Her latest report illustrated Russia's concerted effort to reinvigorate its nuclear stance, unprecedented since START I in 1991. The signing of START I, the first Strategic Arms Reduction Treaty, by the United States and the USSR, had marked a historic moment. The USSR was still a federation back then, but the treaty encompassed all former Soviet republics and remained in effect after the federation dissolved.

START I, and later START II, limited the number of nuclear warheads and intercontinental ballistic missiles, or ICBMs, on both sides and mapped the road to arsenal reductions. It marked the beginning of a new era, where peace was becoming a possibility. It marked the end of the Cold War.

Henri had anticipated her report would cause some turmoil, being the first report ever to document and argue the rekindling of the arms race, the first of its kind in fifteen years. Within minutes after she had filed it, her phone had started ringing. Colleagues asked her if she was sure. Her boss followed suit immediately and grilled her for an hour on the report facts. Even the CIA's general counsel, whom she'd never met, reached out and asked if she knew what that report meant. He also encouraged her to withdraw it if she wasn't 100 percent sure. Finally, Seiden's chief of staff asked her for more details and her degree of confidence. Now Seiden wanted to see her.

At first, her confidence had been high, the full 100 percent everyone expected from an analyst of her seniority. However, after so many confidence-eroding phone calls and meetings, she wasn't that sure anymore. Still, she knew not many people were able to spot patterns as she could. She had the ability to identify patterns from the fifth data point, in some cases even from the third. It didn't matter what she was analyzing. People's behavior, global events, communication, actions, legislation, she was able to pinpoint immediately what her data points had in common and project a trend based on her observations. Her ability to predict the evolution of the Islamic State of Iraq and the Levant, infamously known to the world as ISIL, although she had never worked in the Middle East Analysis Group, had brought her the promotion to senior analyst. That, of course, had happened only after everyone stopped thinking she was crazy and started seeing her point. She wondered if the same people were thinking she was crazy this time too. She wondered how long it would last.

"You can go in now." Seiden's assistant made eye contact for more than a second, making sure she went straight in.

She took in a deep breath, straightened her back one more time, and walked through the door displaying as much confidence as she could.

Director Seiden sat behind a monumental desk, reading from a report, most likely hers. Heavily built, wearing the frame of a former athlete or weightlifter, Director Seiden looked intimidating in his charcoal suit, white shirt, and loosened silver tie. In his sixties, the director had a receding hairline showing a tall forehead and permanent frown lines. His role, most likely one of the most stressful leadership roles in the US government, must have given him plenty of reasons to frown throughout the years, carving those deep lines in permanent testimony of who knows what crises he had dealt with.

Bushy salt-and-pepper eyebrows shaded his eyes. He focused intently on his reading material, while his right hand absently touched his teacup, probably considering another taste of Earl Grey.

Henri hadn't interacted with Director Seiden that often. Such a visit was an exceptional occurrence, considering there were three levels of leadership between her pay grade and his. She felt anticipation anxiety creep up on her. She wanted to make a good impression, and she only had one shot at it.

"Sir," she said, after clearing her throat, turned dry and scratchy all of a sudden.

"Take a seat," Seiden said, not lifting his eyes from the pages.

She sat in one of the large leather chairs in front of Seiden's desk, careful to not make a sound and break the director's concentration.

"Interesting theory you have here," he said, finally looking at her. "How sure are you?"

For some reason, Henri instantly forgot her carefully rehearsed exposé and blurted out unfiltered thoughts.

"I was very sure when I put that report together, but now I don't know anymore. Everyone doubts me, questions my judgment. I hope I'm right. I thought I was."

She cringed hearing her own words. She sounded like an insecure child presenting her math homework and still somehow questioning whether two plus two equaled four.

"Are you a leader, or a follower, Ms. Marino?"

"Umm...I aim to be a leader, sir."

"Then you shouldn't let your self-confidence drop because people are asking questions. It's their right. But you do have a brain of your own, right?" Seiden's voice was almost encouraging. He wasn't smiling or anything, but Henri didn't sense any disappointment or anger in his voice.

"Yes, sir," she acknowledged, aware she was blushing.

"Let's try again. How sure are you, Ms. Marino?"

"It's Henri, sir." She blushed a little more. Maybe offering her first name was inappropriate? She had no idea, but she was going to worry about that later. She was clumsy with people, always had been. "Yes, very sure."

"On what basis?"

"I have profiled President Abramovich. His detailed profile is on page five, I think. That profile, combined with several actions he's taking, all listed in the summary section of the report, led me to believe he is preparing for war, or for a renewed arms race, at least."

"I can read, you know," Seiden said, tapping his fingers on the report cover. "What can you tell me that isn't in the report?"

"Sorry, sir. Yes, well, Abramovich is a pure sociopath, of the worst kind possible. He's a malignant narcissistic sociopath, who would kill millions over his bruised ego. I started my report from that evaluation and from analyzing several actions the Russians have recently taken. They correlate really well; they form a pattern that spells arms race to me, possibly even changes in Russia's form of government."

"How so?" Seiden took his reading glasses off and massaged the bridge of his nose with the tips of his fingers.

"His entire background speaks to that. He was KGB. No, even worse, he was political KGB. He was a KGB general during Mikhail Gorbachev's reign at the Kremlin, but Abramovich's contempt for Gorbachev was common knowledge. He hated Gorbachev for his glasnost and perestroika, for his pro-West attitude and his willingness to end communism in Russia and bring freedom to the Russian people. Abramovich climbed to power under the self-proclaimed mission to restore Russia's greatness, and he started working on that since his first day as president of Russia, in the typical manner of a sociopath."

"Meaning?"

"Meaning his actions are disrespectful of anyone else's values, human rights, or the law, for that matter. He is the most dangerous kind of sociopath one can imagine. Absolutely no conscience, no scruples whatsoever, combined with holding the supreme power in a powerful country. After all, when did President Abramovich start being on everyone's mind again?"

Seiden didn't answer; just continued looking at her, waiting for her to resume her analysis. He'd probably heard these things before and had no interest in dwelling on them, nor cared to play question–and-answer games with her.

"Right," she continued. "He invaded Crimea, because he needed faster access to the Black Sea, a waterway shortcut. He didn't care that it was in a different country; he just annexed Crimea, erasing the border that stood in his path. Nothing mattered to him, not even another country's sovereignty. Then what happened? We applied sanctions. Abramovich, whose ego knows no limit, found the sanctions insulting. He fought back with his own sanctions, but he's hurting. Along with him, his financial backers are struggling. The Russian oligarchs, who paid him immense bribes in exchange for favorable legislation and the unofficial permission to do whatever they pleased, now are facing bankruptcies and are demanding action. His personal cash flow has almost dried up. That's why President Abramovich doesn't want the sanctions lifted anymore. He wants much more than that. He wants revenge; he wants blood. He wants us to pay for his bruised ego and tarnished image."

"Interesting," Seiden said, "but not all that new. What else do you see?"

"Several other things that correlate. The Russian people like him a lot. They, too, are sick and tired of poverty and uncertainty. Their support for him has created a unique circumstance that allowed him to start on the road of becoming a dictator, to remain in power until he draws his last breath."

"How come?" Seiden's interest was piqued.

"Well, after Russia became so-called 'free' from communism," she said, making quotation marks with her fingers in the air, "one of the first legislative changes was the amending of the Constitution, limiting the number of consecutive presidential terms to two, just like we have here in the States. The first few terms were four years long, until 2012. Then, they amended the Constitution to make them six years long, all during Abramovich's tenure at the Kremlin. Once his first two terms were consumed, no one thought he would be coming back to lead the country, but he did. He was elected again after a short hiatus, the single-term intermission required to satisfy the Constitution limiting him to two consecutive mandates. Very soon after he returned as reelected president, the Constitution was amended again, extending, as I said, the terms to six years. With these changes in place, he already had twelve years ahead of him, during which time many things could happen. That might include, I am postulating, another amendment to the Constitution, opening the door for more consecutive terms. Because he is well supported by the desperate Russian people in search for stability and sustainability, that amendment will be easy to vote in. This is how I see him paving the road to dictatorship."

She stopped talking, swallowing with difficulty. She was painfully aware she spoke too much and too fast.

Seiden whistled and leaned back in his chair, interlocking his fingers behind his head.

"You definitely have my attention now, Henri. Why an arms race though?"

"In the past year and a half, several incidents involving the Russian military took place around Europe and even here, in North America. Forty-seven, to be exact. Near misses, some might call them, or provocative, as others have labeled them, nevertheless they are quite a few. Way too many to be slipups, mistakes, or random acts. These data points form clusters. My analysis isn't finished yet on these specific actions, though."

"Yet you filed a report?" Seiden frowned, the lines on his forehead becoming more visible.

"My report is focused on Russia's nuclear stance, and I've finalized that part of the analysis. I was just giving you conjuncture."

"I see. Then let's talk nuclear threat."

"Well, going back to the forty-seven incidents I mentioned, and how apparently random they were, well, I am positive they're not. I will finish the analysis on those events and substantiate my point. But keeping those so-called random incidents in mind, I will now list nuclear-related, apparently random events that took place in the past few months. A cleanup and restoration operation of their ICBM sites, in no particular order, took place during the past few months. Satellite shows it clearly; they've dusted off the majority of their ICBM sites, even some we didn't know existed. Our satellites tracked the cleaning crews once we knew what they were doing."

"How did you know to look for those? Do you normally track via satellite every convoy they move around?"

"No, but it was what I would have done. I would have cleaned up my existing arsenal, get it ready, train my people, and produce more weapons. Makes sense. So I had satellite surveillance on a few top ICBM sites, and bingo! One day they showed up. Then I followed the convoys."

"Hmm...What else?"

"A few months ago, an exercise drill was conducted, involving 25,000 armed forces in a simulated massive nuclear attack. You'll find the details in Appendix 2."

"That's worrisome," Seiden said, frowning some more. "Keep going."

"Their top nuclear research facilities received some new funding recently. The Moscow facility is building a new wing. They've increased their uranium extraction rate at Priargunsky, Khiagda, and Elkon, their biggest uranium ore deposits. The plan is to double their extraction in the next ten years, under the guise of green energy. And Abramovich recently made changes in the leadership of the RVSN RF, their Strategic Missile Command."

"I see. Keep going, if there's more."

"Yes, there is. They're building a large center, partly buried underground, relatively close to an enrichment facility, the one in Novouralsk. We're not sure what that facility will be housing, not yet. On the political side, they've forged a troublesome alliance with India, another nuclear power. Finally, President Abramovich made a bold statement in the media, stating that North American defenses, specifically NORAD, cannot stop his new and improved nuclear missiles anymore. By his count, we're defenseless. That's unconfirmed, though. The fact, I mean—"

"Henri, we need to get a task team going. I'll assign some more analysts under your supervision. Find the underlying correlation behind those incidents you haven't finished modeling yet, and get me some working scenarios. I'll deploy a resource in the field to find out what's going on at that center they're building. Maybe even find out what the extra funding is supposed to buy them. We need to get ready."

"For what, sir?"

"World War III, most likely. We've already entered Cold War II."

~~~End Preview~~~

Like *The Backup Asset*?

ABOUT THE AUTHOR

Bestselling author Leslie Wolfe is passionate about writing fiction, despite spending a significant number of years climbing the corporate ladder. Leaving the coveted world of boardrooms for the blissful peace of the Florida-based "Wolves' den," Leslie answers one true calling: writing.

Leslie's novels break the mold of traditional thrillers. Fascinated by technology and psychology, Leslie brings extensive background and research in these fields that empower and add texture to a signature, multi-dimensional, engaging writing style.

Leslie released the first novel, *Executive*, in October 2011. It was very well received, including inquiries from Hollywood. Since then, Leslie published numerous novels and enjoyed growing success and recognition in the marketplace. Among Leslie's most notable works, *The Watson Girl* (2017) was recognized for offering a unique insight into the mind of a serial killer and a rarely seen first person account of his actions, in a dramatic and intense procedural thriller.

A complete list of Leslie's titles is available at http://wolfenovels.com/titles.

Leslie enjoys engaging with readers every day and would love to hear from you. Become an insider: gain early access to previews of Leslie's new novels.

- **Email: LW@WolfeNovels.com**
- Follow Leslie on Twitter: @WolfeNovels
- Like Leslie's Facebook page: https://www.facebook.com/wolfenovels
- Connect on LinkedIn: https://www.linkedin.com/in/wolfenovels
- Visit Leslie's website for the latest news: www.WolfeNovels.com